# The Ghost Warriors

## Bill Tippins

Book I in The Ghost Warriors Series

TiogaAndKopi.com

Copyright 2021  William H. Tippins

First paperback edition 2021

ISBN (paperback) 9798645031633

*Dedicated to Karen, my soul mate.*

Maps and cover by the author

# Author's Note

*The Ghost Warriors* is a story about your ancestors. Regardless of your cultural heritage, at some point long ago your forebearers lived in clans or tribes in small fortified villages. They wore animal fur, leather, and woven fabrics for clothing. Metal was not yet in use or was scarce, so they made tools (and weapons) out of stone, wood, and bone. They hunted and gathered food, grew some crops, and domesticated a few animals. They were sometimes threatened by wild beasts and natural disasters—but mostly by other humans.

This book is fiction, but based on facts. We know some foggy truths about Stone Age life from archaeological digs, oral history, ancient texts, and the lifestyles of hunter-gatherers in remote regions. Some of this evidence is troubling—it describes disease, warfare, witchcraft, slavery, and death. To this day, you carry DNA from ancestors who once lived this perilous lifestyle—and for many generations.

While the setting is based loosely on the topography of western Pennsylvania (where I live), the story could have unfolded on just about any continent on the planet—at different points in time. While this novel is set in the distant past, it is written in modern English with modern behavior. This is because the characters didn't live in the past—they lived in *their* present, which was every bit as vibrant, complex, and modern to them as ours is to us. They were just as intelligent as we are—actually, they were way smarter when it came to wilderness survival. Their lives depended on it.

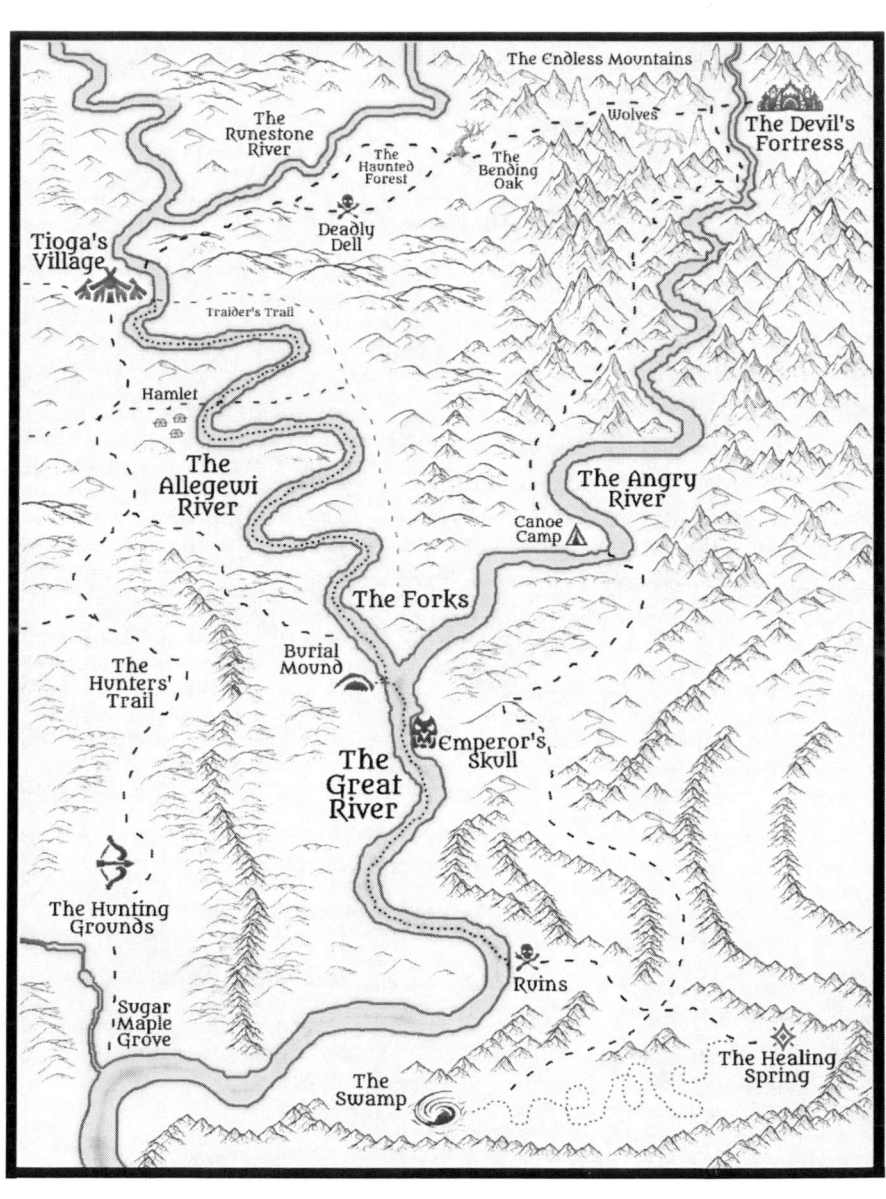

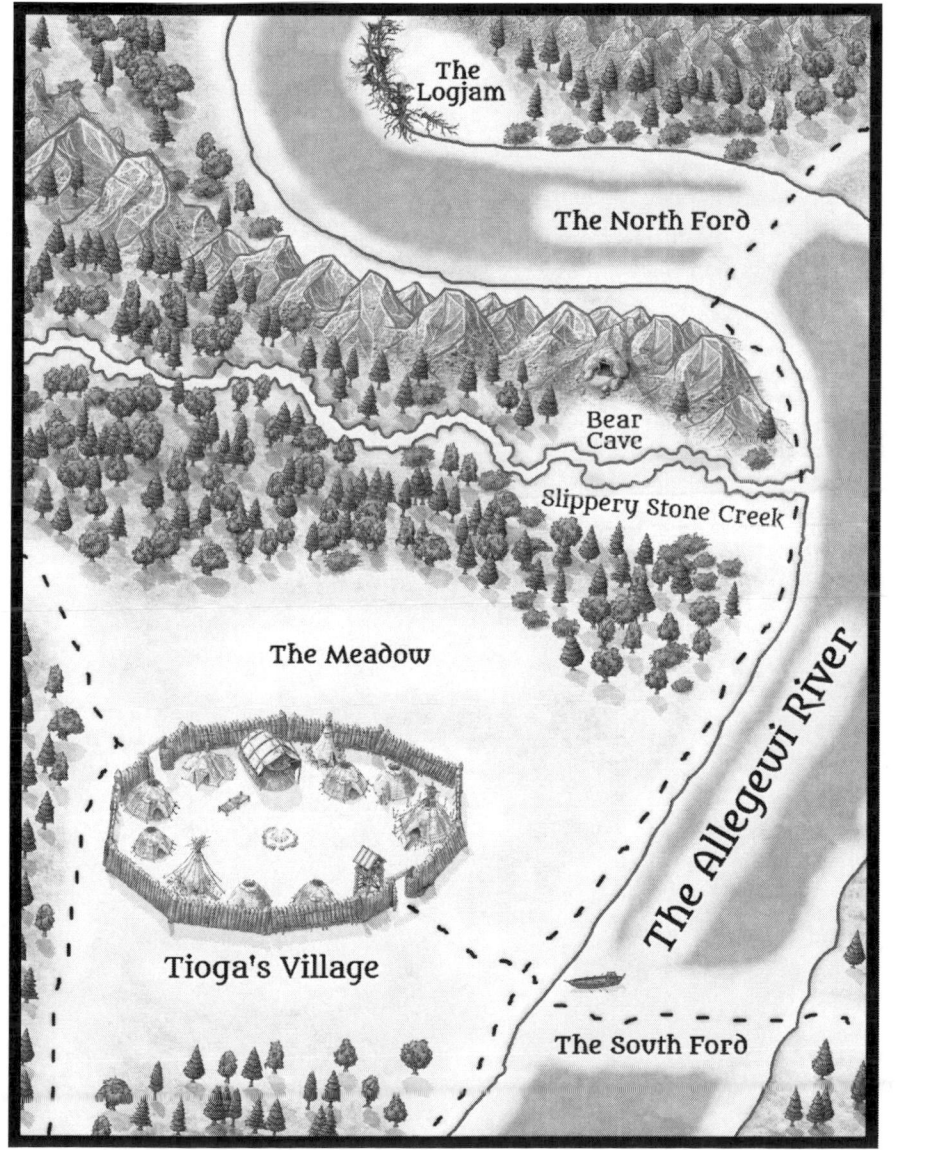

# The Main Characters

## _The Allegewi Tribe:_

**Tioga**: Thirteen-year-old male. Only surviving child of Candowsa and Wroclaw (deceased).

**Kopi**: Twelve-year-old male, best friend of Tioga. Son of Nairobi and Pocano. Has a little brother named Naunu.

**Hanna**: Fourteen-year-old female, only child of Chief Tundra and his wife.

**Candowsa**: Tioga's mother. Daughter of Ötzi (Mononga elder).

## _The Mononga Tribe:_

**Shingas the Terrible (aka. The Mononga Devil)**: Leader of the Mononga tribe.

**Chemung**: Shingas's right-hand man.

**Ötzi (aka. The Iceman)**: _Candowsa's father and Tioga's grandfather._

# *One*

"Come on! Bear Cave is this way," said thirteen-year-old Tioga as he ran through the trees. He stopped at the base of the cliff and looked back to make sure his friend was still coming. Tioga could hear the crack of the branches as Kopi lumbered through the forest. Kopi didn't bother to follow the path. He just bowled through the thicket like a bear sniffing out berries.

Tioga turned and began climbing through the fallen boulders. A moment later Kopi arrived at the foot of the hill. He looked up just as a bramble branch snapped back and hit him in the forehead. "Oh, come on!" he gasped. "How much farther?"

"Right here!" said Tioga. He pointed proudly at the dark crevice in the cliff's rocky face.

"Where?" asked Kopi as he wiped the sweat out of his eyes. It was an unusually warm day for late September.

"Right in front of me," insisted Tioga. "Come up and take a look."

Kopi snorted and began climbing up the moss-covered rocks toward the mysterious opening. As he neared the ledge where Tioga was standing, he looked down at the rushing waters of Slippery Stone Creek and nearly lost his balance. From this height he could even see the girls playing in the tall grass down by the Allegewi River.

Tioga followed his gaze and caught a glimpse of Hanna's purple hair blowing in the breeze. His heart skipped a beat at the sight of her. Once again she cast her spell over him without even trying.

Kopi rudely interrupted his daydream. "I'm not going in there," he said as he eyed the jagged mouth of the cave.

Tioga snapped back to reality and the job at hand. "You'll like it. It's nice and cool inside. And it's not too dark once you get used to it."

Kopi shook his head. "No way."

"You came this far," said Tioga. "At least see my handiwork."

Kopi sighed. He stepped forward and swatted away the cloud of gnats hovering outside the cavern entrance, then bent down and peered into the dark fissure. Its cold, clammy breath blew over his face. He could feel the weight of the stone towering above him, waiting to crush anyone foolish enough to venture inside.

Kopi slowly backed away and looked at Tioga, his best friend since birth. "You're crazy. We'll end up buried alive."

"Think of it," said Tioga. "Once we catch a bear, we'll be the heroes of the village!" An ear-to-ear smile came over his face.

Kopi looked down at the muddy ground and whispered, "There aren't even any paw prints. A bear hasn't lived in there for years."

"Then why are you whispering?"

"Tioga, messing with bears isn't a good idea. Don't forget, that's what got your father killed."

Tioga's smile disappeared. "I didn't forget."

Kopi knew the comment had cut deep. He wished he hadn't said it. "Sorry. I didn't mean it like that."

A moment later the contagious smile returned to Tioga's face. "Forget the bear. We might catch a badger, a bobcat, or even a mountain lion."

"A mountain lion? Not me," said Kopi, as he turned back toward the path. Tioga's twisted left hand landed on his shoulder.

"Please, Kopi? I can't set the trap without you."

Kopi glanced down at his friend's mangled left hand, deformed by a terrible childhood accident. Kopi never thought of it as a disability, except when Tioga asked for help, which was hardly ever. But on that rare occasion when Tioga needed him, Kopi couldn't say no.

Kopi took a deep breath and turned toward the cave. "All right," he said, "but this counts as your birthday gift."

"You didn't get me anything else? It's my thirteenth birthday today!"

"I did, but this counts too. When I turn thirteen in six months, I'll be expecting a double."

"Deal!"

Kopi closed his eyes, and shuffled forward. "I'm not looking. Lead me in."

"If I were you, I'd keep an eye open for snakes."

"Snakes?" said Kopi as one eye popped open. "You know I don't like snakes."

"And be on the lookout for spiders," said Tioga as he disappeared into the crevice. "There are some big ones in here."

Kopi opened both eyes, scowled, and reluctantly followed Tioga into the narrow opening. The walls closed around them. Soon the roof dropped so low that they were crawling single file along the dusty floor.

"It stinks like poop in here," muttered Kopi.

"Don't worry, you'll get used to it," said Tioga as he scurried ahead. "You're not afraid of bats, are you?"

"Vampire bats?" Kopi stopped dead in his tracks and squinted into the darkness.

"No, regular bats. Just think of them as cute, nocturnal squirrels."

The passage began to slope downward. The walls constricted to the point that they hugged Kopi's broad shoulders. The light faded and the air felt colder. Kopi's apprehension grew, and claustrophobia started to set in. It didn't help that Kopi was the huskiest young person in the village. There was no hiding the fact that he loved to eat.

"We're almost there," said Tioga, sensing his friend's uneasiness. "It's much roomier up ahead."

Kopi moved blindly toward Tioga's voice. "I can't see a thing."

"Your eyes will adjust," said Tioga. "Look back. You can still see the entrance."

Kopi gingerly bent his neck to avoid the stone ceiling and glanced over his shoulder. A blinding white light was there at the end of the tunnel. In fact, it was only about thirty feet away. But going backward up the slope would be difficult. A clammy sweat broke out on his forehead.

He decided to trust his friend and crawled forward, hoping the space was larger ahead. After a few more feet, he was rewarded. The walls receded and the ceiling disappeared into the darkness. Kopi stretched out his arms to judge the space, and his hand bumped into something strangely out of place. He ran his fingers along its rough surface.

"What's a log doing in here?" he asked, looking at the object in the dim light.

"It's part of a deadfall trap," said Tioga. "It's the best trap to kill a bear."

Kopi's eyes slowly adjusted to the darkness. The cavity was just large enough to hold the two boys, the six-foot long tree trunk, and a bear. Kopi could see Tioga kneeling beside him. His fingers seemed to fly over a mix of ropes and sticks like a spider spinning its web.

"Just exactly what are you doing?"

"Building the trap."

"How did you get that log in here?"

"It wasn't easy. It took me all afternoon," said Tioga. "Where were you? I could have used some help."

"I was training Scooter."

"Your turtle?"

"Yeah. He comes now when I whistle."

"I can't wait to see that."

Kopi scanned the walls of the cavern. The stone was covered with painted figures. He could make out some human forms throwing spears at mystical animals, and some strange beings from another world.

"I see you aren't the first person to find this place," said Kopi. The dancing shadows in the cave made the markings look even creepier.

"The Ancients," replied Tioga.

"Why would they crawl way back here?"

"They probably were asking the Creator for good luck on the hunt. Hopefully, it will work for us too."

"Humm," huffed Kopi. "I prefer praying from the comfort of my bed." He squinted at the crevice in the back of the cave and inhaled the dank odor of animal droppings. A cold, wet fluid dripped onto the back of his neck. He looked up and shuddered at the sight of several furry forms hanging from the ceiling a few feet above him.

"Bats!" hissed Kopi. "I think one just peed on me."

"Maybe, but it was probably just dripping water," said Tioga. "Even so, don't look up with your mouth open." He reached down to the log and wrapped his good arm around one end. "Alright. Help me lift it into place."

Kopi grabbed the trunk with his thick arms. From its girth he could tell that this was going to be a challenge.

"Now lift," grunted Tioga. Kopi followed the order. One end of the oak timer rose to the height of his straining chest.

"Hold on while I get the support stick," said Tioga. He reached down and rummaged in the dust.

"Hurry! I can't hold it much longer," gasped Kopi.

Tioga grabbed a pole and wedged it upright under the log. Kopi started to relax.

"Wait," said Tioga. "I've got to put in the trigger." Tioga grabbed a stick carved just for this purpose. He opened a small clay pot he had stashed in a corner and dribbled its contents along one end of the bait stick.

"Whew! What's that smell?" asked Kopi.

"Beaver oil."

"You couldn't bait the stick before I lifted this?"

"I was afraid you'd turn and run out."

"You're probably right," said Kopi. "Why do bears like that stinky stuff?"

"I don't know," said Tioga. "But according to my dad, nothing attracts them better." Tioga positioned the stick so that the slightest touch would trigger the trap.

"Let it down easy," said Tioga as he withdrew his hands. Kopi gingerly released his grip. The log teetered for a moment and then stabilized. Tioga crawled backward and smiled.

"That's it. The bear pulls on the bait stick, and the timber comes crashing down, breaking the bear's neck."

"I have to say your father did a great job of teaching you how to trap," said Kopi.

Tioga nodded and thought back to the wonderful hours he had spent with his father in the woods. *He was the best trapper that ever lived*, thought Tioga. *The other boys didn't dare pick on me then, not when Dad was still alive...*

A girl's distant scream suddenly echoed through the chamber, interrupting Tioga's thoughts. Kopi jumped up, and his head brushed against a sleeping bat. It dropped from the ceiling and landed in his hair.

"Bats! They're all over me!" screamed Kopi as he clawed at his head. He lurched forward in a frantic attempt at escape. A dull *thud* could be heard as his skull impacted the rock ceiling. He stumbled backward and brushed against the trigger stick. A crash vibrated through the cave as the wooden beam fell to the floor, just missing him and Tioga.

"Ugh!" cried Kopi as he tumbled back onto the rolling log. Bats swirled through the cave and dust clouded the air.

Tioga pulled Kopi to his feet. "Are you alright?"

Kopi coughed and spit out a glob of dust. "Stupid girls! I could have been killed!"

Even in the faint light, Tioga could see Kopi's face turning red with embarrassment. He was relieved his friend was unharmed.

Kopi bent down and grabbed the log with surprising strength. "Come on," he said. "Let's get this thing back in place." He singlehandedly lifted the heavy weight into the air. A moment later Tioga had the trap reset.

"I'm leaving," said Kopi, already crawling up toward the exit. "I've got that stinkin' beaver oil all over me. Next time use honey!"

Tioga took one last look at the deadfall trap. "Perfect!" He smiled and followed Kopi out.

Kopi was glad to be back outside. The fresh air smelled wonderful and the sky was ablaze with a beautiful sunset.

"Let's go," said Kopi. "It's dinner time!"

Just as Tioga emerged from the cave, another shrill cry pierced the forest. He looked down and spotted a small girl running toward the village in a panic.

"She's in trouble!" said Tioga. "Come on!" He bounded down the rocks, leaving Kopi far behind. At the bottom, Tioga sprinted across the stream and through the trees after the girl. He caught up with her just as their village came into sight. He reached out and grabbed her waist. She shrieked in fear and struggled to break free.

"Sitka, it's me, Tioga." The girl fell sobbing into his arms. "What happened?"

"It took her!" cried Sitka, as tears streamed down her cheeks. "It took Hanna."

"What took Hanna?"

The girl looked up into Tioga's eyes. "The Mononga Devil! The demon with one arm!"

A jolt of terror went through Tioga. All the children had heard of the Mononga Devil, the legendary warlord of the Mononga tribe. They were the most feared clan in the valley, known for their savage and ruthless acts. Every child had nightmares of encountering a Mononga warrior along the trail, let alone their infamous one-armed leader.

Kopi stumbled up just as Tioga came to his senses. Tioga left Sitka with Kopi and bolted toward the river, where the girls had been playing. Up ahead he heard a muffled cry in the field. There, in the tall weeds, someone or something was struggling.

Tioga's heart raced as he rushed into the towering plants. He charged through the brush, splintering the stalks as he went. As he sprinted forward, his foot caught on an unseen rock. He fell with a grunt, knocking the wind out of his lungs. He gasped for air and tasted the sandy dirt.

Finally, a shallow breath came. And then another. As he rose to his feet, he noticed a strange smell: the stench of rotting flesh. He looked ahead but stopped dead in his tracks. A chill ran up his spine.

A grotesque human face, painted in fearsome red and black war paint, glared at him through the grass. Its eyes seemed to penetrate his soul. A queer smile curled over its lips. Just below the face, the stump of an amputated arm glistened in the sunlight. Pus dripped from a rancid wound at the end of it. Tioga shuddered and closed his eyes.

When he opened them, the monster was gone. For an instant, he saw the flowing strands of Hanna's purple hair. Then they vanished. Tioga stood frozen in place, too terrified to move. He stared at the waving grass, where only a moment before she had been.

The sound of Kopi's voice in the distance broke his trance. He looked down at his shaking left hand, curled in toward his chest like an eagle's talon.

She was gone. The girl of his dreams was gone. And he had failed to save her.

# *Two*

Word of the abduction spread instantly through the village of the Allegewi tribe. The news of losing any child to the Mononga was appalling, but this time the girl taken was Hanna—Chief Tundra's only daughter. The place was in an uproar.

The Allegewi village was surrounded by a ten-foot high wooden wall to deter attack. Although the one hundred or so villagers slept inside the fort, during the day most would venture outside to hunt, fish, gather, and garden. The need for firewood alone was huge— children routinely scoured the forest for it. This was when you were the most vulnerable.

A raid by a rival clan was always disheartening, but not completely unexpected. In Tioga's lifetime there had been many violent raids. Most often these attacks were not full-scale assaults, but rather surprise ambushes. The raiders sprung upon the victims in an instant, did their brutal work, and then disappeared into the wilderness. The motivation for the attack was often to avenge a previous loss, or simply to take a child to replace a death in their own village. If the abducted boy or girl was lucky, they would be initiated into the raiders' tribe and accepted by a family as one of their own. Otherwise, they could expect a life of slavery, or worse.

The Mononga, who lived in the mountains to the east, were notoriously bloodthirsty. They would raid, murder, and kidnap for sport. And their leader, the Mononga Devil, was the most feared of the bunch. Not only was he a merciless killer, he was rumored to have mystical powers.

The Allegewi village had moved to this riverside terrace thirty years ago. The location was near a crossing spot on the river and was ideal for trade and travel. But the site was not the best for defense, as it had few natural barriers. The man-made timber wall, also called a palisade or stockade, was the only obstacle to stop invaders.

Thankfully, the Allegewi we were at peace with all the tribes in the lowlands—or what was left of them.

While there had been skirmishes with Mononga war parties for decades, in recent years these had increased in frequency and intensity. More troubling were the rumors that the Mononga had begun wiping out entire villages. The elders believed it was only a matter of time until they launched a full-scale assault on the Allegewi.

That evening Tioga, Kopi, and the other boys met around the central campfire. The fate of fourteen-year-old Hanna was the only topic of discussion.

"She doesn't stand a chance," said fifteen-year-old Lenni, as he roasted a piece of deer meat over the flames. "She'll be running the gauntlet by the full moon, and you know what happens after that." The rumble of distant thunder rolled through the night, emphasizing his point.

"What happens after that?" asked six-year-old Naunu, the youngest of the eight boys sitting around the fire.

"Oh, it depends," said Kopi to his little brother. Kopi enjoyed being the oracle of knowledge to little Naunu. "Running the gauntlet is a test of strength and courage. She'll be forced to run between all their warriors as they try to beat her with sticks. If she does well—"

"They'll roast her," intruded Lenni, as he pulled the sizzling meat from the blaze. "The Mononga won't pass up the chance to torture an Allegewi, let alone the chief's daughter. Once she gets there, they—"

Tioga interrupted, "She won't get there. Chief Tundra will send a rescue squad!"

"Shut up, Claw!" screamed Lenni. Tioga hated the nickname, but didn't dare respond. Lenni continued, "Just cause your stinkin' mother is one of them doesn't make you an expert on those barbarians."

Tioga shifted uncomfortably on his log seat. He looked across the village at the chief's house. Blue smoke curled out of the top and disappeared into the night. Inside, the elders of the village were discussing what to do about the kidnapping.

Lenni took a bite of the hot venison. "As I was saying, once she gets there, they'll tie her to a stake and—"

"Our rescuers will save her!" blurted out Tioga again. Lenni was so shocked that he choked on his meat. Tioga took advantage of the opportunity and continued, "The Mononga fortress is deep in the mountains. There is still plenty of time for our warriors to rescue her before she gets there."

"Deep in the *Endless Mountains*," said Lenni, finally catching his breath. "No one would be stupid enough to follow them there. The wolves are as thick as a swarm of mosquitoes. And there are ghosts, goblins, and zombies in those mountains. Lots of them." The boys listened intently to Lenni's description.

"The mountains aren't really endless," said Tioga. "My father trapped there many times."

"Your stupid father is dead," said Lenni. "Besides, even if a rescue team made it to the mountains, they'd still have to get by the Mononga Devil. He has super powers. That's why he only has one arm. He traded the other to the underworld for black magic."

"They say the Mononga Devil can feel a man's heart beat from miles away," said Kopi. "He has the claws of a cougar, the nose of a bear, and the eyes of an eagle."

"He is only a man," interjected Candowsa. The boys looked back in surprise. They hadn't noticed that Tioga's mother had walked up behind them.

A wave of embarrassment came over Tioga. "Ah, Mom! You know you're not supposed to listen to boy talk."

Candowsa ignored the rebuke and stared into the fire. "I know this man—whom you call the Mononga Devil. He is bad. He is cruel. He is ruthless. But he is just a man."

A commotion outside the chief's hut broke the tension. "He has decided," said Candowsa. Chief Tundra emerged from his house, followed by his advisors.

The boys ran to join the growing crowd at the center of the village. Tioga stayed back by his mother's side. The aging chief slowly climbed the stage with the help of Master Dudley—Lenni's father—who was second in command. Chief Tundra turned to address the sympathetic crowd. The chief had lost his first wife and young children in a horrible house fire twenty years ago, while he was away fighting the Mononga. He was blessed to marry again and have a beautiful daughter. But now she too was gone.

"People of the Allegewi." Chief Tundra paused and wiped the sweat off his brow. Tioga looked proudly at their leader. His courage and wisdom were unmatched. He knew the chief would spare no effort to free Hanna. Over the last forty years, he had tracked countless raiders and freed many captives. Songs were sung about his bravery. Tioga hoped he would be allowed to go on the rescue mission.

Chief Tundra continued, "It has been a very difficult year. First, the fever took many of our loved ones. Then the late frost ruined our crops. We are struggling to survive. We must rely on hunting to make it through the coming winter. As you know, a week ago I sent our strongest men off to the hunting grounds. While they are away, we are especially vulnerable."

The chief paused, and Tioga held his breath. A look of pain came over the chief's face. "With this in mind, I have made my decision regarding young Hanna. To send out a rescue squad now would further weaken our defenses. Therefore, we must leave it to the Great Spirit—the Creator—to protect her."

Hanna's mother burst into tears. "I should never have let her color her hair purple!" she sobbed. "It made her an easy target!"

Chief Tundra looked tenderly at his wife. Then the warrior welled up inside him. He looked up into the night as lightning streaked across the distant horizon. "Her loss will be avenged!" he cried in anguish. The chief staggered for a moment and then climbed down from the stage with Master Dudley's assistance. Chief Tundra took his wife by the arm and led her away to mourn in the seclusion of their home.

Tioga looked at his mother with tears in his eyes. He could hardly believe what he just heard. "They're not going after her?"

Tioga's mother placed her hands on her son's head. "She is gone," she said. "There is nothing more we can do for her." Another flash lit up the sky, followed by a drumroll of thunder. "Let us go. A storm is brewing."

Tioga looked over his shoulder at the wooden stockade. When he was younger, the palisade had given him a feeling of security. Now it felt more like a prison wall, designed to lock him in.

# *Three*

Candowsa and Tioga sat solemnly inside their dimly lit hut, the smallest house in the village. Knowing that her son was upset, Candowsa prepared his favorite drink, sassafras tea, over the hearth. The patter of raindrops started on the thatch roof just over their heads.

Tioga took comfort in petting Schnitzel, his dog, who seemed to instinctively know his master needed him. This was the worst birthday Tioga could remember. All he could think of was Hanna— alone in the storm. The most beautiful girl in the world, alone with *it*—the Mononga Devil. Tioga tried to reign in his runaway thoughts and focused on the positive. *Not all Mononga are evil*, he thought as he looked at his mother. She had been born Mononga. He studied her face in the firelight. She was still beautiful after all she had been through.

Tioga decided to broach the forbidden subject. "Mother," he asked, "will you tell me about the time when you were Mononga? And how you were taken by the Allegewi?"

She looked at him sternly across the fire. He didn't back down. Something in him had to know—for Hanna's sake.

Candowsa nodded slowly as her mind drifted back through the years. She normally didn't allow her thoughts to go there, but this time was different. She knew her only child needed her.

Silence filled the room. Then, as if in a trance, Candowsa whispered in her native Mononga tongue, "I hardly remember."

Tioga understood, as his mother had taught him to be bilingual. She had wanted him to know the language of his ancestors.

"I had a happy childhood," said Candowsa. "For the most part, things were good. There was peace in the valley. It wasn't until I became a teenager that life became difficult."

"What happened?"

She shifted uncomfortably. "I ran away."

"Why?" Tioga could see that his mother didn't want to talk about it, but he pressed the issue. "Why did you run away?"

Candowsa's back stiffen. The rain drummed on the roof above them. "I was to be married to a Mononga man I did not want. He was unbearable. I could not stand the thought of a life with him."

Tioga was fascinated by the story. His mother never spoke of her time as a Mononga. He sat silently, hoping she would go on.

"So, I ran away. I ran for days. Then, as I grew weak, I walked. Then I crawled. I came upon a spring and took one last drink before I died." Candowsa closed her eyes.

"But you didn't die," said Tioga thankfully. "How did our men kidnap you?"

"By chance, a group of Allegewi warriors found me. Your father, Wroclaw, was the youngest among them. I am thankful I met your father. He was a good man and treated me kindly. The warriors picked me up and brought me here."

"Did you try to escape?"

"No. I was too weak. And they were expert trackers. When I saw the Allegewi village, I knew I would never see home again."

"Did they make you run the gauntlet?"

Candowsa flinched. Tioga knew he had hit a painful memory.

"Yes." She paused, then she slowly continued, "I remember looking down that line of foreign faces. They were so angry. Yelling and screaming, waiving clubs, fists, and knives." She unconsciously rubbed the thick scar on her shoulder. "I said a prayer to the Creator... and then I stumbled into the line with my head held high."

Tioga pictured beautiful Hanna running into that brutal line. He had renewed respect for his mother as a survivor.

"You made it through?"

"Yes. Barely. I was so weak they must have taken pity on me," continued Candowsa. "Then the cleansing ceremony began. They washed away my Mononga blood and I became Allegewi."

"Were you treated well?" asked Tioga, again thinking of Hanna.

"The first few years I was little more than a slave. It wasn't until your father married me that things became better."

"Did you miss your old family and friends?"

"Of course! I missed them all—well, all but the one." She hardened at the thought. Then she relaxed and said, "I especially missed my father." Candowsa smiled. She seemed to melt at the memory. "Father Ötzi was a wonderful man. I wish you could have known him."

Tioga wondered what it would be like to have a grandfather—even if he was Mononga. Someone special who could teach you the old ways. It just wasn't the same with the other elders of the village, who often looked past him. All of Tioga's grandparents had gone to the spirit world before he was born.

"I missed my father so much," continued Candowsa, "You see, I was an only child. My mother died giving birth to me. When I became Allegewi, Father Ötzi was left alone, without a wife or child. My loss must have broken his heart. I never saw him again."

"Did the Mononga try to rescue you? They must have followed your tracks."

She stared at the swirling fire, as the wind howled through the thin bark walls of their hut. "They tried once, shortly after I was taken. But the rescue party was ambushed by Allegewi warriors in the Deadly Dell."

"The Deadly Dell? Where is that?" asked Tioga. He thought he knew every inch of the forest around their village.

"Across the river and to the east. In the foothills of the mountains. It is a place where the path passes through a narrow valley—a canyon."

"What happened?"

"A scout detected the approaching Mononga and alerted the Allegewi warriors. They hid atop the cliffs that bordered the dell. When the rescuers entered the canyon, they fell upon them like a pack of wolves. The man you call the Devil was one of the those caught in the ambush."

"The Mononga Devil?" asked Tioga, clearly shocked by the news.

She nodded yes, and went on, "At the time, he was a young man, just a few years older than you. His name was Shingas. His father was chief of the Mononga."

"Shingas the Terrible?" whispered Tioga. He remembered his father saying the name.

"The Mononga were much less violent back then, even peaceful most of the time. We lived in a village similar to this in the foothills. We grew crops, hunted and fished, and traded with the other tribes. Life was good. Shingas's father was a good man. But sadly, he died in the ambush."

"It's too bad Shingas wasn't killed," said Tioga.

"He nearly was killed. Your father severed his arm with a hatchet in the fight. He took his first war trophy."

"Father cut off the Devil's arm?" asked Tioga in disbelief.

Candowsa nodded and continued, "Somehow Shingas escaped and made it back to their village without bleeding to death. As rightful heir, he became the new chief of the Mononga. But he was so traumatized by the ambush that he ordered the village to be moved deep into the mountains to the head of the Angry River. There he built an impenetrable stone castle on the ruins of an ancient fortress."

"He built the castle because he was afraid of the Allegewi?" said Tioga in amazement.

"Or so I heard. But the mountain soil was weak and rocky. They could no longer grow crops. So Shingas ordered his men to raid and take from the other tribes. They took so much food and so many slaves that they became the most powerful tribe in the land."

"Dad beat the Mononga Devil," said Tioga, lost in thought.

Candowsa broke into tears. "It is my fault so much blood has been spilled! If I had not run away, none of this would have happened. Hanna would be home safe in her bed!"

Tioga tried to process all he had heard. But it was beyond belief. He reached out and hugged his mother, as intense thunder shook the frame of the house. The roof sprang a leak and rainwater trickled in. Schnitzel licked at the growing puddle on the clay floor.

Candowsa began sobbing uncontrollably. A long repressed dam of shame and guilt had been breached. "I am the reason Shingas the Terrible rose to power! I am the reason your father was killed by a bear! I am the reason your sister died of a fever! I am the reason your arm was burnt! I am the reason entire villages have been destroyed! All because of my selfishness. Now the spirits have cursed me. The ghosts of the innocent haunt me. It is my lot to live and suffer while my loved ones die. I am the reason the Allegewi will fall!"

"Mom, no! It's not your fault! You were just a young girl. Shingas is to blame. He is the one who kills and maims. He is the one who turned the Mononga to stone!"

Tioga's words seemed to break her trance. Candowsa's voice hardened as she switched back to the Allegewi language. "Shingas will not rest until he has conquered us. He hates the Allegewi more than any other tribe. I have witnessed his brutality. I know the coldness of his heart. After all, I was once engaged to marry him."

Tioga shuddered at this revelation. He exclaimed, "You were going to marry the Mononga Devil?"

She calmly responded, "Not if I could help it. The marriage was arranged by the elders. My father objected, but he was overruled. He could see that the marriage would kill me, so he told me to run. It seemed like the only way out. But by doing so, I triggered the curse and the suffering began. The curse grows stronger each year I live."

Tioga looked up at the ceiling of their small house. Swinging from the rafters was a unique decoration—a Mononga charm. Tioga had always been embarrassed by his mother's race. Now he realized the Mononga had once been peaceful, and she would have been the Mononga queen. For the first time he respected her and *his* heritage. He was also astounded by her courage. Running away from any arranged marriage would be extraordinary. But rejecting the Mononga chief's son would have been punishable by death.

Just then there was a knock on the wood frame of their hut. Schnitzel barked and Tioga jumped at the sound. Chief Tundra's dripping face appeared in the doorway. "Mrs. Wroclaw, may I enter?"

Candowsa quickly pulled herself together. "Of course, Esteemed Leader. What an honor it is to have you in our humble dwelling. Please sit by the fire and have some tea. And sir, please call me Candowsa."

The chief bent down and stepped inside, soaked to the skin. "Thank you Candowsa, but I am here for the business of war, not pleasure." She bowed her head as Tioga looked on in awe. The chief's furrowed face seemed to have aged ten years in the last four hours.

"Tioga, I have come for you," said Chief Tundra. Tioga was shocked. He didn't even think their leader knew his name. The chief continued, "A message must be sent to the hunting party to order their immediate return. Tioga, I have selected you as the messenger."

Before Tioga could answer, Candowsa said, "Esteemed Leader, this is a very important mission. Why send a boy instead of a man?"

"When the Mononga raiders took my daughter, they must have scouted our weakened defenses. I have no doubt they are returning to their fortress now to prepare for an assault. If they attack in force, we will not be able to defend the village. Most of the people here are women and children, and the old and the crippled."

The chief glanced down at the boy's disfigured hand. "Tioga may not be able to use a bow and arrow, but he can run the trails. It's only a three-day journey to the hunting grounds, and he is a fast runner."

Tioga sat up in excitement. His heart was pounding.

"But he is only twelve-years-old," said Candowsa.

"I just turned thirteen!" interjected Tioga.

His mother continued, "Tioga was never taught the hunting trails, due to his limitations." Candowsa gestured to Tioga's arm, which was now hidden behind his back.

"He is the son of a trapper," said the chief. "I'm sure he knows his way around the forest."

"He was still young when my husband died," responded Candowsa. "He does not know the way to the hunting grounds. He will surely get lost, or captured, trying to find the men. It is too important a mission to fail."

Tioga's heart sank.

"Hmmm," said Chief Tundra, pondering the situation. "May I sit down?"

"Of course," said Candowsa.

Tioga scurried and brought the chief a stool. He watched their leader intently. He had never seen the man this close before.

Chief Tundra rested for a moment, then said, "If Tioga does not know the trails, he can travel down the river by canoe. Come to think of it, with this storm swelling the waterway, it will be faster than the hunters' trail."

Tioga nodded enthusiastically. His hope was renewed. He imagined himself paddling into the unknown.

"But he cannot paddle well," said Candowsa. She pulled her son's clawed fingers to the light. "The flames have spoiled his flesh." Tioga broke free and hid the cursed appendage under his knee.

"I see," said the chief.

"And sir, the river south of the Forks is Dracul territory," said Candowsa. "Surely it is not safe."

"The Draculs left that area decades ago," said the chief. "That is not a concern. But a messenger must be able to paddle. Perhaps Tioga is not the best choice."

"I agree," said Candowsa.

"Very well, Candowsa. I will send Kopi then. With those beefy arms, he can certainly paddle. And as the son of a fisherman, he knows the river. Plus, he won't be much good here in an attack. He is a terrible shot."

"Kopi is a much better choice," agreed Candowsa. Tioga's hopes were dashed.

The chief rose to exit the hut. "Thank you for your hospitality and a mother's wisdom. I will go inform Kopi."

"Thank you, Esteemed Leader," said Candowsa with a bow. "We are so sorry for your loss."

The chief nodded in sorrow. Just as he turned to leave, Tioga spoke up. "Esteemed Leader! Two boys are more likely to succeed than one. I would be honored to assist Kopi on the mission."

His mother scowled at him. She opened her mouth to speak, but the chief responded first. "I admire your courage, Tioga. You may be of some use to Kopi. He is a fearful boy. Maybe your presence will bring out the warrior in him." He nodded and smiled. "The two of you will leave at dawn."

"Yes, sir!" exclaimed Tioga, jumping to his feet.

Candowsa knew she could not question the matter further. She bowed her head in submission.

"Very well then," said the chief. "I must be going."

Tioga decided to press his luck. "Chief Tundra, once we bring the hunters back, can I join the rescue squad?"

The chief's demeanor changed in an instant, as sadness overcame him. "As I said earlier, there will be no rescue. By the time you return with the men, it will be too late for Hanna. But not too late to save our village." Chief Tundra turned and disappeared into the storm.

Tioga dropped his head in despair. But a small voice echoed in his brain: *Maybe it's not too late. We will travel like the wind and the men will save her!* The excitement of his selection for such an important mission flooded back. He smiled sheepishly at his mother.

"I am cursed," said Candowsa, on the verge of tears. "You will never come back alive. The ghosts will take you from me."

"I will come back! I promise. Mom, I will break the curse!"

Candowsa sulked away to her bed, where she sobbed into her pillow. Tioga had never seen her act like this before—she was always so strong. As much as he wanted to comfort her, he now had other priorities. The fate of the village was in his and Kopi's hands. He immediately sharpened his flint knife, and then coiled up his favorite rope. After packing a few other supplies, he crawled under his covers and closed his eyes. But it was several hours before his mind slowed enough for sleep to finally come.

# *Four*

Two men and two boys knelt in the dim morning light in the center of the village. Tioga fidgeted as Kopi repeatedly yawned. Kopi was jolted out of his daze by the stern, gravelly voice of Gron, a village elder.

"Let's go over it one more time," said Elder Gron.

Kopi's father, Pocano, knelt beside the boys and the old man. It was barely light enough to see the crude map scratched in the mud.

"Here we are," said Elder Gron, pointing to one head of what looked like a two-headed snake. "Take the Allegewi River downstream to where it meets the Angry River." He traced the path of the river with his finger to the Y on the map. "Here are the Forks— the confluence where the two rivers become one. From this point on it is called the Great River."

"The Forks," said Pocano. "Remember, Kopi? The most famous landmark on the river?"

Kopi stared at the ground and yawned. All he saw was a two-headed snake. He blinked his burning eyes. He had been up all night worrying about the journey.

"The Forks," said Tioga, "where the Allegewi River and Angry River meet."

"Why do they call it the Angry River?" moaned Kopi.

"It's headwaters are turbulent. That's all, son," said Pocano. "Some people call it the Mononga River. You can call it that if you prefer."

"The Mononga River? That's even worse," said Kopi.

"Forgot that evil river!" hissed Gron. "You won't be going there. You will pass it by."

"I hope so," said Kopi.

"Camp near the Forks the first night," said Gron, continuing the lecture. "In the morning, continue downstream for another day. You will pass by the Emperor's Skull, then—"

"An emperor's skull?" interrupted Kopi, his voice quivering.

"It's just a rock formation," said Pocano. "It happens to look like a skull."

"The Emperor's Skull is another famous landmark," said Elder Gron. "Above it is Fort Ancient."

"Fort Ancient?" chirped Tioga. Now he was the one asking questions.

"An old stone fort of the Draculs. But that is *not* your destination," said Elder Gron, growing impatient. "After you pass the Emperor's Skull, continue down the Great River until you see a huge grove of sugar maple trees. Their leaves will be turning bright red."

"We used to make maple syrup there when I was a child," said Pocano.

"I love maple syrup," muttered Kopi.

"Hide the canoe at Sugar Maple Grove and camp there the second night," said Gron, sternly.

"Camp the second night at Sugar Maple Grove," repeated Tioga, but his mind was still focused on the ancient fort.

Gron pointed to the tail of the snake map and continued, "Maple Creek enters the river at Sugar Maple Grove. The next morning, hike up the creek until you reach the waterfall. The men should be camped nearby."

"You will be sleeping with the hunters the third night!" exclaimed Pocano. "And they will lead you back home by the land trail," he added, knowing of Kopi's fear of water.

"Why did they go so far away?" asked Kopi in anguish. "We are surrounded by forest right here!"

Kopi's father responded, "Son, these woods have been hunted out for years. The hunting grounds are just three days away. Just a hop, skip, and a jump, or in this case just a paddle, a paddle, and a hike."

"Three days?" groaned Kopi. "I might starve."

Pocano looked at his portly son with embarrassment. He certainly wouldn't starve, not with all the food his mother had packed for him. As the village healer, she was constantly receiving food as gifts for her services.

"We've got it," said Tioga, boldly. "Thank you Elder Gron."

The old man laughed and placed his hands on Tioga's shoulders. Tioga had always loved the old tracker. After his father's death, Gron had spent countless hours teaching him the art of tracking.

"Tioga, after this journey is over, it will be time for your spirit quest," said Elder Gron warmly. "It is then that your animal spirit—your totem—will show itself. In the meantime, keep a watchful eye. You may spot it watching you."

"Yes, sir!" said Tioga, smiling.

The two men and two boys stood up. Just then a woman came running toward them. It was Nairobi—Kopi's mother.

"Mom!" said Kopi as he gave her a hug.

"You almost forgot this!" said Nairobi, as she handed Kopi a packet of herbs. "In case you get a tummy ache."

Kopi dropped his head in humiliation. But the two men nodded their approval. No one questioned Nairobi's ability to heal. She knew every plant in the forest and had saved many lives with her medicine—treatments that had been passed down in her family for generations. If you were sick or injured, she was the most important person in the village.

Nairobi squeezed Kopi tight, kissed him, and said, "Safe travels, my son." Then she turned and walked away. She knew the mission was too important to interrupt.

"Remember, no matter what happens, do not let yourself be afraid," said Elder Gron. "Fear is the real devil, not a man with one arm. Fear can make a smart man do stupid things. Trust in the Creator, use your head, and calmly think things through."

"Yes, sir," said both boys in unison.

Pocano leaned down and hugged his son so firmly that he lifted Kopi's feet off the ground. "You will be back home before you know it. And after this trip, maybe you will want to come fishing with me! Some of the biggest fish in the river live down at the Forks."

Tioga watched with a strange sense of jealousy, wishing his father was still alive. He shook off the familiar rush of emotions that often came when he thought of him.

Elder Gron lifted his wrinkled arm and pointed to the gate. Sensing the boys' hesitation, he chuckled and led the way in a slow shuffle. Pocano ran ahead to open the heavy door.

Kopi looked fearfully into his best friend's eyes. "Tioga, I don't think I can do this."

"Come on. You'll be fine," said Tioga as he pushed Kopi forward.

Before they had taken ten steps, laughter erupted from the shadows. Tioga knew who it was without even looking. That voice had teased him as long as he could remember.

"I can't believe they're sending a cripple and a coward," said Lenni, stepping out from the shadows. Tioga ignored the comment and moved forward with Kopi.

"Why are you going along, *Claw*?" taunted Lenni. "To change Tubby's diapers?"

"Leave us alone, Lenni," said Tioga as he tried to move by his nemesis.

"Oh, look at the brave warrior! What are you going to do, scratch me to death with your talon?" The bully stuck his clawed fingers in Tioga's face.

For the first time in his life, Tioga was ready to fight back. He wasn't going to let Lenni spoil their mission. His right hand balled into a tight fist, and his arm tensed. He was about to let loose when Kopi grabbed him. Lenni seized the opportunity and punched Tioga in the gut, who fell to his knees and gasped for breath.

"You don't even know how to fight!" laughed Lenni. "You'll never be anything more than a one-armed skunk trapper!"

Elder Gron croaked through the morning mist, "Tioga! Kopi! It is a bad omen to begin a journey in conflict. Lenni, leave them alone. Your strength is needed to fight men, not boys."

"Crazy old man," muttered Lenni under his breath. "My father says he's nuts." He turned and disappeared between the houses.

Tioga rose from the ground gasping for breath. Elder Gron reached out and pulled him close. He had a surprisingly strong grip for an old man.

Gron whispered in Tioga's ear, "I see the fire in your heart. When used wisely, the blaze can give warmth. But when used carelessly, the inferno will burn. You know this, as the flames have touched you deeply." He ran his fingers along Tioga's scarred arm down to his disfigured hand. Tioga felt the old man place something into it.

"This is a charm of protection," whispered Elder Gron. "One day, it may save your life."

Tioga looked down at his hand and saw he was holding a peculiar old bone hanging from a leather necklace. It was about eight inches long, decorated with feathers, and had swirling lines carved into it. Tioga recognized it as the dusty Mononga talisman that had hung from the ceiling of his hut for as long as he could remember.

"Wroclaw, your father, was a brave warrior, in addition to being a great trapper," said Elder Gron. "He took this as his first war trophy. In the famous battle at Deadly Dell."

Tioga looked down at the bone with renewed interest, wondering what the old man meant. "This was my father's?"

"Yes, but back then it was not just a bone, but a human arm," hissed Gron. "The arm of the Mononga Devil!"

Tioga stared into the old man's bloodshot eyes in disbelief. The elder released his grasp and pushed the boys through the gate. A second later, it closed behind them. They were alone.

"What did he say to you?" asked Kopi. "And what is that thing?"

Tioga was too stunned to answer. He twisted the bone in his hand as visions of his father cutting off the Devil's arm flashed in his head.

"Nothing… It's nothing," said Tioga. He refocused on the task at hand. The river valley below them was cloaked in a thick blanket of fog. It was time to venture into the unknown. He led Kopi into the mist without saying another word.

# *Five*

Tioga paddled as best he could in the front of the canoe, while Kopi rowed in the back. The chief had allowed them to take his valuable light-weight birch bark canoe, rather than a more common dugout canoe—so called because they were literally dug out of a log. Tioga was glad they were engulfed in fog, as the boat was an embarrassing sight. Due to Kopi's weight, the back of the canoe was deep in the water, while the front beneath Tioga was nearly in the air. Lenni would have had a field day making fun of them.

The mist took away all features of the landscape except for the ripples of dark water around them. It felt like they were traveling through the sky in a cloud. A fast-moving cloud—the river was running high from last night's storm. For several minutes, neither boy said anything, as they had been instructed to remain quiet. The Mononga could still be nearby.

The rear of the canoe bounced off a submerged boulder, and the swift water swirled menacingly around them. Kopi moaned, as he did every time the canoe bumped something. To Kopi, the river was just as sinister as any Mononga warrior. Despite the best efforts of his father, Kopi had never learned to swim. Well, he could doggy-paddle a little, but if the canoe tipped over, he would never make it to shore. Kopi had been too ashamed to mention this to the chief the night before. If he did end up in the water, he would just try to cling to the canoe and hope for the best.

All of a sudden, Kopi let out a lengthy burp, reminiscent of a bullfrog's croak. "Excuse me," said Kopi, sheepishly. "I had a big breakfast."

"You're excused," said Tioga, who followed it up with an equally dramatic fart.

Kopi chuckled at his friend's response.

Now that the silence had been broken, Tioga decided to share what was on his mind. "Doesn't it feel good?"

"Doesn't what feel good?" said Kopi. "This is horrible. I hate the river."

"Doesn't it feel good to be free, away from everyone telling us what to do," said Tioga. His spirits were soaring. He had finally gotten his chance to go on an adventure. He had been passed over too many times to count.

"Yeah, I guess," said Kopi. "But I miss my parents and my little brother."

"Kopi, we just left! The village isn't even out of sight."

"Yes, it is."

Tioga looked back and saw it was true. The fog masked not only the village, but even the shore. "I can't believe it. I'm finally out of sight of my mother," laughed Tioga. Just then he noticed something in the water behind the canoe: a small head with a pointed snout. "Look! A snapper!" said Tioga, in the Mononga tongue. "He's watching you."

By the time Kopi looked, the turtle was gone. "Where?" he replied, also in Mononga. Ever since they were young, Tioga had been teaching Kopi the Mononga language. It was in effect their own secret language, as none of the other boys in the village could understand it. There had been many times when Tioga insulted Lenni and the bully never knew it. Only Kopi got the inside jokes.

"You missed it," said Tioga. His words hung in the early morning fog. The phrase made him think of Hanna. He decided to share his feelings with Kopi, his only true friend.

"I really miss Hanna," said Tioga, switching back to Allegewi.

"She was a beautiful girl," said Kopi.

"I've never seen anyone more beautiful," said Tioga. "There's no one else like her."

"Well, that's certainly true," said Kopi. "No one else has purple hair."

Hanna did have the most unusual hair in the village. Her mother was the town's top weaver. Since the flax thread that was used to make cloth was bland, the weavers sometimes added dye to make their garments more colorful. When Hanna was helping her mother, she sometimes took a moment to color her hair. The practice was unusual, as dye was expensive and girls were expected to appear conservative. But Chief Tundra had a soft spot in his heart for his independent daughter and looked the other way. This month a trader had brought a rare purple dye made from snails in a distant land. After trying it, Hanna's hair glowed like a purple sunrise.

Tioga continued his daydream. "Hanna is so special. You know Kopi, she's the kind of girl I'd like to marry someday."

"It wouldn't have worked," said Kopi.

"What do you mean?"

"She's the chief's daughter. She would have married a man of high standing."

The comment troubled Tioga. He'd figured he had as good a chance as anyone to marry Hanna one day. After all, he watched her a lot, and sometimes she even looked back at him.

"She might pick me," said Tioga.

Kopi chuckled. "Did you ever talk to her?"

"Yes."

"I mean *really* talk with her," said Kopi.

"Yes."

"When?"

"Last month, when we were gathering nuts."

"What did you talk about?"

"Squirrels," said Tioga. "We talked about squirrels."

"Well, I guess that puts you ahead of all the rest!"

Kopi's words sank in. *She'd never want a nobody like me*, thought Tioga. *She'd want a fighter. Someone who could protect her. A tough guy, like… Lenni.* The thought turned his stomach.

"It doesn't matter now, anyway," said Kopi. "She's gone for good."

Tioga's mind went numb. The stark reality of Hanna's kidnapping hit him. *She is never coming back. I'll never again see her brilliant eyes. I'll never again hear her melodious voice. I'll never touch her beautiful purple hair.*

To Tioga, the river no longer looked like the magical pathway to freedom. The spark of the journey vanished into the mist. He wished he was home in his bed. There he could have mourned her loss in peace. He gripped the paddle as best he could and rowed on in silence.

Kopi didn't notice the change in his friend's demeanor. He was too busy watching for boulders that would suddenly materialize out of the mist. He also sensed that the waterway was unusually quiet, even for a foggy morning. Normally fishermen and traders traveled the river. Their voices and laughter carried up from the water and into the village. But not today—not with news of the Mononga on the warpath. Today, the river was empty.

Hours later, the canoe rounded a bend and the boys finally saw other people. Up ahead, in the shallows, some children from a nearby hamlet were gathering freshwater clams. At first the kids didn't notice the approaching travelers. But as soon as one spotted the canoe, they dropped a full bag of clams and ran screaming for the hills.

"What are they afraid of?" asked Kopi.

"They know," responded Tioga.

"They think we're Mononga?"

"Word spreads quickly whenever the Mononga go raiding. Nobody wants to run into a Mononga war party."

"You were lucky," said Kopi. "Not many have seen the Mononga Devil and lived."

"He didn't look that ferocious," said Tioga. "He only has one arm and the stump on the other looked infected."

"Oh, he is ferocious," said Kopi. "The Devil has a taste for human flesh. Lenni said he ate a boy last month up on the plateau. All that was left was his hair and his toenails."

"That's ridiculous. Why would you believe anything Lenni said?"

"It just might be true. There are cannibals out there. My Dad told me so."

An instant of uncertainty passed over Tioga. Could the Mononga Devil be so wicked as to eat people?

"Kopi, be quiet and row," said Tioga. Although he tried to pretend otherwise, the thought of the Devil rattled him. He did a quick inventory of their weapons. Kopi had his bow and a quiver full of arrows, and each boy carried a knife. Tioga also had the old hatchet that his mother had given to him after his father died. The blade of the stone ax head was so dull it barely chopped wood. *Was it once a sharp enough to cut off a man's arm?* wondered Tioga. He had never really thought of it as a weapon before—just a tool to gather firewood. For fun, he sometimes threw it at old clay pots placed on a tree stump. Every now and then he even broke them on the first try.

The current carried them onward. The fog began to thin, and the sun warmed their shoulders. The river seemed like an enormous snake, slithering through an endless forest. Turn upon turn, a bend to the right, then a bend to the left. Occasionally a stream would merge with the river, making it even stronger. As they passed by, Tioga would peer into the mysterious hollows and wonder what secrets were hidden in their depths. He had never been this far from home before.

In some places the river became shallower and rushed over the rocky bottom. Tioga knew these were fording spots—places where people could walk across the river if the water wasn't too high. Important trails often crossed at these shallows. Tioga knew to be especially watchful for strangers at such spots, as they could literally walk right up to their boat. The canoe passed through a riffle, then glanced off a submerged rock.

"Oh, no!" cried Kopi.

"It's just a bump. We're fine."

"I dropped my paddle!"

Tioga looked back and saw it was true. The escaped wooden paddle bobbed in the water a few feet behind them.

"Take mine," said Tioga, as he stripped down. A moment later he slid over the side. Kopi was embarrassed that Tioga had to do his dirty work. He watched as his friend closed the gap in a few strokes and retrieved the lost paddle. Tioga laughed and even took a swim around the canoe.

"Quit showing off," said Kopi. It was well known in the village that Tioga was one of the stronger swimmers. In the water, his injury somehow became an asset. No one really understood it—including Tioga.

It was also well known, at least among the boys, that Kopi wouldn't go near deep water. Ever since his older brother had been swept away in a flood, he avoided the river—at least until today.

Kopi reached down and pulled Tioga back into the boat. The boys paddled on as they basked in the sun.

Several hours later they were both soaked in sweat. They opened their backpacks and ate their lunch as they floated downstream.

"Hey, where's your birthday present?" asked Kopi. "The bowl I gave you. You didn't bring it?"

"I didn't have room for a turtle shell. But I really like it. It was too nice to bring along."

Kopi was a little let down, but understood the decision. "So what's it feel like to be thirteen?"

"A lot like being twelve, except with more responsibility. Mom made up a whole new list of chores that I'm supposed to do when we get back."

"Hmmm, I think I'll stay twelve for as long as possible."

Time slowly passed. The sun began to sink low in the sky. Tioga was actually bored. The river did most of the work. They mainly went along for the ride.

"Weren't we supposed to be at the Forks by now?" asked Kopi. "Elder Gron said to camp there."

Tioga had been thinking the same thing for hours, although he was afraid to admit it. Daylight was fading fast. Thoughts raced through Tioga's brain. *Did we miss the Forks? Should we turn back?* Suddenly, to their left, he saw a broad expanse. In the span of a moment, the river had grown twice as wide.

"The Forks!" exclaimed Tioga. "That's the Angry River up there!"

The words sent a shiver up Kopi's spine. He knew the Mononga controlled that river and the mountains from which it flowed.

"Keep going," said Kopi. "There is no way we're going there." The last rays of the sun illuminated snowcapped mountains far in the distance. To Kopi, they looked like dragon's teeth that towered over the landscape.

Tioga's heart began to race. Hanna was likely somewhere up that dark river, heading into Mononga territory. She must be terrified. Part of him wanted to turn the canoe and head toward her. But his blistered hands reminded him that wasn't an option. He could barely hold the paddle as it was. They drifted past the confluence and continued downstream.

"We're in the Great River now," said Tioga.

"Let's quit for the night," said Kopi.

Tioga nearly burst into tears when he heard the words. "That's a deal," he said as he guided the canoe toward the shore. When the nose of the boat touched the gravel bottom, Tioga leap out to help beach the craft. Although the birch bark canoe was relatively lightweight, loaded with their supplies, it took all their strength to drag it out of the water and into the forest.

"We can turn the canoe upside down and sleep underneath it," said Tioga.

"Not until we're out of sight," said Kopi, lugging the craft further into the trees. "We're on a secret mission you know."

"This spot is as good as any," said Tioga, lowering his end to the ground. "Let's roll it over and prop one end up on that log. If it rains, we'll still be dry."

Kopi glanced at their surroundings. He immediately spotted an unusual hill just fifty feet away. "Look! A burial mound," said Kopi. "We can't sleep here."

Tioga recognized the large mound of stone and earth, built by the Ancients to house the bones of their dead. Burial mounds or cairns were common along the river terraces. While they were familiar, everyone avoided them. It was well known that these places were haunted. As if to drive home the point, a single standing stone stood in front of the mound of earth. The narrow boulder was as tall as a man. In the faint light it looked like a ghostly guard standing at attention.

Tioga's legs were cramping. He collapsed in the leaves and tried to message the knots in his calves.

"Ouch! Leg cramp," groaned Tioga. Although he thought he was in good shape, his body wasn't used to canoeing. "I'm done for the night. This is our camp spot."

"What do you mean?" asked Kopi in distress. "We can't sleep here. That's a mound for the dead!"

"It's almost dark. I can't go any farther," said Tioga. His body had decided enough was enough.

"But there might be ghosts."

Tioga's legs cramped even harder than before. "I can't do it."

"I'll carry you."

"Kopi, stop. We can stay here. Listen to the frogs."

They were surrounded by a chorus of croaking frogs.

"The frogs?"

"Yeah. They're like birds. They'll let you know if anyone is around. The frogs will stop chirping if someone comes close."

"How are we supposed to listen to the frogs while we're sleeping?"

Tioga knew Kopi had a point. But he was in no shape to move. He decided to use his secret weapon. He reached into his shirt and pulled out the decorated bone necklace.

"Relax. We have this for protection."

"What is that?" asked Kopi, squinting at the mysterious object. "A turkey bone?"

"No, definitely not. It's a powerful charm of protection. Elder Gron gave it to me." Tioga decided he'd better not tell his friend the whole story of the Devil's arm.

"It really works?" asked Kopi. "Against ghosts?"

"Of course, it works. He wouldn't have given it to me if it didn't."

The sight of the charm seemed to calm Kopi. He removed their supplies, flipped over the canoe, and placed one end on the log. Tioga crawled into their den and molded his aching body into the sandy soil.

"Goodnight, and sweet dreams," said Tioga. He knew Kopi didn't have the courage to go off and sleep by himself.

"I'll build us a fire," said Kopi.

"No fire. The smoke or light could attract attention. Remember the secret mission?"

Kopi huffed in disappointment, but the last thing he wanted was to bring on trouble.

Tioga took a last look at the burial mound that loomed over them in the fading light. He wondered if the charm really worked, but was too exhausted to care. He closed his eyes and tried to relax. He could hear Kopi rummaging around the camp. He was surprised Kopi wasn't as tired as he was. Tioga soon drifted off into a deep slumber.

Minutes later, Kopi nudged him in the side. "Tioga, wake up."

"Kopi, let me sleep."

"Give me your hands," said Kopi as he grabbed one of Tioga's blistered palms. "Just as I thought…"

Tioga was embarrassed to show his raw fingers to his friend. Kopi's own hands were calloused from gardening—one of his favorite activities.

Kopi began to apply first aid to Tioga's blisters. Apparently, while Tioga was dozing, Kopi had managed to gather some medicinal plants.

"How did you find those in the dark?" asked Tioga.

Kopi grunted. "My nose. Can't you smell the witch hazel?"

Tioga didn't bother to reply. He was too tired to smell. Kopi lifted his friend's hands and applied a poultice to the blisters. Tioga immediately felt relief from the pain.

"Thanks, buddy," said Tioga. "I don't know what I'd do without you."

"My pleasure. I want to make sure you can do your share of the paddling tomorrow. We've still got a long way to go."

A cool wind blew through the trees, bringing the first hint of autumn. Tioga pulled his blanket around him for warmth and was soon fast asleep. Images of Hanna turned over and over in his head. Then the Mononga Devil appeared, with his amputated stump of an arm oozing pus. Panic jolted Tioga from the nightmare.

He sat up with a start, banging his head against the bottom of the canoe. He couldn't see much, but heard Kopi snoring beside him, and the frogs were still chirping. Tioga ran his fingers along the human bone hanging from his neck. He could feel the ridges that had once pulsed with blood. *What if the Devil can sense that I have his arm?* wondered Tioga, his heart beating faster. *What if it draws him to us?*

Tioga took off the necklace. He seriously considered throwing it into the river. Then he thought of Elder Gron. His trusted mentor would never lead him astray. The charm must have some power and it had once been his father's. The thought calmed him.

Tioga rolled over and stroked the charm of protection. It wasn't long until he fell back asleep.

Hours later, the ghost of a dead warrior climbed out of the mound to talk with him. The skeleton mumbled a message, but Tioga couldn't quite make it out. He leaned in closer, but all he heard was clicking coming from the skull. *Click, click, click...* As he peered inside the bony jaw, a spider crawled out and leapt onto his face.

Tioga awoke again with a jerk. He felt something crawling on his cheek. He reached up and flicked a wolf spider off his face. The rhythmic clicking sound continued. He reached out to where Kopi was supposed to be sleeping. Kopi was gone. The sound wasn't coming from his dream. A bright spark lit Kopi's face, a few feet away.

"What are you doing?" said Tioga.

"I heard something," hissed Kopi. "And the frogs stopped croaking." The clicking sound grew louder, and another flash illuminated the night. Tioga recognized its source. Kopi was trying to start a fire with a piece of flint and pyrite.

"You know we shouldn't make a fire," said Tioga.

Suddenly, something snorted in the bushes. Tioga scurried from under the canoe and arrived at his friend's side. Kopi clicked harder, and sparks flew from his hands. A small red ember glowed beneath them.

"Blow on it," urged Tioga.

A moment later the smoldering tinder burst into a tongue of flame. Kopi quickly fed the tiny blaze. The fire lit up their grove like sunshine.

Tioga scanned the surrounding forest. He could see a pair of eyes glowing faintly in the shadows. A stomping sound came from the thicket.

"Shoot it," whispered Tioga.

Kopi reached down and picked up his bow. With shaking hands, he placed an arrow in position. He pulled back the string and aimed. Then he closed his eyes and released the tension. *Boing!* The arrow fell harmlessly on Kopi's lap.

"Darn it!" cursed Kopi. "These stupid arrows never work."

Tioga reached down and grabbed a round river stone. He whipped it with surprising force and accuracy at the bush. A large buck bolted into the night.

"It was only a deer," said Tioga.

"Yeah, but it could have been something—or *someone* worse," said Kopi, adding wood to the fire.

"You've got to toughen up. We've got two more days of travel ahead of us. You're acting like a scared little girl."

"Tioga, you don't know who's lurking around these woods. The Mononga Devil could be watching us right now. I want to go home."

"Kopi, in less than a year you'll be going on your spirit quest. If you can't handle this, how are you going to handle a week alone in the wilderness?"

Kopi shrugged, but didn't answer.

"I can't wait to go on my spirit quest," said Tioga, with a smile on his face. "A week away from Mom—that's called paradise. Kopi, she is always riding me. 'Clean up that mess, take out the trash, pluck that turkey.' And if I'm out of her sight for more than an hour or two, she freaks out. A week alone in the woods will be awesome."

"Yeah, but don't forget, you have to fast on a spirit quest," said Kopi dejectedly. "I can't think of a worse torture. I can't handle a week without food."

"You only fast for a few days," said Tioga as he glanced over at Kopi's belly rolls. "Don't worry, you've got plenty of meals stored up there. You'll survive."

"I hope so."

Tioga leaned back and stared at the flames. The only sounds were the crackle of the fire and the cadence of the river frogs. Before long, the fire had burned low, and their eyelids grew heavy. Even Kopi's fear was replaced by exhaustion. Soon the loudest sound in the forest was Kopi's snoring.

# *Six*

The boys pushed off from the shore and started their day on the Great River under a brilliant sunrise. "Goodbye, Forks!" said Tioga from the front of the canoe. He felt refreshed by the cool morning air and the singing of the birds. He had learned the calls of all the local species long ago. Tioga could read the mood of the woods just from the tone of the birds.

The confluence of the two rivers created the largest gap in the forest canopy that the boys had ever seen. In the hazy morning light, they could observe the strange behavior of the two sibling rivers as they met for the first time at the Forks. The muddy green water of the Allegewi River and the milky blue water of the Angry River stayed separate, flowing side by side, as they continued downstream in the Great River. It would be quite some distance before the two rivers trusted each other enough to truly merge as one.

Tioga took a moment to drop over a fishing line. He was about to tie it to his ankle when he passed the string to Kopi. "Here, you give it a try."

Kopi took the line grudgingly and tied it to his belt. "With my luck, it will snag the bottom and pull me in."

"We should make it to Sugar Maple Grove by sunset."

"Can we make some maple syrup?"

"Sure, why not?" said Tioga, knowing full well there would be no time for that. The promise of food was the best way to keep Kopi motivated. With Tioga's sore hands, that was critical.

Kopi licked his lips and started paddling faster. Just then, he felt an unexpected tug on the fishing line. "Hey, I got something!"

Tioga turned back and watched Kopi pull on the thin woven line. It was stretched to the point of breaking.

"It's something big!" said Kopi. "There aren't river monsters around here, are there?"

"I don't know," said Tioga. "You're the son of a fisherman."

Kopi paused. He was embarrassed that he didn't know much about fishing. He had heard his father talk of monster fish but didn't know whether the stories were true.

"Should I cut the line?" asked Kopi. He really didn't want to see what was thrashing at the other end.

"No way! Pull up that fish before it throws the hook. It's probably good eating."

The thought of fresh food energized Kopi. His thick arms began whirling as he reeled in his catch. A minute later, a huge catfish broke the surface and flapped its tail against the side of the canoe. It took all of Kopi's strength to pull the massive creature into their craft. It was nearly as big as he was.

"That's breakfast, lunch, and dinner for a week," said Tioga, with a chuckle. "Great job!"

"I *am* a fisherman!" said Kopi, beaming. "This river isn't so bad after all."

Tioga smiled at his friend's good fortune. Of course, it wasn't really luck at all. Tioga was one of the best fishermen in the village. He had baited the hook with his secret catfish bait—ground-up grubs mixed with acorns and raccoon fat. Whether by fishing or trapping, Tioga could always put food on the table.

After they secured the fish, they turned their attention back to paddling. This morning, before they left shore, Kopi had crafted some makeshift mittens for Tioga from a spare buckskin. They helped protect Tioga's bandaged blisters and made paddling almost painless. With the river running high, they were making excellent time.

Although the sun was shining, they occasionally passed through patches of river fog that hadn't yet burned away. Whenever they entered a fog bank, the temperature would drop and the mood of the river darkened. The swirling mist seemed to fuel Tioga's imagination. For a moment he thought he saw his father's face, twirling in the distance. Then it faded, only to be replaced by a ghoulish skull. The grotesque gray head grew in proportions. It seemed to rise up from the water. The fog barely covered its jagged teeth.

The strange vision seemed so real that Tioga rubbed his eyes in disbelief. He turned to Kopi, "Do you see anything?"

Kopi looked up and cried out, "A monster!" The canoe nearly tipped from his panic.

For a brief moment, Tioga's heart jumped. Then he took another look at the misty apparition. He laughed out loud, "Relax Kopi, it's just a cliff."

"The Emperor's Skull!" exclaimed Kopi. The strange rock that hung over the river was more than a cliff—it did resemble a giant scowling skull, with haunting hollow eyes. It was clear that long ago a huge face had been carved into the rock. The current pulled them toward it, as if the mystical head was calling them forth.

Suddenly, the canoe took on a life of its own. It began swirling in circles, and couldn't be controlled.

"What's going on?" asked Kopi with concern.

"It's just an eddy," replied Tioga, not sounding particularly concerned. "If you swam more you would see them—little whirlpools."

"Whirlpools? Get me out of here."

"They aren't dangerous, unless the river is flooding." Just then the canoe was swept to the left of the skull toward a natural inlet.

"Look! A lagoon," said Tioga "Let's check it out. It's even got a beach."

"That's not a good idea," said Kopi, as he glanced up at the towering stone face. The emperor did not look happy.

Tioga ignored the comment and paddled into the lagoon. "Elder Gron said there are ruins of a Dracul fort up there—Fort Ancient. Let's investigate."

"No way," said Kopi. "I don't want to see any stone fortresses."

"Kopi, please? I'll never get back here again."

"I'm not going up there. It's probably more haunted than that burial mound. Plus, we have to stay on schedule."

"I'll just take a peek," said Tioga, guiding the canoe toward the beach. "You can gut the catfish."

"Alright, but that won't take me long."

The nose of the canoe made contact with the sandy bottom and they ground to a halt. Tioga smiled. Now this was excitement! He could see the ruins of a stone wall on the edge of the plateau. In his mind he could imagine a line of ancient archers taking aim at them.

"Hurry up," said Kopi. "Go have your adventure!"

Tioga dropped his mittens, jumped free of the canoe, and ran toward the hill, pretending he was an attacker. As he climbed the rocky slope, he wondered how many men had fought and died here. A few minutes later he crested the broken down wall, and jumped to the other side.

He turned back, raised his arms in victory, and shouted to Kopi, "I made it! I conquered the emperor's castle!"

Kopi looked up and waved. "Don't go out of sight!"

Tioga began to explore where the old fortification once stood. It really wasn't much of a fortress any more. Other than the ruins of the wall, there was no sign of any structures. Trees and brush covered the site. He knew from the girth of the trunks that they were only about forty years old. These were babies compared to the giants in the old growth forest. The broken down stone wall looked much older.

Tioga walked out to the top of the cliff that overlooked the lagoon. Below him was the skeletal face that had been carved into the rock. The cliff dropped right into the river. During a flood, the waters would rush around it, and the hilltop might even become an island. From the top of the cliff, Tioga could see up the Great River almost all the way to the Forks. It was no wonder a fort once stood here. It was a strong defensive position, and it commanded the river.

Tioga stepped forward to the crown of the skull and felt the earth loosen beneath him. Suddenly the ground gave way and he fell with a yelp into a pit. Luckily the cavity was hardly deeper than his height. It was filled with debris from fifty years of neglect.

After catching his breath, Tioga looked around the shaft. He realized he would be able to climb out without much trouble, so he decided to investigate. It was clear that the pit had been dug into solid rock by humans—no doubt a difficult endeavor.

Tioga knelt down and reached into the leaves and branches around his feet. He couldn't feel the bottom of the shaft. It clearly went deeper. Visions of buried treasure entered his head. *What if I discovered the emperor's tomb?* thought Tioga. *Maybe it's filled with riches!*

Tioga pulled aside some of the rotten wood and a faint light appeared beneath him. *A light? Inside a rock mountain?* Tioga dug deeper. He encountered chunks of charcoal and bits of charred bone. The light twinkled beyond it. Tioga pushed downward and part of the floor broke away.

The bright light blinded him for a moment. Then he saw water glistening fifty feet below him. Tioga bent down and stuck his head into the hole. There in the distance was Kopi, pulling the guts out of the giant catfish.

*I'm inside the skull! I must be looking out from the eye socket.* Tioga was a little disappointed at the discovery. There would be no buried treasure. He pulled his head back and examined the walls of the vertical shaft. They were charred black. It was an ingenious construct. If someone built a fire at the bottom of the pit, the eyes of the skull would appear to glow at night—at least from the vantage point of the river.

Tioga leaned a charred log up against the wall and used it as a make-shift ladder to climb out. As he emerged from the pit, he noticed the smooth rock all around him was also blackened from countless fires built above the emperor. *Long ago, this must have been an important ceremonial site,* he thought.

Tioga dusted himself off and walked towards what once would have been the center of the fortress. He spotted a muddy game trail that paralleled the wall. He could see shimmering flint chips and broken pottery sherds left behind by the previous occupants. He scanned the bare ground, hoping to find an arrowhead lost in an ancient battle. But his eyes immediately locked on to something else—animal prints.

Tioga instantly knew what had made them. A mountain lion—or as they were called in these parts, a cougar. He dropped down and placed his palm inside one of the prints. The paw was bigger than his entire hand. And worst of all, the print was fresh.

Tioga realized that this was a dangerous situation. The cat was probably still nearby. He nervously stood up and raised his arms above his head, trying to look as large as possible. Then he slowly walked backward, keeping a keen eye on the forest around him. Although Tioga had never seen a cougar, his father had told him to move slowly if he ever encounter one. If you ran, you would be considered as prey.

Suddenly, a swishing tail in a tree caught his eye. A patch of tan fur was visible behind the foliage on a thick low hanging branch. Peeking out from behind the leaves were two intense green eyes. The enormous cat was watching his every move.

Tioga realized his only weapons were his knife and the old hatchet that hung from his belt. He drew the blade slowly from its sheath, but knew it would do little to stop a charging lion.

With his heart racing, Tioga continued to shuffle backward, until he reached the ruins of the wall. He slowly slid between a gap in the stones and carefully began making his way down the steep hill toward the lagoon. He put away his knife so he could use his good hand to grip the trees.

Kopi saw him coming. "Why so slow? You usually move like a mountain goat. Afraid of spraining an ankle?"

Tioga ignored the comment and continued down the slope without a word. When he reached the beach, he sprinted to the boat and jumped in with a sigh of relief.

"Let's go!" barked Tioga.

Kopi picked up on his friend's tension, and looked up at the ruins. "What's wrong?"

Tioga grabbed his paddle and commanded, "Row!"

Kopi followed the order. They were soon moving out of the lagoon toward the main river. The Emperor's Skull seemed to look down on them in judgement as they passed.

"What happened up there?" asked Kopi.

"Nothing," said Tioga, breathing easier. There was no point in stoking Kopi's fears.

"You saw a ghost, didn't you?"

"No Kopi. No ghosts." His pulse was finally under control.

"Tioga, tell me. I know you better than my own brother. I can tell when something has got you spooked."

Tioga knew he might as well tell the truth—or at least part of it. Otherwise Kopi would badger him all afternoon.

"There were cougar tracks. I didn't want to end up as his lunch."

"A cougar? That's not good."

"Well, in a way, it is good. They stay away from people. If anyone was living nearby, they would keep their distance. This area must be uninhabited."

The comment settled Kopi down. He knew people were a much greater threat to them than animals. And in the middle of the Great River, there was zero chance of a lion attack. For once, he was glad they were back on the water.

By midday, the air had warmed considerably. They occasionally heard the roll of distant thunder. The unseasonably balmy weather was stirring up storm clouds again.

Kopi's stomach began growling so loudly that it actually rumbled louder than the thunder. Kopi looked at the dead catfish and his mouth began watering.

"We've got to cook that fish before it spoils."

"A fire isn't a good idea," replied Tioga.

"But we can't waste all that food. That's the biggest fish I ever caught."

"Do you want to end up as lunch yourself?"

Kopi shuddered at the thought. *Are the Mononga really cannibals?* Then he remembered Tioga's necklace. "But we've got the charm! Elder Gron's charm of protection. A little fire won't hurt."

Tioga hadn't forgotten the charm. It bounced against his chest with every stroke. *It did protect us last night. And it stopped the cougar.* Fresh grilled catfish would be way better than the dry acorn bread and stringy deer jerky in their packs.

"Alright," said Tioga. "A short lunch break."

"There's a nice beach!" said Kopi, pointing to his left. "The perfect place for a picnic."

As the boys landed the canoe, they both agreed it was an inviting spot. In addition to the sandy shore, there was a nice clearing on the rise above the bank. This was a rare sight in the continuous forest that normally ran to the water's edge. The boys climbed up the bank to the terrace. It soon became apparent that it was more than just a clearing.

"This is a village," said Tioga.

"It *used* to be a village," said Kopi. The burned-out remains of a town shimmered in a field of waving grass.

"Let's explore," said Tioga, regaining his spirit of adventure.

Kopi shook his head. "That's not a good idea. Someone might be living here."

"Look at the place. There's not a house left standing."

"I'm starting a fire. I've got a fish to cook."

"Better do it on the beach. With all this dry grass you might start a wildfire."

"Sounds like a plan," said Kopi, heading back down the bank. "Stay in earshot."

Tioga agreed and began exploring the plateau. As he wandered through the brush, a strange feeling of apprehension came over him. He shook it off and stepped over the burned out remains of a wooden house. By the looks of the overgrown vegetation, the village must have been abandoned for at least a year.

He suddenly felt very alone. Tioga looked back to make sure Kopi was still there. He was glad to see his friend already had a small fire going. The sight emboldened Tioga to continue the search. He had hardly traveled a few steps when his foot landed on something brittle, breaking it with a *crack!* He bent down and searched the underbrush. He emerged holding the remains of a man's skull.

*What in the world?* thought Tioga. The skull's teeth shined in the sunlight like a string of freshwater pearls. It looked happy to see him.

"Kopi, come up here!" shouted Tioga. "Now!"

"I'm busy. I don't want the fire to go out!" responded Kopi. On cue, thunder roared in the distance.

"There's someone here you need to meet."

Kopi looked up in concern. The thought of Tioga with a stranger was motivation enough. He dropped the firewood and barreled up the bank.

Tioga stood alone. There was no one in sight.

"You made me climb up here for nothing?" huffed Kopi.

"Is this nothing?" Tioga handed Kopi the smiling skull.

"Ahh!" Kopi dropped it, and it rolled away into the weeds. "Where did you get that? You know it's bad luck to disturb the dead."

"It was just lying here." Tioga knelt and searched among the leaves. He pulled out several more bleached bones, then another skull, a miniature version of the first.

"It's a child," said Tioga softly. The somber sight reminded him of his little sister. Tioga still missed Antara terribly. He had never understood why the Creator had taken her when she was only four years old. His lip trembled as he gently placed the skull back in the waving grass.

"There are bones all over the place," said Kopi as he scanned beneath the brush. "No one even buried them." Kopi's fear of ghosts crept back into his mind.

"Something terrible happened here," said Tioga. "Everything is burnt to the ground. They didn't make it out."

The thunder rumbled again, this time closer.

"A lightning strike?" said Kopi, prompted by the sound. "Or a forest fire?"

"I don't think so," said Tioga. "The people would have fled to the river."

"Then they were massacred," said Kopi.

"By who?" wondered Tioga. But as soon as he said it, he knew the answer—and so did Kopi.

The boys looked at each other. The warm sun vanished behind the darkening sky. Tioga reached down and felt the cold bone hanging from his neck.

Kopi finished the thought, "The Mononga Devil!" He bolted toward the river. "Let's get out of here!"

Tioga wasn't far behind. In a few strides he passed by Kopi and jumped down to the beach. As he hit the sand, he hesitated— something caught his eye. Kopi ran by him and hopped into the canoe. Tioga stared down the shore. *What is that?* A wind gust blew sand into his face, making it even harder to see.

"Let's go," pleaded Kopi. "A storm is coming. And this place is haunted!"

Tioga walked down the beach without taking his eye off the object. A bracelet of colorful shell beads was lying in the sand. Tioga starred at it for a moment, then it hit him.

"Kopi! Come here!"

From the tone of Tioga's voice, Kopi knew it was important. He grabbed his bow and arrows and leapt from the canoe. A moment later he arrived beside Tioga with his bow drawn and loaded, ready for action.

"What is it?" asked Kopi.

Tioga reached down and gingerly lifted up the bracelet. He could barely contain his excitement.

"Some beads?" said Kopi. "That's it?"

"It's Hanna's bracelet!"

"You're imagining things. It's just a bracelet from the lost village."

"Look at them," said Tioga as he handed the strand to Kopi. "The string is brand new. There's no way they've been sitting out in the weather for a year."

"Well, that doesn't mean it's hers."

"Look at the pattern and colors. Those are Allegewi markings."

"Maybe so, but traders go this way all the time."

"Kopi, I saw Hanna wearing it!" said Tioga earnestly. "Just a few days ago. The day she was taken."

"Are you sure?"

"Yes, I'm sure. I never miss a chance to look at her."

Kopi had to admit it was a strange coincidence. "What would her bracelet be doing here?"

"She must have dropped it," said Tioga. "They must have come this way."

"She escaped?" asked Kopi.

Tioga was hardly listening. He was scanning the beach for signs. "Here!" He pointed to a faint shape in the sand. "A footprint!"

Kopi fell to his knees and scrutinized the mark. He had to agree with Tioga this time. There was no doubt it was a large man's shoe print. Tioga gingerly probed the grainy surface of the impression. He even went so far as to smell the soil.

"Someone was here," said Tioga. "And not long ago."

"Who?" asked Kopi, nervously scanning the hillside above them.

Tioga didn't respond. He continued his methodical search of the beach, his face only inches from the surface. Elder Gron had taught him well. As he looked closely, he found several more prints.

"She was here," said Tioga. "But she didn't escape."

"What do you mean?"

"The girl's print is Allegewi. The others are Mononga."

"The others?"

"Two men. They're wearing leather shoes—Mononga moccasins."

"How can you be sure?"

Tioga pointed down at his own boots made by his mother and said, "The Mononga stitch. No one else around here uses it."

Kopi nodded. "I never noticed that before."

Tioga continued his survey and more signs seemed to magically appear. "Here's where they landed their canoe." He pointed to a U-shaped gouge in the sand at the water's edge. "They hit hard and fast—in a heavy dugout. After they climbed out, they set the boat adrift in the river." Tioga looked up at the dark forest. "Then they headed for the hills."

Kopi strained to perceive the tell-tale signs in the sand. He thought he saw one, then two more footprints. Was his mind playing tricks on him or were they really there? He wanted to believe his friend, but something didn't make sense.

"Tioga, the tracks head *toward* the water, not away from it," said Kopi. "They were getting into the canoe."

"No, they were backtracking. You know, walking backward to conceal their direction. If you look closely you can tell. See how there's no dust mark coming off the heel?"

"Why would they backtrack?" wondered Kopi aloud.

"In case someone saw these footprints," said Tioga. "Backtracking is quicker than trying to cover your tracks. And it can send a pursuer off in the wrong direction."

"But the girl's print isn't going the same way."

"They were carrying Hanna. But she must have struggled to get one foot on the ground. Smart... And she dropped the bracelet to leave a sign. She must have been fighting hard. They didn't notice the bracelet."

Kopi was amazed at Tioga's perceptions. He had known his friend could track, but not this well.

Tioga continued, "I doubt they thought anyone would even see these prints. After all, why would a rescue squad be searching down here? The mountains are up the Angry River to the north."

"Maybe the Great River gave them a quicker escape," said Kopi. "They must have had a canoe stashed near our village."

"That makes sense. Kidnap the chief's daughter and paddle downstream all night, making sure to go well past the Forks. Any pursuers would turn up the Angry River and paddle toward the mountains."

"But why stop here?"

"I'm not sure," said Tioga. "Maybe because they knew the place." Both boys looked up at the destroyed village, as the first thick drops of rain started to fall. "A place they had scouted many times before they destroyed it."

"Why did they abandon the canoe?" asked Kopi.

"They wanted to get off the river. Too many eyes. Plus, paddling upstream on the Angry River at flood stage would be more work than hiking."

Kopi nodded, thankful that they weren't going that way.

"If it wasn't for the bracelet, we would have missed her," said Tioga. "Hanna is so smart. She dropped it as a sign."

"It worked. Too bad there's no rescue squad."

"These tracks are only about a day old. They probably just got off the river yesterday."

Kopi gripped his bow tighter and again scanned their surroundings. "They could be watching us right now," he whispered.

Tioga ignored the comment and continued, "If a rescue team was here, they could catch up. Remember, they're traveling with baggage. I'm sure Hanna is doing her best to slow them down."

"What a shame," said Kopi. "It will take us a day and a half to reach the men. And once we find them, it will take at least as long to get back here—paddling upstream."

"That will be too late," said Tioga. "Their trail will be cold. Another storm and the tracks will be washed away." Thunder echoed through the valley, emphasizing his point. "Her only hope is a rescue team today."

The thought depressed both boys. Kopi sighed. Suddenly, Tioga shot up like an arrow.

"There *is* a rescue team here today!" gushed Tioga. He shook Kopi by the shoulders and smiled. "There's a rescue team here right now."

"What do you mean?" said Kopi suspiciously. He knew that look in Tioga's eye—when he got a crazy idea. "Oh, no," groaned Kopi.

"We can follow her trail."

"You'll get us killed."

"Where's your courage, Kopi? It's her only chance!"

Kopi sat down on the warm beach. "We are boys, Tioga. We're not fighters. Even if we did catch up to them, then what? Do you think we are going to march in and take her away from two Mononga warriors? One of which is the Devil himself? Even if we did steal her away, they'd just track us down."

"But she's so close," said Tioga.

"We can't do it—not without the men," said Kopi.

Tioga fell back into thought. Kopi used the lull to continue his case. "I hate to say it, but a bracelet and a few scuffs in the sand aren't enough to abandon our mission. After this storm passes, we must go get the men. They will know what to do next."

Lightning flashed across the sky, followed instantly by intense thunder. Kopi scurried for the shelter of the overhanging river bank. Tioga stood alone on the shoreline and studied the steep, wooded hillside behind the village. *She could be just over that ridge*, he thought.

Kopi seemed to read his mind. He shouted, "Tioga, she is only one girl! The entire village is depending on us."

"That's just it," said Tioga emphatically. "Look at this village!" He swept his arm at the ruins above them. "This could be our village in a few days. We must stop the Mononga Devil before he can gather his army!"

"We must get our message to the men!" said Kopi with equal determination.

Tioga stewed for a moment, then backed down. Kopi was right. They had been given a mission, and it would be wrong to abandon it. Plus, maybe he was mistaken about the bracelet. He tried to remember if he really had seen her wearing it. The raindrops were falling hard enough now to obliterate the footprints in the sand. The trail was vanishing. A wave of depression came over him like the dark clouds that blanketed the hilltops. Tioga hunched over and crept to Kopi's shelter.

But just before he crawled in, a new idea popped into his head. "You go get the men, while I follow the trail!" Tioga exclaimed. "I'll leave blaze marks that no one could miss."

Kopi didn't like the thought of splitting up, but he instantly saw the merits of the plan. "That might work, but it still will take me days to lead the men back here. Hanna will be in the Endless Mountains by then. There is no way a rescue party could catch up before they reach their fortress."

"I'll find a way to slow them down," said Tioga, ever the optimist. "You take the canoe and head to the hunting grounds. We don't have a moment to spare!"

A powerful gust of wind whirled down the beach and blew sand in their eyes. The stinging grit hit Kopi like a slap in the face. "Tioga, wake up! You don't even know for sure it's her. This could all be in your head. And in your heart..."

Just then Tioga's eye caught something waving in the bushes above them. He raced up the bank and reached into the branches. He pulled out a shimmering purple hair.

"I knew it!" shouted Tioga. Even Kopi couldn't argue with this evidence.

"It *was* her," muttered Kopi, as he crawled out of his den. His chest puffed out, and he stood at attention. "How far to the hunting grounds?"

"You should be there tomorrow," said Tioga excitedly. "If you hurry, you might even spot the men tonight!"

The prospect of spending the night with the hunters was all the motivation Kopi needed. "I'd better get moving," he said. "I'll bring them back as soon as possible."

"I know you will," said Tioga, just as the heavens let loose.

There was an awkward pause, while the two friends stood face-to-face in the downpour. Tioga could sense that the foul weather was already weakening Kopi's resolve. He had to move now, before Kopi changed his mind.

"I've got to go," said Tioga, "As soon as the lightning stops, get in the canoe." Tioga turned to climb the bank. "Tell the men to follow my trail."

Kopi nodded. "Take care of those blisters."

"Don't worry. I won't be paddling anytime soon."

Kopi rushed forward and wrapped his arms around his best friend. He hugged him so firmly that Tioga could barely breathe. Sometimes Kopi didn't realize just how strong he was. He released the bear hug and said, "Be careful. The Devil has special powers." .

Tioga nodded. His hand instinctively went to the charm hanging on his chest. As soon as he touched it, a bolt of lightning flashed from the sky and shattered a tree only a hundred feet away. An incredible blast of thunder came instantly. Both boys instinctively fell to the ground.

The lightning bolt momentarily sapped Tioga's courage. Doubt slipped into his mind. He knew that if he left, there was a good chance they would never meet again. He blinked away the rainwater and stared at the wide river, which was rising with alarming speed. His stomach dropped at an unexpected sight.

"The canoe!" shouted Tioga in shock.

There, in the distance, floating peacefully downstream was their canoe, set adrift by the rising river. The two boys ran down the beach in the downpour. They watched helplessly as the canoe disappeared around the bend.

"My catfish," mourned Kopi. "It's still in the boat."

"Why didn't you pull it up on shore?" whined Tioga.

"The catfish?"

"No, the canoe!"

Kopi shrugged. Tioga shook his head and sat down under the overhang of a large tree. Losing the canoe was going to be a major embarrassment. It was the chief's birch-bark canoe—a nearly irreplaceable watercraft. Birch trees didn't grow in Allegewi territory. Even a dugout canoe took a team of experts nearly a month to craft. It might take Tioga and Kopi a year to attempt to replace it. Tioga pictured his winter spent canoe making. And there would be Lenni, continually reminding them of their incompetence.

"We're stranded, you know," said Kopi in despair. Losing the canoe was like losing his lifeline to civilization. The river stood between them and the trail home. Both the men and their village were on the other side.

"We can't let the loss of a canoe stop us," said Tioga. "You'll just have to swim." As soon as the words left his mouth, he knew it wasn't going to happen. "Or I'll swim and you track the Devil." He quickly realized that wasn't going to work either. Kopi would end up lost or worse.

"Look at the river," said Kopi, eyeing the flash flood. "Even you might drown trying to cross it now."

Tioga had to agree. He was shocked at how quickly the peaceful waterway had transformed into raging rapids.

"We'll just have to wait until it goes down," said Kopi. "In the meantime, we can make a raft."

Tioga eyed the storm, which showed no sign of abating. "It could take days for the river to calm. And it won't be easy to build a raft without rope. All our supplies were in the canoe."

"Including our food," lamented Kopi. "At least I still have my bow and arrows. And my fire-starter kit. I even have a pair of dice to pass the time. We can camp here until the river is safe."

"I'm not worried about us," said Tioga, thinking about Hanna.

"Forget about splitting up," said Kopi. "We're better as a team anyway."

"I agree," said Tioga. "We'll just have to go back to our original plan."

"Our original plan?"

"Yeah. The one where you and I rescue her."

"Now, wait. I never said that."

Tioga stepped out into the rain and started up the bank. "Come on!" he said. "That river isn't going down anytime soon. In the meantime, we've got a trail to follow." *And a girl to save*, he thought. *And if I save her, she'll want me.*

# Seven

"She's slowing them down," said Tioga as he knelt, feeling the damp earth on the forest path. "See? She's limping." He pointed to a muddy streak in the green moss.

"She's hurt?" asked Kopi.

"No, she's faking it," said Tioga. "A little while back, as we crossed that slippery spot, the limp disappeared. She's pretending to be hurt."

Kopi bent over and tried to see the clues. The rain drummed on his back and ran into his eyes. He was seriously out his element.

"They're heading east," said Tioga.

"They should be heading north, toward the mountains," said Kopi. "I'll bet they're trying to confuse a rescue team."

"I don't think they're worried about being followed," said Tioga, as he moved along the trail. "They're not even trying to cover their tracks. Look, here's 'Three Sticks' again." Tioga placed his hand on a group of three indentations in the mud.

"Three Sticks?"

"That's my nickname for him. Every time he stops to rest, he leaves these marks. Like he's leaning on a cane of sticks. Three sticks, each with a point on the end."

"You sure can tell a lot from those footprints," said Kopi with new admiration for his friend's tracking skills. He reached down, picked a wild mushroom, and popped it in his mouth.

"Tracking is about a lot more than just footprints," said Tioga. "You have to use all your senses—sight, hearing, smell, and touch."

"What about taste? I love to taste new things."

"I'll leave that one to you."

"Look, see that broken twig? And notice that loose pebble? Once you get used to it, you see all kinds of signs." Tioga resumed following the path, which passed over a stretch of exposed bedrock.

"Hey, here's another hair!" Kopi pulled a long purple strand from a branch. He handed it to Tioga, who added it to the others.

"She's trying her best to show us the way," said Tioga, admiring the silken threads. "She plucks out a hair at each fork in the trail."

"I have to say she's pretty smart—for a girl."

"Good eye spotting it. I wasn't sure which way to go. These smooth rocks don't show footprints."

The boys had been following their adversary for several hours, leaving unmistakable trail blazes as they went. Kopi was especially focused on this, as he wanted to make sure they could find their way back to the river. He reached out and broke a sapling in two like it was a twig. An earsplitting *crack* echoed through the hills.

"Quiet!" hissed Tioga. "Break plants, not trees."

Kopi snapped back to reality. "Are we getting that close? You said the tracks were from yesterday."

"They are, but they're human. They have to stop and sleep like the rest of us."

"Speaking of sleep, I'm beat. Haven't we gone far enough for today?"

Tioga was also exhausted, but he didn't want to say it. The adrenaline rush had worn off hours ago. He looked up and estimated that there was about an hour of daylight left. To catch up, they needed to use all of it.

"Tioga, let's head back," whined Kopi.

"It's been raining off and on all afternoon," said Tioga as he continued down the trail. "The river will still be flooded."

Kopi shut up and continued to mindlessly follow his friend. He realized he was in no position to negotiate.

"Look at this," said Tioga, pointing to a glob of yellow goo smeared on the side of a sapling. He decided to show off a bit. "Kopi, I'll bet you a turtle dinner that you don't know what that is. Give it a sniff."

Kopi leaned over and took a whiff. He recoiled in disgust. "Aww, gross! That's putrid pus!"

"How did you know?" said Tioga. Then he remembered Kopi had spent countless hours by his mother's side giving health care to the villagers. If there was one smell he knew, it was infection.

"She's hurt," said Kopi, with concern.

"It's not from Hanna," said Tioga. "It's from Three Sticks. He's been dripping bloody pus the entire way." Just then, Tioga made the connection. He remembered the sight of the Devil's raw stub of an arm when Hanna was taken. "Three Sticks is the Mononga Devil!"

"Really? That's a bad infection," said Kopi. "He's got to be feverish. And in a lot of pain."

The comment emboldened Tioga. "If he's injured, and Hanna is slowing them down, maybe we can catch them tonight!"

"Now wait a minute," said Kopi.

Tioga ignored the comment and began to move faster. The trail was easy to follow in the mud. He hoped they could catch up and sneak a glimpse of their enemy—and Hanna.

Kopi had never realized before just how noisy he was in the woods. He seemed to make a thunderous racket compared to Tioga, who moved through trees like a forest cat. He carefully watched his friend's movements and tried to mimic them. Every few minutes Tioga would stop, listen, and raise his nose to the air.

"Do you smell it?" whispered Tioga.

Kopi sniffed the breeze, but detected nothing. "Smell what?"

"Smoke. To the east. From up that hollow."

"A village?"

"No. A single fire," said Tioga. "Something doesn't make sense. They should be a lot further along than this if they got off the river yesterday."

"Are you sure it's them?"

"It's their tracks. I haven't seen any others."

"Maybe it's a nice camp spot and they decided to stay a while."

"That's strange behavior for raiders heading home with the chief's daughter."

"I'll bet you the Devil is too sick to travel!" exclaimed Kopi. "I'm telling you that's a bad infection."

"That would explain it," said Tioga, as ideas raced into his head. "If he is too weak to travel, we should be able to sneak right up on them."

"Sneak up on them?" Kopi's heart jumped.

"There are only two of them—and one is sick. They probably haven't even posted a lookout."

"Are you crazy?"

"We'll wait until dark," said Tioga. "Don't worry. We won't attack tonight. That will take some planning."

"Attack? Now that we know where they are, we need to get help."

"No time for that," said Tioga. "It's getting dark. We need to scout the area." Tioga reached down to the ground and dug beneath the leaves. He pulled up two handfuls of dark, wet soil and held them out to Kopi. A black beetle scurried out of the dirt and crawled up Tioga's arm.

"Here, take some," said Tioga.

"What for?"

"So we can take a look tonight."

Kopi paused. He didn't know what Tioga meant, but he didn't want to look stupid. He watched as Tioga smeared his face and body with mud.

"Camouflage!" said Kopi. He got the idea and enthusiastically covered himself in muck.

"How do I look?" asked Kopi.

"Like a giant turd," grinned Tioga, barely holding in his laughter.

"It takes one to know one," said Kopi with a smile.

"Come on. We've got work to do." Tioga branched off from the trail and disappeared into the shadows.

Hours later, Kopi nervously waited underneath a rock overhang in the darkness. *Where is he?* thought Kopi for the hundredth time. He had been waiting alone for what seemed an eternity. He was terrified. The sounds of the forest at night surrounded him. An owl's ghostly hoot echoed across the hills. *Is that really an owl?* wondered Kopi. *Or is it a warrior, mimicking an owl, as signal to attack?* He heard a snap behind him. *What if they captured Tioga? And now they're coming for me?* A feeling of panic rose in Kopi's chest. He was just about to bolt when he heard a comforting whisper.

"Come with me," said Tioga. "As slow as a turtle."

Kopi felt an enormous sense of relief at his friend's return, but it was short-lived. Tioga had vanished again.

Kopi followed, but had never felt so clumsy. He couldn't understand how Tioga could see. It seemed pitch black to him. With every move, he bumped into a tree or snapped a branch. His anxiety grew until he could hardly contain it. A hand suddenly closed on his shoulder.

"Ahh!" squeaked Kopi in shock. Tioga gently pushed him to the ground.

"Crawl on your belly," said Tioga's disembodied voice.

Kopi obeyed the order and dropped to all fours. He followed Tioga more by sound than sight. It dawned on Kopi that Tioga could see much better in the darkness than he could. He'd never realized it before, but it was almost like Tioga had the night vision of the owl that was haunting them.

To Kopi it felt like they were crawling way slower than a turtle—more like a snail's pace. He could feel that they were moving uphill. Before long, Kopi's arms were aching. He ignored the pain and pulled his body through the wet leaves. Pull, then rest. Pull, then rest. The sweat dripped down his forehead and burned his eyes. He closed them. There wasn't much point in having them open anyway. Every now and then, Tioga would reach back and guide Kopi in the right direction.

A strange smell hung in the air—like rotten eggs. Kopi knew that odor from somewhere. Then he remembered that his mom had a stinky yellow powder in her medicine kit. She called it sulfur and said there were sulfur springs in distant lands.

The owl hooted again, much closer this time. Kopi looked up into the trees but saw nothing. He felt like he was stuck in a horrible nightmare.

Tioga inched them forward to the top of the hill. When he reached the crest, he froze like a fallen statue. Kopi watched anxiously. A faint light reflected off the trees. Kopi could barely make out his friend's features.

Tioga even seemed to stop breathing. But his eyes were watching something. They darted back and forth like a cougar stalking its prey. Kopi held his breath too. He knew they were close.

Tioga turned his head and motioned for his friend to come up. Kopi, moving as slowly as a slug, arrived beside his leader.

They were at the top of a cliff. Kopi leaned forward and peered over the edge. A mysterious warm mist, strong with the smell of sulfur, floated up from beneath them.

Tioga pointed to something in the valley below. Kopi followed his gaze and spotted a glow in the shadows. At one end of the ravine, a narrow stream of water tumbled over a ledge, forming a delicate waterfall. Beneath the waterfall lay a dark void—a hollow under the falls. Kopi could see red coals glowing inside.

Something moved in the shadows. Kopi's heart pounded in his ears. Slowly his eyes focused on the faint light. *Is that her?* he wondered. Then he saw the silhouette of a man. A man with two arms.

Tioga was also having a hard time seeing. The foliage was obstructing his view. He had to get closer.

The owl hooted again, just above and to their right. Tioga looked to the pine tree where the owl must be sitting. It wasn't long until he spotted the creature perched in a gap in the branches. The tree grew on the edge of the cliff and leaned precariously over the gorge. Tioga began to crawl toward the leaning tree—the perfect vantage point. Suddenly a hand gripped his calf so hard that he almost cried out. Tioga looked back and saw Kopi shaking his head, *No!*

Tioga pulled free. He wasn't about to stop without seeing her. He inched forward along the cliff edge and worked his way to the tree. He made a final push and slid behind the trunk. But his foot dislodged a pebble, which fell over the cliff and hit a rock, which hit another, and another, and in an instant, there was a small landslide crashing to the valley floor. Both boys froze, and the owl spread its massive wings.

The response was immediate. A projectile flashed by Tioga's head, and a blood-curdling screech came from above. Seconds later, the dead great horned owl fell from the tree, pierced by a slender spear. It disappeared into the ravine.

"Good shot, boss," said a thin, ghostly voice from below in the Mononga tongue.

"There was no way I was going to let that damn owl keep me up another night," said a deep, gravelly voice in response. "Go recover my spear."

"Yes, sir."

The glowing coals behind the waterfall burst into bright flames. The entire valley was blasted by light. Tioga heard a girl whimper.

"Get back to sleep!" roared the Devil. The order was followed by the crack of a hard slap.

*Hanna!* thought Tioga. He could hear her crying. He held perfectly still and waited, then looked back to where Kopi had been. All that remained was a large, round rock. Tioga watched the rock intently. It was breathing! He swelled up with pride. The camouflage worked! Kopi was nearly invisible. The sight gave him renewed confidence.

He slowly stood behind the pine tree, which was just wide enough to conceal his slender body. He peered around the trunk, but his view of their camp was blocked by branches. He looked up into the tree and spotted the gap where the owl had been perched.

As slowly as possible, he placed his foot on the lowest branch. Then he raised a hand to another. The pine tree offered a natural ladder. As Tioga moved higher, he felt the tree bend under his weight. He knew he was pushing it to the limit. The tree's roots and the rocky soil had been weakened by the rain. If he climbed any higher, the entire tree might uproot and fall into the gorge.

Tioga stopped and assessed the situation. He could hear people moving in the chasm below him. The breeze shifted, and he was engulfed in the pungent sulfur mist. He had to hold his breath for a moment to keep from coughing. Tioga couldn't see the camp, so he listened. The sound of crying had stopped. A gust of wind blew through the forest. The pine branches swayed and moaned. This was it—his chance to move higher. He lurched upward into the gap.

The view was astounding. He could see into the cave. *There she is!* Her purple hair glowed in the firelight. She was sleeping in the dirt in the hollow beneath the waterfall. Just then a man returned to the grotto. He had two arms and a slender frame. *Where's the Devil?*

Tioga held his position but the light was fading. Fear coursed through his brain. His eyes darted the length of the ravine. *What if he's sneaking up on us?*

Tioga heard a wheeze in the shadows, forty feet below him. Someone was there, nearly submerged in a misty pool at the base of the cliff. It was him—the one-armed Mononga Devil. Strange water leaked from the cliff, leaving a blazing yellow trail on the rocks. Bubbles floated and popped on the surface of the pool.

The Devil looked even larger than Tioga remembered. He could plainly see the inflamed stump of an arm beneath his left shoulder. It rose in and out of the water with each breath. Tioga again felt the outline of the bone charm as it pressed against his chest. *Is it my heartbeat or is the bone pulsing?*

The wind swirled again, and it began to rain. The Devil raised up from the pool and climbed the bank. He threw a bearskin cape over his shoulders and strode toward the waterfall. Then he disappeared into the void behind it.

The warlord seemed to be as strong as ever. He had dispatched the owl with incredible force and accuracy.

Tioga had seen enough. He slowly descended from the tree and reached the top of the cliff. The rain began to fall harder. He crawled back from the edge and headed toward Kopi.

Kopi sensed his approach and looked up for guidance. Tioga motioned for him to follow. The breathing rock ever so slowly vanished into the darkness.

# Eight

The two boys stayed hidden under their stone shelter for the rest of the night. After they made their retreat, Tioga insisted on total silence. He needed time to think.

Kopi drifted off into a deep slumber. He slept like a rock. Six hours later, the first birdsong of the new day woke him. He saw Tioga's shadowy form sitting beside him in the faint predawn light.

"Good morning," whispered Kopi.

Tioga whispered back, "We need to talk."

Kopi nodded and sat up. He looked down at his muddy body. He had never been so dirty.

Tioga started his lecture, "Kopi, it's our duty as warriors—"

Kopi interrupted, "I know why they came here."

Tioga paused, with a curious look on his face. "Why?"

"A healing spring. My mother told me of such places. The water runs rich with purifying powers. Did you notice its strange color and odor?"

Tioga responded, "Yeah, it smelled like rotten eggs."

"It's a sulfur spring. Some say it's strong medicine."

"So that explains it. The Devil's been soaking his infected stump in medicine water for the last two days," said Tioga, processing the new information. "Do you think it worked?"

"I don't know," said Kopi. "Some wounds never heal." He glanced at Tioga's twisted left hand as he said it, but quickly looked away.

"This is it," said Tioga. "This is our moment."

"Our moment?"

"It's the perfect place for an ambush."

"Maybe so, but we aren't ready," said Kopi.

"Yes, we are. I've been up all night preparing. I've got a plan that can't fail."

Kopi could see Tioga was serious. He listened more intently than ever before. Fear seemed to sharpen his senses.

"That's a dead-end ravine they're in," said Tioga. "They've got to come out the way they went in. And when they do, we'll be waiting."

"It's too risky."

"We won't get a better chance. It's two against two, and one of them is missing an arm."

Kopi's eyes were again drawn to Tioga's hand, but he fought off the urge to look. He dared not mention the obvious parallel.

"And we've got the element of surprise," continued Tioga. "See those huge boulders over there? The ones that straddle the ravine?"

Kopi strained in the darkness to see. Again, it was clear that Tioga's vision was something special.

"It's the perfect place for a trap," whispered Tioga. "A natural funnel. They'll have to come through single file between the boulders. One of the men will be in front and one in back. They'll put Hanna in the middle."

"But we've only got one bow and just a few arrows!"

Tioga chuckled. "Oh, we've got a lot more than that. What do you think I've been doing while you slept? Come on, we need to get into position. I have a feeling they're going to leave this morning." Tioga stepped out into the dew-laden air.

"Wait! This isn't a good idea," hissed Kopi, as he nervously followed. Then he stopped dead and made a stand. "I'm not doing this!"

Tioga ignored the comment and kept going. He knew Kopi's fear of being alone in the dark woods would get him moving. Tioga headed downhill, and stopped at the first giant boulder. Sure enough, Kopi arrived beside him.

"Now listen here," said Kopi, sternly.

"You climb to the top of this rock and hide," said Tioga.

"Climb to the top? This thing is bigger than my house. You know I'm afraid of heights."

"It's got to be you. You're the archer. You'll have the perfect shot from up there."

Kopi could see it was an ideal spot for an ambush. Their adversary had to pass just below the boulder.

"You know I can't shoot," said Kopi. "Forget about it."

"You shoot fine. Just don't hit Hanna."

"Tioga, what are you thinking? It would take a master archer to hit two running men with a hostage between them."

"They won't be running. The Devil is sick. And you only need to hit one. He will be standing still, right beneath you."

Kopi glared at Tioga with contempt. "How can you be so sure?"

"I've set a trap for the leader at the other end of the funnel," explained Tioga. "When you hear him go down, you shoot the second man. I guarantee he will be standing here, frozen in shock."

"What if the second man is the Devil?" asked Kopi. "What if arrows don't hurt him?"

"He's just a man, Kopi, not a warlock. And a wounded man at that. The arrows will stick. Once they're down, we can use our knives."

"Our knives? We can't expect to beat them in hand-to-hand combat!"

"It won't be hand-to-hand. I tied our knives to the ends of some sticks."

Kopi reached down and felt for his knife. It was gone. Tioga must have lifted it while he was sleeping. Tioga pulled out two makeshift spears from the brush. He handed one to Kopi, who examined it in the faint light.

"You want to kill them?" asked Kopi.

"No. Once they're down, they'll see that we have the upper hand. They'll surrender. Hanna will be free and they'll be our prisoners!"

"Tioga, this is crazy. We can just watch them leave and follow them."

Tioga set his spear aside and grabbed his friend by the shoulders. "Kopi, this is our moment! There will never be a better spot. Don't you realize what's at stake?"

"At stake?"

"The survival of our tribe! If we do nothing, our families will die at the hands of the Mononga army."

"But we can follow them. Or go get the men."

"Either way, it will be too late to save the village. This is our only chance. The Great Spirit put us here for a reason. This is our destiny."

Kopi stood in confusion, trying to sort out all he had just heard.

Tioga looked up the path, with his nose to the breeze. "They just peed on the fire. I can smell it."

"What?"

"They're leaving. They'll be here in a minute."

Kopi's eyes grew wide. He felt an uncomfortable rush of adrenaline.

"Good luck, brave warrior!" said Tioga as he gave Kopi a hug. Tioga began to move down the path, dragging a leafy branch behind him to cover his tracks.

"Wait! Where are you going? said Kopi, trailing after him. "You're coming up there with me. You can hand me the arrows."

"I can't," said Tioga, feeling rushed. "I've got to be down at the snare."

"Snare? You said it was a trap! You said it would take out the first man!"

"It will take him down, but it won't take him out. I'll have to be there to do the rest," said Tioga coldly. "Now get up on that rock. This is war!"

Kopi had never heard his friend give orders like a commander. Part of him resented it, but the bold tone of Tioga's voice gave him a strange confidence.

Kopi looked up at the towering boulder. When he looked back, Tioga was gone. Kopi was alone. He stood there for a moment, racked with indecision.

He heard a branch *crack* from up the path. It broke him loose from his anguish. *I can do this,* he told himself. He followed Tioga's example and brushed away his prints as he moved to the rear of the boulder. Then he said a quick prayer, and began to climb.

A moment later, Tioga burst from the gap in the rocks at the other end of the natural gauntlet. He knelt in the path and took a close look at his snare loop. Although it was getting lighter, it was almost impossible to spot it, even from two-feet away.

His eyes followed the braided line he had made of thin, but strong hemlock tree roots. The rope led to a sapling that he had bent over to serve as a spring. When a foot landed in the loop and pulled, the tree would release, launching the victim into the air. Well, at least that's how it worked for Tioga's normal victims—rabbits and squirrels. He had upsized this snare so it would at least trip up a human. Tioga had positioned a large, leafy branch just before the loop. With the recent storms, branches were down everywhere. The first man would step over the obstacle, right into the loop.

Dawn was breaking and the forest was coming alive. Tioga heard voices from the ravine. He scurried to his hiding place behind the last boulder. But as he squatted down, he spooked a chipmunk. It burst from a crevice and took off down the trail with its tail held high. An instant later, the screaming chipmunk was catapulted upward and out of sight.

"No!" hissed Tioga. He watched helplessly as the sapling swung violently back and forth. The root rope trailed behind it like a spastic rat's tail. The trap had been sprung. *I have to reset it!*

Tioga jumped into the path and looked into the boulder gap. No sign of them yet. He grabbed the sapling spring and pulled with all his might. The trunk bent into position and Tioga jammed it into the notch he had cut in another tree during the night. He wished he could re-chip the notch, but his old stone hatchet had shattered hours ago.

"Stay!" he whispered under his breath. The bent sapling obeyed his command. He gently gathered the root rope and attempted to place the loop back in the path. His hands were shaking. Pain shot through his fingers every time the line touched his blisters, which were raw from the night's work.

Tioga looked up and eyed the path. The sound of footsteps echoed off the rocks. *They're coming.* Tioga was on the verge of panic. He almost called it off and ran away, but then he remembered Kopi. He had to stand with his friend. He tried again to put the snare back into position.

*Stupid hands! Why don't they do as I say?*

He re-formed the loop and placed a stick to keep it open. It stayed in place. Tioga glanced up the path and saw a shadow moving in the gap. Heart thumping, he slid back toward his hiding place.

He watched the bent sapling and held his breath. The footsteps grew closer. *Please step in the loop, please step in the loop, please step in the loop...* Tioga instinctively reached for his spear. His hand felt nothing. *My spear! It's gone!* He scanned the ground, which was now clear in the misty morning light. There was no spear in sight. *I left it at Kopi's boulder!*

*Snap!*

The tree flew upward. A shocked face smashed into the ground in front of him. The man groaned and opened his eyes in surprise. A girl screamed.

Tioga jumped over the warrior and ran into the gap. Hanna was standing in the path a few feet in front of him. Their eyes met.

"Tioga?" she gasped in disbelief.

He looked over her shoulder. *The Mononga Devil!* He had something in his hand. *A spear?* The Devil's arm cocked back. A smile curled over his lips. Tioga was the target. There was no place to hide!

Just as the Devil was about to launch his weapon, an arrow flashed from above. The Devil jerked forward with a grunt. He twisted and saw the arrow shaft impaled in his buttocks.

"Aaahh!" the Devil screamed in fury. He turned and scanned the forest to find his unseen attacker.

"Shoot him again, Kopi!" yelled Tioga. "Shoot the Devil!"

Another arrow flashed by, just missing its mark. The Devil quickly recovered his senses. He dropped his spear and lept toward Hanna. He pulled his knife and wrapped his arm around her neck, with the blade just under her ear.

"Stay back!" he screamed in Mononga. "Stay back or I'll slice her throat!"

Tioga stumbled backward and fell over the other man, who was cutting the snare free from his ankle. He reached out and grabbed the boy's leg.

Tioga kicked wildly and broke free. He panicked and ran into the timbers. Tioga flew through the trees in terror. Tears streamed down his cheeks. He had never been so afraid. The forest grew thicker. He became even more frightened when he heard branches breaking behind him.

Tioga looked for an escape. His only hope was a thicket of brambles. He bolted into it at full speed and fought through the branches, the thorns ripping his flesh. In his panic he didn't even feel them. But the vines snagged him and he slowed to a crawl. There was no way out.

Then he spotted a huge rotten log on the ground that was hollow at one end. He was about to dive in when he remembered his tracking skills. He had left a clear path right to the log! It would be a death trap.

Tioga jumped back into the thicket and pushed past the log, hoping he could lead them away. The noise of his pursuers came closer. It sounded like a stampeding herd of elk.

The vines thickened to the point that he could go no farther. There was no more time. He backtracked to the log. To his right he spotted a moss-covered boulder. He grabbed the edge of the moss and peeled it away from the stone like a soft green blanket.

Tioga kneeled before the hollow log and backed in. There was just enough room to squeeze inside. He was hyperventilating. He reached up and did his best to drape the sheet of moss over the opening.

His hideout instantly turned dark. Rotten, dusty debris and a shower of red ants rained down from above. The angry insects crawled all over him as their pinchers found his skin. Tioga ignored the bites, but the dust made it difficult to breathe. He fought against the urge to cough. A thin beam of light poured in from a small open knothole just above his head.

He could hear the enemy's approach. Tioga held his breath. The sound of footsteps stopped. His heart pounded like a drumbeat. Then the footsteps resumed. Thankfully, his pursuers continued past the log. The thrashing sound grew faint. *It worked!*

Tioga gasped for air. He couldn't believe it. He thanked the Creator and his ancestors for their protection. He even said a prayer of thanks to Elder Gron for showing him the moss trick. *Maybe it was the charm of protection*, thought Tioga. He reached up and held it.

Then his heart dropped. He could hear them coming back to the log. The sound grew closer. Suddenly, the light went out and an eyeball appeared in the knothole. He was about to scream when Kopi whispered, "Tioga?"

# Nine

The sharp call of a Blue Jay awoke Tioga with a start. He sat up with a jolt, but relaxed when he saw the tall grass that surrounded them. Somehow, they had made it.

Tioga moaned as he felt the pain of the scratches, bites, and bruises that covered his body. He looked over at Kopi, who was still fast asleep and snoring up a storm. Tioga was surprised to see a massive bullfrog sitting right on top of his friend's chest. The frog must have been attracted to Kopi's mating call.

Tioga's stomach growled at the sight of those beefy frog legs. He slowly moved toward Kopi in hopes of catching them breakfast.

The wily old frog sensed the danger and lept off into the reeds. Now that the catch of the day was gone, Tioga took a closer look at his friend's condition. Kopi was a wreck. His cloths were torn and he was caked in dried blood. *He looks like he was wrestling a bear.* The thought flooded Tioga's mind with images of his father's tragic death.

While nearly all his memories of his father were good, when Dad drank wine, his entire personality changed. The kind and caring man that he loved so much vanished, and he became boastful and argumentative. Whenever Dad was under the influence of that bad medicine, Tioga had spent the night at Kopi's house.

Thankfully, those times were few and far between. But one day long ago, when Tioga was seven, his father captured a live grizzly bear. It happened to be on the summer solstice—the longest day of the year—which was celebrated in the village. His father, who was named Wroclaw, was drunk by nightfall. He boasted to the crowd that he was could out-wrestle the bear. Lenni's father, Dudley, called him a liar and bet a year's worth of hides that he couldn't pin the bear.

Tioga was hanging out with Kopi at his house when it happened. He didn't see the matchup, which was apparently short-lived. When they carried his father into Kopi's house to see Nairobi the Healer,

Tioga barely recognized him. His hair and half of his face had been torn away. Blood gushed from a wound in his neck. He remembered holding his father's mangled hand as he struggled to breathe. *Daddy, please don't die.* His father's last words were, *"Tioga, I'm sorry."* Kopi's mother had tried her best, but his father had stopped breathing. She said he had gone to be with the spirits of his ancestors. Tioga vowed that day to never drink the evil brew that had cost his father his life.

A female Blue Jay's chirp interrupted that terrible nightmare and brought Tioga back to the present. He looked up at the blue sky and wondered if his father was hiding in the clouds. The sun above almost blinded him.

Tioga snapped to attention. "Kopi, wake up!"

Kopi moaned in pain. "What? What is it?"

"We overslept! Look at the sun. It's almost noon!"

Kopi rolled over and groaned. It took him several breaths to gather the strength to sit up. "Relax," he said. "We lost them. We can sleep all day in this beautiful swamp."

Tioga reflected on the statement. It did appear that they had lost them—if they had ever been followed at all. He shook the cobwebs from his brain and began to review the details of the most terrifying day of his life.

After Kopi had pulled him from the hollow log, they had run. Tioga couldn't remember for how long, but he recalled it was to the point that he couldn't run any more. Since Tioga had been in a state of shock, Kopi had led the way. He made no attempt to conceal their trail and paid no attention to the direction; his only goal was to put as much distance as possible between them and the Devil.

Eventually Tioga's mind had cleared and he had taken over the escape. He had known that if they were being followed, they would have to use deception to throw off their enemy. He used all of his skills—including backtracking, covering their tracks, and false trails—in an effort to conceal their true path. His goal was to return to the river. Tioga knew that if they followed water downhill, they would eventually come back to the river, and from there they could make their way to the men or back home.

After wandering all that day, they still had not found the river. But as the sun began to set, they'd caught a break. The stream they were following slowed and grew into a marsh. A family of beavers had made a large dam downstream. The result was a beautiful pond full of cattails and tall swamp grass. From the edge of the marsh, Tioga had spotted a small, grassy island—the perfect hideout for the night.

After some convincing, Tioga had led Kopi into the waist-deep pond. No one would be able to see footprints through that murky water. The boys slept that night on soft grassy beds in the middle of their own private island. A war party could have walked right by and not seen them.

In hindsight, Tioga could see the ambush had been a massive mistake. Attempting such a maneuver was beyond the capabilities of two inexperienced boys. He was so humbled that he could barely talk to Kopi this morning. But he knew what had to be said.

"Kopi, I owe you an apology." Tears welled up in Tioga's eyes. "I'm sorry that I screwed up so badly. You were right. We should have stayed by the river."

"Don't worry about it," said Kopi. He patted Tioga on the leg. "Years from now, we'll laugh about how we once tried to ambush the Mononga Devil."

Tioga's mood lightened a bit. "I can't believe you shot the Devil. In the butt of all places!"

"It was a lucky shot," said Kopi.

"Lucky or not, it saved our lives. If he had been able, I'm sure he would have tracked us down yesterday."

"I'm not afraid of him," said Kopi boldly. "Did you see how he hid behind Hanna for protection?"

Tioga recalled the terror in Hanna's eyes as the warlord held the knife to her throat. "She was depending on us to save her," said Tioga in despair. He curled up in the fetal position. "We failed her."

"We did all we could. We're just not cut out for this warfare stuff. We've got to go find the men and let them handle it from here."

The comment reignited hope in Tioga's heart. "With that arrowhead in his butt, the Devil is probably limping home. Maybe the men could catch them!"

"Okay, that's the plan," said Kopi, as he rubbed his restless stomach. "But first I need to eat something. I'm starving. Let's gather up some snails."

"Better yet some frogs," added Tioga. "They're some big ones around here. They've been croaking up a storm."

Kopi stood up in the chest-high grass and surveyed their surroundings. A female Blue Jay squawked in the distance, perturbed at the intruder in her marsh.

Tioga took a moment to appreciate the beauty of the fall colors shining in the sun. In another moon or two, the leaves would be gone and winter would set in. He listened to the mating call of the male Blue Jay, as it responded to its companion.

"Kopi, I have to say you are turning into a great woodsman. Maybe you can guide us—" Something about the bird's call stopped Tioga in mid-sentence. He grabbed Kopi and pulled him down to the ground.

"What are you doing?" asked Kopi.

"Did you hear the Blue Jays?" whispered Tioga.

"Yeah, so what?"

"Blue Jays don't mate in the fall."

"What do you mean?"

"Those aren't real birds!"

A shocked look came over Kopi's face, just as the female Blue Jay chirped to their right, closer this time. They froze and eyed the thick grass that surrounded them. Tioga noticed the frogs had stopped croaking. The swamp was eerily silent.

Then they both saw something moving in the reeds in front of them. Tioga held his breath. The grass slowly parted, and the Devil's yellow eyes appeared, accompanied by that gruesome smile. A thin spear quivered in his right hand, ready to impale them. There would be no escape without the wings of an eagle.

# *Ten*

For a fleeting moment Tioga's despair turned to excitement. *It's her! And she's alive!* He could see Hanna clearly now, gagged and bound to a tree. As Tioga and Kopi were brought into camp, she barely looked up at them. She slumped back against the ropes and lowered her head.

Tioga was disappointed at her reaction. During the march through the forest, he had tried to convince himself that being captured was actually an advantage. Now he would be with Hanna. Now he would be able to observe the Devil up close, to find his weaknesses. When the time was right, they would break free and overwhelm their captors.

*Why isn't she happy to see me?* he wondered. Before Tioga could think more on the issue, the Devil grabbed him and threw him to the ground. The other man quickly tied the boys to two trees, while the Devil stoked the smoldering fire.

Tioga took the opportunity to study the infamous warlord. While he was larger than most men, he didn't seem to possess special powers. One weakness was already clear: the tyrant had an ugly wound on the end of his arm stump. Flies buzzed incessantly around the pus-covered sore. Tioga remembered the healing spring. If it did have medicinal powers, it seemed to reserve its magic for others. The infection in the Devil's stump was worse than ever. The smell alone gave away the severity of the condition.

The warlord noticed Tioga's stare. He looked down at his stump, brushed away the flies, and turned his gaze toward the skinny boy. His cold eyes came to rest on the thick scars that covered Tioga's left arm. He followed the discolored flesh up to Tioga's face. He studied the boy's features for a moment and then walked over to him. He bent down and shouted in broken Allegewi, "Where men? Where MEN?"

Tioga glared back at him in defiance. Hanna's presence bolstered his courage. He could see now that his mother was right. The Devil was just a man. Tioga raised his chin in pride.

The Devil turned to his accomplice, smiled, and said in Mononga, "The skinny boy doesn't want to talk."

Tioga understood the language perfectly, but he didn't want them to know that.

The Devil said, "Well, we'll see about that." He reached down and pulled a burning twig out of the fire. "Such a little stick can make even a hardened warrior talk."

Tioga stared at his tormenter. He had felt the flames bite into his flesh before. As a toddler he had stumbled into the fire. By the time his mother pulled him free, his left arm was blackened. For many days and nights, he screamed in pain as the skin peeled off in sheets. Thanks to Kopi's mother, his arm and his life were saved. But Tioga had been left with a twisted claw for a hand and grotesquely scarred skin to his shoulder. From that day on he had been treated as a cripple in the village.

The Devil moved toward Tioga with the burning ember. He circled the boy and stopped beside Tioga's right arm. The Devil knew the value of a good arm. He slowly moved the flame under Tioga's wrist.

Tioga grimaced, but the only sound was from Kopi, who seemed to moan for his friend. The Devil pulled back the flame as the smell of burned skin wafted through the camp. "Where is the rest of your force?" he asked in Mononga. Then, realizing his mistake, he switched to Allegewi. "Where MEN?"

Sweat beaded on Tioga's forehead, but he continued to stare off into the distance. The Devil rolled the twig in his fingers to keep it burning. He was clearly losing patience with the stubborn boy. In frustration, the Devil switched back to Mononga. "Maybe I should cut off your arm and leave you here in the wilderness!" screamed the tyrant, inches from Tioga's face. "Would you know how to stop the bleeding? Would you be man enough to press the stump into red hot coals until it sizzled and smoked, as I had to do?"

Sweat rolled down Tioga's face. His wrist throbbed in pain as the seared skin started to blister. Tears leaked from his eyes. If the flame returned, he hoped he would pass out before breaking down in front of Hanna.

"Trial by fire is a wonderful thing, is it not?" said the Devil to his audience. No one answered, not even the other warrior. The tall, lean man seemed bored by the interrogation, a procedure he must have witnessed countless times in the past.

The Devil slowly moved the burning stick forward, this time under Tioga's chin. Just as the flames licked his friend's skin, Kopi broke down. "We were alone!" he screamed in Mononga. "There is no rescue force!"

The Devil dropped the flaming stick in the dirt and turned to Kopi. A smile exposed his rotting teeth.

"Shut up, Kopi!" shouted Tioga in Allegewi.

Kopi burst into tears. "We are just messengers," he sobbed in Mononga. "Tioga and I were sent to retrieve the men from the hunting grounds. We just happened across your trail. And once we lost our canoe, we decided to try and rescue the girl. We are alone. There are no men."

Tioga dropped his head in despair. Kopi had told them everything, and in surprisingly good Mononga.

The Devil froze for a moment and then burst out laughing. "You thought you could outsmart us? Two little boys?" He turned to the other warrior. "It is a funny story, isn't it, Chemung?"

The other man laughed awkwardly at his leader's joke.

"Too bad I don't believe it," growled the Devil, turning to Kopi. "Let us see if your comrade—what is his name, Tioga? Let us see if he comes up with a different story. Fat boy, you translate."

"He speaks Mononga," muttered Kopi.

"Kopi!" barked Tioga.

"Tioga, just tell him the truth. It's our only chance."

The Devil turned to Tioga. "You understand me? Yes?" Tioga stared back at the evil man with no response. "This will make things much easier," said the Devil. "I want to hear your story. You are the leader of the fat boy?"

"His name is Kopi, not fat boy," said Tioga, in Mononga. It bothered him to hear his friend described that way.

"So, what is your story?"

"It is as Kopi told you."

"You are messengers? You are not scouting for the men?"

"We are just messengers," said Tioga dejectedly. There was no point in lying. He hoped their deaths would be quick and painless. He decided to go out with a bang. "And I've got a message for you. The

71

Allegewi will hunt you down! They will never rest until you return Chief Tundra's daughter!" As soon as the words left his lips, Tioga realized he had said too much.

"We have Chief Tundra's daughter?" said the Devil, looking over at Hanna. "That is a valuable prize indeed!"

Although Hanna couldn't understand the conversation, she did recognize her father's name. The Devil grabbed a fresh torch from the fire, this one much larger than the last.

"An interesting story, but we must test it by fire," said the Devil with a smile. "Let's see if the crippled boy is telling truth." He slowly raised the flame toward Tioga's face.

"Great Leader," interrupted Chemung. "If you burn him too badly, he won't be much use as a slave."

"He is already of no use! Look at his arm!"

Chemung thought this was a strange statement from a man missing an arm, but of course he couldn't say it.

The Devil paused for a moment in contemplation. "These boys are full of information on the Allegewi. They deserve a slow and thorough interrogation."

Chemung looked around the woods nervously. "Great Leader, of course, you are right. But we are still far from the safety of the mountains. Perhaps they are lying and a rescue squad is nearby. Maybe it is a trick to delay us."

The Devil pulled back the flame and thought about the issue. He nodded and tossed the torch back into the fire. "Thank you for your wise council, Chemung. Sometimes I do get carried away while I'm enjoying myself. Let's break camp and hit the trail. There is plenty of time ahead for interrogation."

Tioga and Kopi both breathed a sigh of relief.

The Devil bent down and picked up three slender lances from the ground. Tioga noticed they were unlike any weapon he had ever seen before. The spears looked like long, thin arrows, but were as tall as a man. With them was some kind of spear-throwing device. Tioga remembered cave drawings showing the Ancients with similar weapons.

The Devil said to Chemung, "If these two boys are the best the Allegewi can send after us, they are truly weak. We will head home and gather my army. Then we will destroy the Allegewi once and for all!"

Tioga's heart sank. They had not only failed in their mission to reach the hunters; they had passed on valuable information to the enemy. Due to his foolish plan, Tioga had triggered an attack on his own people. Tears welled up in his eyes. He turned his face away from Hanna.

"Gag them, bind them, and get them on the trail," said the Devil to Chemung. "We have no time to lose."

Chemung quickly complied. Tioga and Kopi soon experienced the tenacious pace that the Devil set. It was no wonder Hanna had little energy left for personal interaction.

After two hours of hard travel, they stopped at a small spring. Chemung removed the prisoners' gags and allowed them to drink. Tioga found himself face-to-face with Hanna as they bent down over the shallow pool. Her purple hair brushed against his cheek. He studied every line of her flawless face. She looked beautiful, even in her frayed condition. As she raised her tender lips from the cool water, their eyes met. Her mouth opened...

"You idiot!" she hissed. "Why didn't you bring the men?"

Tioga was dumfounded. He could feel the anger in her stare. He could taste the rage in her voice. His mind was frozen. All he could do was stammer, "I... I... I..."

"No talking!" The Devil pulled the two apart. He dragged Tioga to his feet and looked him in the eye.

"Are you planning an escape?" asked the Devil. "I hope so. For there is no better sport than chasing down a captive." The Devil laughed. "Isn't that right, Chemung?"

"Yes, Great Leader."

"I'll think up something special for this boy," said the Devil, licking his lips. "Something very special." He snickered and shoved Tioga down the trail. The others fell in line.

Tioga stumbled down the path in shock. Her voice echoed in his head. *You idiot!* His lip quivered. Then he burst into tears. He sobbed uncontrollably as he staggered forward into the seemingly endless forest.

# Eleven

The Devil and his prisoners stood on a dramatic overlook watching the Great River. Tioga instantly recognized the location. Several hundred feet below them was the famous Emperor's Skull. From this spot, they not only had an outstanding view of Fort Ancient, but also the Great River all the way to the Forks. Tioga looked longingly at the tail of the Allegewi River. Both it and the Great River were empty. There was no sign of a rescue party or any other travelers.

Tioga remembered the cougar he had seen in the old fort just a few days before. He wondered if the creature was still lurking in the forest below them. Upon reflection, he wished the lion had sprung on his back and ended this nightmare before it started.

"Nice view of the Emperor's Skull from up here," said Chemung, as he sat down on a log and pulled out a piece of deer jerky. "If I had a girlfriend, I'd bring her up here to show her the sights."

"Shut up you fool," said the Devil. "I didn't come up here for a picnic. You need to start thinking like a warrior. You should always be watching for the enemy."

Apparently satisfied that there was no threat from the river, the Devil pushed them down the hill and back on the path. Tioga realized they must be paralleling the waterway, and were moving north.

They had started on the trail before dawn, after the worst night of sleep Tioga could remember. Each of the captives had been tied to a tree. Despite his exhaustion, it had been nearly impossible to sleep with painful bindings digging into his wrists and ankles, not to mention the throbbing burn on his arm. Neither of the boys had eaten in two days. Tioga was growing especially weak.

It was clear that he wasn't the only one who was slowing down. The Devil had backed off the rapid pace he had set the day before. He seemed to be stopping more and more often to rest. And he was frequently drenched in sweat, even when a chilly wind blew.

That afternoon they came to a bluff overlooking another river. Tioga could see its complexion was different than both the Great River and the Allegewi River. He knew it must be the Angry River. He had heard many times of the famous waterway, but had never seen its winding course. The river did look agitated, but not quite angry. Its swirling milky waters looked strange compared to the more docile Allegewi River. Tioga wondered what evil force lay at its source to make it so disturbed.

The Devil led the group to the riverbank, where riffles in the water signaled a crossing place. He scanned the river and the surrounding terrain. Satisfied that the coast was clear, he motioned them forward. Tioga glanced over at Kopi, who was on the verge of tears.

Kopi started whining and Tioga tried to shout through the gag in his mouth. Both of the boys were clearly upset.

"Chemung, remove their gags," said the Devil. "They can scream all they want. We are in Mononga territory now."

As soon as Tioga's gag was cut free, he blurted out, "Kopi can't swim. With his hands tied, he might not make it."

"I guess you'll just have to hold him up," said the Devil. He pushed Kopi rudely into the river. Tioga jumped in after him. Hanna stumbled in next. The water was ice cold due to its source high in the mountains. Tioga's bones ached as they worked their way across. The Devil led the way and Chemung brought up the rear. As the water got shallower, the Devil froze.

"Why are we stopping?" moaned Kopi through chattering teeth. He wanted out of the water as soon as possible.

"Shut up," hissed the Devil. "You're going to cost me my dinner." He leaned over to the other man and whispered, "Watch them. And hold my extra spears." The Devil sank low in the water and slithered off toward the far side of the river.

Tioga spotted his target, a large elk grazing in the grass in a clearing above the riverbank. The Devil moved closer. Only his head was exposed above the shimmering surface. It was an amazing display of stealth. Soon he was so close Tioga was sure the elk would see him.

Then, in an instant, the hunter sprang up and unleashed a blistering shot. The spear flew through the air with unbelievable speed and accuracy. It hit the elk with such force that it passed right through its rib cage and emerged on the other side. The huge animal dropped without taking another step.

Tioga was stunned. He had never seen a spear fly with the velocity of an arrow. And it wasn't just the spear that was impressive, but the powerful way the man propelled it. He drove it forward with a hooked wooden stick. Tioga had heard of such a device, called an atlatl. It was a weapon of the Ancients, used long before the bow and arrow were created. He had never actually seen an atlatl before. The bow and arrow had replaced it generations ago. Tioga was fascinated by its effectiveness and, more importantly, by the way it could be operated with just one arm. With that weapon, a one-armed man could be just as dangerous as any archer.

By the time the group climbed out of the river, the Devil was feasting on the elk's bloody heart. Chemung tied the prisoners to a tree and began butchering the massive carcass. He even passed some of the organs to Hanna, Kopi, and Tioga. They wolfed down the raw meat like it was the best meal they had ever tasted.

In a few moments, Tioga felt somewhat renewed by the fresh nutrients. He turned his attention to the Devil. The man sat gingerly on a tree stump, careful not to rest his weight on his left buttocks. Although the wound was unseen, clearly it was causing him some discomfort. But this must have been nothing compared to the pain in his inflamed shoulder. The infection was spreading from his stump into his torso. Tioga wondered how someone could function in that state. Mononga warriors were known for being tough, but this was beyond tough.

The Devil was working to replace the broken flint tip of his killing spear. He carried three of these spears, each as tall as a man. Tioga now recognized these were the "three sticks" that made the dimples he had spotted on the trail days before. Each spear, or lance, was built like an elongated arrow, with feathers at the end and a notch that matched the hook on the spear throwing device—the atlatl. He wondered how the man had learned to use such a mysterious weapon, but dared not ask.

Kopi was also watching the Devil. But he wasn't focused on the lance. He was studying the infected shoulder, which was crawling with flies.

The Devil pointed his spear at Tioga, smiled, and said, "Now is a good time to finish our talk. Shall we make a fire?"

Before Tioga could answer, Kopi blurted out in Mononga, "Soon you will not be able to travel."

The Devil seemed as surprised as Tioga that the fat boy had addressed him. He looked at Kopi suspiciously. "What did you say?"

Kopi nodded at the wound. "Soon you will not be able to travel. That infection will spread and make your blood boil. Then you will die."

Tioga, as well as Chemung, was shocked that Kopi had made such a bold statement. At any moment Tioga expected the Devil to run him through with the spear. Even Hanna raised her head at the tone of his comment, though she didn't understand the language.

The Devil turned to Chemung and growled, "I should never have let the Gangas Witch touch me!"

"Is the seed growing?" asked Chemung.

"Nothing is growing but the pain in my shoulder."

Chemung had noticed the pus was more profuse, yet not even a single finger had sprouted on the stump. "Maybe you didn't water the seed enough," he said. "It takes a lot of magic water to grow a new arm."

"She put a curse on me!" said the Devil. "The fat boy is right. The witch's curse will kill me."

"Why would the Gangas Witch betray you?" asked Chemung. "She is a trusted healer."

"There are many who would pay to see me dead."

"She must know that if a new arm doesn't grow, you will track her down and kill her."

"If I live long enough to make it back to her," said the Devil, looking very depressed. "She must have known that the poison would spread. That crafty old witch…"

Chemung was clearly perplexed. He stood up and paced around the elk carcass, lost in thought. He couldn't imagine life without his leader.

Tioga was stunned. The Gangas Witch, whoever she was, had poisoned the warlord. This changed everything. When the Devil died, it would be three against one!

"It might not be too late," said Kopi. "With the right medicine, you could be saved."

Tioga looked at Kopi in shock. How could he be so stupid? *Let the witch's poison finish him!* Then Tioga's anger turned to amazement. *Kopi must know something. Maybe the wound won't kill him. He must be planning an escape!*

"What medicine?" said the Devil.

"If you get out the poison and apply the right medication, it may heal," said Kopi, thinking of the times he had helped his mother treat infections. "Try willow root and the leaves of the bearberry."

"You should listen to him. He's the son of a doctor," said Tioga, assisting with the plan. "He knows which plants have strong medicine."

"I can treat the wound if you wish to be my patient," said Kopi calmly.

The Devil studied Kopi carefully. His cold eyes never blinked as he sized up the heavy-set boy. He turned to Chemung and said, "Cut the fat one loose."

"Sir, it could be another trick," said Chemung, with concern. "This boy is less trustworthy than the Gangas Witch! He is the one who shot you with an arrow!"

"Cut him loose!" said the Devil as sweat beaded on his brow. "And help him gather whatever he needs. He is in charge now."

Chemung warily did as he was told. A moment later he followed Kopi into the forest.

Tioga was buoyed by the development. Kopi knew a lot about herbs and plants. He would surely find some that would poison their captors. *What a plan!* thought Tioga. *It's just a matter of time until we're free!*

After what seemed an eternity, Kopi and Chemung returned carrying a variety of flowers, green leaves, roots, and mushrooms. He set them on a slab of stone and began to grind them with a smooth rock.

"I'll need hot water," said Kopi, hardly looking up from his work. "Boiling water. And an earth basin to place it in."

The Devil nodded at Chemung. Kopi's new assistant immediately began the task of starting a campfire. While it was heating up, he went to the riverbank and gathered several fist-sized cobblestones. He placed them in the fire to heat them.

Kopi hummed a familiar Allegewi song as he continued his mysterious preparations. At one point, he looked at Tioga and winked. Tioga tried to gather his remaining strength for the upcoming escape. His life was now in Kopi's hands.

Chemung sliced a large swath of hide from the elk carcass. He dug a shallow basin in the sand beside the fire and lined it with the bloody hide to hold the water. Kopi looked at the setup and nodded his approval.

"I'll need about two canteens of water in the basin," said Kopi, with the authority of an expert healer.

Chemung dumped the contents of their gourd canteens into the makeshift pot. Kopi began adding his ingredients.

"Now the rocks, please," said Kopi.

Chemung looked to his leader, and the Devil nodded. Using a pair of sticks as tongs, Chemung grabbed each glowing river cobble from the fire and slipped it into the brew. The rocks hissed and steam rose from the strange cauldron.

Tioga watched the scene intently. While he had boiled water with hot rocks before, he had never noticed the potential of superheated stones as weapons. He pictured a war party scattering as a barrage of fire rocks landed on them. Of course, he would have to invent a way to heat and launch them.

All eyes were on Kopi, with the exception of Hanna, who was curled in a ball on the ground. She was still shivering from the river crossing. Her fighting spirit had been broken by the ordeal of the last week.

After several minutes, Kopi finally announced, "Alright, I am ready." He motioned to the Devil and said, "Sir, please lie down."

The Devil nodded and followed the order.

"The Gangas Witch," said Kopi to his patient, "she promised she could grow you a new arm?"

"Yes. She planted a magical seed."

"Where did the seed come from?"

"I do not know."

"She is known throughout the uplands," added Chemung. "She has great powers. We heard from a scout that she was traveling down the Allegewi River. So, we rushed to find her. It is said she can repair damaged bodies, break strong curses, and even raise the dead. It was a special opportunity."

"She can raise the dead?" asked Kopi, skeptically.

"Yes!" responded Chemung, enthusiastically. "Long ago, one of our tribe members was frozen in ice. He was as stiff as a dugout and as blue as the sky. They took him to the Gangas Witch and she brought him back to life. He still lives with us today. We call him the Iceman."

"Interesting," said Kopi. He had studied his mother's medicine since he was a small child. He had never heard of raising the dead or growing a new arm. He wanted to comment on the foolishness of it, but bit his tongue. He knew better than to insult a patient. It did explain why two lone warriors were such a long way from home. Raiders normally travelled in greater numbers. The capture of Hanna must have been an unexpected bonus on the way to the healing spring.

"I need your knife," said Kopi to his patient. The Devil reached down and pulled it from his sheath.

Chemung blurted out, "Sir, no! The boy can't be trusted!" Chemung sprang forward with his own knife drawn.

The Devil responded, "Back off, Chemung. The fat boy—" He stopped mid-sentence and corrected himself. "Kopi—is right. I can feel the fever spreading. If he slits my throat, it will just be a quicker death than the witch's poison." The Devil handed Kopi his knife.

Neither Chemung, Tioga, nor Hanna could believe what they were seeing. Kopi moved over top of his patient as the blade flickered in the sunlight. He knelt down and examined the wound.

Tioga could barely contain his excitement. Now Kopi didn't even need the poison! If he was quick about it, he could plunge the dagger into the Devil's throat, then turn and charge Chemung. Tioga tested the strength of his bindings. There was some give. He might be able to break free and help.

Kopi moved the knife forward. He passed over the Devil's neck and gingerly probed the putrid stump. Pus oozed from the wound and dripped into the grass.

Tioga waited to see the patient's reaction. Kopi was toying with him. The pain must be excruciating. But the Devil didn't even flinch. He calmly looked out at the river as if he was watching for a fish to jump.

Kopi scowled and dug deeper. Finally, he found his target. The blade emerged with a strange purple sphere balanced on its tip—a cherry pit. Kopi studied it for a moment then flicked it into the fire. It landed in the red-hot coals and sizzled. Everyone watched as the pit took on a life of its own. It jumped, rolled, and squealed in the intense heat. The shell finally burst open with a loud *pop!*

"The witch's seed was cursed!" said Chemung.

"I knew it! I'll roast that Gangas Witch!" roared the Devil.

Kopi methodically cleaned the wound, removing several squirming maggots. After it cooled a bit, he poured his strange medicinal brew over the damaged tissue, then made the Devil drink the last of it.

Tioga waited for the warlord to lurch over in agony. Instead he lay peacefully in the warm afternoon sun. Kopi wrapped the wound in a poultice of aromatic leaves and soft cattail down beneath a leather sling.

"It is done," said Kopi. "Do you wish me to look at the arrow wound?"

The Devil ignored the question. He stood up and stretched his legs. Although the arrowhead was still embedded in his buttocks, the wound was barely a scratch compared to what he had been through. A witch's curse was a serious situation. He doubted the fat boy had the power to break such a spell, but maybe it was possible. His stump was beginning to feel better already.

"You should rest," said Kopi.

"Chemung, move them to the camp," said the Devil.

The warrior immediately complied, and moved the captives from the elk carcass to a cleared area a hundred paces away. A half dozen empty huts stood waiting for them. For the first night since they left home, they would have a roof over their heads.

Tioga was perplexed. The Devil didn't seem to be getting worse. In fact, as he walked to the camp site, he looked fresher than he had in days. Could Kopi have actually helped the man?

Tioga realized he might have to lead their escape. He closely studied their surroundings. They were standing on a wide level terrace between the river and a tall cliff. This was obviously a significant camp site. Although he couldn't be sure, it looked like there were a dozen or more dugout canoes stored upside down on blocks in the tall grass that surrounded them. If they could somehow get free, they could steal one of the canoes and go down river to get the men.

The idea gave Tioga new hope. He starred at Kopi, trying to get his attention. Kopi finally made eye contact. Tioga used his head to gesture to the boats. He even mouthed the word *canoe* to make Kopi aware of the opportunity.

Kopi nodded and turned to Chemung. "What's up with all the canoes?"

Tioga scowled. He didn't want Kopi to alert the enemy!

"This is what we call Canoe Camp," answered Chemung. "You cannot paddle the Angry River upstream of here, due to the rapids. So, we keep the boats here." Chemung chuckled. "If you had one, you could paddle all the way home to your village."

Tioga was steaming. Kopi had gone and leaked his plan!

"Aren't you concerned someone will steal them?" asked Kopi.

Chemung pointed at one of the vessels. "They all carry the mark of the bear. Anyone caught with a stolen Mononga canoe wouldn't live to see the sun rise. Every trader knows it."

"Chemung, quit chattering like a little girl," said Shingas. "Get busy and cook my dinner."

"Yes, Great Leader."

"Kopi, do you like roasted elk?" asked the warlord to his new doctor.

"I love it! I've got a really good recipe. If we can find some wild mushrooms, onions, and herbs, I could make it."

"You cook?" said the Devil, who actually had an appetite for the first time in days.

"Oh yes," said Kopi. "It's one of my favorite hobbies."

"Chemung, help Kopi prepare the meal."

The man paused and looked at the Devil with surprise. "Sir, are you sure?"

"Do it!" bellowed the tyrant. "His cooking can't be worse than yours."

"Yes, sir."

The Devil walked to the beach and scanned the horizon. Chemung joined him and washed the elk blood from his hands.

Noticing that they were just out of earshot, Tioga leaned over toward Kopi.

"Kopi!" he hissed. "What are you doing?"

Kopi responded, "Cooking dinner. Wait until you taste my elk chops. I've got a special rub—"

Tioga interrupted. "You helped the Devil. He was dying!"

"I'm the son of a doctor. It's my duty to help the sick."

"Your duty?"

"Silence!" barked Chemung from the riverbank. He cracked a leather whip to add emphasis to the threat.

Tioga's outlook turned bleak. He looked up the river and could see distant snowy peaks. Tomorrow they would climb into the mountains. They looked as dark and ominous as Lenni had described them. Tioga had often heard stories of distant villages and faraway places, but until now, he never realized just how big the world was. It made him feel small and naïve. He longed to be back in their humble village overlooking the Allegewi River.

# Twelve

Tioga followed Hanna in silence. As she climbed over a fallen tree, the rope between them drew tight, causing Tioga's right wrist to burn. At least his left hand was free. *A hand so useless that it wasn't even worth tying.*

As Tioga crossed the tree trunk, his foot slipped and he fell to his knees. He had barely hit the ground when the Devil's spear point prodded him in the ribs. He let out a yelp and slowly rose to his feet. Hanna glanced back and looked at him without emotion.

"Eyes forward," ordered the Devil. "Keep moving." In the three days since their capture, Tioga had grown numb. After marching for ten hours a day, he had little feeling left for the Devil, or for Hanna. They had crossed a river, countless streams, and thick forests. But then had come the mountains.

Tioga couldn't see the mountains, as the trees blocked their view. But he could feel them. Every step was higher, and colder, than the last. The path seemed to go up and up without ending.

Depression clouded his thoughts. *What is there to live for? Torture in the Mononga fortress?* He shuddered at the thought of what lay ahead. There was no way out. With each step, Tioga fell deeper and deeper into despair. *What's the point of going on?* He slowed down and nearly stopped. *I don't care anymore. The worst he can do is kill me. Go ahead, get it over with!*

Just then the travelers burst into the sunlight as the trail emerged atop a rocky overlook. Tioga was stunned. He could see farther than he had ever seen before. For a moment he tasted the glory of an eagle's view. The incredible vista freed him. A strange energy coursed through his veins. He breathed in deeply and the cool mountain air filled his lungs.

A memory suddenly swirled in his brain, like the clouds that twisted below them. He remembered his mother saying something—

something important about her life with the Mononga. He thought back to their talk on that rainy night when the chief had come to their hut. It seemed so long ago. Suddenly, he recalled a name. He turned his head back and looked the Devil straight in the eyes.

"Get moving!" said the Devil. The spear nipped Tioga in the shoulder. He didn't even flinch.

"Your name is Shingas," said Tioga. "Shingas the Terrible."

Shingas stared back at Tioga. "What did you say?"

"Your name is Shingas!"

"Stop!" ordered Shingas. The group ground to a halt. Kopi and Hanna fell to the ground in exhaustion.

Shingas walked beside Tioga and bent down to his ear. His stump was directly in front of the boy's face. Tioga could see that Kopi's medicine was working. The wound was healing.

"Where did you hear this?" whispered Shingas.

*Is that fear in his voice?* thought Tioga.

"Who told you my childhood name?"

Tioga studied the man's face. Something about him had changed. The immortal Devil was gone. Before him stood an ordinary man. A man with fears, just like everyone else.

"My mother told me," said Tioga.

Shingas looked at him suspiciously. "Who is your mother?"

"Her name is Candowsa," said Tioga.

Shingas's eyes opened wide. He seemed to gasp for air. "Candy? She is alive? Candowsa is alive?"

Tioga nodded proudly. "She is Allegewi now."

Shingas's eyes softened. "They told me she was dead." He staggered back and nearly stepped off the edge of the cliff. The revelation seemed to penetrate his soul. He began to wander aimlessly around the group as his mind struggled to comprehend the news.

Chemung watched with concern. *What could the boy have said to affect him so?* He pulled an arrow from his quiver and loaded his bow—an unconscious habit he had developed over the years when faced with uncertainty.

After several tense moments, Shingas stopped pacing. His stoic demeanor slowly returned. "Get up and get moving," he said. The hostages took to the trail without a word. They had learned to follow the warlord's orders or suffer the consequences.

As Tioga moved along the narrow path, he stole a glance over his shoulder. Shingas was again lost in thought. Tioga noted the pronounced limp in his stride. He wondered how someone could travel so far with a flint arrowhead in his buttocks. Or for that matter with a wounded arm. Shingas was a living display of a warrior's ability to suppress pain.

Regardless of the discomfort, Shingas quickened the pace. It was plain to see that he traveled with renewed urgency. They re-entered the forest, and the trees closed around them.

Tioga wondered whether he had made a mistake. He was proud of his secret knowledge of Shingas's past. It gave him a sense of control in an otherwise hopeless situation. But he regretted telling the warlord his mother's name and where she lived. He hadn't expected that Shingas would remember her.

Several hours later, after dusk turned to night, the group finally made camp in a rocky hollow near a babbling brook. Hanna and Tioga were tied back to back with a small sapling between them. The temperature of the thin mountain air plunged when the sun went down. Hanna shivered on the damp ground.

Shingas and Chemung sat close to the fire as Kopi worked on the warlord's stump. In addition to nursing his patient back to health, Kopi was now Shingas's private cook, making him medicinal tea and healthy food every time they stopped. Tioga resented Kopi's care for the enemy and the preferential treatment he received in return. *Could it be?* wondered Tioga. *Has Kopi become a traitor?*

Kopi finished dressing the wound and meekly retired to the far side of the fire. As a formality, Chemung tied the boy's hands, but it was clear they no longer viewed Kopi as a threat.

Tioga tried to make eye contact with his friend, but Kopi seemed to be avoiding his gaze. Tioga leaned back against the tree in a futile attempt to get more comfortable. His shoulder accidentally touched Hanna's back. She tensed and pulled away. He ignored her reaction. She was a spoiled brat, not worth thinking about. Instead he kept a keen eye on their captors.

Shingas was especially talkative this evening. Normally he kept to himself, saying little even to Chemung. Now he was chattering away. *He must be excited to be nearing home,* thought Tioga.

The warlord was in a festive mood. His strength was returning. He hadn't felt this good since that witch had messed with his stump.

The fat boy must have broken the curse after all. He smiled at the thought of an Allegewi boy outsmarting the famous Gangas Witch.

Chemung sensed the positive change in his boss's demeanor. He dumped out a bag containing the items they had confiscated from their captives. He picked out a small pair of dice, hoping a game would break the boredom.

"Commander, do you want to roll the dice?" asked Chemung to Shingas, as he jostled the small bone squares.

"No," answered Shingas. "Games of chance are a waste of a warrior's time."

Chemung nodded and began to place the objects back in the bag. One item caught Shingas's eye. "What is that?" he asked.

"This?" said Chemung as he held up an odd-looking bone, adorned with strange carvings and old feathers. "It must be a charm. I took it off the skinny boy when we captured them. He wore it as a necklace. Remember?"

"Let me see it," said Shingas.

Chemung tossed it across the fire.

Shingas made a weak attempt to catch it, but he fumbled it and the charm landed in the dirt. The medicine tea was making his head spin. He picked up the bone and examined it closely.

Tioga's heart pounded in his ears. *Could he know? Could he sense his own marrow?*

Chemung was surprised his leader would bother with the old fetish. It was well known that the commander believed in strategy, not sorcery, to win in battle. The longer Shingas studied the charm, the more Chemung wanted it back. Maybe it possessed strong magic after all.

"What do you think it is?" asked Chemung impatiently.

Shingas didn't answer. He seemed to be in a trance as he ran his fingers along the bone's polished surface.

Chemung noticed that Tioga was watching them intently. "Let's ask the cripple who wore it," he said. "He can barely walk without it!"

Shingas snapped out of his daze. "Chemung, never underestimate a man with one good arm," he said slyly. "In the middle of the night you might find it wrapped around your neck."

Chemung simmered at the insult. Did he honestly believe the cripple was dangerous? Or was his leader threatening him?

Shingas looked over at Tioga. It was hard to imagine the boy as Candowsa's son. He felt a strange emotion pass through him. *Envy?*

The tyrant turned his gaze to the girl with the purple hair. She looked tired and beaten, but something about her was mesmerizing. Due to the language barrier, he had never interrogated her. But now it dawned on him that Kopi could serve as translator. The daughter of the chief might have insider information on the Allegewi.

Shingas stood up and limped over to the captives. He passed by Tioga and looked down at Hanna. "You are a rare catch," he said with a smile. "Valuable in so many ways." He brushed the hair off her cheek.

Hanna kept her eyes to the ground, knowing her best chance to avoid further abuse was to hold perfectly still. She couldn't understand his language, but she could sense his intent.

"It is time we talked," said Shingas warmly. "Come over to the fire." A knife flashed through the darkness and Hanna was suddenly cut free. Shingas dragged her cowering body into the light and threw her in the dirt.

He held up the strange bone charm and waved it over her. "Look, Chemung, do you think this charm will bring me luck?" Shingas burst into laughter.

Chemung scowled, still bitter from the previous rebuke. He quickly faked a chuckle to avoid incurring the warlord's wrath.

Shingas turned to Tioga to see if he, too, saw the humor in the situation. Tioga glared at him with obvious contempt.

"Here, boy, you could use a little backbone," said Shingas. He threw the charm at Tioga. The cold bone smacked him in the cheek and fell into his lap.

Kopi sat there wide-eyed and frozen. While he might treat the warlord's wounds, he wouldn't help him hurt his friends. He sensed the situation was turning ugly.

Tioga felt the blood rush into his cheeks. "Get away from her," he growled, as his protective nature took over.

"Don't worry, boy," said Shingas. "I'll deal with you when I'm finished with her." He returned his attention to Hanna.

Tioga strained at the ropes that bound him. The only item within his reach was the charm. With the claw of his left hand, which had been left untied, he grabbed the bone and shouted, "Shingas, you could use a little arm bone! After all, it is *your* arm bone!" He whipped it at the back of Shingas's head. It ricocheted off the warlord's skull and landed in the glowing coals at the base of the fire.

The bear of a man turned and rushed the boy, grabbing him by the throat. Shingas's first reaction was to strangle him on the spot. But curiosity overcame his rage. *What did he say about an arm bone?* He held back from crushing the boy's windpipe.

Kopi watched the confrontation in horror. Hanna lay frozen in the dirt. Chemung sat enjoying the show. *The boy is brave*, he thought, *but stupid.*

"What did you say?" screamed Shingas. Tioga gasped for air. Shingas broke off the attack when he remembered the charm. He rushed back to the fire and kicked it out of the coals. The feathers had been burned off and it was a little blackened, but otherwise it was undamaged.

He juggled the steaming bone in his one hand as it cooled down. Then he charged back to Tioga. "Where did you get this?" he snarled.

"A village elder gave it to me," said Tioga fearfully.

"Why?"

"To protect me," said Tioga.

"It is an arm bone? A human arm bone?"

"Elder Gron said it was. My father took it as a battle trophy."

"Your father?" said Shingas. "Who is Candowsa's husband?"

"Wroclaw," said Tioga softly. "My father was Wroclaw the trapper."

"You are the son of Wroclaw the trapper?" asked Shingas. "The idiot who died wrestling a bear?" Shingas burst into laughter. "He was the joke of the valley. Even the Mononga know the tale. How could Candowsa have married such a fool?"

The insult was more than Tioga could stand. His fear turned to anger. "He was no fool! He cut off your arm with a hatchet at Deadly Dell! My mother told me so!"

The statement staggered Shingas. He looked down at the charm. *Am I holding my own arm bone?* Memories of the Allegewi ambush flooded into his brain. He recalled the flash of an axe and the searing pain in his shoulder. Then there was the panic of his escape, and the sorrow of losing his father. He had never learned the name of the warrior who had taken so much from him—until now.

"Your father was a coward!" yelled Shingas "The Allegewi were afraid to fight us face-to-face. They ambushed us with no honor!"

"Just like you ambush young girls?" said Tioga.

Shingas stumbled to the far side of the fire, as he tried to process all he had heard. The medicine tea made it difficult to think. A foggy haze was coming over him.

Kopi whispered to Tioga in Allegewi, "Your father cut off the Devil's arm? Why didn't you tell me?"

"Silence!" screamed Shingas in Mononga, attempting to regain control of the situation.

Chemung stared at the warlord. *Could what the crippled boy said be true? The commander lost his arm to Wroclaw the fool?* Chemung clicked his tongue in judgment.

Shingas snapped out of his daze and scowled at Tioga. "You are a fool, just like your father. Little boy, the elder was wrong. This bone won't protect you from death. It has *brought* your death!"

Tioga turned ice cold at the comment.

"A very slow and painful death," said Shingas, as the dreaded smile returned to his lips. "But not just yet. After all, what better bait to catch a mother bear than its cub?"

The words upset Tioga. The last thing he wanted to do was involve his mother in this nightmare. Did Shingas still have feelings for her? Were they of love or hate?

Shingas's good mood was long gone. He yelled at Chemung, "Tie the girl to a tree. And tie both arms of the skinny boy—tight!"

Chemung immediately followed the order. He grabbed Hanna by the hair and led her to a sapling a few feet from Tioga. After tying her hands behind the tree, he turned his attention to the boy, making sure that both arms were secure.

The camp soon fell silent and the fire dimmed. Tioga sat with his back to the tree, feeling very alone in the cold night. He was facing unimaginable torture in the enemy's fortress. He fought to hold in the sorrow that welled up inside him. Just as a lonely tear ran down his cheek, something warm pressed against his leg. It was Hanna's foot.

*What is she doing?* he thought. *Why is she touching me?*

Her toes softly stroked the side of his leg, sending ripples through his body. He wanted to pull away, but something kept him there. He slowly lowered his guard and gave in to her caress. His strained muscles relaxed. Tears of joy streamed down his face. He could hardly believe it. Her touch was as wonderful as he had ever imaged it to be.

# *Thirteen*

"Whoop, whoop, whoop!" Shingas's war cry boomed through the mountains. Tioga looked at Hanna and waited for the response that he knew would come.

An eerie response echoed across the wilderness, answering the warlord's signal. Then another voice joined it. Then another. The high-pitched calls seemed to come from all directions. Hidden sentries were posted on every peak.

The tribal screams were not the only unusual sound in the forest. With each step, a curious vibration grew louder. Soon it transformed from a hiss into a thunderous roar that reverberated around them. As the trail exited the trees and traversed a rocky ledge, Tioga saw the origin of the sound. Far below, a tortured river leapt and fell over enormous boulders on its journey down the mountain gorge. Tioga stopped to stare at its brilliance. Now he knew why they called it the Angry River. He had never seen such a dramatic landscape.

The path followed the canyon rim for some distance as it paralleled the course of the river. As the group turned a bend, a strange apparition appeared over the misty abyss. Tioga studied the bizarre and delicate object—a suspension bridge. A web of thick ropes stretched across the canyon. A series of wooden planks were tied between them to serve as a walkway.

"Oh, no," said Kopi at the sight. He stopped dead in his tracks. A push from Chemung got him moving again.

Tioga looked in awe at the construct. His eyes followed the ropes and the trail beyond it. For a split second, the clouds parted and he caught a glimpse of the Mononga mountaintop fortress. Then the mist closed and it vanished from sight. A chill ran down Tioga's spine. While he didn't see much of the castle, its sheer size dwarfed their small village.

The group paused at the entrance to the span. On the other side stood an armed guard of a dozen warriors, waiting to escort their commander home. The suspension bridge was the perfect defensive device. If an attacking army arrived, the defenders could cut the ropes. The only other way in was a full day hike around the canyon, and that would be loaded with ambush opportunities.

Shingas confidently strode onto the swinging planks, raised his arm in triumph, and let out a blood-curdling war cry. He reached back and grabbed the rope that bound Hanna and Tioga and pulled them forward. They stepped carefully onto the rickety wooden slats and began the crossing. Tioga felt the eyes of countless sentries watching the procession.

As they moved forward, Tioga held the side rope with his good hand to stabilize himself. He looked down and noticed the finest rope he had even seen. Clearly a master rope-maker lived in the fortress.

Kopi turned to Chemung with fear in his eyes. "I can't do this. I'm afraid of heights."

The warrior chuckled. His commander was already halfway across, with the other hostages in tow. Chemung had a rare moment alone with Kopi. He didn't miss the opportunity to teach the spoiled fat boy a lesson. *Crack!* He snapped Kopi in the back of the legs with his leather whip. Kopi fell to his knees in pain. Chemung grabbed him by the hair and threw him out onto the bridge. Kopi looked down between the rungs at the chasm below. The sight made his head spin.

*Crack!* The whip cut through his pants and burned into his butt. "You want more?" roared Chemung. "Get moving!"

Kopi rose up in pain and gingerly took his first step. Chemung could see that his leader and the captives were already across.

Shingas looked back to see what was causing the delay. Chemung hid the whip behind his back. Now that the boss was watching, he would have to use other methods to motivate Kopi.

He took the boy by the arm and began helping him negotiate the unstable planks. By the center of the span, Kopi was ready to throw up. The wind howled through the canyon and rocked the bridge back and forth. Kopi closed his eyes in an effort to stop his dizziness. He blindly felt for each board with his feet. More than once his foot slipped between the slats, but Chemung arrested his fall. Finally, he felt the crunch of solid earth. He nearly dropped to his knees to kiss the ground.

After the crossing, the path grew steeper and Shingas drove them even harder. Soon they were running uphill. The prisoners struggled to keep up the pace—especially Hanna and Tioga, as their feet were lashed with barely enough slack to take a normal step.

Shingas was visibly excited. They were almost to their destination. The clouds parted and Tioga got his first clear look at the Mononga castle. For days he had tried to picture it, but its reality exceeded even his vivid imagination.

The fortress was perched on a flat-top mountain and was surrounded by steep cliffs. In areas where the bluffs weren't vertical, evergreen trees clung to the rocky soil like a strip of thinning hair around a bald man's head. As if the crags weren't enough protection, a wall encircled the fort. The Mononga flag whipped angrily at the top of an enormous flagpole. Eager faces peered over the stockade at the approaching band.

The travelers arrived at the bottom of a winding wooden staircase that led up to the fortress. Tioga had never seen such a construct. While he had climbed ladders, he had never seen stairs that literally rose into the clouds. They began the arduous climb up to the fortress.

By the time they reached the top, Tioga's legs were burning. Kopi wheezed behind him, on the verge of collapse. Tioga looked up at the fortress walls. The sections on either side of the massive gate were made of cut stone, matched perfectly together. But apparently such material was in short supply, as the palisade on the river side was made of upright timbers. That side of the fort hardly needed defenses. Below the wooden wall, the gorge fell two hundred feet to the thrashing river.

As they stood before it, the heavy gate slowly opened. Tioga had tried to prepare for the trauma of entering the enemy's village. But he hadn't anticipated the deafening roar of four hundred people. His ears rang with their rhythmic chanting.

Hanna stumbled back against him and looked into his eyes. She was trembling uncontrollably. He pulled her close to comfort her as best he could. Kopi was frozen in terror.

The excited crowd was massed in the central plaza. Tioga had never seen so many people. Hundreds of angry faces shouted at them. Shingas pulled them forward.

"Mononga people! Your leader has returned!" yelled Shingas. The mob roared. "And I have brought captives for your enjoyment." A festive atmosphere spread through the throng.

Shingas bellowed, "Quiet now! I have much to tell you!"

The crowd instantly obeyed his command for silence.

The warlord continued, "I have had a very successful journey! Our conquest of the valley is nearly complete. Only one obstacle remains in our way—a small village on the Allegewi River. They are so weak it is an embarrassment. The only force they could send to combat me were these helpless children!"

The horde roared again. Shingas raised his hand, and they hushed. He continued his speech. "Tomorrow we go to war to finish the Allegewi! We shall fall on their little village like a cougar leaps on a newborn doe!"

The people cheered with delight. Then they began to call for the prisoners. They formed into two angry lines that waited to engulf the captives. The dreaded gauntlet appeared before them. Tioga thought of his mother as he stared into the mouth of the tribal monster.

Shingas turned to his prisoners. Judging by his expression, he was enjoying the moment. He bent over Kopi and said in his ear, "You broke the witch's curse. I therefore give you the honor of entering the gauntlet first."

Kopi looked back in terror. It was an honor he didn't want! Shingas took the stocky boy by the arm and led him forward. Kopi was shaking with fear.

The tyrant spoke to his people. "Here we have a young Allegewi *man*, named Kopi." Tioga was surprised Shingas had called Kopi a man—clearly a term of respect. Shingas continued, "He is a great healer! A man of much value! Is he courageous enough to meet the Mononga gauntlet?"

The crowd responded, "Bring him on!"

Shingas leaned down and spoke to Kopi again. "You know the rules of the gauntlet. Run down the center as strongly as you can. Your life depends on it. If you make it through, run to the house with the red door. There you will find safety. Now run, and make me proud!"

He pushed Kopi toward the mob. Kopi hesitated and looked back at his friend. Tioga gritted his teeth and nodded. With his friend's encouragement, Kopi turned and attacked the line with surprising speed and power.

The blows fell on him from all sides. He stumbled, but kept running. He raised his hands to deflect the assault. Tioga thought he saw blood splash as one of the clubs struck home. Kopi kept going.

His legs churned up the dust as he powered through the human barrier. Tioga soon lost sight of Kopi in the mob. Just when he thought his friend had fallen, Kopi reappeared near the end of the line. He was nearly through. Only one man remained in his way.

Kopi ducked as the man swung a war club at his skull, then responded by smashing his fist into the man's crotch. The crowd cheered, and the warrior crumpled to his knees. Kopi jumped over him and staggered to the hut with the red door. He wiped the blood from his eyes and looked back. Tioga raised his arms in pride as Kopi disappeared behind the deerskin flap. The villagers applauded his strong performance.

"Well done!" said Shingas. "A surprising effort for a member of such a feeble tribe!"

Next, he grabbed Hanna and pulled her forward. As he was slicing the ropes that bound her hands and feet, she looked back at Tioga.

"You can do it," he said. She started to nod, but burst into tears. She quickly regained her composure as Shingas announced her arrival.

"Today we have a special guest—with purple hair no less!" yelled Shingas with a laugh. "This is Hanna, the daughter of the chief of the Allegewi!" The people roared with delight. "Listen carefully!" The crowd quickly quieted. Tioga was surprised at the villagers' obedience. He wondered how many Shingas had killed to gain such control.

"She is a rare prize," he continued. "I may use her as bait to draw out her weak-hearted father, who—." Before Shingas could finish the sentence, Hanna broke away and sprinted toward the gauntlet.

"Run to the house with the white door!" yelled Shingas. He admired the girl's daring assault. It was smart thinking to hit the line while he was still speaking.

Tioga prayed for her deliverance. He quickly noticed a difference in the crowd's treatment of Hanna. The people barely touched her as she ran through their ranks. They had gotten the message not to damage the valuable hostage. Other than the loss of a few handfuls of hair taken by curious woman, she arrived unscathed at the hut with the white deerskin doorway. She stopped outside it and waited for Tioga.

Tioga stepped forward without hesitation. The warlord grabbed him by the hair and pulled him toward the line. The crowd swelled, and their excitement grew to a fever pitch.

Shingas shouted, "Hanna is not the only visitor who merits special treatment! Here we have Allegewi Tioga, the son of the fool Wroclaw." A murmur traveled through the crowd. "Do you recall the story of Wroclaw the trapper? The idiot who died wrestling a bear?"

The crowd laughed remembering the old tale, which had even been made into a song. The children started chanting the lyrics, "Wroclaw, Wroclaw, come wrestle a bear! He did just that and lost his hair! Wroclaw, Wroclaw, do you feel my jaws? Yes, I do, and I feel your claws..."

Shingas chuckled at the taunts, but raised his arm. "Quiet now, there is more to tell you." The crowd obeyed. "This boy is not only the son of a fool, but also the son of a coward. Do you not remember it was the Allegewi who killed my father?" The crowd roared in anger. "Wroclaw was one of the cowards who ambushed us!"

The crowd gasped and began chanting for Tioga.

"Will the Mononga avenge my father's death?"

"Yes!" came the unanimous response. "Give him to us!"

Shingas looked Tioga in the face and smiled. "Run," he said calmly.

"But my hands and feet," said Tioga, looking down at his bindings.

"Run," said Shingas as he pushed him toward the mob.

"To which hut?"

"It does not matter. You will not reach any of them."

Tioga looked up and saw the crowd falling upon him. He stumbled into the mass and tried to block their blows. The assault came from all directions. He tried to cover his head, but was quickly knocked to the ground. His eyesight flooded red. He clawed at the dust and curled into a ball. There was no escape from the vicious kicks and punches.

The pain swallowed him. The attack was so severe that he couldn't even think to breathe. A ringing sound vibrated through his brain. From a distance, he felt himself go limp. Then he floated away into the darkness.

# *Fourteen*

Tioga awoke to a wet burning sensation on his forehead. He tried to open his swollen eyelids. Only his left eye cooperated. Through the narrow slit, he saw the wrinkled face of an old woman leaning over him. She dabbed his face with a piece of fur, blackened with charcoal paint. He moaned at the throbbing pain that enveloped him.

"Will he survive?" The familiar voice of Shingas made his heart skip a beat.

"He will," said the old woman. "You are lucky you stopped it when you did. A few more seconds and he would have been dead."

"He's not getting off that easy," said Shingas. "I'll be back for him shortly." He left the hut, leaving Tioga alone with the old woman.

She gingerly lifted his head and spooned warm broth into his mouth. The soup tasted good, but it barely quenched his insatiable thirst.

"Water," he moaned in Mononga. "Please."

"You speak our language?" said the old woman in surprise. She lifted a cup of cool spring water to his lips. He overcame the pain to drink it down.

"More, please." Tioga gulped down another cup then fell back, exhausted. "I'm so thirsty."

"I'm not surprised," said the old woman. "You've been asleep since yesterday." She got up and hobbled toward the door. "I'll get some more water. You wait here." She departed, knowing that he was in no condition to go anywhere.

Tioga strained to look around the small house. He was alone. He fought off the urge for more sleep and took inventory of his body. He flexed his arms, his legs, and his torso. Everything hurt, but nothing seemed to be broken. His head was the biggest problem. Whenever he moved it, his vision swirled, and the pain was nearly unbearable. The reality of his situation slowly dawned on him. He was alive. He was in the Mononga castle. He was in danger.

He opened his good eye again and struggled to sit up. As he looked down at his body, a sense of dread came over him. He had been painted completely black. Tioga knew a captive painted black was to be burned at the stake. An uncontrollable fear rushed through him. His twisted left hand began shaking uncontrollably. It still remembered the bite of the flames. Even though he had been very small at the time, he would never forget that agony.

*I have to get out of here*, he thought. He crawled toward the door, but heard someone coming. He collapsed and pretended to be comatose.

Shingas burst into the room, followed by Chemung. "He's back asleep," said Shingas in disgust. "Where is that old woman? We can't wait any longer. The sun is going down. Let's take him."

"But he's still unconscious," said Chemung. "The crowd won't like it."

"What would you have me do, Chemung? Put off the attack for another day just so we can torture one prisoner? We should have been on the trail this morning."

"If you hadn't stopped it, the gauntlet would have finished him."

"Are you questioning my judgement?"

"No, Great Leader," said Chemung, but in truth he was. The commander had been acting very strange the last few days. He was even slurring his words like a man drunk on wine.

"He deserves a death as excruciating as the pain I have carried all these years," said Shingas. "Tonight, we will finish the job properly. Then tomorrow morning we can leave in a good mood."

Just then the small old woman came through the door with a fresh jar of cold water.

"Give me that," said Shingas. He took the clay pot and dumped the contents on the boy. Tioga jerked at the unexpected shock. The paint ran and burned in his eyes. He held them tightly shut.

"He moved!" said Shingas. "Even if he isn't completely awake, he'll still squirm in the flames. Grab him."

Tioga felt himself being pulled to his feet and dragged out of the hut. He remained limp as his heart pounded in his ears. Warm fresh air filled his lungs. It was an unusually balmy night in the mountains. He heard an occasional curse from a passing villager as he was dragged through the plaza.

*I've got to try to escape*, he thought. He heard the rumble of thunder overhead. A raindrop landed on his shoulder. And then another. Before he could think of a plan, Tioga felt his hands and feet being tied to a pole. He squinted through puffy eyelids at his captors.

"A storm is coming," said Chemung to Shingas. "He won't burn well if it's raining."

"Another delay. What else can go wrong?"

"Maybe it's a sign. Maybe this isn't a good time to go to war," said Chemung, hoping to get another day of rest before beginning the long journey. "Did you seek the advice of the shaman?" The village shaman, the mystical high priest of the tribe, was to be consulted on any important decision.

"Forget the shaman," said Shingas. "I know it's a good time. This boy told us so. Their men are away hunting! Now is the time to burn their village to the ground."

Tioga cringed at the conversation. Shingas's words cut into him more than the ropes Chemung was pulling tight around him.

"Great Leader, how many warriors shall we mobilize for the attack?"

"Sixty should be enough. No, make it eighty. We will crush the Allegewi even if their hunters are back."

"But sir, that will only leave twenty warriors to guard the slaves and defend the fortress."

"We will be gone less than a week. Who do you fear, Chemung? We control the mountains and the rivers."

"Yes, sir," said Chemung as he stacked wood around Tioga's legs.

"We will move like lightning. And we won't have this cripple slowing us down," said Shingas as he tried to kick Tioga in the shin. Due to the inebriating effects of Kopi's medicine, he missed completely. Chemung caught him before he fell to the ground.

Shingas continued, "Now that we have the Allegewi chief's daughter as a bargaining chip, I don't need this misfit to lure out his mother. In just a few more days those mongrels will be ash and my princess will be back in my arms."

"Your princess? What princess?"

"Princess Candowsa," said Shingas softly.

"Who?"

"Candy!" screamed Shingas, as thunder echoed through the mountains.

"The girl who ran away when we were young? She is alive?"

"Yes, you moron. Did you not hear this boy say she is his mother? And she didn't run away—she was kidnapped."

"If she is alive," said Chemung, "she is no longer Mononga. She has turned Allegewi."

"She is Mononga!" screamed Shingas as he struck Chemung in the face, knocking him to the ground. Tioga listened to the confrontation as he hung limply at the pole. "She will always be Mononga!" Shingas stood over Chemung, trembling with rage. "And I want her back. We were to be married. It was arranged!"

Tioga was sickened at what he had just heard. It was bad enough that he had put the village in danger. Now he realized that Shingas's goal was not only to destroy his tribe, but also to marry his mother.

Chemung looked down as the blood dripped freely from his nose. The wind of the coming gale carried off the drops before they even reached the ground. Heavy rain began to fall.

"No woman could take her place," said Shingas. "The day she was taken, I vowed to have none other as my wife. Now I will have her, as it should have been."

Chemung was shocked, but he dared not utter a word. His boss's love life was the least of his concerns. He was more worried about the commander's abnormal behavior. He seemed to be making some bizarre decisions. Chemung noticed his leader's pupils were fully dilated. Was he possessed? Was it a spell by the Gangas Witch or that boy-mystic Kopi?

Shingas's breathing slowed as he regained his composure. "She should have borne me a son—an heir—instead of having this mutant from another man." Shingas slapped Tioga across the face. Lightning flashed across the horizon, as a jolt of pain rocked his swollen head.

The concussion, along with the words, was more than Tioga could take. His stomach heaved, and he vomited on Chemung. Then Tioga passed out. His limp body was held upright by the ropes.

"Ha!" said Shingas to Chemung. "You got what you deserved." Chemung tried to wipe the foul liquid off his body. The pouring rain soon did the job for him.

"Look at this weather. The wood is soaked," said Shingas, as if the confrontation with Chemung had never happened. He sighed in resignation. "Leave the boy tied here for the night. We'll burn him at dawn, before we set off. It will brighten my day to see his flesh bubble."

"Yes, Great Leader," said Chemung.

"Go gather the elders in my lodge," ordered Shingas. "It is time to begin the adoption ceremony."

"What adoption ceremony?" asked Chemung, with hesitation. He didn't want to trigger another attack, but his curiosity got the better of him. "Who is being adopted?"

"The other boy, Kopi. He has turned out to be a pleasant surprise. Strong, courageous, and a proven healer—whom I can trust! He will be a fine Mononga warrior."

"Who is adopting him?"

Shingas stared Chemung in the eye as the rain drummed on the ground. "I have decided to take him as my son. The preparations are already underway."

Chemung looked back in horror, but didn't dare respond. While it wasn't unusual for a tribe member to adopt a captive, it was unheard of for the chief to select his successor in such a manner. *Has he gone insane?* thought Chemung.

Shingas continued, "I will train him to follow in my footsteps. He will learn to be ruthless and cunning. Above all, he will be fearless!" Shingas looked up at the swirling storm clouds. "Hurry! I want the adoption completed tonight. There is no reason the rain should delay it."

"Yes, Great Leader." Chemung immediately ran off, the blood still streaming from his nose.

Shingas glared at the unconscious boy lashed to the pole. He tried to see Candy's features in the boy's battered face, but couldn't find her there. Tioga was just a cruel reminder of her rejection. He wondered what her reaction would be when she learned he had burned her son to death.

"It is her turn to feel the pain," said Shingas. "Then we will be even. Then we can begin again." He turned and walked off, leaving the boy hanging from the old timber.

# *Fifteen*

Tioga was pulled back to consciousness by the sound of drums mixed with distant thunder. He opened his swollen eyes and saw hundreds of dancing fireflies. Then he realized that they weren't fireflies, but torches glowing in the darkness. A ceremony was underway in the village plaza. Tioga hung limply on the pole, at the center of it all. His first thought was that they were coming to burn him, but it was still raining, and he was being ignored. The focus of attention was on the other side of the village, where a procession was exiting Shingas's opulent lodge. Tioga watched the proceedings from his humble perch, making sure that he appeared to be comatose.

Hanna was brought into the plaza with her hands tied. Tioga was shocked at her appearance. Her long, beautiful purple hair was gone. It had been cropped short and smeared with white grease. Her body was clothed in pale furs and her skin was painted in ash. A hue so colorless that it was only found in the hearth of a forgotten fire.

*Ash?* thought Tioga. *What does it mean?* A wind gust made his eyes water. He blinked away his blurry vision just in time to see Kopi exit the big house and join the procession.

Kopi and several of the tribal elders entered the plaza. Other than a loincloth, Kopi was naked. He seemed bewildered and dazed. It was obvious he had been given strong medicine. They led him toward the center of the village. A group of gyrating dancers circled him, as the shaman chanted his mysterious song.

A group of old women surrounded Kopi and washed him from head to toe to purify his spirit. Tioga knew they were symbolically washing away his Allegewi blood to replace it with their own.

Another band of females arrived to prepare his soul for the transformation. They painted his skin blood red, the color of rebirth, adorned him in fresh clothes, and placed his feet in a new pair of

Mononga boots. Kopi seemed to be entranced, barely noticing those around him.

The rain picked up, and the wind howled through the mountains. No one moved from their positions, although the gale made it difficult to hold steady. Sparks swirled through the air from torches that were struggling to stay lit. Kopi was led to a stage on which the Mononga shaman stood. The old sorcerer had taken on the appearance of an immense wolf. His eyes peered out from its massive jaws. Shingas appeared beside him, wearing a grizzly-bear cape. Tioga noticed something dangling from Shingas's neck. He was wearing the charm made from his own arm bone.

Shingas signaled to the women to bring Kopi onto the stage. The drums stopped, but the thunder continued. Tioga shivered in the cold. He strained to hear the shaman's song, but the wind carried it away. Tioga tested the ropes that bound his limbs, but they were well tied and he was very weak. He wanted to break free to stop this nightmare, before it was too late. Kopi would not only become Mononga, but the blood of his new father would pump through his veins—or so the people believed. Tioga had been taught by his mother to respect the ancient ways and their magic. But as he grew older, he wondered whether the magic was real. Would Kopi really become Mononga?

Tioga raised his head and opened his eyes as wide as his swollen cheeks would allow. He was surprised to see Hanna looking back at him in sorrow. Lightning flashed across the sky, followed by a thunderous roar. The villagers looked up in fear. The old shaman hesitated for a moment and then continued his incantation.

Tioga wanted to scream. He tried to lock eyes with Kopi, but his friend was too dazed to notice. Salty tears began streaming from Tioga's eyes, mixing with the fresh rainwater.

Shingas stepped forward and placed his hand on Kopi's shoulder. "Stand tall! You will soon be the son of the greatest warrior in history!"

Intense thunder shook the village and the crowd cowered in response. The shaman leaned forward against the tempest and reached his arm toward Kopi. Tioga felt the hairs on his head straighten up, as if the Creator himself had come to witness the spectacle.

A powerful gust of wind whooshed across the plaza and knocked the old priest away from Kopi. The roof of one of the houses lifted off its frame, spiraled upward, and flew over the wall. The villagers gasped at the apocalyptic sight.

"Continue!" yelled Shingas. "Complete the adoption!"

The shaman paused for a moment, and then staggered back into position. Once again, he raised his wrinkled hand to Kopi's forehead. Just as he touched it, a lightning bolt flashed down from the heavens and struck the flagpole of the fortress. The pole exploded in flaming splinters, and the wooden wall beneath it was split to the ground. The gap smoldered and hissed in the downpour.

The blast was so powerful that it knocked Shingas and Kopi off their feet and the old shaman completely off the stage. The villagers screamed, dropped their torches, and scattered in panic. They bolted for the protection of their houses. Tioga stared in wonder at the smoking gash in the wall.

Shingas jumped up and yelled over the torrent, "Come back! We will finish the ceremony!"

No one heeded his command. Even the shaman ran for cover. Another lightning bolt raced across the sky and crashed into a nearby mountaintop. Within seconds the plaza was empty, except for Shingas, Chemung, the cowering captives, and dozens of sizzling torches on the ground.

Shingas looked up at the storm with contempt and spit. Once again the spirits had robbed him. He hated them for interfering with his plan. Disgusted at his people's cowardice, Shingas grabbed Kopi and led him off. Chemung followed with Hanna in tow.

Tioga stood alone in the deluge. He looked to the heavens in gratitude. He had never felt so close to the Creator. He watched in awe as lightning lit up the mountains and thunder shook the village. He hoped the next strike would hit his pole and end his torment. But it wasn't meant to be. The storm slowly moved away and the thunder became a distant rumble.

In time, the clouds parted and stars appeared in the night sky. The orange moon peeked over a mountaintop and slowly rose higher. The air grew colder and the village was eerily silent. In the distance, a lone wolf howled—its call echoing off the granite cliffs. Tioga shivered uncontrollably as hypothermia began to set in.

For the longest time there was no movement. Then Tioga heard the shuffling of feet. He saw the ghostly form of two old tribesmen coming in his way. The elders passed him by without a word and continued to the charred gap in the stockade. They ran their hands along the shattered timbers. Then they slowly backed away toward Tioga. He strained to hear their conversation.

"It is the work of the fat boy—the healer," said one of the men. "He commands strong magic. He brought down the bolt of lightning."

"Dangerous magic! He controls fire," said the other man, nodding in agreement. "It happened just as the high priest touched his head. It is a clear sign. He must not be brought into the tribe until he can be cleansed further by the shaman. We must speak with the leader..." The two men wandered off out of earshot. The conversation sickened Tioga. He had hoped the explosion would save Kopi. Now he realized it had only delayed the adoption.

Tioga collapsed against the ropes and began to lose consciousness. The forest mist crept through the walls of the fortress and seeped into his aching brain. His mind wandered to the thought of riding a spark on its reckless journey from the hearth to the heavens. His mother had told him that the stars were the campfires of their ancestors. Tioga felt himself rising above the castle and moving toward those distant fires. Higher and higher he flew, away from the Mononga nightmare.

But something was holding him back. His hair. His hair was pulling him softly back down to earth. As he fell lower and lower, the pain in his body returned. His wounds ached and the ropes burned.

As he returned to the world of the living, he realized someone was stroking his hair. Someone was touching his cheek. He opened his eyes, hoping to see Hanna before him. Instead, a ghoulish face appeared in the faint moonlight.

Tioga jumped in shock. "A zombie!" he hissed.

The zombie chuckled. "You are feverish. Drink this," said a raspy voice layered in wisdom and experience, but still soft and nurturing.

Tioga realized it wasn't a monster standing before him—but a disfigured old man. He was heavily scarred and had no nose! In its place was a gaping hole. The man's top lip was torn away, as well as one of his ears.

*Was he once mauled by a bear?* thought Tioga. He was wary of the elder and his brew, but his thirst was overpowering. Tioga drank down the bitter liquid. Warmth flowed into his body.

The strange visitor looked Tioga straight in the eye. "I curse you!" he screamed. Tioga jumped at the sudden change in demeanor. "I curse you for the pain the Allegewi have brought on our village!"

The angry old warrior lifted Tioga's chin up with one hand. Tioga cringed as his other hand swung toward his bruised face. The crack of flesh against flesh echoed through the fortress. Tioga felt no pain, so he opened his eyes. The old man had smacked his own hand.

Tioga studied the ruddy features beneath the scars on the elderly face. Something was familiar. The old man looked around to see if anyone was watching.

"I can tell you are a good boy, and soon to be a good man," whispered the sage. "Be strong and you will live."

Tioga felt his chin rise up again. "I curse you to die!" screamed the old man. "To die a thousand deaths!" The air split with the sound of another false blow.

Chemung's voice rang out from the darkness: "Iceman! Quit beating the captive. We want him alive at dawn. You are disturbing the village. We need our sleep!"

"He is almost dead from exposure already," replied Ötzi the Iceman, with a cackle. "Let me finish him!"

Tioga heard a man approaching. It was Chemung. Tioga slumped against the ropes and pretended to be unconscious.

"Get away from him," barked Chemung to the elder. Chemung wrapped an old beaver-fur blanket around Tioga's shoulders to protect him from the cold.

"He and his father are a curse to the Mononga," replied Ötzi. "Let him freeze as solid as an icicle. Then we can melt him in the fire in the morning."

"He'd better not die tonight," said Chemung. "The chief wants him to squirm in the flames at dawn."

"But the ice will be an equally painful death!"

"Iceman, get back to your cave. We hit the trail in a few hours— as soon as the boss is finished with this runt."

"Very well. Just give me a moment to place a curse on him."

"Fine, but no more beatings. And leave him covered!" Chemung stormed off, and the village grew silent.

Ötzi the Iceman leaned down and whispered in Tioga's ear, "You have a long journey ahead of you. And you will need this to begin." The old man reached around the pole and placed a sharp stone blade in Tioga's hand—a piece of flint freshly chipped to a fine cutting edge.

Tioga was shocked. *A knife that can cut through my bindings? The old man wants me to escape?*

"Why are you helping me?" whispered Tioga.

"Because you are my own flesh and blood."

"Flesh and blood?"

"You are the son of my daughter. You are my grandson!"

"Grandfather Ötzi? I thought you were dead."

The old patriarch smiled. "Don't speak. Save your strength." He continued in a tone reminiscent of a practiced orator. "Long ago, the Mononga and the Allegewi were at peace. Evil on both sides brought war, with its demons of selfishness, greed, and foolish pride. For decades we have battled senselessly in a blood feud. Too many lives have been destroyed. The land is big enough for us all." Ötzi looked up at the stars. "It is my hope that one day, a good man will bring the two sides together again in peace, not war, just as the Allegewi and Mononga rivers join at the Forks. We will live again in harmony."

Tioga was speechless. His battered brain couldn't comprehend all that his grandfather had said, but he somehow felt safe in his presence.

Ötzi stroked Tioga's matted hair. "I must go before they suspect. But drink this medicine first. It will stoke the fire in your heart. You will need a strong flame to get through this night!"

Tioga drank again from the cup that was lifted to his lips. His grandfather continued, "Look at me and listen carefully." The soothing voice was gone, replaced by that of a stern commander. Tioga locked eyes with the old man as best he could.

"Break free and go through the gap in the wall that the Creator prepared for you," said Ötzi, pointing to the charred breach in the wooden palisade made by the lightning bolt. "In the woods, follow the sound of the Angry River. Look for the granite sentinels—you must use them as stepping stones to conceal your escape. They lead to a secret exit."

"Stepping stones?" asked Tioga, confused.

"Yes! The Ancients brought them here. They will glow blue in the moonlight. But before you go to them, you must use the trees to climb to the sky. You must vanish without a trace."

"Vanish?"

"That's right! Then jump along the stepping stones until you see the marks of the Ancients. Use their carvings to climb down to the river. It is your only chance of escape. If you are a strong swimmer, like your mother, it will carry you to freedom. When you are free of the canyon, follow the river to Canoe Camp. Take a boat and paddle back home. Meanwhile, I will work here to stop the attack on your village."

Tioga felt his strength returning. The combination of hope and the medicine was giving him new life.

"I must go now," said the old man. "I will watch you from above." He kissed Tioga on the forehead and backed away.

"Wait, Grandfather!" whispered Tioga. "Why do they call you the Iceman? What happened to your face?"

"As the fire has touched you, I have been touched by the ice. Both leave scars that will never heal."

"Oh," said Tioga. The old man must have had some kind of accident in the cold. "Grandfather, I have one more question."

"Yes, my grandson. What is it?"

"If black is the color of death, and red is the color of rebirth, what will become of the girl who is bathed in ashes?"

"Ash is the color of the ghost spirit. One who is caught between two worlds." Ötzi gently touched his grandson on the cheek. "Tell your mother I love and miss her. I will meet her again at the campfires in the sky." He turned and disappeared into the night. Tioga was sorry to see him go. There was comfort in his grandfather's voice. A comfort he had never known.

# Sixteen

Tioga had been rubbing the flint knife against the thick hemp rope for nearly an hour, with little success. The Mononga made exceptionally strong rope. And with his hands bound, it was an especially difficult task. He was terrified of dropping the blade, which would end any escape attempt. To calm his mind, he thought of his mother as a little girl, sitting on Ötzi's knee. Tioga suddenly felt closer to his mother. They both shared the never-ending pain of losing a father.

Tioga rubbed until his arms ached. The moon worked its way across the stars. Occasionally a distant guard would cough or a forest wolf would howl. And from the valley below came the unrelenting roar of the Angry River.

Tioga struggled to stay awake. Though he knew his life depended on his efforts, his aching head screamed for sleep. Several times he dozed off only to awaken with a start, fearful that he had unknowingly dropped the flint knife. Each time he willed his limbs to fight on.

Finally, he felt his hands loosen. The frayed rope was losing the battle. He cut faster now. Soon he had more room to maneuver. With a final tug, his arms were free. He raised them triumphantly in the faint moonlight.

Just then he spotted a shadow moving through the empty plaza toward him. He quickly clasped his hands behind the pole and pretended to be unconscious.

A lone warrior walked up to Tioga and placed a large stack of dry wood at his feet. The man leaned down and whispered in his ear, "Are you ready to feel the flames licking at your body?"

Tioga could smell his foul breath on the fresh, dew-laden air. The man dropped to his knees and began arranging the pile of wood around Tioga's legs. Dawn must be near. They were preparing to finish him.

The man pulled on his ankle, checking the bindings. Then the warrior reached up and tugged on his good arm. Tioga struggled to hold his hands together behind the pole. The man pulled again, harder. The flint blade slipped from Tioga's palm and fell to the ground with a *clink.* He held his breath, wondering if the man had heard it.

Suddenly, the kneeling man stood up. He spit in the captive's face, then walked off toward the far end of the village.

Tioga breathed a sigh of relief. As soon as the guard was out of sight, he reached down to his feet. He pushed away the wood and searched the surrounding mud for the flint blade. *It must be here somewhere*, he thought.

A dog barked in the distance. The village was beginning to awaken. *Forget the knife,* thought Tioga. *Use your fingers.* He followed the rope wrapped around his ankles until he reached the knot, then began to work on it. Tioga was an expert at knots. He quickly recognized the type.

His feet were numb. The swollen rope that held them was soaked in rainwater and blood. He had unraveled a thousand knots in his lifetime. *Why can't I undo this one?*

The first birds began to sing their morning song in the darkness. Tioga's mind raced. He closed his eyes and took a deep, calming breath. He once again ran his fingers over the rope and followed its twists and turns. He envisioned the rope as a snake. A snake never forgets how to unwind.

He picked up a thin stick and wiggled it in a gap in the knot. He felt the tangle loosen. He pulled harder. The knot gave way, and unraveled. One foot was free. He stretched his tingling ankle and turned to the other foot. The rope finally sensed it had lost the battle and fell away in the dirt.

Tioga stood up. The blood rushed out of his head and his vision faded for a moment. He staggered away from the pole, unsure if he could even walk. The sights of the village slowly came back to him, as the first dim light of dawn appeared in the heavens.

Tioga eyed the gap in the palisade. He could see the shadows of a few sentinels patrolling the narrow catwalk near the top of the castle walls. Luckily there was just a skeleton crew on duty. The majority of the warriors would soon be up, readying their gear for battle.

He lifted the musty beaver blanket over his head, then bent over and shuffled like an old woman toward the split in the wall. He stopped after just a few steps when he spotted a piece of clothing in the mud. He picked up a limp shawl from the ground. Someone must have dropped it in the panic of the adoption ceremony.

Tioga turned back to the empty pole and grabbed a piece of wood about as wide as his shoulders. He quickly tied it to the timber using the leftover rope and draped the shawl over the crossbeam. He grabbed two wooden logs and propped them against the pole as legs for the makeshift scarecrow. It wouldn't fool anyone in the daylight, but it might give him a few extra minutes to make his escape while it was still dark.

Tioga resumed his imitation of an old woman and shuffled to the splintered gash. The guards either didn't see him or ignored the elderly woman wandering alone. The gap smelled of charcoal and fresh pine. He could see the shadowy forest beyond the fractured timbers.

He climbed into the breach, which was just wide enough for his slender body, and started through. The roar of the river intensified as he emerged on the other side. *I can do this*, he thought. *I can make it to the river.*

He hesitated. Images of Hanna rushed through his head. Then he remembered Kopi. His best friend. His only friend for most of his life. *I can't leave them to die or become Mononga*, thought Tioga. He turned back and re-entered the fortress.

*I'll rescue Kopi first, and then we'll get Hanna.* He tried to recall which lodge Kopi had gone into the night before. The choice was daunting. The dozens of houses all looked the same in the darkness. He remembered Shingas leading Kopi away through the rain as the lightning lit up the village. *It must be that one—Shingas's lodge—the largest house in the village.*

Tioga debated on how best to get there. He could cut straight across the open plaza or work his way around the perimeter. Fatigue made the decision for him.

He draped the blanket back over his head and made a beeline for the big house. He didn't have time to waste. The only one who noticed him was a small scrawny dog. It ran toward him and gave him a sniff.

"Good boy," he said in Mononga. The dog wagged its tail. He patted its head and quickly moved on.

When he reached the largest house, he stopped. He was glad to see that Shingas hadn't posted guards. Tioga circled the building and looked for a back door. There was none. He returned to the front door, cautiously opened it a crack, and peered inside. It was pitch black.

There was no time to let his eyes adjust. He knelt down and crawled in. It wasn't long until he bumped into something. Tioga reached out to feel the object and gasped in surprise. He felt sharp teeth—massive teeth. He expected a guard dog to launch at his neck, but the jaws didn't move. Then he realized it was the head of an enormous bear—still attached to a fur rug.

He could hear people breathing. His swollen eyes slowly adapted to the darkness. Several figures were sprawled on the ground inside the sleeping quarters—each on its own fur rug. Tioga could tell they were all females. At the far end of the room, there was an enormous throne made of elk antlers. And beyond it there was a huge bed with a large man sleeping under a bear blanket. *Shingas. Surrounded by his hareem.* He was relieved to see that Hanna was not in this group.

Tioga's eyes were working well enough now that he could see that Kopi wasn't here. He backed slowly out of the house and knelt in the courtyard. The first smoke of a new day rose from several of the houses. Soon the village would be alive with activity.

*How am I going to find Kopi?* His friend the dog trotted by and disappeared behind a hut with a muddy-looking hide in the doorway. *Run to the house with the red door.* Shingas's voice rattled in his head from the gauntlet ceremony. *That's it!* In the faint light, the bright red door looked dark brown.

Tioga moved silently toward the lodge. Suddenly the deerskin flap flew open. He stood perfectly still. A woman emerged from the doorway. She glanced in Tioga's direction, but saw nothing in the dim light. The black body paint concealed his form. She walked off behind the hut to relieve herself in the latrine.

Tioga took a deep breath and crawled inside. The coals of a fire glowed eerily. Several bodies were curled up near the embers. One looked familiar. It was thicker than the rest, but he couldn't see its face. Then he recognized a distinctive sound—Kopi's snoring!

Tioga stepped over a sleeping man, moved to his friend's side, and slipped his hand over Kopi's mouth. Kopi burst to life and fought against the attacker. Tioga leaned on the body and whispered in his ear in Allegewi, "It's me."

The squirming stopped. Tioga removed his hand. He could make out Kopi's confused face in the darkness.

Someone moved on the far side of the fire. Chemung's voice called out, "Who's there?"

Tioga froze. Kopi responded softly, "I was just having a bad dream. Go back to sleep." The hut fell silent. Apparently, Chemung was too tired to question things further.

Tioga climbed off Kopi and crawled out the door. Kopi emerged a second later and nearly tackled his friend in delight. Tioga led him to the shadow of the palisade wall.

"How could you sleep knowing that I was to be burned at sunrise?" hissed Tioga.

"It was the medicine they gave me," said Kopi. "It knocked me out."

"Where's Hanna?"

"Over there, in the house with the white door."

Tioga could see it plainly in the growing light. People were beginning to exit the houses. It was an important day. A day to go to war. Thankfully, the foggy mountain mist still cloaked the fortress and offered some cover.

"Follow me," said Tioga.

The boys silently worked their way along the back alleys of the village until they reached the rear of the house with the white door. Tioga listened. He could hear several women chattering about breakfast.

*It will be impossible to get Hanna out now*, thought Tioga. *Too many people are awake.* Tioga looked down at his shredded leather pants. His mother, Candowsa, made the best buckskins in the village. And she always added Allegewi beading to the edges, a touch that made each pair unique. Tioga reached down and ripped off a fragment of beaded leather.

"What are you doing?" whispered Kopi.

"Give me your arm," said Tioga. He grabbed Kopi's wrist and rubbed the piece of leather along his friend's bicep. Then he did the same on his torso. The leather was soon streaked with the red and black paint.

"Stay here," said Tioga, handing Kopi his beaver blanket. "I'll be right back."

"I'm coming too," said Kopi.

"No, I know what I'm doing. You watch for trouble."

Tioga knew the comment was meaningless, as there wasn't much Kopi could do if trouble arrived. Tioga crawled back toward the hut's entrance. His knees ached as the sandy mud worked its way into his wounds. He dropped the leather fragment just outside the door and moved away. *She will see it*, he thought. *Just as we saw her bracelet on the beach. She will know it's a sign that we'll be back for her.*

As he crawled away, he grabbed a large gourd of water that was leaning against the house. As soon as he reached Kopi, he pulled the plug and quenched his thirst. Never again would he take drinking water for granted. He kept the gourd as a canteen. They would need it on the journey ahead.

Tioga pointed to the gap in the fortress wall. It was only a few houses away. "That's our escape route," he whispered.

"But what about Hanna?" asked Kopi.

"Leave her."

"What? How can you say that?"

"It's too risky. Let's go." Tioga started toward the exit.

Kopi grabbed him by the arm. "You're acting like a coward! She is one of us. We can't leave her here."

"Yes, we can," said Tioga. "I left her a sign. We've got to get home to warn the village. Now come on."

Kopi thought about arguing more, but realized he didn't have a plan to get Hanna out. He followed Tioga to the split in the wooden wall. Tioga quickly climbed through the narrow opening. Kopi followed as best he could. It was a very tight squeeze. Tioga grabbed Kopi's hand and pulled with all his might.

"Exhale!" commanded Tioga.

Kopi popped through. Tioga helped him to his feet and looked up at the towering wall. At least they had made it outside the fortress. But between the wall and the forest was a clear-cut kill zone where archers could pick off any assailants, or in this case, escapees. There was no alternative but to hope for the best and sprint forward.

With fear as their fuel, the boys ran across the open space dove into the relative safety of the trees, which clung to a steep hillside. Now that they were out of sight, Tioga surveyed their surroundings. The forest was thick with evergreen trees—pine, fir, and spruce. The sound of the roaring river was directly below them.

Tioga struggled against his concussion to concentrate. He knew that in a few minutes their absence would be discovered and all hell would break loose. Even in the dim light he could see the footprints they had left in the mud. It would only take a tracker a moment to discover their trail and recapture them.

Tioga instinctively moved downhill toward the river. Kopi followed hesitantly. The slope steepened to the point that Tioga was holding onto trees to keep from falling. A moment later the branches parted. They were standing atop a two-hundred-foot sheer cliff. It was a dead end, unless they jumped. The Angry River churned unseen in the fog below them.

Kopi instantly knew what Tioga was thinking. "I am not jumping off this cliff," he said nervously.

"No, we're not doing that," said Tioga. He recognized the fall would probably kill them. And then there was the matter of Kopi's inability to swim.

Tioga strained to find the answer. His grandfather wouldn't have sent him this way if it was a death trap. He fought hard to remember what Grandfather Ötzi had said: *"In the woods, follow the sound of the Angry River."* They had done that, and it had led to a precipice. *There must be a better way to the river*, thought Tioga.

His grandfather's voice came to him again: *"Look for the glowing granite sentinels—you must use them as stepping stones."*

Tioga was confused. *What sentinels?* Tioga struggled against his racing heart to remain calm. He must have missed something. He had to go back and look for clues to decipher his grandfather's message. The stimulant Ötzi had given him was beginning to wear off. He struggled to summon the energy to continue the escape.

"Kopi, listen to my instructions carefully," said Tioga. "You must follow them to the letter, or else…"

"Okay, tell me what to do."

"Quickly, kick something into the river."

"What?"

"Just do it!"

Kopi followed the order and kicked a fallen log over the edge. It crashed down the cliff and disappeared into the mist.

"Good. Now take four big steps away from me. And kick another object over the cliff."

Kopi, followed the directions. Tioga did the same. They were eight steps apart.

"Listen carefully!" Tioga almost had to scream to be heard over the rapids. "Charge back up the hill until you see the fortress. Make sure the coast is clear, then run out, take four large steps to your left, and re-enter the trees. Then run down the hill to the cliff and repeat the process. Do it three times, then wait for me at the top."

Kopi smiled. "I've got it. You're leaving a bunch of trails! They won't know which one to follow."

Tioga nodded. But he knew this was a beginner's trick. It might only take them a few extra minutes to follow all the trails. Nonetheless, it was all he could think of at the moment. And at the bottom of each trail, at the edge of the cliff, a scuff would make it look like they had jumped into the river. Certainly a deadly plunge, but their pursuers would have to stop, look, and wonder—delaying them for several valuable seconds or perhaps even minutes.

Kopi and Tioga climbed in parallel paths back toward the fortress. With their adrenaline pumping, it didn't take long to reach the top. Kopi broke out of the forest, took four large steps to his left, and headed back down the hill.

Tioga did the same to his right. But before he went back in, he closely studied the wooden wall and the open land below it. He tried to remember his grandfather's instructions. *What did he say about stepping stones glowing in the moonlight?*

Tioga was confused. *It makes no sense! And now there is no moonlight!* He needed more time to think, but time was running out fast. In frustration, he headed down toward the cliff to continue the false-path ruse. There was no point in being quiet in the forest with the roar of the river. And he wanted to leave a clear trail.

A moment later, he arrived at the cliff edge. As he skidded to a stop, he slipped and almost fell into the abyss. He regained his footing, pushed a rock over the edge, took four steps to the side, and turned back uphill.

When he arrived below the fortress wall this time, he stepped out of the trees and went all the way back across the open kill zone to the gap in the wall. Perhaps he had missed seeing a clue. At any moment he expected a barrage of arrows, but once again he wasn't spotted.

From this vantage point, Tioga studied the landscape. Below the wall, the hillside fell away toward the forest where Kopi was making his paths. But to the far right, there was a string of strange boulders, standing tall like guards frozen in stone.

Grandfather's words popped into his head: *"Look for the granite sentinels—you must use them as stepping stones."* Giant stepping stones! The stone pillars exited the forest, paralleled the wall at the forest's edge, then disappeared around the curve of the palisade. While they weren't glowing, they were of different rock than the cliff.

*The stepping stones!* thought Tioga. He remembered the old adage: *"rocks don't show tracks."* But to get to them without leaving footprints would be impossible. The rain-soaked soil preserved their every move. What did grandfather tell me? As if on cue, his ancestor's voice entered his brain: *"Before you go to them, use the trees to climb to the sky."*

Tioga looked at the trees of the forest. Then it dawned on him: *Climb to the sky! Vanish without a trace!* He smiled and rushed back across the clearing and into the woods. As soon as he was within its cover, he took a right and headed to where Kopi should be.

As he moved through the timbers, he could clearly see the various paths that Kopi had made up and down the hill. When he approached the top of the last trail, he heard Kopi wheezing. Kopi spotted Tioga's approach and smiled. Tioga arrived beside his friend and looked up.

The evergreens in this area were tightly packed and roughly of the same size, the result of a landslide that had cleared the slope decades ago. Young trees had quickly filled the space, but competition kept any one tree from outpacing its rivals.

"We've got to get to those boulders," whispered Tioga, pointing to the standing stones that were just visible through the trunks. "We're supposed to use them as stepping stones."

"Whatever you say," said Kopi. He followed his friend's orders without question and headed toward the rocks.

"Wait!" Tioga grabbed him. "We can't leave footprints."

"How do we get there without leaving a trail?"

Tioga pointed upward. "We climb to the sky."

"What? You know I don't climb trees."

"You do now." Tioga tied the beaver blanket across his chest, grabbed hold of the nearest tree, and began his ascent.

Kopi stood below and watched his friend disappear into the canopy. Just then, a blood-curdling scream came from the fortress. It was followed by shouting, then the war cries started. The alarm echoed through the mountains.

It was all the motivation Kopi needed. He grabbed a branch and started climbing. Spotting Tioga twenty feet above, he moved toward his friend as best he could. More than once a branch gave way under his weight, but Kopi held on for dear life. Thankfully, the shouting and the sound of the river covered the crack of the breaking branches.

Tioga was waiting for his friend near the top of the slender tree. Kopi arrived just below him and looked up. "Now what? We don't have wings!"

"Follow me," said Tioga. "Just pretend you're a squirrel." He leaned out until the tree bent to one side, then grabbed the trunk of the adjacent tree and moved onto it. When he released the first tree, Kopi was nearly catapulted off the swinging trunk, but he managed to hold fast.

The uproar in the village had reached a fever pitch. In addition to the war cries, ram horns were blaring. Tioga swung over to the next slender trunk, and then to the next. Thankfully, the forest was so thick here that the trees were right next to each other. And best of all, they weren't leaving prints.

"You've got to be kidding," said Kopi, as he watched Tioga traverse the treetops. But the war cries reminded him that he had no choice but to follow. Kopi climbed higher, and then tried the same maneuver as Tioga. He was surprised to see that under his weight, the trunk leaned twice as far. He was able to move two trees to Tioga's one! Kopi quickly caught up and passed his friend. Although it was dangerous work, they were making good progress.

"Hey, slow down!" said Tioga, before Kopi moved out of sight.

Kopi stopped and looked over his shoulder. "Hurry up! What's taking you so long?"

"I'm trying my best not to fall to my death," said Tioga. He caught up and moved a few trees beyond Kopi. "Look! The stepping stones." The top of a tall gray boulder was directly below him. "That's where we go next."

Kopi nodded in agreement. As Tioga climbed down the trunk, he could see why Grandfather Ötzi had called the tall rocks sentinels. They formed a curving line of stone pillars, each over six feet tall. Tioga dropped down on top of the closest one. He looked up to make sure Kopi was following, then leap to the next one. They could jump along the tops of the boulders without leaving a visible track—at least until someone decided to climb a sentinel to take a look.

Kopi arrived at Tioga's tree and began to climb down to follow his friend. For some strange reason, he noticed that the height didn't bother him anymore. He couldn't believe it! Just when he had become comfortable in the treetops, it was time to head down. He stopped a few feet above Tioga and watched him leap to the next boulder. Kopi dropped to the stone and mimicked the maneuver.

The boys continued to move along the tops of the standing stones, which ran parallel to the curving fortress wall. Tioga imagined his grandfather doing the same when he was younger. He obviously knew every secret of the mountain.

As they jumped from pillar to pillar, it dawned on Tioga that these stones were not a natural feature. Someone must have placed them here long ago—the spacing was too regular to happen by chance. They obviously predated the trees and the wooden wall by centuries. He tried to image who might have placed them here and why they went to the trouble.

Up ahead, the stepping stones exited the forest and headed into the clear-cut kill zone, which was only ten yards wide at this point. The boulders led to a smooth slab of rock on which this portion of the stockade had been built. Below the ledge, the cliff fell away dramatically.

Tioga paused before leaving the cover of the forest. Kopi arrived beside him. "Another dead end!" gasped Kopi.

Tioga sighed. "It can't be. There must be a secret exit." He looked back at the gap in the palisade, where they had exited the fortress, a hundred paces away. Several arms and legs protruded from the split, as a group of warriors tried to squeeze through.

"They're too fat!" chirped Kopi. Just then the sound of axes biting into the timbers rang out. Chips of wood began to fly from the opening.

Tioga knew that they didn't have a moment to spare. "Come on! Just a few more." He jumped to the next boulder, which stood in the open kill zone. Kopi followed. Although they were hopping from boulder to boulder in plain sight, no one had yet seen them. Any guards on the wall must have been focused on the drama at the gap.

They made a final leap and landed on the smooth slab just below the wall. Tioga was pleased to see that their feet weren't leaving marks on the cool stone.

Tioga led the way, following the curve of the palisade until the ledge was too narrow to go any farther. He stopped and looked back. For the moment, the curve of the wall kept them out of sight. Voices echoed off the cliffs, and the sharp *crack* of broken branches could be heard, even over the roar of the river. It was clear that their pursuers were through the wall and had followed their trail into the forest.

Tioga looked up at the palisade, then down at the sheer cliff below them. It looked impossible to climb down safely. The Angry

River tumbled through the canyon, a hundred feet below. It least the drop here wasn't quite as far, but the chances of surviving the fall would be slim.

"Now what?" asked Kopi, in frustration. It looked like their escape had come to a cruel end. It would only be a moment until someone either followed the ledge or looked down from the stockade and spotted them.

Tioga tried to concentrate. *What else did grandfather say? "Follow the stepping stones to the marks of the Ancients. Use the carvings to climb down to the river."* Tioga scanned the landscape in all directions and didn't see any marks. Then he got an idea.

"Hold on to me," he said, stretching out his arm to Kopi. Using his friend as an anchor, Tioga leaned out over the edge. As he peered down, he could see something carved on the cliff face.

"Petroglyphs! The marks of the Ancients," said Tioga in excitement. "This way! It's grandfather's trail!"

Kopi looked at Tioga as if he was crazy. "Grandfather's trail? Your grandfather died before you were born. That bump on your head must be worse than I thought."

Tioga grabbed the edge of the cliff and swung his legs over the lip. His feet probed the rockface and soon found a foothold. He began moving down the cliff like a spider. The Ancients had carved footholds and handholds into the stone. It was a secret exit!

Kopi shook his head in disbelief at his friend's behavior. Then he saw two warriors dash into the forest to his left. The next thing he knew, he was climbing downward. His survival instinct had taken over. As his foot probed the cliff for the next foothold, he was surprised to notice he had no fear of the dizzying height.

The boys were soon out of sight below the lip of the ledge. They slowly moved down the cliff toward the river. The handholds and footholds came easily. Tioga thought of his grandfather and smiled. He began to recognize carvings of animals, people, and spirits. *It must have taken generations for the Ancients to chisel all these figures.* Shingas obviously wasn't the first person to recognize the attributes of this mountaintop.

Tioga led the way down to a narrow ledge fifty feet below the rim. He easily reached it and stopped. A moment later Kopi arrived beside him. Although the ledge was only a foot wide, there was a cavity in the cliff just large enough to shelter two boys.

"Let's take a break and catch our breath," said Tioga, as he moved into the small cave. "They can't see us in here."

"Alright," said Kopi. He nervously looked down at the churning river fifty feet below them. A cool mist rose from the gorge, bathing the boys in a chilling spray. They sat in their grotto with their backs pressed against a wall that was covered with painted markings. The Ancients clearly viewed this as a mystical spot.

"Can I have a drink of that water?" asked Kopi.

"Sure." Tioga handed the gourd over to Kopi, who pulled the plug and drained it in three gulps. Kopi was about to throw the empty jug into the river, but Tioga stopped him.

"Keep it," said Tioga. "We'll need a canteen." Kopi nodded and tied it around his waist.

Tioga evaluated their options. They were presently out of sight and secure. He was confident that this must be the way down. Otherwise, his grandfather wouldn't have sent him here.

Tioga saw something in the air to his right. He turned and caught a glimpse of a golden eagle as it swept by them and floated in the morning light. It screeched and then disappeared down the valley. Tioga smiled at the good omen, but suppressed the urge to screech back.


Far above them and to their left, Shingas stood below the splintered gap in the stockade wall. He stared into the thick evergreen forest. A head popped out of the underbrush, followed by a lean body. Soros, Shingas's lead tracker, approached.

"Well?" said Shingas. He was gripping his three spears so tightly that they were at risk of snapping.

Soros responded, "Your bumbling henchmen trampled through the woods like a herd of buffalo. You should have called me first."

Shingas let the rude remark slide. He was too focused on the escape to reprimand the old tracker at the moment.

"Did they go this way?" asked Shingas.

"Yes, they went this way!" said the annoyed tracker. "In fact, they went this way several times."

Shingas bellowed, "So where are they now?"

Soros recoiled, but knew better than to argue. "Likely in the river. There are no tracks out of this part of the forest. They went in, but they didn't come out. Well, actually, they did come out, but then went back in—several times. Come to think of it, when they saw that this was a dead end, they might have gone back into the village. Maybe even out the rear gate."

Shingas pushed by the man. "Idiot!" He was fed up with the tracker's riddles. He yelled to Chemung; whose face peered over the top of the castle wall. "I want every inch of the fortress searched! And I want this valley scoured, as well as the forest beyond the rear gate. Leave no stone unturned!"

"But, Great Leader, such a search will take all day. What about the Allegewi village? Do you really wish two little boys to delay us further?"

Shingas cocked his arm and almost launched a spear at Chemung's head, but the target disappeared at the sight of the weapon.

"Do as I say!" roared Shingas.

"Yes, Great Leader!" came the response from the other side of the wall.

Tioga could hear people above them, but the shape of the overhanging cliff protected them from view. It would hopefully take a while before the Mononga remembered the ancient cliff ladder. Tioga wondered when it had last been used. Based on the moss in the cracks, it might have been decades.

"Now what?" whispered Kopi. "I'm not swimming." Although his fear of heights had vanished, the same couldn't be said for his fear of deep water.

Tioga leaned out and looked for a safe way down. Below them and to their right, he could see more handholds carved into the rock face. They led to a small beach at the base of the cliff. There was enough driftwood lodged there to make some kind of raft.

"This way," said Tioga, heading back out onto the ledge. "Don't worry. You won't need to swim." In his head, he added, *but you might need to float!* Tioga moved down the ledge in the direction of the hidden exit. Mononga voices floated down from above, followed by a few dislodged pebbles.

"Let's go," said Tioga. "They're getting closer."

"Wait a minute," said Kopi. "I can't hold it any longer." Kopi had to relieve himself. He untied his pants.

"Oh, no," said Tioga, expecting to see Kopi squat. Luckily his friend just had to pee.

Kopi's golden stream arched off the cliff and disappeared in the churning water fifty feet below. "Ahh," said Kopi in relief.

Tioga waited while Kopi did his business. It seemed to take him a really long time.

"Finished yet?"

"Just about. They gave me a lot to drink last night."

Suddenly Kopi's foot slipped on the slick granite. In a split second, his legs flew out. He landed on his rear, bounced off the ledge, and then was gone.

Tioga looked down in shock. Kopi had vanished. The roiling grey water had swallowed him without a trace! Tioga stared, and waited for his friend to pop up. The opaque river churned violently with no sign of Kopi.

Tioga knew there was no time to waste. He rushed back along the ledge to where Kopi had been. He took a deep breath, and without hesitation, stepped forward into thin air.

# *Seventeen*

The impact shocked Tioga, knocking the wind out of him as he plunged deep beneath the surface. The water was much colder and more violent than he had expected. As he flipped head over heels, he opened his eyes to judge his position. All he could see was churning black liquid.

He struggled to regain control, but the river was too powerful. His ribs slammed against a rock. His head was dragged through the gravel. His lungs wanted to explode. The constant tumbling disoriented him. *Which way is up?* He began to panic.

By a stroke of luck, his head broke the surface. He gasped and inhaled a mixture of foam and air. Tioga looked up just in time to see a towering wave crash down upon him. He went under again and fought the urge to inhale. The wild river moved at an unbelievable pace and threw him about at will.

He popped back up and stole another breath. For a split second, he thought he saw Kopi's head downstream, but he couldn't be sure. He slammed into a boulder and went  back under. The frigid water stiffened his limbs. He swam with all his might, and succeeded in breaking the surface. Far above, he briefly saw the rope bridge silhouetted against the sky, but then the torrent swallowed him again. He tumbled down the canyon, catching a breath when he could.

Finally, the water slowed and the roaring sound diminished. The rapids vanished behind him, and he was left treading water in a deep canyon pool where the sun's rays never shined. In this part of the gorge, it was perpetual twilight.

Tioga scanned his surroundings, but there was no sign of Kopi. Just as he was about to burst into tears, he spotted the gourd canteen floating up ahead. He rushed to it and pulled the leather strap. Kopi's motionless body appeared from beneath it.

Tioga grabbed Kopi around the neck and kicked with all his might. He soon felt the gravelly bottom. He pulled Kopi onto a flat boulder near the shoreline. In the faint light, he could see his friend wasn't breathing. *He's dead!* Tioga stared at the lifeless body. *No!* He jumped onto his friend's chest and tried to press the life back into him. He shook Kopi violently as he burst into tears.

"Breathe, Kopi! Please, breathe!"

In desperation, Tioga bent down and tried to blow the life back into Kopi's lungs. Nothing happened. He tried again and again. Nothing. Tioga pulled away and covered his eyes. His body began shaking from shock and the cold. He felt very alone. Then he heard a strange gurgle.

He looked over and saw Kopi explode in a fit of coughing. Tioga jumped for joy and rolled his friend over onto his side. Foam and water gushed from Kopi's mouth as his lungs expelled the fluid.

"Kopi! You're alive!" yelled Tioga.

"Ugh," was the only response, followed by another coughing spell.

A war cry echoed off the canyon walls. Tioga looked above them, but no one was there. He guessed that they hadn't been spotted—yet. This part of the gorge was almost impenetrable, but Tioga knew they couldn't remain exposed on the flat rock. He scanned the canyon for a place to hide, but the sheer walls offered no cover.

"We've got to go back in the water," said Tioga.

"Noooo," moaned Kopi, still with his eyes closed.

Tioga spotted a driftwood log wedged between two boulders. He splashed over and wrapped his arm around it. It took all of his strength to pry it free.

"Kopi!" hissed Tioga. "We've got to move!" Tioga pushed the floating log over to the boulder.

"I'm freezing," groaned Kopi.

"I'd rather be cold than roasting over a fire," said Tioga. "This river is going to carry us home."

Kopi lifted his head and looked up at the canyon walls. He recognized there was no climbing the sheer cliffs. The river was the only way out. At least it was no longer as angry as it had been.

"Hold on to this log," said Tioga. "The rapids are gone. Our only chance is to keep moving."

Kopi whimpered as he rolled off the rock into the water.

Tioga secured the empty gourd around Kopi's waist to provide a little extra flotation. Then he looped the strap around a branch on the log. He didn't want to lose his friend again.

The boys held the thick tree trunk and pushed away from the rock. At the far end of the pool, the current picked up and carried them downstream. Tioga tried to scan the canyon rim for signs of their pursuers. So far, they were alone. The river began moving faster than a man could run.

"This is almost as good as a canoe," said Tioga, with his teeth chattering. Kopi looked at him and promptly threw up. The two floated down the channel together, doing their best to keep their heads above water.

"Stop," croaked Kopi. "I can't take it."

Tioga looked up and noticed the sheer walls of the canyon had given way to cliffs with scruffs of vegetation clinging to the cracks. Soon boulders as tall as trees hung over them. Through the mist, Tioga could see the morning sky was blue far above, but everything was still gray in the canyon. The landscape was spectacular, but Tioga knew the rugged terrain wouldn't stop the searchers.

"We can't go ashore," said Tioga. "Not yet. We're too close. They'd just find us and bring us back."

"No more," moaned Kopi.

Tioga could see Kopi was fading fast. The cold was affecting him too. His bones ached, and he was losing control of his limbs. He began scanning the shore for a place to land.

But the river seemed to have other ideas. It was speeding up again. As they rounded a bend, a hissing sound came from downstream. It quickly grew into a rumble.

"Rapids," mumbled Kopi in despair. He started kicking in a feeble attempt drive the log to the shore. "No more."

Tioga was also concerned at the increasing speed of the river. "Alright, let's head for that big rock." He pointed to a flattened boulder off to one side of the stream. A strange, milky mist hung in the air beyond it.

The two boys held on to the log and kicked with all their might. The water began to roll up and down. The roar became deafening. Explosive rapids appeared before them. The waves were twice as high as before. The river pulled them forward. The boulder they had targeted moved out of reach.

"We're not going to make it!" yelled Tioga. "Turn your feet downstream!" He remembered the instructions he'd been given as a child, when he used to swim the river riffles. "It's better for your legs to hit the rocks than your head!"

A wave broke over Tioga. He fell over an unseen drop and gasped for breath. Then he was under. His feet immediately jammed into a boulder. He lost his grip on the log and whirled around. He was now hurtling downstream headfirst. He pulled up, and his face broke the surface. He took in a shallow breath and was swamped by another wave.

He tried not to fight the river. Fighting would only make the river angrier and exhaust him. He relaxed and slipped under the surface. It wasn't as noisy underwater. He was carried away like a leaf in the wind. When he detected a brief lull, he swam up and grabbed another breath.

Suddenly the river dropped sickeningly as he went over a waterfall. He fell with it and slammed against a submerged rock, losing his breath. The lack of air and disorientation caused him to panic. He tumbled underwater, and the cascade pulled him back beneath the falls. His lungs burned with unimaginable pain. He was about to inhale the liquid when the whirlpool spit him out. He broke the surface and gulped for air.

After two quick breaths he was under again and rushing downstream. He tried to regain his composure. The speed and power of the current was incredible. In some strange way, he felt like he was flying. He was so numb now he hardly felt the cold. Tioga realized this wasn't a good thing. His body was shutting down. In a few more moments he would be dead. *Fight!* he thought. *I've got to fight or die.*

Tioga struggled to awaken his rigid limbs. He broke the surface and noticed the water was slowing. He was able to take several good breaths, which allowed him to regain some energy. Again, the river slackened in a deep pool. Tioga was shaking uncontrollably. It took all of his remaining strength to reach the shore.

*Kopi! I can't leave Kopi.* Tioga turned and splashed back toward the center of the river. Just then the log floated into the pool. There was something beside it. *Could it be?* Tioga swam toward it and saw a waterlogged arm curled over one end, with a mop of soggy hair beside it. Tioga wanted to scream for joy, but knew better than to give away their location. Kopi's nose was barely out of the water. Tioga reached over and pulled his friend free. Kopi's eyes were shut, but he was breathing.

On the western side of the river there was a pebble beach. Tioga kicked with all his might and was able to pull Kopi up on shore. He collapsed beside his friend and tried to catch his breath. Suddenly a blinding spotlight turned on and focused on the escapees. Tioga's heart skipped a beat. Then he realized it was just the sun's rays, which had just crested the canyon rim. He laughed and laid his head on Kopi's shoulder. The sun was doing its part to warm them up. Every bone in his body wanted to stay there and rest, but he knew they couldn't remain in the open.

Tioga had spent most of his life outdoors and was particularly good at spotting hideouts. In the past, these hidden refuges had only been used for play. But now the game was all too real.

Tioga spied a dark void at the edge of the narrow floodplain and knew from experience that it had potential. He dragged Kopi toward it hoping for some cover. He parted the low hanging hemlock tree branches and exposed a small cavity under the side of a massive boulder.

"Yes!" he exclaimed as he pulled Kopi inside their little den. Tioga felt very lucky to find such a nice hideout. The small cavity must have been dug out by the raging waters of a past flood. The cave was just large enough for two people lying down, and had a sandy floor covered with dry leaves and branches. Best of all, its opening was concealed by the sagging branches of the evergreen tree. Of all the trees, Tioga liked hemlocks the best. They seemed to enjoy the same kind of places he did. Cool, wet spots where other trees, or people, didn't like to go. Whenever Tioga felt like being alone, he went to a hemlock grove.

Tioga threw out the sticks and the larger stones to make the ground more comfortable. In the process, he uncovered a dry six-foot long rattlesnake skin that had been shed by a prior inhabitant. Tioga made sure to ball it up and throw it out of sight. Kopi would never consider sharing a bed with a rattler.

Tioga stripped the wet leather buckskins off of Kopi and covered his semi-conscious friend in a thick layer of dry leaves, as well as the remains of his tattered beaver-fur cape—it had somehow stayed with him on the wild river ride. Tioga wished they had a fire to warm their refuge, but that was out of the question. At least the cool mountain air cut down on the mosquitoes. Kopi quickly passed out and began snoring in his sandy crib.

Tioga was nearly as exhausted and wanted to join him, but he knew he had one more job to do. He peered outside to make sure he wasn't being observed, then crawled out into the sunlight. He broke off a hemlock bough, and used it as a broom to brush the beach clear of their tracks. Thankfully, the rocky pebbles didn't capture footprints nearly as well as mud or sand.

Before climbing back into their sanctuary, Tioga did a quick study of their surroundings. The sheer cliffs of the gorge were gone, replaced by steep, rocky hillsides. Tioga immediately knew that it might be possible to climb out, but this also meant that searchers could climb in. He wondered if the Mononga warriors knew of their small rockshelter. He hoped not, as Kopi was in no shape to move. For that matter, neither was he.

Tioga parted the branches and dropped into the cave next to Kopi. He also removed most of his wet cloths and hung them where he could. Tioga looked down at his slender body. The powerful rapids had washed away most of the black paint. Underneath it, his skinny torso was covered with purple bruises, scrapes, and cuts.

Tioga snuggled up close to Kopi to conserve heat, molded his aching body into the sand, and covered himself in leaves. He tried to relax, but his mind was still racing from their daring escape. His brain was flooded with a strange sense of euphoria. Tioga began giggling uncontrollably. They had done it! They had escaped the Mononga Devil!

Then reality slowly set in. The woods above them would be crawling with warriors searching for the renegades. Against all odds, they had made it this far. But Tioga knew they were far from safe. He wanted to formulate a plan to continue their escape, but his head hurt too much to think. He closed his eyes and fell into a deep and badly needed slumber.

Tioga jerked awake when something wet hit his forehead. He was afraid to open his eyes. He prayed he wasn't back in the hut of the old Mononga woman, with his torso again covered in the black mask of death. His whole body was wet and tingling.

When he gathered the courage to look, all he saw was a hand hovering over his face. A lump of green goo dropped from its fingers and landed on his forehead with a smack. It was just Kopi messing with him.

"What are you doing?" moaned Tioga.

"Hold still," wheezed Kopi. He smeared the slimy paste over his patient's face. Tioga grimaced when the stinging liquid seeped into the cuts on his cheeks. He struggled to move his stiffened limbs.

"Quit moving," croaked Kopi.

Tioga noticed that Kopi was having trouble breathing. The raspy sound reminded him of their ordeal. "Kopi! You're alive!" he exclaimed.

"Shhh…" whispered Kopi. "Be quiet."

Tioga barely registered the comment. He struggled to sit up to give Kopi a hug, but the low ceiling prevented that.

"Hey, take it easy," rasped Kopi. "You're knocking off the paste."

"I was afraid I'd lost you," said Tioga.

"I don't remember much of what happened," said Kopi. "Did you pull me out?"

"Oh, you did fine," laughed Tioga. "I should call you Froggy. You should have seen how you swam those rapids. If I hadn't stopped you, I think you would have floated all the way to the Forks."

"Really? I don't remember anything except falling. I must have swallowed some bad water. My lungs and throat feel like a badger ripped them apart."

"Bad water will do that. Your voice sounds like a swamp monster."

Kopi chuckled. "Lay back down. I'm not finished with your poultice."

Tioga looked down at his body. Kopi had covered him with sticky green paste. It smelled like pine needles. "What is this stuff? Camouflage?"

"It's medicine," growled Kopi, taking a moment to cough up some green bile. He leaned over and tried spit it outside, but it hit a branch and hung there like a slime icicle.

"Oh gross! You're coving me with spit?"

"No. Ground up hemlock needles. It's good for scrapes and cuts."

"How did you do all this without waking me?"

"You were out cold. We both slept most of the day."

"Oh," said Tioga, still feeling groggy. It felt awkward being mothered by his friend. If anything, he should be taking care of Kopi. After all, earlier that morning Kopi had nearly died. But Tioga knew that he had come equally close to crossing over to the spirit world. After the beating in the fortress, and the violence of the river, he ached so much that he could barely move. It was a miracle that none of his bones were broken. From the angle of the sunlight shining on the far side of the canyon, Tioga could tell that it was late afternoon.

"It looks like we outsmarted them," said Tioga.

"Not yet," said Kopi. "They're still looking for us. I saw two men on the other side of the river just a little while ago."

"Excellent," said Tioga.

"Excellent? It's just a matter of time until they check here," groaned Kopi.

"That's right, it's a matter of time. They could have been on the way to our village by now, but we got lucky. They wasted a day looking for us."

"Lucky? We can only hope they stop looking."

"The sun is setting. They'll stop searching soon, at least for today. We can rest for the night."

Just then, a warrior's cry echoed through the canyon. Several voices returned the call. Then it seemed like the whole forest around them erupted with screams. Kopi's eyes opened wide in fear.

"Well, that's a good sign," said Tioga.

"How can you say that?" said Kopi nervously.

"They've got the whole village out looking for us."

"It sure sounds like it."

"Since they didn't find us today, they'll assume we drowned. Tomorrow they'll move on."

"Maybe, or maybe not."

"Shingas is in love with my mother. He knows our men will return to the village soon. He can't afford to waste another day searching. They'll head out at dawn."

"I hope you're right." As soon as Kopi said it, he regretted it. He was putting their survival ahead of their village.

Kopi laid back and stared at the sandstone ceiling. He wondered how his family was doing. He counted the days that they had been gone.

"This is our ninth day away from home," croaked Kopi.

"Yeah, we should have been back with the men days ago," said Tioga. "Mom is probably a nervous wreck."

"How are we going to get out of here?" asked Kopi, wheezing heavily. From the roaring sound downstream, it was clear that more rapids were just around the bend. Before Tioga could even think it, Kopi added, "There is no way I'm going back in the water. We have to climb out."

Tioga was surprised at Kopi's initiative. He knew his friend didn't like heights. He guessed climbing was the lesser of two evils.

"When it's safe to look, I'll study the hillside and we'll find a way up," said Tioga, wishing he had his trusty rope with him. It would make climbing a lot easier and safer.

"Once we get out, maybe we can stall them for another day," said Kopi, still thinking about his family.

"Stall who?" asked Tioga. His brain was still suffering the effects of the concussion.

"The Devil and his warriors. I don't want them to get to our village. I heard them talking. It's only a three day march to the Allegewi River from here."

"That's a problem. We'll never beat them home if we head to Canoe Camp."

"Canoe Camp?"

"I was thinking we could hike there and steal a canoe. Then paddle to the Forks, and head up the Allegewi River."

"That's a long trip," said Kopi. He hated the idea of getting back in a canoe. "It'd be quicker to walk home."

"Kopi, you're right. We've got to go on foot," said Tioga, trying to brainstorm. "We'll sleep here tonight. Then, if the coast is clear in the morning, we'll climb out and follow them."

Kopi considered the comment. He was relieved to hear Tioga didn't want to move tonight. His lungs needed more time to recover. But the thought of falling behind the war party was disconcerting.

"There's no way we can get ahead of them?" asked Kopi.

"Not yet. We don't know the way. It's easy to get lost in the mountains."

Kopi sighed. It was clear he was losing hope.

"Don't worry," said Tioga, trying to raise his friend's spirits. "The hard part is behind us. Thanks to you, Froggy, we escaped the Devil's fortress!"

"Thanks to me? I didn't do anything."

"You don't remember the storm? And the lightning bolt?"

"What storm?"

"Or the adoption ceremony?"

"Not really, I think they drugged me."

"I'd say so. You almost had a new papa—Papa Shingas."

"What? No way."

"Yep. You made quite an impression on him. He tried to adopt you. But the lightning bolt put a stop to that."

"Come to think of it, I do remember a flash," said Kopi.

"It was more than a flash. It was a bolt of fire that shattered the wall. They think you did it. They think you're a sorcerer and you can control fire."

"Me? A sorcerer?"

"Hey, if the wizard's cap fits, wear it."

"I guess so," said Kopi, not exactly knowing what this had to do with a wizard.

"So, we'll follow the war party," said Tioga, "and when the time is right, we'll pass them by and warn the village. I'm sure the chief has sent out another messenger to the hunting grounds by now."

"Probably Lenni," mumbled Kopi. "That's who I would send."

The comment stung Tioga, but he pushed past it. "In any event, our hunters will be back and ready to defend the village!"

"That's right! This is all going to work out."

"You bet it will."

"But what about Hanna?" asked Kopi. "We can't just leave her here."

"There's no need to go back for her."

"Tioga, what's happened to you? Have you lost your courage?"

"Relax. They'll bring her home for us."

"How can you be so sure?"

"She's a valuable hostage. Shingas wants to use her as bait. I heard him say so."

"So that's why you didn't try to save her at the fortress."

Tioga nodded. "It was more important that we get out. I left her a sign that we haven't forgotten her. And, if we can, we will rescue Hanna along the way home."

Kopi shook his head in wonder. Tioga was always thinking two steps ahead. He wished he were half as smart as his friend.

"Sorry for calling you a coward this morning," said Kopi.

"Better to be a live coward than a dead hero," said Tioga.

To Kopi, Tioga was a living hero. Somehow, he had managed to get them out of the fortress and led them to safety. And now he had a plan to save the village and Hanna too.

Just then something flashed by their hideout. "An eagle!" said Tioga. The boys watched as it swooped down, with talons extended, and snatched a massive trout from the river pool. The raptor rose gracefully into the air with the prize fish.

Tioga's stomach cramped. He hadn't had solid food in days. A fish would be good eating. He wished he still had his fishing line and hook. He wondered if he should risk searching the hillside for raw materials to make a new fishing kit.

As the bird of prey disappeared from sight, its distinctive cry pierced the air. Tioga crawled forward and looked up between the branches. High overhead he could see a second eagle approaching the first. An even larger bird was attacking the one carrying the fish. They swooped and tumbled in spectacular midair acrobatics.

"They're fighting," said Tioga.

"Get your head back in here," said Kopi, but he couldn't resist the urge to look too.

Tioga was entranced. It was a rare sight to see two eagles battling.

"Why doesn't the big one just get its own fish?" said Kopi.

"I guess there are bullies even among eagles," said Tioga. "We should name him Lenni." Just then the smaller bird gave up its prize. It dropped the trout and veered away toward the cliffs. The fish tumbled toward earth. The larger bird swooped down in pursuit. But even with its incredible speed, it couldn't make up the distance in time. The trout smacked into the side of a boulder at the far end of the beach and disappeared in a crevice. The larger eagle pulled up and landed on a nearby branch. It looked frustrated at the disappearance of its meal.

"That fish is dinner, if I can get to it," said Tioga, his mouth watering.

"We can't risk it until it gets dark," said Kopi.

"You're right," said Tioga. He ignored his rumbling stomach and settled back in.

Kopi coughed up some more bile and leaned back against the rock wall. Tioga wished he knew of some medicine that would help Kopi's breathing. He was still mystified at Kopi's knowledge of healing plants. The subject reminded him of a troubling question.

"Kopi, can I ask you something?"

"Sure."

"Why did you save Shingas's life when we were at Canoe Camp?"

Kopi grew silent. He paused for quite some time before answering. He finally mumbled his response in sullen tones. "Because he was suffering."

Tioga contemplated the answer. He knew there was more to it than that. And he knew that if he waited, he would hear it.

Kopi continued, "I don't like to see suffering. There's too much in the world as it is. I'm not smart like you, Tioga. I can't figure out complicated things. I don't always understand what's right and wrong, or who's good and bad. I just do what I can do. I didn't save Shingas's life. Only the Creator can do that. I only tried to take away the suffering."

Tioga nodded and watched the darkness slowly swallow the valley. The more he knew about Kopi, the prouder he was to have him as a friend.

After a lull, Kopi volunteered some more information. "I did do something to Shingas that I'm not exactly proud of."

"What was that?"

"Well, when we were heading into the mountains, I thought it wouldn't hurt to add a certain type of mushroom to his tea. I started with just a little, but by the time we made it to their fortress, I was giving him a pretty heavy dose."

"What kind of mushroom?" asked Tioga. While mushrooms were prized as a special treat at the village, you had to be careful collecting them, as so many varieties were deadly.

"Oh, a certain speckled type that grows in particular places."

"You poisoned him?"

"Well, not exactly," said Kopi. "They won't kill him, but I've been told they can make you feel really weird. They can even make you see things that aren't there."

"And get crazy ideas?"

"Yeah."

"Like adopting an Allegewi boy you just met as your son?"

"I guess so, now that you mention it," said Kopi. Inwardly, he was a little hurt that Tioga didn't think he was worthy of adoption.

"I wish he was still on that magic mushroom tea," said Tioga.

"He probably is," said Kopi. "I gave Chemung a week's worth of mushrooms and taught him how to brew the tea. I told him it was essential for his commander's recovery."

"Perfect!" said Tioga. "Maybe he'll lead them the wrong way!"

Both boys chuckled at the thought. As they waited for darkness, Tioga's thoughts turned to Hanna. She must have heard that they had escaped. *Does she think we abandoned her? Did she see the beads I left behind?*

An hour later, Kopi broke the silence. "I'm dying of hunger. I think it's safe to look for the fish."

"Alright. You stay here," said Tioga as he grabbed their canteen and prepared to exit their hideout. Kopi didn't argue. He knew Tioga's night vision was superior.

Tioga scanned the surrounding landscape for activity and cautiously stepped out onto the beach in only a loin cloth. His leather clothes were still wet and he would be colder with them on than off. He leaned down and half-crawled over the rocky terrain, swishing his hemlock broom behind him to cover his tracks. He didn't want Kopi to notice, but he was having a hard time balancing. He pushed through the pain and moved on.

His first task was to fill their canteen. Tioga was still dehydrated from their ordeal. In the faint light, he spotted a rivulet of water cascading down the cliff to his left. After quenching his thirst, Tioga returned the full canteen to Kopi. Then he headed back out to get the trout.

As he neared the large boulder where it had landed, he was greeted by the overpowering stench of death. Something way larger than a fish was rotting nearby. Tioga couldn't see the carcass among the shadowy boulders, but he knew from experience that it was close. He was thankful that the breeze blew the smell away from their hideout.

Tioga refocused his mind on finding the trout. He pictured where it had come down. *It must be right over there.* He crept forward, rounded a large boulder, and arrived at his destination. He scanned the gaps between the boulders but saw no sign of a fish. *It must have slid down that rock and into that pile of broken stone.*

He moved forward and reached into a dark fissure, hoping to feel the slimy scales of his target. He pulled away when his hand met a thick spider's web. Shuddering at the thought of a hole filled with spiders, he moved on to the next crevice.

He peered into the dark chasm, which opened into a small boulder cave. The stench of death was so strong he could taste it. It took a moment for his eyes to adjust to the darkness, and then he saw it: not the fish, but a mangled human torso, protruding from a tangle of driftwood. The sight of the dead body made him realize how lucky they were to survive the river. Tioga backed away from the corpse, and his appetite instantly disappeared.

He was about to turn back to their hideout when his brain kicked in. Without food, they wouldn't have the strength to climb out of the gorge. He had to find that trout if they were to have a chance to make it home.

Tioga renewed his efforts to secure dinner. He looked to the next gap in the stone heap. The thought of snakes slithered through his head. It dawned on him that it was not a good idea to be shoving his hand blindly into a rock pile. Rattlesnakes and water moccasins nested in such places.

He backed away and took another look at the huge boulder where the fish had touched down. He moved forward and noticed a streak of blood. He envisioned the fish sliding down the boulder. *It has to be that crack. The one with the spiders in it.*

He returned to the dark hole and thrust in a stick. This might clear out the webs, but any spiders would likely be waiting against the walls. He slid his wrist down into the darkness, through the remnants of the sticky webs. His fingers reached sticks, sand, and something cool and wet. *The fish!*

Tioga pulled out the most beautiful trout he had ever seen. He looked up at the emerging stars and said a prayer of thanks to the creature for giving its life so that they could eat. He used a sharp sliver of stone to gut the fish.

Then Tioga wrapped one arm around the trout and used his other to sweep the pebble beach clear of footprints. He carefully worked his way back to their den, and crawled inside.

Kopi could hear his friend come in, but it was so dark he couldn't see him. "Well?" asked Kopi hopefully.

Tioga jokingly lifted the fish to Kopi's lips. "Somebody wants to give you a kiss!"

Kopi smelled food, and was so hungry that he bit off a chunk of the fish's head and crunched it down.

"Hey, wait for me," said Tioga, as he took a bite out of the tail.

The boys ate it raw. A meal had never tasted so good. Tioga didn't mention the decaying body he had seen in the rocks. There was no point reinforcing Kopi's fear of water with news of the sobering discovery.

After dinner, Tioga took a final look at the night sky before going to bed. He was glad to see the stars shining so brightly. He knew that if another storm came, and the river flooded, their hideout could be inundated.

Tioga relaxed and crawled under his leafy covers. For the first time in days, he was going to bed on a full stomach. By the time he got comfortable, Kopi was snoring loudly in his ear. While the sound was annoying, it also concerned Tioga. This was unlike Kopi's usual snoring. Now he was wheezing, snoring, coughing, and moaning in rapid succession—all while being fast asleep. Kopi sounded like a possessed demon.

Tioga realized his friend's lungs were damaged. *What if he gets worse?* he thought. *What if Kopi stops breathing during the night? He could be dead by morning! Should I stay up and watch him?*

While Tioga listed to Kopi's labored breathing, his eyelids grew heavy. Somehow the continuous roar of the river was soothing. In his mind, he pictured the canyon walls, and tried to figure the best way to climb out.

Tioga plotted his course and began the ascent. The cool mountain air filled his lungs. He began jumping from rock to rock effortlessly. He had never moved so gracefully.

Then he spotted it—a wild bighorn sheep clinging to the side of the gorge. He instinctively crouched and began stalking his prey. Tioga's whiskers twitched and his tail swung from side to side. He expertly calculated the distance, then sprang forward!

By the time the ram saw him coming, it was too late. Tioga flew through the air and hit his target at full force. He buried his sharp claws into the animal's back and sunk his fangs into his victim's neck. The warm blood tasted glorious. The ram squirmed frantically, but Tioga held tight. It soon stopped moving. Tioga dragged his meal up onto a ledge. Then he looked out over the rugged canyon and roared.

# Eighteen

A single Mononga "whoop" carried over the wall. The fortress gate opened in response, and the exhausted search party dragged into the village. Shingas counted the shadowy forms as they passed through the entrance. He let out a low growl as Chemung sheepishly walked toward him.

"Well?"

"No sign of them," said Chemung, breathlessly. "We've looked under every rock, up every tree, and down every trail within an hour of here."

"You're telling me two little boys outfoxed an entire tribe of Mononga? I should have your head on a spike." Shingas walked away disgusted. He wandered through the darkened village, tormented by thoughts of the escaped prisoners. He had never lost a captive before.

He soon came upon the Allegewi girl and her female attendant sitting by a campfire. Hanna whimpered as she caressed a small piece of beaded leather, streaked with red and black paint. He yanked it out of her hand, and looked at the grimy fragment. Something about the beading caught his eye.

"Allegewi trash," said Shingas with disgust. He tossed it into the fire. Hanna burst into tears as it burned.

Chemung appeared out of the darkness and handed his leader his nightly cup of medicine tea, then sat down by the fire to warm his chilled feet.

"Who said you could sit down?" barked Shingas. Chemung jumped up and stood at attention. Shingas continued, "The search will not be over until you find them, dead or alive."

"Yes, Great Leader," said Chemung, who paused then softly asked, "Sir, permission to give council?"

"Proceed."

"They must be dead," said Chemung. "We followed their trail to the cliff. To the very spot where we throw the weak-minded and infirm into the river. They must have jumped. Many prefer death to recapture. No one has ever survived the fall and the rapids. The skinny boy was almost dead before the escape, and the fat one can't swim."

"So where are their bodies?"

"The river is running high. Their bodies could be half way to the Forks by now."

"You searched the canyon, from top to bottom?"

"Yes, sir, all the areas that could be reached."

"Did you send a team down the river?"

"In the rapids?"

"Yes, you imbecile! Did they go in the water?"

"Well, no sir. That would be a suicide mission."

"Gather the torches and send the men back out."

"But, Great Leader, the men have been searching all day. They are exhausted. We should rest and prepare for war. You said that we will leave at sunrise."

"Are you refusing my orders, Chemung?"

"Of course not, Great Leader!"

Shingas thought he almost detected a tone of sarcasm in Chemung's response. "Very well then," said Shingas. "Renew the search. If they are still alive, they probably hid until dark and are now running for their lives."

"Yes, sir," said Chemung in resignation. "We will renew the search."

"Good," said Shingas. "I will reward the men for their efforts. The moon is just beginning to rise. Tell them they must only search until the moon is directly overhead."

Chemung did the math in his head. "Sir, that will only give them a few hours of sleep before dawn."

"That is more than enough for a Mononga warrior."

"Yes, Great Leader." Chemung turned and sulked away. As he called his men together, their audible discord drifted through the village.

Shingas felt the tea begin to take effect. His fingers tingled, his heart beat faster, and his vision blurred a bit. While he did not really like the feeling, he was glad to know the strong medicine was working. His stump was healing nicely. Although he would have liked to grow a new arm, he now appreciated a healthy stump.

He staggered a bit as he watched the torches spring to life and depart through the stockade gate. Shingas turned back toward the campfire. His eyes were again drawn to the Allegewi girl painted in ash. Her nonstop crying reminded him of another girl he had once known. A girl who had disappeared a week before their wedding. His heart still ached from the memory.

Hanna noticed the warlord staring at her. He looked larger and meaner than ever dressed in his grizzly-bear cape, with its massive claws still attached. She turned away to hide her tears from his prying eyes.

"What's wrong with her?" asked Shingas to Tatami, the eighteen-year-old woman assigned to mind the captive. He was beginning to reconsider his decision to bring Hanna on the warpath. The last thing he needed was a sniveling girl to slow them down.

"I do not know, Great Leader," said Tatami with her head bowed in submission.

"You speak the Allegewi tongue?"

"Yes, Great Leader. My grandmother was Allegewi before she became Mononga." The comment reminded Shingas that the war with the Allegewi had been going on for many decades. It was time to finish it.

"Good. Tell the girl that her two friends are dead. They drowned like rats in the river."

"Yes, Great Leader," said Tatami. She conveyed the news to Hanna in Allegewi. The shock on Hanna's face was evident to all. Tears streamed down her cheeks.

"She is mourning the deaths of those two weaklings?" said Shingas to Tatami, slurring his words. "Tell her we have much better men in our tribe for her to marry."

Hanna looked down at the fire as the woman translated the comment. "No," said Hanna. "NO!"

Shingas considered striking her for her insolence, but he was too tired to bother. His head was spinning from the tea. He watched as sparks rose from the fire and flew up into the night sky. Never before had he found sparks so interesting.

He was broken from his trance by the throbbing in his rear. Earlier that day, he had finally allowed the tribe's medicine man to remove the small flint arrowhead from his buttocks. It had been bothering him more than he cared to admit. He hoped his men hadn't noticed his diminished stride. To receive such a wound from a child was embarrassment enough.

Shingas addressed Tatami. "I am retiring early. No one is to wake me unless the search party finds their bodies."

"Yes, Great Leader."

Shingas staggered off toward his lodge. Hanna remained by the fire and wiped the tears from her face.

"Please stop," said Tatami. "You are smearing your paint." She moved forward and dipped a brush into a bowl containing ash mixed with bear grease.

"I don't want to be painted again," said Hanna as she turned her face away.

"Please allow me," said Tatami. "If I don't keep your paint in proper shape, our leader will beat me."

Hanna reluctantly turned her face toward the young woman who had shadowed her for the last two days. Tatami smiled and gingerly dabbed her face with the milky paste.

"My father—our tribe's leader—never lifts his hand in anger," said Hanna. "He leads with wisdom and courage."

Tatami looked around to make sure no one else was listening. "I have been told that we too used to have such a wise leader. In the time before I was born."

Hanna appreciated having someone to talk with. She even felt that in another time and place, the two girls might have been close friends.

"It is wrong for him to beat you," said Hanna.

"I know," said Tatami. "But it is his way. We must endure it." The young woman mustered enough courage for another confession. "It is his treatment of Pox—my husband—that troubles me the most. He drives the men very hard, sometimes to the point of collapse."

Hanna listened with sympathy. "Pox? That's an unusual name."

"He had a different name when he was born. But even he does not remember it."

"How is that?"

"He was born in a small hamlet to the east. A terrible plague wiped out their people when he was a baby. An old Mononga trapper found him barely alive and brought him home, as he had never had a son. But the Great Leader kicked them both out, saying the boy was diseased and cursed. The man raised the child in the far meadow until he was well. Since the trapper never got sick and the boy grew stronger, the shaman said the curse was broken. They were both welcomed home. But my husband was forever covered with hundreds of scars from the illness. His name became Pox. Some say he is ugly, but the scars never bothered me. I love him just the way he is."

"I understand," said Hanna, thinking of Tioga.

"He is a good husband. But every time he walks out that gate, I wonder if he will ever come back. The life of a warrior is often short."

The comment made Hanna burst into tears. Tatami was confused by her reaction at first, but then nodded.

"You cared deeply for him, didn't you?" asked Tatami. "The one who was painted black?"

Hanna looked up, surprised that the woman could read her thoughts. But even more startling was the aching feeling in her heart. She had never felt that way about anyone before.

"He was very special to me," said Hanna softly. "But I never knew how special until now."

"I could tell by the way you looked at him," said Tatami. "The other night my heart felt for you. Nothing could be worse than to see your man die by the flame."

Hanna nodded. *At least his pain is over*, she thought. She broke down and sobbed on her friend's shoulder.

"Come," said Tatami. "Let us go to bed. Tomorrow you will begin a difficult journey."

"Where will they take me?" asked Hanna.

"To war."

"Will you be going with us?"

Tatami smiled but shook her head. "Mononga women are not permitted to go to battle. You must be a very important woman to be taken on the trail."

"No, Tatami, I am not important. I am just an ordinary girl, afraid and far from home. I'm caught in the middle of a horrible game that I don't even understand."

"I don't understand the game either. But I do know that if you leave tomorrow, I'm going to miss you, Hanna."

"I will miss you too, Tatami."


Hours later, as Tatami and Hanna slept in their lodge, nineteen-year Pox stood at the rim of the canyon watching the night sky.

"Look, a shooting star!" said Pox, to his comrade Bongo. "That's a good sign."

"Quit dreaming and get back to searching," said Bongo. "There is a beach down there that we should check. There are some caves there too."

"I'm not climbing into the gorge at night," said Pox, looking into the black abyss. "That's way too dangerous."

"Think of it," said Bongo. "If we find those boys, we'll be the heroes of the village!"

"They're dead," said Pox. "What's the point of risking our lives?"

"Great Leader said he wants them back—dead or alive. If we find them dead, it will be even easier. We can cut off their heads and leave their bodies to rot. Imagine the reward when we present their heads to the commander!"

"Look at the moon," said Pox, with a yawn. "In another hour it will be directly overhead and we can go back and sleep. Let's sit here and relax. We've got to hit the trail at dawn."

"Fine, you lazy coward. I'll go by myself," said Bongo. He held his torch out over the edge of the canyon and tried to determine the best route down. He set his bow and quiver of arrows on the ground and crawled over the ledge.

"You're not bringing your bow?" asked Pox. "What if you run into them?"

"Arrows don't work on ghosts," responded Bongo, with a chuckle. He carefully picked his way down the cliff, holding his torch in one hand.

"What if they aren't dead?" asked Pox, leaning over the rim of the gorge.

"If they aren't dead yet, they soon will be," said Bongo from below. "Can you imagine swimming those rapids? If I find one alive on the riverbank, it will be no problem finishing him off. I still have my knife."

"It could be two against one."

Bongo looked up and said, "Pox, what kind of a warrior are you? You're afraid of two little Allegewi boys who have no weapons? Wait until your wife hears this. I'll bet she asks for a divorce."

"You wouldn't tell Tatami!" said Pox, nervously.

"I just might. She is my cousin. I owe her the truth. I doubt she'd want to stay with a coward."

"Hold on," said Pox. "I'm coming!" He left his bow and arrows on a rock and gingerly followed Bongo into the canyon.

The two men cautiously worked their way down the steep slope, which at times was nearly vertical. It wasn't easy with only one free hand. They needed to hold their torches with the other.

"You've been down here before?" asked Pox, a body length above Bongo.

"Yeah, a couple of times—when I was a kid."

"Why in the world would you come down here?"

"I liked to play on the beach. Can you think of another beach anywhere near here?"

Pox thought about it and said, "There's a nice sandy beach down at Canoe Camp."

"That's days away," said Bongo. Just then a fist sized stone whizzed by his head. "Hey! Watch the rocks! You nearly killed me."

"Sorry! Wait for me. You're getting too far ahead."

Bongo paused and looked across the canyon. He could see dozens of other torches twinkling across the landscape. Few were in the gorge, but there were only a couple of places that could be reached. If those boys did somehow survive the river, he knew this was just about the only place they could crawl out.

Fifteen minutes later they arrived at the bottom of the canyon.

"You call this a beach?" said Pox, holding out his torch.

"Be quiet!" hissed Bongo. He bent down and examined the pebbles in the torch light. There were no obvious footprints, but they might have covered their tracks.

"This way," whispered Bongo. He led Pox upstream toward a pile of large boulders. "There are places here to hide."

"Whew! What's that smell? It stinks!" hissed Pox.

"Something died around here," said Bongo. He followed the stench until he found the right cavity. He thrust his torch into the gap. "Look! A dead body!"

"Really?"

"Yes!"

Pox held his nose and peeked inside. "That's a body? There's hardly anything left."

"Those rapids can rip a man apart."

"It looks too small to be a man. I think that's a woman."

"Or a boy? Come on, we've got to get him out."

"I'm not going in that cave. It's not a good idea to disturb the dead."

"Hold my torch, you little baby. A man shouldn't be afraid to get his hands dirty." Bongo crawled in. Even he gagged at the overpowering stench. His stomach heaved, but he swallowed his vomit. If he lost it now, Pox would be the one telling stories. He pulled several branches off the corpse to free it from the tangle. Then he grabbed its legs and pulled.

The rotting carcass wasn't coming out without a fight. Its head was lodged firmly between two boulders.

Bongo leaned back and pulled with all his might. The head decided to stay, but the torso jumped back toward him. Bongo slipped and the decaying body landed on top of him.

"Aww, gross!" shrieked Pox.

Bongo struggled free and dragged the headless victim to the beach.

Pox took one look and threw up.

"It's not one of them," said Bongo, covered in putrid slime. "This body has been here a while."

"I could have told you that," said Pox.

Bongo ignored the comment as he rushed to the water's edge and frantically tried to wash off the stink. Pox arrived beside him and placed their torches on the ground. He too began to wash his hands with vigor.

"What are you doing?" said Bongo, in astonishment. "The torches could go out!" He turned and grabbed one of them just before it was extinguished. The other smoldered in the wet pebbles.

"Oh, sorry about that." Pox picked up his torch and relit it from Bongo's flame.

"You could have ruined us!" growled Bongo. "If the torches go out, we'll be stuck down here until morning. We'd be the laughing stock of the fortress."

"Let's get out of here," said Pox. "This place is creepy. And the ghost of that headless corpse is probably nearby."

"Alright, but there is one more spot we need to check. This way!"

The two warriors suppressed their fatigue and trotted down the shoreline. They arrived outside of a large boulder at the far end of the beach. An ancient hemlock tree leaned out and seemed to embrace the rock with its branches.

"There's a small cave under there," said Bongo.

"Where?"

"Under the branches."

"Are you sure?"

"Yes, I'm sure. I used to play in there. It's your turn to go first," said Bongo, still shaken from his encounter with the dead body.

Pox slowly moved forward with his torch. He reached out to pull aside a branch, but suddenly stopped cold. His arms and legs began to tremble. Then he turned and rushed back to his friend's side.

"There's something in there!" hissed Pox as he pulled his knife. "It's alive. I heard it growling!"

"What is it?" said Bongo. He knew Pox was prone to exaggeration. But just to be safe he reached for his knife too.

"I'm not sure," whispered Pox. "But it's something big. You're the brave warrior. Go check it out."

Bongo moved cautiously forward toward the cave with his knife in one hand and his torch in the other. It was tough to hear over the sound of the rapids, but as he got closer, he did hear something strange coming from the grotto. It sounded like a low growl mixed with heavy breathing. Then there was a sharp bark unlike anything he had ever heard before. He jumped back and distanced himself from the den.

"Did you hear it?" asked Pox.

"Yes. There's an animal in there."

"What do you think it is?"

"Could be a badger," said Bongo, straining to identify the unusual growl.

"I don't think badgers live at the bottom of canyons."

"Then probably a bear."

"I'm not messing with a bear with only a knife. We should have brought our bows!"

"I'll bet it's a mountain lion," said Bongo, upon further reflection. He slowly started moving backward. "I've seen them hunting bighorn sheep in the gorge before."

"They can see at night. He's probably watching us!"

"Don't panic. If you run, a lion will attack."

Just then an unworldly moan echoed from the cave. The bizarre sound was unlike any known animal, but also couldn't be called human. It was followed by a spastic barking cough and a protracted groan. The spine-chilling sounds could only be made by a tortured spirit.

"It's the ghost of the headless corpse!" cried Pox. He turned and ran for the exit.

Bongo was right behind him. When they got to the cliff, Bongo passed him by and frantically moved up the canyon wall.

"I told you not to mess with that body," hissed Pox. "It's haunting us!"

Bongo was too busy climbing to respond.

# Nineteen

Tioga and Kopi cautiously crawled out of their cave well after the sun was up. Both boys had slept like the dead. They had badly needed the rest. Tioga was actually beginning to feel human again.

As he moved onto the beach, he looked down at the pebbles and froze. In the morning light, two sets of footprints were clearly visible, and they weren't his or Kopi's. He grabbed Kopi and pulled him back to the hideout.

"Footprints!" cried Tioga.

Kopi looked back in terror. "They must have come by in the night."

"Somehow they missed us."

"They're still looking for us?" gasped Kopi.

"I don't think so. I haven't heard any calls this morning. They must have given up during the night. Even if they are still searching, they've crossed this spot off the list."

"Do you want to stay here for another day?"

Tioga mulled the question over in his head. "No. The war party is heading to our village. We don't want them to get too far ahead. And now we know the easiest way out. We can just follow the searchers trail up the cliff."

"Alright," said Kopi as he went into another coughing spell. "Just give me a moment to catch my breath."

When Kopi was ready, Tioga crawled out and surveyed the landscape. After filling their gourd again with fresh water, Tioga waved Kopi forward. They followed the footprints along the beach in the direction of the rock pile.

Kopi spotted something strange ahead of them. Tioga instantly recognized it as the corpse from the boulders. The stench of the cadaver greeted them.

"What is that?" said Kopi at the sight. He quickly figured it out. "That's a dead body!"

"Yep. I saw it last night in the boulders. But I didn't want to worry you. You know, with your fear of ghosts and all."

"Who is that and what happened to them?"

"Probably a flood victim... or worse," said Tioga, thinking of Shingas. "Last night, the searchers must have wondered who it was, as they moved her body." He picked up a tree branch and walked toward the cadaver.

"Come on, we've got to go," said Kopi, as he gagged from the stench.

"Just a second." Tioga prodded the corpse with the stick.

"What are you doing? Disturbing the dead is wrong. You'll cause the ghost of that poor soul to haunt us."

"She's not going to haunt us, she's going to help us."

Kopi shook his head and turned away. Tioga continued to poke the body. Soon he found what he was looking for. The purple skin gave way and a stream of squirming maggots fell to the sand.

Tioga grabbed a large green leaf and made a makeshift pouch. He gathered the maggots inside. He said a silent prayer of thanks to the fallen person and turned back to Kopi.

"Let's go," said Tioga.

"What did you take from her?" asked Kopi with concern.

Tioga opened the leaf and showed the wiggling occupants. "Bait!"

"We don't have time to go fishing."

"Maybe we will tonight," said Tioga. "These mountain streams are loaded with brook trout. And there is nothing a trout likes better than a maggot."

"From a dead body?"

"I hate to tell you this, but fish don't believe in ghosts."

"Maybe so, but I do. And now we'll have a ghost following us."

"Kopi, we are not our bodies. The soul who was in that body is finished with it. That's why she gave it to the maggots. And the maggots will give up their bodies to the trout. And the trout will give up their bodies to us. Once they leave their bodies, all the spirits are happy to help the next in line. This is how it works in the spirit world. My father taught me this."

Kopi nodded. He suddenly realized that the cycle of earthly life and death was all part of the Great Spirit's plan. There was no death of the spirit. The thought of happy spirit helpers cheered him up.

The boys followed the searchers footprints to the wall of the gorge and looked up. From further away, it looked like a steep hillside. But now it seemed more like a vertical cliff.

"It took some guts to climb this in the dark," said Tioga.

"Forget about the dark, how are we going to climb this in the light? It looks impossible."

"If they did it, so can we. We'll take our time and be careful."

"You go first," said Kopi.

Tioga eyed the warriors' tracks and started up the cliff. Kopi stood at the bottom of the canyon and watched his friend slowly work his way up. He coughed up some mucus, then joined him on the climb.

Meanwhile, at the same moment less than a mile upstream, Shingas stood at the rim of the same canyon and stared into the misty abyss. His eyes were focused on the suspension bridge—a marvel of Mononga ingenuity. The only problem was that it was no longer suspended. The rope bridge had collapsed, and was hanging from the far rim of the canyon. Someone had cut the ropes during the night. The war party had been stopped just after it had started.

"There is a traitor in the fortress!" screamed Shingas.

None of the eighty warriors massed behind him dared utter a word. Shingas scoured his brain for who it might be, but his morning medicine made it hard to think. Someone wanted to slow down the war party. His mind kept returning to the escaped Allegewi boys. *Could they have pulled off such a feat?*

"I want those boys found!" roared Shingas. "Chemung!"

"Yes, sir?"

"Send half our men down the valley to search for them!"

"Sir?"

"That's an order! And they are not to come back without their heads!"

"But sir, their bodies could be floating all the way to the Forks."

"Then the men will go there and wait for them!"

Chemung looked at his commander in horror. The order would weaken the attack force by half. Something very strange was going on with the Great Leader.

"Do it!" barked Shingas. "And bring me the Iceman!"

"Yes, sir," mumbled Chemung in shock. He split the troops and sent half the puzzled warriors south along the canyon rim. With the bridge out, they wouldn't even be able to search the western side of the gorge.

Chemung then led Ötzi the Iceman to the front of the remaining group. The old man looked at the fallen bridge and clicked his tongue in judgement.

Shingas starred Ötzi in the eyes. "You are a rope maker. Did the lines fail or were they cut?"

Ötzi walked around the support posts and examined the frayed ends of rope at the top of the span. "They were cut."

"Who did this?" asked Shingas in anger.

"Did you see footprints?" asked the elder in response.

Shingas's ears turned red. He realized then that he forgot to order his tracker to search for clues. "There were no tracks," said Shingas in frustration.

"Then it must have been the ghosts of the two dead boys!" shouted Ötzi, loud enough that everyone could hear. An audible gasp went through the ranks.

"Forget those boys!" said a flustered Shingas. "How long will it take to fix the bridge?"

"To do so will require a large amount of rope."

"Do we have enough in storage?"

"No. It will take me and my apprentices quite a while to make that much." Ötzi was the master ropemaker in the village. As an expert alpine climber, he had developed a unique way of making strong but flexible rope that could survive the harsh winters in the mountains.

"How long until the bridge is fixed?" roared Shingas.

"A week or more."

"Unacceptable. We will hike around the canyon. We can be back to the other side in a day."

Ötzi looked up at the sky. "Yes, if the weather holds. And if the ice pack above Howling Pass does not break loose."

The men listening in looked at each other nervously. They knew the detour included a difficult climb high into the mountains. And it meant they would have to cross Howling Pass—so called because the winds howled through the high and often deadly gap. That is where the Iceman had earned his nickname. He was the only survivor of a storm in Howling Pass that took the lives of a dozen men decades ago. If not for the magic of the Gangas Witch, he too would have perished.

"I think it is better to fix the bridge," said Ötzi. "Otherwise, after the battle, we will have to return by the same route. If a winter storm blows in while we are gone, the pass may become impassable."

"We will not wait!" bellowed Shingas. "You are a fearful old man. Chemung! Get the troops ready. We move out now!"

"Yes sir," said Chemung warily, as he looked at the icy peaks that surrounded them. Moments later, the remaining force began the circuitous trek around the gorge.


Far downstream, the boys slowly progressed up the western side of the canyon. The ascent was difficult, but not impossible. Tioga could easily follow the searchers' trail. Kopi was doing surprisingly well. He hadn't complained once about the height. But they did have to stop frequently to let him catch his breath.

Thirty minutes later, they were just below the rim. It was clear that the final stretch would be the most challenging. The last twenty feet were nearly vertical with just a few good holds. There was a ledge about halfway up which would serve as a rest stop. Tioga pointed out where to grab, and Kopi followed along bravely. As Tioga reached for the ledge, he heard a rattling sound. He froze instantly. Every tribe member knew that sound.

"Rattlesnake," he whispered, bringing his hand back.

He looked down into Kopi's ashen face. Although they couldn't see the snake, it was obviously right above them.

"Back down," said Tioga.

Kopi nodded. The two boys dropped a few feet lower.

Tioga looked at the ledge above them. A beam of sunlight was focused there. "He must be warming up in the sun," said Tioga.

"We've got to find a way around him," wheezed Kopi.

Tioga quickly surveyed the landscape and evaluated their options. To their right and left, the cliff walls were sheer. Any other way would involve some very dangerous climbing. The easiest route went right by the snake.

"I'd rather deal with a rattler than a fall from those cliffs," said Tioga. "Do you know a good remedy for a rattlesnake bite?"

"No," said Kopi. "The best remedy is not to get bit."

"Let me take another look."

Tioga began climbing up toward the serpent. As he crested the ledge, he cautiously eyed the obstruction. A small diamondback rattlesnake was coiled a few feet away. It rattled with renewed intensity and flicked it's forked tongue in the air, judging the distance to Tioga's face.

Tioga backed down a few feet. "It's just a baby."

"The babies pack just as much venom as a full-grown adult," responded Kopi.

Tioga scanned the hillside for a tool. "Please hand me that stick."

Kopi complied. When it came to handling critters in the forest, there were few better than Tioga.

"I'm going to give him a little nudge," said Tioga. "Hopefully he will move along."

"Be careful," said Kopi from below.

Tioga climbed up again and peered over the ledge. The snake rattled loudly. Tioga reached the trembling stick toward the rattler's face. In an instant, it flashed forward and bit the wood. Tioga jerked it back, and noticed clear yellow venom was dripping from the end. Tioga moved lower.

"What happened?" asked Kopi.

"He struck the stick."

"Did he move?"

"No, he's sitting tight."

Tioga scanned the canyon again for another way out. From this vantage point he could see the Angry River twisting and turning downstream in another set of vicious rapids. He also noticed how exposed they were at the moment. If the Mononga were out looking for them, the boys would be easy to spot.

"We've got to get by it," said Tioga. "I'm going to throw the snake off the cliff."

"With your bare hand?"

"Of course not. I'll fling it with the stick."

Tioga climbed back up to the ledge with renewed determination. When he peered over the rim, the snake was still there in the sunny spot. It began to rattle again.

Tioga reached out the branch. The snake didn't bother to strike it this time, so Tioga gently slid it under the coiled form. He tensed his arm got ready to heave it over the cliff.

He counted, "One, two," but before he could say, "three," the snake unwound and headed straight toward him. "Oh, no!"

One wrap of the snake's body remained on the stick, so Tioga flipped it skyward. The branch snapped under the strain, but it had just enough energy to fling the rattler over Tioga's shoulder.

A split second later Kopi cried out, "Ahh! Snake!"

Tioga looked down and saw Kopi thrashing about with the squirming snake draped over his shoulder. Kopi lost his balance, and they fell together and landed with a thud at the base of a tree stump a body length below—the only obstacle which could have saved him from a horrible fall.

The snake scurried free and disappeared into the rocks.

"Are you alright?" asked Tioga.

"Yeah, I think so," said Kopi, checking his limbs. "Why did you do that?"

"The stick broke. Sorry."

Tioga remembered when one of the hunters was struck by a rattler. His foot had swelled up twice its normal size and turned dark purple. It was months before he could run again. And that was a full-grown man. Tioga hesitated to think what a bite would have done to Kopi.

"Didn't I ever tell you I don't like snakes?" said Kopi.

"I think you did," said Tioga.

"Unless they're cooked, of course," said Kopi as he rose to his feet and dusted himself off.

"Are you sure he didn't bite you?"

"Yes, I'm sure," said an annoyed Kopi. "Now let's get moving. The ledge is clear."

This time Kopi took the lead. Somehow the encounter with the snake gave him a burst of energy. He found a grip and moved upward. After a difficult ascent over the ledge, the pitch lessened. Soon they were climbing easily and the rim of the canyon was in sight. But before they reached it, Kopi stalled.

"Can we take a break?" he wheezed.

"But we're almost to the top," responded Tioga.

"Please? My lungs hurt."

Tioga still felt exposed, but Kopi was clearly winded. "Okay, but just for a moment. Then we need to get out of here."

Just as he said it, Tioga spotted movement on the far side of the canyon. With his keen eyesight, it only took a second to identify what it was.

"Warriors!" hissed Tioga. He grabbed Kopi and pulled him down behind a fractured boulder. The two boys pressed their bodies into the sharp fragments of stone on the sloping ground. The boulder was barely large enough to hide them both.

"Where?" whispered Kopi. His wheezing increased with his heart rate.

"On the far side of the canyon."

"How many?"

Tioga shimmied forward and peeked through a crack in the rock. He could clearly see a column of men, walking single file along the trail on the other side of the gorge.

"A lot," said Tioga. "Dozens."

"Dozens? What are they doing here?"

"They're moving south."

"But our village is to the west."

"I know," said Tioga. "It doesn't make sense."

Kopi shifted uncomfortably. "Are they gone yet? These rocks are sharp."

Tioga ignored the discomfort and kept his eye on the enemy. He breathed a sigh of relief when the warriors moved out of sight. "They left. We're good."

Kopi reached down and grabbed a glossy sliver of stone that was poking him in the belly. "Flint! We're laying on flint!"

"We can make some tools," said Tioga, as he gathered up some fist-sized chunks that had eroded out the shattered limestone block.

"We can make some weapons!"

"Yes! Kopi, I like the way you think. You really are becoming a warrior!"

After making sure the Mononga were gone, they resumed their upward trek, loaded with an ample supply of flint. Nearly an hour after they had started, they reached level ground beyond the canyon rim. Tioga was shocked at what he saw. Hundreds of footprints zigzagged in every direction as far as the eye could see. The search had been extensive.

"Well, at least we don't need to worry about our prints," said Tioga. "They will blend right in with all the rest."

"What about those warriors?"

"They are on the other side of the gorge."

"What if more come this way?" asked Kopi.

Tioga found it hard to believe that Shingas was still looking for them. But it was better to be safe than sorry.

"Okay, we can hide for a bit," said Tioga.

"Good," croaked Kopi. "Cause my lungs are killing me."

"You're voice sounds like it could use some help too."

"Look at you," said Kopi. "You're in even worse shape than me."

It was true. Tioga was still beat up from his ordeal in the fortress and the violent river. They looked for a suitable hiding place. Before long, Tioga spotted a dense grove of bushes beneath an old oak tree. They worked their way through the twisted branches and took refuge there. The canopy above them blocked out most of the light. In a way, they were back inside a cave, but this time the roof was made of leathery leaves, not sandstone.

Tioga noticed several large feathers on the ground. A raptor's cry pierced the air from above them. He stood up and parted the branches. High above, in the ancient tree, there was a massive nest. Tioga watched a beautiful eagle land in her impressive home. *Thank you for last night's meal,* he thought.

Tioga bent down and picked up two eagle feathers. He admired the way they caught the gentle breeze that was flowing through their grotto. He tied one feather to a lock of his hair and let it hang down over his shoulder.

"Nice," said Kopi. "You look like a real fighter."

"I've got one for you too," said Tioga. He stepped behind Kopi and began to tie it into his friend's hair. Kopi stood at attention as if he were receiving an award for bravery.

Then Tioga spotted something on the side of Kopi's neck—two small, bloody puncture wounds. Even a child would have recognized the bite of a snake. Tioga opened his mouth, but no sound came out. His entire body started to shake. He stumbled backward.

"What is it?" said Kopi. "What's wrong?"

Tioga raised a trembling finger and pointed at Kopi's neck. A rattlesnake bite on the neck would surely be fatal.

"A spider?" Kopi convulsed in panic. "I hate spiders!" He swatted feverishly at his neck and back.

"No!" said Tioga. "Worse. The snake bit you!"

"What?" said Kopi. "No, he didn't."

Tioga stepped forward and grabbed his friend's hand. He guided Kopi's fingers to the bite. Kopi felt the puncture wounds with the expertise of a doctor.

"That little bugger did bite me!"

Tioga nodded in shock. He studied Kopi for the first signs of his coming death.

Kopi looked concerned for a moment and then smiled. "I feel fine. That was nearly an hour ago. He forgot to inject the venom!"

Tioga had seen shamans handle live rattlesnakes. There were even stories of some of them getting bit, but the poison didn't hurt them. Only a very formidable mystic could overcome snake venom. Tioga looked at Kopi in awe and with newfound respect. Was his friend a powerful shaman in the making?

"Kopi, you'd better lie down."

"Nonsense. Look, here are some tasty mushrooms. I'll make you a snack."

Tioga watched suspiciously as Kopi gathered food. He didn't appear to be dying. Then a dark thought entered Tioga's head. *Maybe Kopi's already dead! Maybe he drowned in the river and he's a zombie!* Kopi had a smile on his face and was whistling a tune. As far as Tioga knew, zombies didn't smile or whistle. He began to realize that it was just the same old Kopi. Maybe the snake hadn't injected its venom after all.

Other than his breathing and his raspy voice, Kopi was as good as normal—actually, better than normal. Over the course of their journey, Kopi had lost a considerable amount of fat and gained a lot of muscle. He really did look like a warrior.

Tioga waited a few more minutes to make sure Kopi didn't drop dead. During that time he also listened for sounds of people, but heard no one. The birds were chirping happily. The searchers had apparently gone in another direction. Tioga felt like they were safe, at least for the time being.

"Well, if you're not dying, you might need a weapon," said Tioga. "I'll chip us some new knives with this flint."

"Great. I never liked chipping flint. I always seem to end up with slivers in my pants."

While Tioga went to work crafting them blades, Kopi ventured out to gather more plants. He came back chewing something fragrant.

"What have you got there? It smells good."

"It's called wintergreen." Kopi passed over a few small berries. "It will make your breath smell fresh. You don't want stinky breath when you rescue Hanna."

"True," said Tioga. He chewed one of the waxy red berries. "Wow. That's really neat." The tingling in his mouth was invigorating.

"Yeah, my mom uses them for tooth paste. And for lung infections. I'm hoping it will help my breathing."

After sharing his snacks, Kopi dressed Tioga's numerous wounds. The food and the medicine helped. Tioga felt like he was getting his strength back. During their rest, he continued to listen intently to the sounds of the forest, but heard nothing unusual. It was almost like the boys didn't exist.

"We're dead, you know," said Tioga.

"What?" Kopi jumped up as if the enemy was approaching.

"I mean to *them* we're dead. They must think we drowned in the river."

"Yes!" responded Kopi. It was liberating to feel they were no longer being hunted. "That means we're ghosts!"

"That's the good news," said Tioga. "The bad news is that Shingas is hours ahead of us and heading to our village."

"But you saw warriors heading south."

"That was only half of their force. The rest are probably heading west. Forty warriors is more than enough to destroy our village if the men aren't back."

Kopi frowned, thinking of home. The Mononga weren't the only ones who probably thought they were dead.

"Let's get moving," said Tioga. "We have to catch up."

"Then what?" asked Kopi, with concern.

Now Tioga was the one frowning. "I'll figure out something." His mind was working intently. "In the meantime, we've got to find their trail."

"Don't you think it's too dangerous traveling in broad daylight?" said Kopi, looking around nervously.

"It's a risk, but we've got to find the path they took."

Tioga led Kopi out of their hiding place and into the footprint-covered forest. The sound of the roaring rapids allowed him to get his bearings. Thankfully, they had climbed out of the river on the western bank. He knew the fortress was upriver to the north. And he knew their village was to the west. A departing war party would likely leave by the main gate and cross the suspension bridge. Beyond that he couldn't be sure, as there were no doubt several possible trails. But if he and Kopi headed northwest, they should cross their path.

From the angle of the sun, Tioga could plot their direction. When it was behind the clouds, the moss on the rocks and trees told him which way was north, as it grew where the sun never shined. Tioga confidently led them through the forest toward his objective.

Kopi had a much poorer sense of direction. He trusted Tioga's judgment and followed along without complaint. While Tioga focused on the big picture, Kopi focused on the smaller details around them. From time to time he picked plants that might be of use on the journey. Some of them were food and others were medicinal. Each young man had his own specialties, and was willing to trust his life to the other.

Tioga did his best to walk in a straight line, but that was impossible in the mountains. The hills were steeper, the waters ran quicker, and the underbrush was thicker than at home. It wasn't long until they came upon a gorge which was nearly as deep as the main canyon. The rushing waters below were clearly a feeder stream to the Angry River.

"I'm not going down there," said Kopi.

"Yeah, that water is moving," agreed Tioga. "I'll bet there is a bridge. We should follow the tracks and find it."

"Look at all these footprints," said Kopi, noting they were still within the search zone. "How do you know which way to go?"

Tioga scratched his head. "Well, if there's a bridge, it's either to the right or the left. We should probably move upstream, as then we'll be heading west."

"Lead the way," said Kopi.

For the next two hours, Tioga and Kopi hiked parallel to the gorge. It seemed to go on forever. If there was a bridge, it had been in the other direction. Finally, the canyon waned and became a ravine shallow enough to cross. Just then they came upon a north-south trail, but there was no sign of recent prints.

"I remember this spot," said Tioga. "We took this trail from Canoe Camp to the fortress."

"It leads to the bridge over the Angry River," said Kopi. "I'm not going back there again."

"We'll cross the stream here, then head northwest," said Tioga. "I'm sure we'll come upon their path soon." The creek was so shallow that they could actually jump from rock to rock without even getting their feet wet.

Tioga led the way for another hour. Daylight began to fade as the sun fell toward the mountain peaks.

"I don't understand it," said Tioga. "We should have found their trail by now. I've seen deer prints, wolf prints, and bear prints, but no human footprints for the last few hours."

"Maybe they haven't left the castle yet," said Kopi. "Or maybe they went another way. It's going to be dark soon and I'm worn out. Let's stop for the night."

Tioga agreed. While he was feeling better, he was far from feeling normal. He glanced around at their surroundings. He pointed to a nice level spot overlooking a small stream. "That's as good a place as any," he said.

"Looks like home to me," said Kopi.

As soon as they got there, Kopi plopped down and took off his boots. "I'm feeling good about this, Tioga. Something tells me you'll find their trail first thing in the morning."

"I hope you're right," said Tioga. He was a bit surprised at Kopi's optimism. His friend had never been one for positive thinking. Tioga cut some tall grass and began braiding it for use as a fishing line. Then he found a hawthorn tree and pulled off a few thorns. He quickly made a fishhook. Before long he was ready to fish.

"I'll be back with dinner," said Tioga confidently, as he strode off. He studied the picturesque brook and picked an inviting pool. Once there, he pulled the maggots from his pocket and placed one firmly on the hook. He leaned over a boulder and lowered the hook into the water. The bait had barely touched the surface when a small trout hit. After landing that one, Tioga moved downstream and caught five more. He expertly gutted the fish with his new flint knife and strutted back into camp, proud that he was the breadwinner. He hid the string of fish behind his back, so he could surprise his buddy.

Kopi looked up at the returning fisherman and said, "No luck? Well, don't worry, I gathered us dinner!" He pointed to a spread of food laid out on a flat rock. "We've got chestnuts, mushrooms, some wild onions, and best of all some tasty roots."

"Looks good, but I'll bet they don't taste better than fresh trout!" Tioga held up the fish.

"Awesome! Wait until you taste my cooking."

"Sorry, but we can't risk a fire," said Tioga. "We're eating raw again tonight."

"Well, at least we're eating!"

It was a very satisfying meal. As soon as they finished, they were ready for bed. The evening sky was clear and there was no threat of rain. They gathered a large pile of dry leaves to serve as insulation from the cold. The boys crawled into the pile and left only their heads poking out.

Kopi looked up at the stars that sparkled through the branches. He realized he had never paid much attention to stars before. The scent of fresh pine drifted on the breeze.

Kopi had a revelation. *I can smell! I can really smell!* He sniffed the air around him. There was the earthy odor of dry leaves and moist earth. He could even detect the scent of the wintergreen berries in his pocket. It dawned on him that he had spent his entire life around campfires and smoky lodges. Even when he had been outside the village, his cloths, skin, and hair were saturated with the smell. This was the first time in his life that he had been away from fire for more than a few hours.

Kopi breathed in deep. Although his lungs weren't back to normal, they felt a lot better than before. The clean mountain air seem to be helping. He would never take breathing for granted again.

As he lay there in the dark, he also noticed the sounds of the forest. It seemed like his hearing had vastly improved. In the village he was always around the hustle and bustle of other people. Now his hearing had adjusted to the quiet—well, not actually the quiet, but the *noise* of the forest. It was almost as noisy as the village, but in a different way. Everywhere there was sound—mostly soft sound—but now that his hearing had adapted, it seemed quite loud. He closed his eyes and listened.

He could hear the wind gently moving through the leaves, the *plop* of falling acorns, and crickets chirping. He even listened for the sounds of the night animals, whether they be mice, raccoons, or possums. Most often these sounds were unhurried, but sometimes the shrieking cry of prey or predator echoed through the darkness. In the past, Kopi would have jumped in fear at these sounds, but now they no longer worried him. For the first time, Kopi was in tune with Mother Earth. As he drifted off to sleep, somehow the wilderness felt like home.

# Twenty

Tioga yawned in the early morning light. He felt like he had just closed his eyes. *How could it be morning already?* He wanted to sleep some more in his warm cocoon of leaves. But his slumber was disturbed by a strange, rhythmic sound. *Distant drum beats? No, not drum beats—footsteps!* He opened one eye and was shocked at the sight.

Only a hundred feet away, on the other side of the trout stream, he saw a column of Mononga warriors. They were running through the forest. A moment later they were gone.

He urgently elbowed Kopi in the side.

"Please, Mom… let me sleep a little longer," moaned Kopi, still in a beautiful dream.

"Wake up!" hissed Tioga.

Kopi recognized the voice and its urgent tone, and immediately sat up. Tioga grabbed him and pulled him back down into the leaves.

"Now what?" said an exasperated Kopi.

Tioga tunneled deeper and pulled Kopi in with him until they were invisible. "The war party," whispered Tioga. "They just ran by. The warpath must be just on the other side of the stream."

It was a sobering thought. They had slept all night with their necks out.

"You said they were way ahead of us!" whined Kopi.

"I thought they were," said Tioga, worried at his miscalculation.

The boys stayed under the leaves for half an hour, listening for any sound out of the ordinary. After what seemed an eternity, Tioga led them out of their hiding place and across the creek. Kopi stood watch while Tioga read the trail for a hundred feet in both directions. Finally, he led Kopi back across the stream and behind a large boulder.

"Well?" whispered Kopi impatiently.

"It was a large group of warriors—probably close to forty. Three Sticks, I mean Shingas, is with them. He's limping and unstable. Sometimes he uses his three spears like a crutch. He's having a difficult time, thanks to your marksmanship."

"And that medicine. I'll bet he's still drinking my tea," said Kopi.

"Apparently so."

"Is Hanna with them?"

"She has to be," said Tioga wistfully. But he hadn't seen the footprints of a fourteen-year-old girl. He didn't want to voice the possibility that Hanna might still be back in the Mononga stronghold.

"Now what do we do?" asked Kopi. "Wait here until dark?"

"No, we can't let them get that far ahead. We'll follow them, but we can't get too close."

"In broad daylight?" said Kopi. "I don't want to get recaptured."

"Me either. But this might be a second group of warriors. Maybe the first group went ahead yesterday. I heard Shingas say that he was sending eighty men."

"Eighty warriors… that's an army."

"We'll follow this group today, then sneak by them tonight and check the trail ahead of them. But for now, it's one step at a time."

Tioga and Kopi followed the war party at a brisk but cautious pace. From the tracks in the soil, Tioga could tell whether the warriors were running, walking, or sitting. Most of the time they were running, which meant the boys had to run too, to keep up.

The rhythm of the trail took Tioga's mind off his problems. While he was still in pain from their ordeal, he was able to work through it. He realized now the secret of a warrior's endurance. A strong will. The will to survive. The will to reach one's goals. With determination, anything was possible. He drove Kopi hard. After an hour of pursuit, Kopi slowed to a stop.

"Tioga, I need a break," said Kopi, panting.

"Alright, but just for a minute. And we'd better move off the trail. More warriors could be coming behind us."

The boys cut into the thick forest. After they were safely out of sight, they sat down on a log.

"Hey, look here," said Kopi as he bent down and picked up an oval shaped object. "A box-turtle shell." He held up the empty shell of a tortoise that had died years before. "Lots of good uses for this. We could use it as a cup, a soup bowl, or even a helmet." Kopi placed it on his head. The shell was a little small for his big skull, but in some strange way it fit him.

Tioga laughed. "I guess you never know when an acorn will hit you in the head."

"That's right!" The acorns were falling and the leaves were turning bright colors.

"It's getting colder," said Tioga as he pulled his beaver fur tightly around his shoulders. "You know, it could snow up here in the mountains."

"Relax. You worry too much," said Kopi.

Tioga was shocked at the statement. *What did they do to him in that hut?* Kopi was usually the worrywart. But truth be told, Tioga was worried—not about the weather, but the situation. If they fell too far behind, they might never catch up. But if they moved too quickly, they could run right into the rear of the enemy. *And even if we can get ahead of them, then what?* thought Tioga. *We still don't know the way home.*

He didn't want Kopi to see his anxiety, so he stood up and acted like he wasn't concerned. "Time to get back at it. You know Kopi, these mountains really aren't that mountainous."

"Yeah, they're just big hills," said Kopi, following Tioga toward the path. "I kind of like it up here. The air is so refreshing. Much better than the stink of our village."

Tioga wondered where the old Kopi had gone. Deep down he missed his fearful friend. There was something different about Kopi now—something formidable yet mysterious. *Is Kopi a mystic? Did the snake sense it and hold back its venom? Is it possible that Kopi brought down the lightning bolt in the fortress?*

Just as Tioga pondered these questions, Kopi tripped and fell face first into a mud puddle. His shell helmet rolled by Tioga and bounced off a tree trunk. Tioga picked it up and helped Kopi to his feet. "Mystic or not, you are still my best friend." He respectfully crowned Kopi with the royal turtle shell.

"Mystic? I don't know what you're talking about," said Kopi as he wiped the mud from his face. He accidentally slung a clump right into Tioga's eye.

"Great! Now you've blinded me," said Tioga, half joking. The mud did sting and his vision was temporarily blurred in one eye. "Your turn to take the lead."

"But I don't know how to track," said Kopi.

"Sure you do. Just use your senses."

"But I don't know the signs."

"You know what a footprint looks like, right?"

"Of course."

"Well, just follow the tracks. There's dozens of them."

Kopi stumbled back to where he thought the war path should be. While a group of warriors had gone by, they were experts at stealthy travel. They moved in a single line and avoided leaving obvious signs. As Kopi focused, he did notice some marks.

"Look, a footprint!" said Kopi, excitedly.

"Alright tracker Kopi, lead the way. But don't go too slow," said Tioga, looking behind them. "We're supposed to be closing ground on them."

As Kopi followed the marks, his awareness of the forest diminished. He was totally focused on the trail. After a few minutes, he realized that he wasn't so bad at tracking after all.

Before long the boys came upon the fresh carcass of a deer. Feeding a war party took a lot of food. Apparently, this unlucky deer had wandered across the path and a warrior had promptly shot it. It was clear that they were in a hurry. By only taking the choicest cuts of meat, they had unknowingly left a meal behind for Tioga and Kopi.

"Can we cook up some ribs?" asked Kopi, licking his lips.

"Maybe later," responded Tioga. "We can't risk a fire now. Let's take it to go."

The boys took out their flint knives and collected their share of the unexpected bounty. Since they didn't have anything to carry it in, Tioga stripped off the hide and made a sack out of the bloody skin.

The sight of Tioga's bloody arms reminded Kopi of the scene at the gauntlet. He had felt powerless when Tioga disappeared into the angry mob. He tried to shift his thoughts to another topic. Then Hanna popped into his mind.

"She was painted white, you know," said Kopi. "What does it mean?"

Tioga instantly knew who he was talking about. "My grandfather told me ash is the color of the ghost spirit. She is caught between two worlds."

"Your grandfather again?" asked Kopi. "Are you seeing ghosts?"

"No. He is alive and well," said Tioga. "Grandfather Ötzi—my mother's father—is a Mononga elder. He came to me in the castle when I was tied to the pole. He gave me a knife and some medicine. And he coached our escape."

"I was wondering how you got off that pole. It's a miracle!"

"Yeah. That and your lightning bolt. We might need a few more miracles before this is over."

"Don't worry, I've got a plan to rescue Hanna from the fortress," said Kopi.

Tioga realized then that Kopi must have been studying the trail closely. "You noticed she's not with the war party, huh?"

"Well, I didn't see her footprints."

"Me either."

"So, after we save the village, we'll just have to go back and rescue her. Except this time with the men. We can use the secret entrance!"

"That's a deal," said Tioga, smiling. The burden on his heart was a little lighter at the thought of returning for Hanna. He nodded to Kopi and they began to trot along the trail. But deep down, Tioga doubted he would ever pass this way again.


In the late afternoon they came across the empty lunch camp of the enemy. There were three fire pits, one of which still emitted the faintest trace of smoke. In addition, there was another deer carcass.

Tioga gathered some dry leaves and gently placed them on the ashy charcoal. He blew on them until a small orange flame sprung to life. Then he gingerly added dry twigs.

"I thought you said a fire is too risky," said Kopi.

"They're ahead of us and moving forward," said Tioga, as his stomach growled. "And they left us the gift of some glowing embers and more deer meat. We don't want to offend our hosts."

"Certainly not," said Kopi. He couldn't wait to taste the roasted venison.

A minute later a small fire was crackling away. The sight of it warmed the boys' hearts more than the actual heat. They cooked some skewers of deer meat and enjoyed a hearty meal.

"They should be farther along than this," said Tioga, between bites.

"Maybe Shingas's sore butt is slowing them down."

"Maybe. I need to scout this camp for more clues. You can tell a lot about an army by what they leave behind." Tioga began to study the ground around them. "They are traveling with an old man. See his fallen arches?"

Kopi took a look but had a hard time seeing it. Tioga widened his search.

"Another has diarrhea," he added. "See, Kopi, the key to tracking is just using your eyes."

"And your nose," said Kopi. "Speaking of smell, that deer hide you brought along is starting to stink."

Just then a long, lonely wolf howl echoed through the forest. It was followed by the returning call of the pack.

"Wolves," said Kopi, nervously. "They can smell a dead deer a mile away. I don't like wolves."

Tioga laughed to himself. The old Kopi was back.

"They won't bother us," said Tioga, half wondering if it was true. "Not with a fire going."

"So, we're staying here all night?" Kopi started gathering more firewood.

"I'm afraid not. We can't let the war party get that far ahead," said Tioga, as he methodically worked his way around the area. The camp was smaller than he expected. There couldn't be more than fifty people in the group. And he saw no signs of two different war parties. Everyone seemed to be traveling together. Tioga was puzzled that there weren't more warriors. He had seen three times as many men in the fortress as seemed to be on the trail. *They must know our village is weak to attack with such a small force*, he thought.

Tioga scavenged the camp for anything useful and found a few items including a boar hair toothbrush and a discarded piece of string. In their current state, even the simplest things were worth keeping. Tioga looked forward to brushing his teeth for the first time in over a week.

Kopi decided to get his mind off of the wolves by joining Tioga on his survey. It wasn't long before he made his first find.

"Hey Tioga, check these out!" Kopi lifted a huge pair of moccasins into the air. "They were stashed under a bush."

"I know people lose stuff," said Tioga, "but how could you forget your shoes?"

"Maybe they were causing blisters," responded Kopi. "They look brand new."

Tioga glanced down at his own hands, which were still recovering from the ordeal of the last two weeks. Then he looked down at his toes. Several were poking through his tattered boots. "If you don't want them, I'll give them a try."

"Be my guest," said Kopi, as he tossed the footwear to his friend.

They were so big that Tioga could easily slip them over his own pair of boots.

"Do they fit?" asked Kopi.

"Too big," said Tioga. "But if I put padding in the ends, I could probably wear them. Maybe we can use them down the road. Once we pass the war party, we'll need to conceal our tracks. If anyone spots my prints, at least they'll think it's a big man. A big Mononga man."

The unexpected finds encouraged the boys to expand their search.

"Did you see this?" said Kopi. He was stopped at a small tree on the fringe of the camp.

"No, what is it?

Kopi held up the ends of two leather straps that were still tied to the sapling. "They tied a dog to the tree?"

"I've seen wolf tracks, but no dog tracks," said Tioga, as he headed over to his friend. Tioga arrived beside Kopi and looked closely at the leather bindings. They were cut at the ends. He knelt down and examined the soil.

"Someone was here—tied to the tree," said Tioga.

"A slave?" asked Kopi. "I saw a lot of them in the castle. They have a whole slave prison."

"A small person, who was resting. Look at this elbow print in the mud. It's too small to be a man's." Tioga's heart raced. "Hanna is with the war party!"

"I think you're seeing things. It's probably just a water boy," said Kopi, remembering how many times he had carried water for the men.

"Tied to a tree? I haven't seen any boys' footprints on the trail," said Tioga.

"Or a girl's, for that matter," said Kopi, skeptically.

Tioga gingerly lifted the leaves, looking for more clues. Then he spotted it—a thin, delicate hair.

"Look! It's her hair!" said Tioga as he held the strand up to the light.

Kopi peered closely at the evidence. "That's a gray hair. It's from an old woman."

"No, it's not," said Tioga. He wiped the hair along its length and the ashy gray paint was stripped away. A beautiful purple thread glowed in the afternoon sunlight.

Kopi couldn't argue with that. "She *is* with them. But why aren't her footprints on the trail?"

"They must be carrying her," said Tioga.

"So she wouldn't slow them down!" agreed Kopi.

A rush of energy flowed through Tioga's body. "Let's go! We've got to catch up. Maybe we can find a way to rescue Hanna!"

"Or slow them down," said Kopi, thinking again of his family.

Tioga quickly packed up their meager supplies.

"Just a second," said Kopi as he sliced off a few more chunks of meat from the deer carcass. "I'm not leaving behind all this food for the wolves."

"A meal for the wolves," muttered Tioga. "That's a good idea! Let's take as much meat as we can carry." He stripped the deer hide off the second carcass and used it as a sack. Tioga glanced over at Kopi. Between the deer blood, the various bruises, and the dirt of the trail, Kopi hardly looked human.

"Wow, you look like a scary zombie," said Tioga, with wide eyes.

"Really?" said Kopi with a grin.

The sight gave Tioga an idea. "Hey, watch this." He went over to an abandoned hearth and gathered up some pale ashes, then began rubbing them over his face and body.

"Let me guess," said Kopi. "More camouflage? You'll stick out, not blend in, with that ash."

"We're supposed to be dead, right?"

"Dead?"

"They think we drowned in the Angry River. We'd better look the part."

"We're zombies?"

"No, ghosts," said Tioga. "Ghosts can move a lot better than zombies. Although, I have to say with your new raspy voice, you sound more like a zombie than a ghost."

"I have come to eat your brain!" moaned Kopi, doing his best zombie imitation. He gleefully followed Tioga's lead and covered himself with ash.

"Hold still," said Kopi as he moved toward Tioga with a chunk of charcoal. He drew black circles around Tioga's eyes and shaded in hollow cheeks. Tioga's face soon resembled a ghoulish skull. The sight of his friend as a specter was a little unsettling to Kopi. He had seen fighters with war paint, but never with ghost paint.

"We're ghost warriors!" said Kopi, as he handed the charcoal to Tioga. "Do me!"

"Ghost warriors," said Tioga, deep in thought. "That just might work." He quickly did Kopi's makeup. Then, as if on cue, the howls of a dozen wolves rumbled through the forest.

"They're getting closer!" said Kopi in a panic.

"They *are* getting close," said Tioga calmly.

"What if the pack comes and eats us? We're both covered in blood!"

"That's what I'm hoping for. Well, not the eating part."

"Are you crazy?"

"I want them to follow us."

Tioga reached down and picked up a long rope of stinky deer intestines. He quickly tied it to a tall walking stick.

"Come on, Tioga! You already look like a ghost. You don't need any more props."

"This isn't a prop. It's a lure."

"A lure?"

"Alright, let's go!" said Tioga as he tested out his new walking stick. He picked up his sack of meat and boldly strode down the trail, dragging a ten-foot section of deer intestines behind him.

"Wait for me!" said Kopi as he grabbed his bag of meat. He stumbled after Tioga while nervously glancing over his shoulder.


Two hours later, once the sun was down, the wolf pack cautiously approached the camp and eagerly devoured the scraps that had been left behind. As the moon rose over the horizon, they began howling in excitement. Then they moved down the trail following the irresistible scent of the kill.

# *Twenty-One*

"Warriors, halt!" commanded Shingas. "We camp here for the night!"

All of the troops were relieved. They had been running most of the day, but at least today they were running in the right direction. Yesterday had been a disaster. Well, not a complete failure—as they had survived the climb through Howling Pass—but the detour had seriously sapped their strength.

Even with Shingas driving the men hard, it had taken them an entire day to go around the canyon and come back to the other side of the fallen bridge. By that time, the men were exhausted, so they camped there for the first night. It was an embarrassing start to the campaign. The entire fortress could see that they hadn't even made it out of sight.

This morning the war party had started their march west, exactly one day behind schedule. Shingas had pushed them to make up time. The exhausting pace put the troops in a foul mood.

Chemung watched the men as they made camp for the second night. At least they did that efficiently. They were a battle-hardened group. Very few things could throw them off their game, but Chemung noticed that on this mission, there was unusual friction in the ranks. He slowly made his way behind a group of grumbling warriors to eavesdrop.

"The commander is acting strange," said one of the more experienced fighters, whose nose had been broken so many times that it was profoundly crooked.

"No doubt about it," said another, rubbing his sore bare feet. "How could he lose his shoes at lunch and then not notice it for an hour? My feet are killing me. I'll never make it without my boots. Just my luck that our feet are the same size."

"That's not the worst of it," added Crooked Nose. "Why would he send forty men down the Angry River to look for two dead bodies? We are half the force that we were when we left the fortress."

"Those dead Allegewi boys really have him spooked."

"They have me spooked too," said one of the men. "What other explanation is there for the bridge collapse?"

Crooked Nose agreed. "Did you see the fat boy command the lightning? He has powerful magic! And that was when he was alive. His ghost is probably twice as powerful."

Chemung stepped away. He had heard enough. He looked over at his leader. The boss *was* acting strange. Clearly his mind was being bent by the Allegewi boys—no doubt a curse. Nothing had been going right since they captured them.

Chemung headed back up the trail to collect some speckled mushrooms he had spotted just before they made camp. They were the same type that were used for the commander's medicine tea. They seemed to be healing his stump, so a fresh batch might work even better.

He slowly began to make sense of the puzzle. The fat boy must have been a young shaman. He had saved the commander's life in order to control his mind. After the boy died, his spirit had continued the mission. Only now, as a ghost, he could torment them at will. It was not a good scenario.

As he picked the mushrooms in the fading light, Chemung thought he heard footsteps. Not the sound of men, but the patter of boys' feet. He strained to see who was coming down the trail in the twilight. For a moment, he thought he spotted two ghoulish forms, then—in an instant—they vanished. He could have sworn he saw the decaying corpse of the fat boy leading the way. He panicked and raced back toward the camp.


Tioga violently pulled Kopi off the path and into the bushes. He waited to see if the alarm would be raised.

"Did you see him?" whispered Tioga.

"Yeah. There was definitely someone there."

"I think it was Chemung," said Tioga. He regretted letting Kopi lead the way when they were so close to their adversary. *I should have been more cautious!* he thought.

Tioga slipped on the giant Mononga shoes and led Kopi away from the trail into the darkest part of the forest. He knew the size of his prints would make little difference at this point. If they had been spotted, the entire war party would track them down by torchlight.

The boys stayed perfectly still as the sounds of the night echoed through the tall timbers. The most chilling were the howls of the wolves in the distance. The pack was clearly on the move—and in their direction. Though, at the moment, the wolves were the least of their worries.

After a few minutes of silence, Tioga's confidence grew. When he smelled roasting meat, he breathed a sigh of relief. Kopi's stomach growled at the rich scent.

"Do you smell that?" whispered Tioga.

"Of course," said Kopi, a bit annoyed. "One of my favorites—roasted venison."

"Kopi, my friend, that is the sweet scent of freedom."

"What do you mean?"

"If Chemung had seen us, they wouldn't be eating deer meat for dinner."

"They'd be eating us?" asked Kopi nervously. "Lenni was right? They're cannibals?"

"No, I didn't mean that," said Tioga, recognizing that he had accidentally triggered one of Kopi's numerous fears. "I meant that they wouldn't be cooking dinner. They would be out searching for us."

Once again, the wolves howled.

"I hope the wolves aren't following us," said Kopi.

"They'd better be."

"Tioga, I'm not messing with a pack of wolves."

"I don't want to tangle with the wolves, I want the wolves to tangle with the Mononga."

"Another one of your plans?"

"No, it was your idea. You said you wanted to slow down the war party."

"And just how does a wolf pack do that?"

"Well, I've been leading them in by dropping bits of meat all evening. Hopefully, they're still a hungry bunch. We've still got plenty of bait. Now we just have to get them to the camp."

Kopi looked down at the bloody sack of deer meat that he had been carrying all day. "Ah, at the moment, I think we're the bait."

"Yeah, you're right. But see that cliff over there? I'll bet it's wolf proof."

"If you say so," said Kopi. He could barely see its dark shadow in the fading light.

"Let's go check it out."

"From now on, you lead the way," said Kopi. "That was too close for comfort."

Tioga didn't argue. When it came to tracking, Tioga's skill rivaled Kopi's knowledge of medicine. But the tracking part of their mission was over. They had caught up to the war party. Now the tough part of the plan went into effect.

Tioga arrived beneath the rocky cliff and found more than he was hoping for. He pointed it out to Kopi.

"An ancient cliff dwelling," said Tioga. "That's home for tonight."

Long ago someone had built a small stone shelter on a wide ledge about half way up the overhanging cliff face.

"Why would anyone want to live up there?" asked Kopi.

"Protection," said Tioga, as he began the climb to check out the shelter.

"From wolves?"

"I hope so, and probably from people too." Tioga arrived at the ancient stone house and peered inside. "This is the perfect hideout. We'll spend the night here. But first we've got to bait the wolf trap. The timing is going to be tricky."

Tioga climbed down and led Kopi through the trees in the direction of the Mononga camp. It was too dark for Kopi to see, so he placed his hand on Tioga's shoulder and followed as best he could.

The Mononga cooking fires soon appeared as distant twinkling lights. As they made their silent approach, the fires seemed unbelievably bright. Tioga knew that the warriors sitting near the flames would be blinded by the light, but lookouts would be another matter. Tioga hoped they hadn't posted any. After all, they were still in the mountains. And the war party would never expect to be followed. If there were sentries, they were probably well ahead of the camp.

Apparently, Chemung had either not seen them earlier or never reported the sighting. In any event, the camp seemed calm at the moment. Tioga could see the silhouettes of people preparing for bed.

He and Kopi moved very slowly toward the camp. Kopi's stealth had improved dramatically. He was now nearly as quiet as Tioga in the forest.

The boys sat at a safe distance and watched the fires grow low. Tioga worked diligently to cut up the remaining deer meat into smaller bites. From time to time, they heard the howls of the wolves. The pack seemed to be coming closer.

Tioga was thankful there were no dogs in the war party. Any canines would have barked up a storm at their scent. Tioga thought of his pooch Schnitzel. He would be nipping at their heels for a taste of the deer meat.

"Remember, Kopi, we are ghosts," whispered Tioga. "We've got to be invisible."

Kopi wasn't sure how to do that, but the thought of being a ghost somehow made him lighter on his feet.

"Here's the plan," continued Tioga. "We work our way around the camp dropping bits of meat as close to them as we can."

"Bait for the wolves?"

"That's the idea."

Tioga used hand signals to direct their movements. They moved at a snail's pace. As they went, Tioga tossed tasty treats just outside the circle of light. These morsels made no more noise than a falling acorn when they landed. Every now and then, Tioga left a nice chunk of hide or a piece of intestine wrapped tightly around a tree.

As they made their orbit, they could see the outlines of the warriors sleeping around the fading fires. The war party looked weary. Tioga strained to spot Hanna, but the shadowy figures all appeared to be men.

It took them an hour to complete the circle. When they finally reached the point where they had started, all the meat was gone. The trap was set. Only time would tell if the wolves would take the bait.

The camp looked so peaceful that Tioga decided to press his luck. He crawled over and whispered in Kopi's ear, "Everyone is asleep. Let's go closer. Let's see if she's with them."

Kopi shook his head emphatically and pointed away from the camp. Tioga ignored the gesture and crawled toward the glowing red coals. As he moved in, he studied each slumbering body. He counted over forty men, but couldn't find Hanna. He was about to give up when he spotted her delicate form sleeping in the shadow of a fallen tree.

For several moments he laid there transfixed, watching her every breath. A change in wind carried the smoke from a dying fire into his eyes. He accidentally inhaled the noxious fumes and snapped out of his trance. He turned away, but a shallow cough escaped his lips.

He froze, waiting to see the camp's reaction. No one seemed to notice. Tioga realized he had pushed his luck too far. He was about to crawl backward when something moved near the glowing coals. An old man slowly rose to his feet. He hobbled away from the group and walked directly toward the intruder.

Tioga held perfectly still. The firelight was very dim. If he stayed put, the elder might pass him by. But if he bolted, even an old man would surely see him. Tioga lowered his nose into the musty leaves and held his breath. A tattered moccasin missed his head by inches. The man stopped a few feet away and urinated.

Tioga tried to slither away, but there wasn't enough time. He heard the man finish and turn back toward the fire. Tioga was directly in his path! The next step would be on him.

He glanced up at the man's head. There was no mistaking the heavily scarred face.

"Grandfather?" hissed Tioga. The groggy old man looked down at the apparition at his feet. An expression of shock rolled over his face, and his mouth opened to sound the alarm. Then a smile overcame it, exposing a toothless grin. Grandfather Ötzi lifted his foot and stepped over Tioga. The patriarch chuckled softly as he shuffled back to the fire.

Tioga snuck away from the camp as fast as he could. He grabbed Kopi and led him in the direction of the cliff dwelling. Tioga realized he had taken a foolish risk. It had nearly cost them their lives.

Off to his left he heard a sharp yelp, and then a deep growl. Several gray shadows flashed through the trees.

"Wolves!" hissed Kopi fearfully. "They're on to us!"

Tioga's heart beat faster. He had expected they would be sleeping in the cliff dwelling when the wolves arrived. But they were still five minutes away from the safety of the shelter. If they were caught by the pack in the open, they wouldn't stand a chance.

Tioga guided Kopi to a maple tree. "Climb!"

Kopi started up the trunk without hesitation. He was thankful wolves couldn't climb trees. Tioga followed after him into the treetop. From their vantage point they had an excellent view of camp and remained invisible to the war party. Tioga watched closely to see whether his wolf trap worked.

Before long he saw the wolves at the edge of the dim firelight. They were moving in close, sniffing out the gamey bits of meat. It didn't take long for a scuffle to break out in the pack. Angry growls erupted as two young wolves fought over a scrap.

A moment later a campfire sprung to life, illuminating the forest. The wolves backed off, but kept circling the camp. More fires burst to light. Another wolf fight broke out, this time over a bloody piece of deer hide. Men waved torches to scare off the hungry beasts. The entire camp was soon awake and watching the spectacle.

Tioga leaned toward Kopi and smiled. "The wolves will keep them busy for a while. Let's go get some rest." Tioga began moving down the tree.

"Are you sure it's safe?"

"The pack will stay together," whispered Tioga, hoping it was true. He needed sleep so badly that he was willing to take the chance. "There's plenty more meat for them to find," he said, praying the statement didn't include the two of them.

The boys took a last look at the chaos in the camp, and moved away into the darkness. Kopi nearly burst into tears when they made it inside the cliff dwelling. As Tioga closed his eyes for the night, the forest was still alive with the sound of growling wolves and shouting men. He smiled and drifted off to paradise.

# *Twenty-Two*

"Everybody up!" yelled Shingas to the sleepy group. The sun had already risen above the horizon. The late start further aggravated the ill-tempered tyrant.

"I've never seen a wolf pack act like that," said Chemung. "They circled us for hours."

"Very strange behavior," added Ötzi the Iceman. "It's not a good omen. Some of the men are saying the mission is cursed by the ghosts of those Allegewi boys."

"Shut up, old man!" said Shingas, nervous that the sage's words might spook his troops. He took a sip of his medicine tea and unconsciously rubbed the wound on his buttocks. For whatever reason, it was bothering him more than his stump.

Ötzi ignored the rebuke and continued smoking thin strips of wolf meat over the coals of the fire. When the wolves wouldn't go away, the warriors had made the best of the disturbance and shot several of them.

Shingas walked over to Ötzi and kicked dirt over the coals. "Forget that stringy wolf meat. Get ready to move out."

"The men will need food on the trail," said Ötzi. "The meat will be ready in just a few more minutes."

"Leave it," said Shingas. "We'll shoot game as we go."

"It never hurts to have extra in the mountains. A winter storm can change things in a flash."

"We will soon be out of the mountains. If you don't get moving, I'll leave your bony carcass behind for the wolves!"

Shingas stormed away from the respected elder. Chemung followed and asked, "Why did you even bother to bring along such an old man? He is slowing us down."

"Why do you always question me, Chemung?" snapped Shingas. "Do you think I'd bring that useless old windbag if I didn't have a reason?"

Chemung sulked, wishing he had kept his mouth shut.

"We've got to pick up the pace," said Shingas. He yawned involuntarily. "We should have made it to the Allegewi River by now. I've never seen such a lazy war party."

Chemung stared down at the ground. His commander was in an unusually foul mood for being at war. He normally reveled at the thought of combat and conquest.

Shingas looked over at the small Allegewi girl. He was beginning to wish he had left her and the old man back in the fortress. "Get the girl up on the stretcher," he said to the two slaves who carried her. "Chemung, tie her tight. Yesterday she squirmed off too many times."

Although she couldn't understand the language, Hanna could see that the warlord was talking about her and guessed the meaning. "I can run as fast as any man," she boasted in Allegewi. "Let me go on foot today. It will be easier on your men than carrying me."

"What did she say?" said Shingas to one of the warriors who knew some Allegewi. Normally he wouldn't have responded to the girl's comments, but this was the first she had spoken in two days. He was curious to hear more. The warrior translated the message.

Shingas laughed, "So you can intentionally slow us down? Or so we can spend hours chasing you if you run off? I'm not that stupid." The translator passed on his words.

"Maybe you are," said Hanna in Allegewi. "You fell for the boys' trap at the healing spring and got shot in the butt!"

Shingas waited for the translation. The warrior hesitated, knowing it would upset the commander.

"What did she say?" bellowed Shingas.

The translator chose his words carefully. "She said you suffered an unfortunate wound at the healing spring."

Shingas's ears turned red in anger. He was about to lash out at her when he realized it was just another one of her delay tactics. The girl was smart. She knew what lay ahead.

Shingas turned away and barked to his men, "Move out! Tomorrow we destroy the Allegewi!"

The weary fighters responded with a feeble cheer—way less enthusiasm than would normally be heard from a Mononga war party. Shingas noticed the weak response, and his ears turned even redder.

After Chemung tied her tight, the slaves lifted Hanna's stretcher into the air. The slaves had fed her and treated her kindly. She certainly trusted them more than the warriors, who often looked at her with lust in their eyes. In a way she even felt a kinship with the two slaves.

Just then two scouts, Bongo and Pox, came running up the path. The bigger of the two men approached the commander.

"Sir, Scout Bongo asking permission to report!"

"Proceed."

"I'm pleased to say that the trail is clear."

"Very good," said Shingas. "Now let's get moving. Break camp!"

Everyone scattered and rushed to get their things. Chemung noticed a small group of fighters was gathering around the scouts. He quietly moved behind them to hear their conversation.

"One buck hide per rattle, payable when we get back home," said Bongo.

"A buck for a rattlesnake rattle? That's expensive," said one of the men.

"You won't pay a buck to save your soul?" responded Bongo.

Several men immediately agree to his price. The scout reached into a pouch and passed out his product.

Chemung burst into the circle. "Just what are you selling?"

Bongo hid the bag behind his back, as Pox and the others slipped away. "Ah, nothing sir."

"Give me that!" said Chemung. He grabbed the pouch from the man's shaking hands. Chemung dumped the contents into his palm. Four bloody objects rolled out.

"Rattlesnake charms!" said Chemung. He noticed Bongo was wearing a freshly severed rattle around his neck on a string. "Where did you get these?"

"Sir, Scout Pox and I came upon a den of snakes. We took the opportunity to secure their charms." It was well known that snake rattles offered excellent protection against evil spirits.

"You spent the last hour searching the rocks for rattlesnakes instead of scouting the trail? You should both be executed for dereliction of duty!"

Bongo responded, "We did both, sir. The trail is clear."

Chemung huffed as he returned the rattles to the pouch. "I'm confiscating these as evidence!"

Just then Shingas bellowed, "Mononga fighters! Forward!" He led the way down the path. The men straggled out of camp and followed.

Chemung was the last to leave. He eyed the thick forest with suspicion. "Crazy wolves," he muttered to himself. "What got into them?" Suddenly he remembered the ghost sighting from the night before. Had he really seen the spirits of the two dead boys or did he imagine it? He reached into the scout's pouch and pulled out the largest rattlesnake rattle. A moment later it was hanging around his neck. Chemung took one last look at the eerie forest, then turned and ran down the trail.

As soon as it was quiet, Tioga's ghoulish head peeked out from underneath a bush. "All clear."

Kopi's face and arms appeared from behind a large, rounded boulder. It looked like a giant turtle coming to life.

The boys moved cautiously into the vacant camp. Tioga walked up to the fire and pulled a piece of wolf meat off the smoking rack. "It sure was nice of grandfather to leave us breakfast," he said.

"That's enough for ten men," said Kopi, licking his lips.

"That's not all that he left us," exclaimed Tioga. "Look at this rope!" He pulled a coil of the finest Mononga line from the leaves.

"I wish I had a grandfather like yours," said Kopi as he wolfed down a strip of meat.

Tioga laughed. "Kopi, I barely know him."

"I'm a pretty good judge of character. It's a shame he's Mononga though. I've never met a Mononga I liked."

"Well you're looking at one," said Tioga. "Don't forget I'm half Mononga by blood. You know about my mom."

"That's different," said Kopi, embarrassed. "I mean, your mother—she's one of us now. And you were always one of us." For the first time, Kopi recognized that the lines between tribes were more blurred than he had realized.

Tioga thought back to that horrible night when he was tied to the stake in the castle. "Kopi, come to think of it, I think you're half Mononga too!"

"Me? Mononga? What are you talking about?"

"Back in the fortress, they almost made it through the adoption ceremony. They washed away your Allegewi blood and replaced it with Mononga blood."

"Really?" Kopi thought hard on the subject. He had no recollection of what had happened that night. But after their escape, he had noticed he was painted red—the color of rebirth.

"I'm Mononga?" asked Kopi in confusion.

"Not officially. They never completed the ceremony," said Tioga. "You kind of got stuck half-way."

"Sounds like ash really is our color!"

The boys ate their share of wolf meat and searched the camp for anything else they could use. A shortage of sleep, combined with exhaustion, had resulted in a number of lost objects.

"Here's a bag of walnuts!" said Kopi with excitement.

"Grab it. We could use the sack."

"And some snacks! I love walnuts," mumbled Kopi as he opened a shell with his knife. Before long, Kopi looked like a greedy chipmunk as his cheeks bulged with nut meat.

Minutes later Tioga pulled a fine Mononga war club from the leaves. "Check this out!" He passed it to Kopi. "That thing is perfect for you. It's way too heavy for me."

"Tioga, I could never use this," said Kopi, holding the club awkwardly. "Hitting people isn't my thing."

"Well, at least give it a swing."

Kopi scowled and swung it through the air with surprising ease.

"Woo, I wouldn't want to be on the receiving end of that," said Tioga. "Keep it. It makes you look mean."

Just then a cold breeze blew in from the north.

"Burrr," said Kopi, with a shiver. "Did you see those snowflakes this morning?"

"A storm could be coming," said Tioga, concerned at their lack of winter clothing. "We should use the gifts we've been given. I'm going to cut us some wolf fur blankets."

"Those are some big bad wolves," said Kopi eyeing the dead animals around them.

Tioga used his knife to quickly strip the hides off of two wolf carcasses. As a trapper, he was an expert at such tasks.

"Can I wear mine as a cape?" asked Kopi. "I always wanted to wear a cape."

"Good idea. Bloody wolf capes would be a good addition to our ghost costumes."

Tioga used a bit of rope to attach neck loops to the furs. Meanwhile, Kopi gathered some ash and cinders and freshened up their ghost makeup. They really were a haunting pair.

The boys gathered up their bounty and moved along the trail. It wasn't long before they noticed the path seemed to be going downhill. While it still had its ups and downs, there was no doubt they were dropping in elevation.

Eight hours later, they were still moving lower. Tioga could sense they were leaving the Endless Mountains behind. The dramatic scenery had been replaced by more familiar forest. Every so often, Kopi asked Tioga whether he recognized a certain stream, hilltop, or fork in the path—any landmark that might lead them home. Always, Tioga's response was the same. He shook his head or just shrugged his shoulders.

After their previous close call, Tioga made sure they followed the war party at a safe distance. He was surprised that they were able to keep up so easily. A group of seasoned fighters should have quickly outpaced them. Something was slowing the war party down. Maybe it was the wound in Shingas's rear. Or maybe his grandfather or Hanna was responsible. He hoped the wolf attack in the middle of the night had sapped the warriors' strength. Whatever was causing it, Tioga was grateful for the slower pace. Every hour that slipped by was another hour of life for the Allegewi tribe.

In the late afternoon, the sky darkened and the wind began to blow. The temperature dropped quickly. After three days of beautiful weather, storm clouds rolled in.

"They've stopped for the night," whispered Tioga when he smelled smoke on the breeze. "I'll bet they're making rain shelters. We should look for a dry place to sleep." The thought was intoxicating. They had been up much of the prior night.

"Look at that ridge," said Kopi, pointing to their left. "I think I see a rockshelter."

Kopi was getting good at spotting these natural features, which provided instant shelter in bad conditions. But unlike last night, this refuge was on ground level, and was far from wolf proof. The boys took cover under the overhanging rock just as the rain began. It felt wonderful to stretch out as daylight faded. They ate their fill of wolf meat and walnuts for dinner and settled in, using their new furs as blankets.

Tioga fought off sleep long enough to say, "We can take a nap, but then we need to get back to work."

"Back to work? Another visit from the wolves?" asked Kopi.

"I hope not," said Tioga. "With these bloody hides, it would be our turn to face them. Hopefully, they got enough of humans last night. And I doubt the pack would come down from the mountains."

Kopi nervously scanned their surroundings. "I think I'll sleep in that sycamore tree tonight."

"Suit yourself. I think we're safe here. I haven't heard any howls all day," said Tioga with a yawn.

"Well, even if the wolves don't come, we need to watch out for bears. They like meat too."

"Kopi, last time I checked, bears can climb trees."

"Oh," said Kopi, scratching his head. "That's right."

"I'm going down for a nap," said Tioga, craving rest. "We've got another long night ahead of us."

Kopi was still too anxious to sleep, so he tried to keep up the conversation. "So, the ghost warriors are making another visit tonight?"

Tioga hesitated. "Yeah, once it gets really dark."

"Can you at least give me a clue about what you've got planned?"

"I don't want to ruin the surprise. Get some sleep. You're gonna need it."

Kopi took the hint and settled down. While Tioga was mum about their plan, the truth was he didn't have answers to Kopi's questions. He'd spent the entire day thinking of ways to stop the war party and rescue Hanna. His brain threw out countless crazy ideas, but he knew none of them would work. Now they were a day closer to home and he still didn't have a plan. He yawned and tried to think harder. But instead, he drifted off into a deep dreamless slumber.

# *Twenty-Three*

The next thing he knew, Tioga awoke with a start. He hadn't realized it, but for several hours his mind had been working on the problem while he slept. When it figured out the solution, it woke him up to tell him. *There is no way to stop the war party! Sneak by them while they sleep. Warn the village and hope for the best.* While they might not be able to stop an attack, they could at least stop a *surprise* attack. With the hunters back, the village walls might hold. The thought of Lenni returning with the men as a hero turned Tioga's stomach, but it was no time to hold a grudge.

Tioga nudged Kopi. "Wake up sleepy-head."

Kopi opened his eyes and looked at the pitch-black night. He couldn't see the rain, but he could hear it.

"Nasty weather tonight," said Kopi, wishing he didn't have to leave the comfort of their shelter. "It feels like we barely slept an hour."

"I'd guess two hours," said Tioga, enthusiastically. "That's plenty of rest for a ghost warrior!" Now that he knew what to do, he was buzzing with energy.

Kopi picked up his turtle shell helmet and squeezed it on his head. He knew they had a job to do and rose without complaint. "Lead the way, Chief."

"I'm no chief. Please don't call me that."

"How about General Tioga?"

"Alright, but only if you're General Kopi."

"That's a deal!" said Kopi with a smile. "So General Tioga, what are the ghosts warriors up to tonight?"

"They're going to do what ghosts do best."

"Oooh, let me guess. Scare people?"

"No. Be invisible."

Kopi was puzzled by the comment, but figured Tioga had something exciting planned. The boys stepped out into the rain and headed in the direction of the Mononga camp. By now, Kopi knew the routine. They had developed a keen sense of stalking their prey.

This time Tioga gave the camp a wide berth. There was no point in risking another encounter. They would sneak by and head for home.

Although he didn't know the way for sure, he knew that if they headed west, they would eventually hit the Allegewi River. And from there they could easily find the village. Now that they were out of the mountains, they had much less chance of getting lost.

There was only one problem with this plan. On a rainy night, he would have a very difficult time plotting their course. Without the stars as guideposts, they could walk for hours in the wrong direction. He decided to worry about that once they got by the war party.

As they moved by the camp, they came to a point where the cover was thin. Tioga stopped for a minute and used the opportunity to study the enemy. He tried his best to spot Hanna, but there was no sign of her in the distant firelight. In fact, the only person he recognized was Shingas. He was pacing back and forth, ranting and raving about something. Two young men stood rigidly before him. Then they saluted him in Mononga fashion, picked up their packs, and headed out of camp on the main trail to the west.

"He's sending out scouts," whispered Tioga, in despair. He watched as the two men disappeared into the night. "They'll spy on our village and then report back to the war party."

"Do you think you can follow their trail?"

"I guess I could try."

"Then they'll show us the way home!"

"Kopi, scouts are often the fastest runners in the force. We might be able to outrun a slow army, but we'll never keep up with a couple of seasoned scouts."

"Hey, they're human. They have to eat, sleep, and poop like the rest of us. And how can they see where they're going in the dark? No human has night vision like you do."

"They probably know these paths so well that they could run them blindfolded," said Tioga, feeling hopeless.

"What if they don't report back?" asked Kopi. "Maybe we can scare them off."

"Scare them off?"

"Yeah! Remember, we are ghosts."

"Kopi, you're on to something," said Tioga. He perked up at the possibilities.

Kopi added, "Even if they spy on the village and head back, as long as we stay hidden, we can warn the chief before the war party gets there. Let's go!"

The boys left the Mononga camp behind and were soon following the trail of the scouts.

Elder Ötzi had sensed their departure. He had not seen or heard them. But he had sensed them. It was a feeling a good woodsman developed over a lifetime in the forest.

Ötzi had journeyed over these paths for decades. Long ago, he used to scout the Allegewi village in hopes of catching a glimpse of his daughter. After several years of looking in vain, he gave up the search. But whenever he could, he still spent time alone in the wilderness. When he was away from people, he became one with the forest. He could feel its heartbeat and the rhythm of its breath. And he could tell the subtle change when a stranger was in its midst.

Grandfather Ötzi chuckled at the boys' bold initiative. Trailing the scouts was a wise choice. He was proud of his grandson's cunning intelligence. With the proper teaching and maturity, he would become a strong leader.

His grandson was not the only one with unusual potential. The other boy had a unique aura. One he had rarely sensed in all his years—the uncommon gift of a mystic. But it was too early to tell if it would fully develop. To become a true shaman, the pupil had to have a master. It was uncertain if Kopi would ever find such as mentor.

Even with these talents, he doubted the boys could stop the bloodshed. Ötzi would do all he could to do just that—in fact, he had already done quite a lot. He had snuck out the night before they left the castle and cut the suspension bridge. Then he had started the rumor that the ghosts of the dead boys were haunting the war party— not realizing that the boys actually were trailing the group. And he had slowed down most of the men by secretly adding buckthorn bark to the camp stew. Now they spent more than their fair share of time squatting in the bushes. It felt good to finally resist the evil tyrant. He was not going to sit by idly and watch his daughter and her people get slaughtered.

Ötzi fanned the flames of his small fire and glanced over at Hanna. She sat shivering in the rain. The sight reminded him of the last time he had seen his own daughter. He had never forgotten the look in Candy's eyes as she ran away in tears. Telling her to go had been the hardest thing he had ever done. He had known she would be taken by the Allegewi. He had seen it in a vision. That fate was far better than being married to the evil one who had chosen her as his bride. That one had the aura of death. He wished he could have stopped the wedding in some other way.

Ötzi added a log to the fire and hobbled out of his rain shelter. He stopped behind the small Allegewi girl and cut her bindings.

"You are a brave girl to weather the journey without complaint," said Ötzi softly, in Allegewi.

"What do you want?" said Hanna, warily eyeing the bizarre old man without a nose. He had clearly been in a fight and took the worst of it. She was surprised he spoke her language.

"I thought you could use a dry bed," said Ötzi.

"Not with you, or any other man," said Hanna, defiantly.

Ötzi chuckled. "Not like that, silly girl. You are a friend of the family!"

Hanna was puzzled at the statement. She had no friends among the enemy, and certainly no family. Then she remembered the Mononga girl who had cared for her.

"Are you Tatami's grandfather?" asked Hanna.

"No. I am not related to Tatami. But I would be honored to be. Her heart is pure."

"Then who are you? I have no other friends among the Mononga."

"Ah, but you do," laughed Ötzi. "One old and one new. One and the same."

"Why do you talk in riddles?"

"Relax, my child. Tomorrow will be a busy day. Come sit by my fire."

Hanna wondered whether she could trust the strange old man. Up to this point, she had viewed him as just another one of the cruel monsters that surrounded her. But there was something about him that seemed so familiar. She hoped his intentions were good. She followed him to the comfort of his shelter.

The bold move raised more than one eyebrow amongst the men. But Ötzi wasn't worried, as Shingas was too drugged to notice. He'd watched the preparation of the warlord's medicine tea that night and was surprised at the potent hallucinogenic ingredients. On that brew,

Shingas would be more interested in the sound of the crickets than the hostage girl.

Nonetheless, Ötzi knew that treating a captive so kindly was a risk—a risk he was willing to take. He wanted a chance to speak with the girl privately. If questioned by Shingas, he could always play the part of the senile old man.

Ötzi leaned close to Hanna's ear. "There is something I think you should know. Your friends Tioga and Kopi are still with us."

"The ghost stories are true?" she said, wide-eyed. "Their spirits are haunting us?"

"No," giggled Ötzi. "They are alive and well. They have been following us the whole time."

*Could it be true?* thought Hanna. The old man seemed to read her mind.

Ötzi grinned and nodded. Then he whispered, "Tioga the tracker—he is my grandson!"

Hanna's mind was blown. *How could that be?* Then she remembered the stories about Tioga's mother—that she had once been Mononga. *Could this man be Candowsa's father?*

"Why should I believe you?" she asked. "How do I know this isn't a cruel trick?"

"I would never lie about my family. Especially not about my one and only grandson."

Hanna was shocked. The old man must be telling the truth. *Tioga and Kopi are alive!* She wanted to shout for joy, but settled for a broad smile. For the first time since she had been captured, she felt safe.

"Your father is Chief Tundra?" asked Ötzi.

"Yes," she said softly, embarrassed that the daughter of such a famous chief had been kidnapped so easily.

"He is a good man."

"You know him?"

"Yes, long long ago. We were very good friends. Best friends, you might say."

The comment puzzled Hanna. She nodded as if she understood, but she had no earthly idea how bitter enemies could be best friends. As long as she could remember, her father had warned her about the Mononga—the most dangerous tribe in the land. She wanted to ask more, but the warmth of the fire was like a sleeping spell. Her eyelids grew heavy, and within moments she fell into a deep slumber.

Ötzi also closed his eyes. But he held back from allowing sleep to fall over him. Instead his mind floated upward, into that space between the world of reality and the world of dreams.

His soul gradually took flight on the wings of his totem—his animal guide. He felt it rise on the moist air currents, high above the trees and deep into the night. Before long the vision developed. From high above, he could see the boys moving through the darkness.

He swooped down until his wings fanned the hairs on his grandson's head. He could sense the fear of the unknown in Tioga's fragile mind. He could feel the blood rushing through his youthful veins. Blood that was partly his own. He merged his spirit with that of his grandson.

Tioga suddenly felt safe. A warm, calming sensation came over him. The darkness became less intimidating. The forest path became an old friend.


Tioga led the way along the muddy trail. He had removed his boots so he could feel the scouts' footprints with his toes. It took a master tracker to be able to follow such a trail at night with no torch to light the way. They had tailed them for over an hour when they came to a fork in the path. Tioga hesitated.

"Which way?" asked Kopi.

Tioga dropped to his knees and gently probed the soil with his fingertips, like a blind man studying the face of a child. The rain pounded mercilessly on his slender frame.

"I don't know," said Tioga. "I can't tell which way they went. Not at night in this weather."

"Maybe in the morning," yawned Kopi. He was so tired he was ready to drop.

Normally Tioga would have been frustrated at the setback. But something deep within him told him to relax and take life as it comes. "There's no point in going on tonight," agreed Tioga. "We could end up lost. Let's try to get out of this rain." Even with the wolf fur cape and beaver shawl, he was chilled to the bone. He scanned the shadows for any place that might offer a dry spot.

"Look!" said Kopi, pointing down the trail.

A weak light twinkled in the darkness. For a second it was there, then it vanished into the fog. The two boys crept forward and the light re-appeared. A small fire sputtered under the shelter of a massive oak tree hanging over the trail. Over the course of three centuries, the trunk had leaned far to one side in search of sunlight. Now it provided just enough shelter for two men and a small fire.

"The scouts!" whispered Tioga. He studied the tree closely. "They're camped under the Old Bending Oak. It's a famous landmark. I've been here before!"

Kopi's heart lightened. "That means we're not lost! We can run ahead and warn the village."

Tioga didn't answer.

"So which way is home?" asked Kopi.

"Ah, I don't remember," said Tioga.

"You said you've been here before."

"I have, but I was very young. I was here with my father," said Tioga. He had nearly forgotten about the time they camped here. He smiled at the warm memory.

"At the fork, the scouts picked the path on the right," said Kopi. "The village must be that way."

"Not necessarily. They probably knew about the tree and went there for shelter. They might take the other path in the morning. If we go the wrong way," said Tioga, "the village could end up in ashes."

Tioga stared at the embers glowing eerily in the distance. He could see the two men sitting with their backs up against the tree. Tioga wondered aloud, "Why would they risk a fire in Allegewi territory?"

"It's the ghosts, of course," said Kopi. "Everyone knows that ghosts don't like the light."

"That's right!" said Tioga. "I nearly forgot about the ghosts." Tioga looked over at Kopi. He would never have believed his friend could look so terrifying. "Maybe our ghosts should make an appearance."

"Yeah! Let's scare them!" said Kopi. *What was that feeling? Confidence?*

"Oh, I want to do better than that," said Tioga. He loosened the rope from his shoulder. "I want to see if we can snare us a couple of Mononga scouts."

"You think you could set up some snares?"

"Yes indeed, General Kopi," said Tioga, manipulating the braided rope by feel. "We have them right where we want them. Once we capture them, they will lead us home. And best of all, they won't return to the war party. Shingas will really be spooked."

"The ghost warriors strike again!"

Tioga reached down and searched the ground for a suitable branch. It wasn't long until found what he was looking for. He picked up a sturdy stick with a Y at the end.

"We'll use a couple of choke snares," said Tioga as he sliced the rope into two equal lengths. "The harder you pull against it, the tighter it gets. And it doesn't loosen back up. Once it's around an animal's neck, the more it struggles, the quicker it chokes. It's a silent death." Thunder rumbled through the night, adding an eerie emphasis to the statement.

Kopi didn't respond. There was an uncomfortable silence between them as Tioga worked on the snares. *Those aren't animals up ahead,* thought Kopi. *They're humans—young men with families.*

"Here's yours," said Tioga, passing his comrade a forked stick with a loop on the end. Tioga went to work crafting a second snare.

"You want to choke them to death?" asked Kopi, nervously.

"No," said Tioga, with a chuckle. "If we did that, we'd have to get their ghosts to lead us home."

"So how does it work then?" asked Kopi, trying to examine the strange contraption in the darkness.

"Once they recognize a choke snare is around their neck, they'll stop fighting. Everyone knows about choke snares."

"I didn't, but I guess I know now," said Kopi. "And what kind of trap do you use to get it around both of their necks at the same time?"

"The ghost trap, of course."

"The ghost trap?"

"Yeah. I just invented it. Since a ghost is invisible, he just walks up and puts the loop around the man's neck, then gives it a tug. The snare will do the rest."

"That's not much of a trap," said Kopi, more than a bit concerned with the plan.

All of a sudden the wind picked up, and the heavens let loose in a downpour. The swirling leaves nearly blocked out the flickering fire in the distance. Thunder rumbled overhead.

"For the trap to work, we have to drop the loops over their heads at exactly the same time," said Tioga, almost shouting into Kopi's ear. "Once they stop fighting, I'll tie them up and we can sleep for the night. Got it?"

Kopi didn't answer, so Tioga knocked on his helmet. "You in there Kopi?"

"It seems risky."

"Not in this thunderstorm. A bear could walk up behind them and they'd never even hear it."

"Why don't we wait until they're asleep?" said Kopi.

"The storm might pass by then," said Tioga. "Plus, one of them might stay up on guard duty. This is the perfect time for an attack. Trust me. It will be as simple as snaring a rabbit."

"I've never snared a rabbit."

"Well, then a box turtle."

Kopi huffed. "I don't need a snare to catch a turtle. I just go and pick 'em up."

"Well, it will be almost that easy," said Tioga, hoping he was right.

Kopi reached down and felt the heavy war club tucked in his belt. He hoped he wouldn't have to use it.

"Follow me to the back of the old oak," said Tioga. "When I squeeze your shoulder three times, you run around one side of the tree and I'll sneak around the other side. Drop the loop over your scout's head as soon as you come around, then hold on for dear life. I'll do the same for the other man. Simple!"

Kopi was shocked at Tioga's confidence. It was almost like his friend was possessed by the spirit of an ancient warrior.

"Now's the time," said Tioga. He started toward the rear of the famous landmark. Kopi nervously followed.

The forest was so alive with the noise of the gale that there was no need to be quiet. But a new problem presented itself. Lightning flashed across the sky with troubling frequency. One moment it was pitch black, then the next, Kopi would be staring at Tioga wide-eyed—in broad daylight! Tioga knew they needed to move quickly. If one of the scouts happened to look back during a flash, the boys would be finished.

They danced through the brush and moved closer to the massive oak. Its swaying limbs looked like an evil monster reaching out to devour them. A heavy branch broke free and crashed to the forest floor just in front of them. Tioga jumped over it and continued toward his objective.

He breathed a sigh of relief when they arrived undetected at the back of the tree. They pressed their bodies against the rugged bark, as the rain drummed on their backs. It was a strange feeling to be so close, yet so far from their target.

Tioga double-checked his snare by feel to make sure it wasn't tangled, then took a deep, calming breath. He reached out his left hand and squeezed Kopi's shoulder. On the third squeeze, they would spring the ghost trap.

He could feel Kopi's muscles twitching. He gave another squeeze. Kopi tensed at the touch. Tioga said a silent prayer for courage. Then he gave the third squeeze and rushed around the tree.

Tioga burst into the firelight. It was blinding compared to the darkness of the forest. But the head he had expected to see was gone!

He saw Kopi thrust his loop over the other scout's head. The man's hands jerked up to his neck, but Kopi held tight and gave it a quick tug. The snare engaged as intended.

Tioga searched the shadows for the other warrior. The man had vanished! At least Kopi had things under control. His scout fell to the ground and froze, hoping the attacker didn't pull the loop tighter. When he looked up and saw the ghoul above him, he let out an audible gasp.

Suddenly an angry growl rumbled from the darkness. Tioga looked up just in time to see the other man charge. Tioga didn't think to pull his knife. Instead he instinctively held the stick out in front of him. The scout punched it aside and flashed by the smaller boy to rescue his comrade. He dove forward and drove his shoulder into Kopi's chest. Kopi sailed through the air and crashed against the tree trunk. He collapsed in a heap among its twisted roots.

The warrior pulled his knife to slice the bigger boy's throat. Just before his blade found the mark, something brushed against his cheek and fell around his neck. Recognizing the threat, the scout twirled in self-defense and swung his knife. Tioga leapt back just in time, but kept hold of the rope, hoping the loop was still in place. The sharp blade just missed his belly and snapped when it struck the tough tree bark.

Tioga felt the snare take hold. The man also felt its bite, and sprung away into the night. The rope burned through Tioga's hands and disappeared into the darkness.

Tioga's heart dropped. His scout had escaped! Then he heard a crash, followed by a thud. The man was down. Tioga followed the sound and saw the scout thrashing against the choke snare, which was buried deep in his neck.

"Stop fighting, or you will die!" shouted Tioga in Mononga.

The man was in full panic, losing the battle as the snare tightened. A flash of lightning lit up the scene. The scout's eyes bulged and his face was turning blue.

Tioga screamed again at the struggling figure. "Quit moving and you will live!" The man was desperate for air. His fingers dug under the line, trying to break it free. The tough fibers didn't budge. The man looked at Tioga with wide eyes and then lost consciousness.

Tioga quickly lashed his captive's hands and feet together and then cut the choke snare free. Though unconscious, the man gasped for breath.

Tioga ran back to Kopi, who stood growling over his prisoner with his war club in one hand and the rope in the other. The man had wisely realized fighting the choke snare was useless. And the demon boy guarding him looked plenty dangerous too.

"We did it!" yelled Tioga, as he dropped to his knees and tied up the second scout.

Kopi huffed. "That's the last time you're talking me into one of your plans." He threw aside his club and reached up to feel the bloody gash on his chin. Although he was cut, it was nothing too serious.

"You *are* ghosts," said the junior scout in astonishment. "You are the boys that drowned in the river!"

"No," said Tioga. "We are just Allegewi warriors."

For the first time in his life, Tioga felt like a real warrior. He noticed a rattlesnake charm hanging from the scout's neck. He removed it and walked over to Kopi.

"General Kopi, please stand at attention," said Tioga.

"What are you talking about?" said Kopi, who sat on the ground nursing his wounds.

"Come on, stand up. Please?"

"Alright," said Kopi, as he rose. "What now?"

"Kopi, I hereby present you with the ghost warrior award for bravery!" He proudly tied the charm around his friend's neck.

"A rattlesnake rattle? Will this protect me from ghosts?"

"You don't need protection from ghosts. You're one of them!"

Kopi laughed at the thought. "I guess I don't need protection from rattlesnakes either."

"Nope. They work for you too!"

The boys relaxed in the protection of the old oak's trunk, leaving the men hog-tied a few feet away. They were secure for the night.

Tioga hated to leave anyone in that uncomfortable position, but if one got free, it would be disastrous.

Kopi took inventory of the scouts' supplies. They had food, water, a new rope, extra cloths, bows and arrows, and a fine knife. The ghost warriors were now well stocked for the road ahead. They agreed to take turns sleeping and guarding their captives, with Tioga taking the first watch. Though he had hardly slept in the last two days, he knew it would be a while before he could rest. For the first time since they were captured, Tioga felt like they really had the upper hand. Now he just needed a plan to take advantage of it.

# Twenty-Four

Shingas stood in the morning mist under the Old Bending Oak in disbelief. The footprints circled through the forest in maddening fashion. "They obviously camped here," he said, perplexed. "Then something went wrong. There is no sign of any other men?"

"No," said Soros, the lead tracker. "There was clearly a fight. Much disturbance to the area. Blood, a broken knife blade, a damaged rattlesnake charm, and wolf fur."

"Wolf fur?" said Chemung. "The zombie wolves!"

"Shut up, Chemung!" said Shingas. He focused his attention on Soros. "Are there wolf prints? Were they attacked by the pack and their bodies devoured?"

"No, sir, there are no wolf prints—just a few tufts of fur. The only clear footprints are those of the scouts. They wandered aimlessly through the forest like two blind men."

"Where did they go?" asked Shingas to Soros.

The old tracker shrugged. "They vanished." He hated to admit it, but he had lost their trail in all the footprints of the war party. By now, the entire force was mulling around the Bending Oak speculating on what had happened.

Shingas shook his head as he tried to comprehend the scene. His mind struggled to break through the haze of the medicine tea. He stole a glance at Hanna, who watched the commotion from atop her wooden stretcher. Did he detect a faint smile on her delicate lips?

"They must have gone insane," said Chemung. "Why else would they run through the woods in circles?"

"They became possessed by Allegewi ghosts," said old Ötzi as he stepped into the conversation. "Just like the wolves. Now they too will crave human flesh."

A murmur of fear ran through the ranks. Several of the men touched the charms of protection hanging from their necks.

"Nonsense!" said Shingas, trying to regain control.

"Look," said one of the men, "a sign!" He pointed to a beech tree far down the trail. A large portion of the bark had been stripped away, leaving a fresh surface with strange symbols painted on it. The troops began to move toward it.

"Everyone freeze!" ordered Shingas. "Soros, get over there before they spoil the prints."

Shingas held back his men and let the tracker do his work. After a few minutes, Soros waved them forward.

Shingas and half the force walked down the trail and inspected the pale wood. It was covered by a bunch of symbols written in blood.

"What does it say?" asked Shingas to the tracker.

Soros shrugged, "I don't read Allegewi."

"Bring up the girl and a translator!" shouted Shingas to the group back at the oak.

While they waited for the slaves to carry her forward, Shingas turned again to Soros. "Who made the sign?"

Soros scratched his head. "The only tracks are those of the scouts. They must have done it. And there are no tracks further up the trail. Whatever happened, ended here. The scouts didn't go forward."

A hush fell over the crowd of onlookers. This mission was getting stranger and stranger.

Just then a thick drop of blood landed on Shingas's neck. He looked up to see where it had come from.

Chemung followed his gaze. "There is something in the tree! A dead animal?"

"What is that?" asked Shingas. "Chemung, climb up there now!"

All eyes looked to the treetop. There, hanging from an upper branch, were two bloody furs blowing in the wind.

Chemung hesitated for a moment, and then began shimmying up the tree. It was not an easy climb. More than once, he nearly slipped and fell.

When he finally reached his target, he pulled on a fur and it dropped to the ground. A second wolf pelt fell a moment later. The men were visibly shaken by the sight.

"Bloody wolf skins?" said Shingas, puzzled. "Where did they come from? And how did they get up there?"

"It's another mystery," said Soros, shaking his head.

"Enough of these mysteries!" growled Shingas.

Just then two slaves trotted up carrying Hanna on her wooden stretcher. Her eyes lit up as she looked at the sign.

"These are Allegewi symbols, yes?" asked Shingas.

She studied the markings while the translator explained the question.

"Yes. They are Allegewi," she responded.

"What is the meaning?" said Shingas.

A crowd had gathered around them. Hanna boldly spoke in Allegewi, and the translator said, "It is a warning to travelers. It says the forest is haunted. Anyone who goes further will face an army of ghost warriors!"

"It is written in the blood of the scouts," said Ötzi the Iceman. "The ghost warriors and the ghost wolves got them!"

Whispers spread through the crowd of nervous observers. "We should turn back," said one of the men. Many of the others agreed.

"Never!" bellowed Shingas. "The scouts probably ran into some Allegewi sentries. It is unfortunate, but such things happen."

"Sentries that come out of nowhere and leave no tracks?" asked Soros.

"This is just a scare tactic to keep us from going forward." Shingas turned to his men. "If the Allegewi were strong, would they resort to such a trick? They are weaker than ever!"

"We have lost the element of surprise," said Chemung, as he dropped from the tree. He was glad to be back on solid ground.

"We do not need surprise!" screamed Shingas. "We are the Mononga! The Allegewi village is only a day away. Move out!" Shingas staggered down the trail.

The group followed, but clearly with hesitation. Several men stood firmly by the Old Bending Oak, still bothered by the mysterious disappearance of Bongo and Pox. They were all friends or relatives of the lost scouts.

"Let's go!" yelled Chemung. "That's a direct order!"

Hanna took one last look at the markings made by her supernatural friends. The last symbol, one she had intentionally failed to translate, was that of a girl's beaded bracelet. It was a symbol only she would understand. It gave her comfort to think the boys were near.

Ötzi chuckled to himself as he passed by the sign. Those boys were surprising even him.

After the war party moved out of sight, tranquility returned to the forest. It was soon broken by a loud thrashing sound. Tioga and Kopi appeared over the hill, riding piggyback on their two captives. Their steeds were rigged with gags and choke collars. The scouts knew they had to cooperate or face the consequences.

Two hours earlier, the boys had worked diligently to brush away their footprints. Then they had climbed on their prisoners' backs and drove them in wild circles around the Old Bending Oak. After leaving an untraceable maze of prints, they rode to the beech tree, stripped the bark, and painted the bloody message. Then Tioga had scampered up the tree and discarded their wolf capes, which were beginning to smell. He figured the bloody hides might further confuse the enemy. When finished, they backtracked up the trail on the backs of their captives. When they reached the thickest part of the forest, they branched off and hid to await the passing of the war party.

Capturing the scouts had been a sweet victory, but it also presented a big problem. If they went ahead with the scouts, four sets of footprints would give away their position. If they rode the scouts all the way home, the men would fatigue and might double-cross them. Riding piggyback was a vulnerable position. Tioga didn't want to have his head bashed against a passing tree.

Tioga also considered leaving the scouts tied out of sight and sprinting ahead, but the men might die of exposure and he still didn't know the fastest way home. If they went off course, the war party might beat them to the village. It was Kopi who came up with the plan to ride the "zombie scouts" in circles and hope the ruse scared the attackers enough that they turned back.

As they arrived at the Bending Oak, Kopi said, "I think it worked. I think we've really got them spooked."

"But it *didn't* work," said Tioga dejectedly. "They didn't turn back. And now they're ahead of us again."

"At least now we know which way to go," said Kopi. "We just need to follow the war party."

"Yeah, follow them home and watch them burn our village. We're back to where we started from."

"Hold up a minute," said Kopi. He dropped from the back of his prisoner and motioned for Tioga to do the same. Then he leaned over and whispered in his friend's ear, "They might understand Allegewi."

"Good thinking," said Tioga. He tied both men to separate trees, and secured their leashes in such a way that if they moved or struggled to break free, the snares would engage. He waved Kopi to move out of earshot of their captives, but stayed close enough to keep an eye on them.

"We have to watch what we say around them," said Tioga.

Kopi nodded in agreement. "So what's the plan going forward?"

"I don't know," said Tioga, with a sigh. "It's all my fault. We shouldn't have captured the scouts. We should have slipped by them last night and sprinted for home. We would have made it to the village by now!"

"If we didn't go the wrong way at the fork," said Kopi. "I think we made the right decision. Shingas still doesn't know we're here—alive and well. The war party is only a little bit ahead of us. We can catch up. And now we have two prisoners. They might have information on the plan of attack. That could make the difference, especially if the hunting party isn't back yet."

"You want to interrogate them, like Shingas would do?"

"No, but we could ask them some questions. Nicely."

Tioga scoffed. "They are battle-hardened Mononga warriors. They aren't going to help us. And it's too late. The war party could be at the village by sunset."

"If it's a full day's march, then they'll stop for the night," responded Kopi. "Everyone knows that the best time to attack is at dawn. We still have time. And if Shingas is still drinking that tea, he might miss the village altogether."

"We can't count on that," said Tioga sadly. He looked up at the blue sky. "I wish my dad was here. He was a great scout. He knew every possible trail. I'll bet he would have known a shortcut." Then it hit Tioga. *Maybe the scouts know a shortcut!* Tioga straightened up.

Kopi noticed his friend's spirits brighten. "You got something? What are you thinking?"

"We've got to interrogate our prisoners!"

"Interrogate? You mean ask them questions."

Tioga pulled out his knife. "No, I mean interrogate. We've got to get them to tell the truth."

Kopi shifted uncomfortably at the sight of the blade. He wanted to ease misery, not cause it. "Tioga, stop! You're not a cold-blooded killer."

"Kopi, I'm not going to hurt them. But they need to *think* that I could hurt them."

"Why?"

"Because that's what a Mononga warrior would do in our situation—without hesitation. They need to think of us as ruthless warriors—not little boys. Otherwise they'll just lie."

"I don't understand."

"Kopi, think of it as a skit or a play—like those ghost stories we used to act out for the kids of the village. Except this time our audience isn't the little children—it's the two scouts. We need to scare them enough that they believe the only way to save their necks is to lead us home as quickly as possible."

"I guess it couldn't hurt. Do you think I look like a tough guy?"

"With that raspy voice, you certainly sound like one. Now you just need to act like one."

Tioga went on to explain the details. Kopi was worried that he would flub his lines, but agreed it was worth a try.

When they were ready, Tioga strode confidently back toward the men, doing his best imitation of Shingas. He spoke in Mononga and hoped the captives wouldn't wonder why.

"Kopi, we have no need for prisoners! It's time to finish them and move on." Tioga pulled his glistening knife from its sheath. The scouts looked at him with panic in their eyes.

"Great Leader, they may still be of some use to us," said Kopi awkwardly.

"Use to us? Look at them. They are exhausted and their backs are broken. They will only slow us down." Bongo and Pox looked on in fear as Tioga moved toward them. "It will just take a moment to slice their throats, and then we'll be on our way! It's a shame we don't have more time to torture them."

"Yes, torturing them would have been fun," growled Kopi, as he pulled out his war club and gave it a mighty swing. "And perhaps useful. No doubt they know the battle plan."

"Humm," said Tioga, appearing to be lost in thought. "You may be right, Kopi. It might be worth a few minutes of our time to *interrogate* them."

The younger of the two scouts began shaking in fear. Death was bad enough, but death by torture was far worse. Tioga stepped up to the man and raised his knife. Pox shut his eyes, expecting the worst. Tioga sliced off the gag in his mouth, and quickly did the same to Bongo.

He shook the blade in front of them. "You men understand the situation, correct?"

Both men nodded.

"You either tell the truth, or die."

"Yes sir. We will speak the truth," said Bongo.

Tioga laughed. "I'll bet you take me for a fool! You will talk, but you will talk lies! Do you think I'm that stupid?"

"No, sir," responded the scout. "We will be truthful."

"There are ways to test if you are lying."

The captives' eyes grew large. They had witnessed countless interrogations—all of them cruel and beyond painful.

"What are your names?" asked Tioga.

"My name is Bongo, sir. And this is Pox."

"I'll give you one chance. Tell us what you know."

"We were to scout the Allegewi and report back to our commander," said Bongo. "If the village was weak, the war party would attack tonight. If the village defenses were strong, we would rest and attack at daybreak."

"Ha! Even a child would know that!" Tioga raised the knife again.

Kopi held Tioga back. "Great Leader, if you butcher them too quickly, we won't learn the details."

"Very well," said Tioga. "Prisoners, start talking!"

Bongo was flustered. "That is the plan. I speak the truth."

Tioga point the knife at Pox.

"Yes, he speaks the truth!" stuttered Pox.

"What path will they take?" asked Tioga.

"The northern trail to the river," said Bongo.

"They will avoid Ambush Gulch," added Pox.

"Ambush Gulch?" asked Tioga.

"I believe the Allegewi call it Deadly Dell," said Pox. "Long ago, there was a famous battle there."

Bongo interrupted, "An infamous ambush... A dark day in Mononga history."

"How will they avoid Ambush Gulch?" asked Tioga.

"By taking the northern trail," said Bongo. "It isn't quite as fast as the southern branch, but it is safer from ambush."

"And easier for a group traveling with an old man, a hostage girl, and..." Pox hesitated.

"And what?" said Tioga.

"And a commander who is ill," said Pox.

"What's wrong with him?" asked Kopi, curious if they had figured out his mushroom trick.

"His mind is bent," said Pox. "By a curse or a spell." He looked at Kopi warily, knowing that many believed Kopi the Sorcerer had done it.

"The girl captive is with the war party?" asked Tioga, trying to keep his voice from showing any emotion.

"Yes, sir," said Pox.

"And you know who she is?"

"Yes, sir, the daughter of the Allegewi chief."

"Quite a valuable hostage," said Tioga, with a smile on his lips. "Much more valuable than two scrawny scouts."

The men didn't respond, but they knew it was true.

"But good scouts are valuable too, especially if they know the enemy's trails," said Kopi.

"Yes, sir!" said Bongo. "We know all these paths, from the largest to the smallest."

"Then I should kill you on the spot!" bellowed Tioga, as he raised his knife. The men jumped at his aggressiveness.

"Wait, Mr. Leader!" stuttered Kopi, trying to remember his lines. "The girl… she presents… she is opportunity."

Tioga glared at Kopi. "Are you trying to say, 'the girl presents an interesting opportunity?'"

"Yes!"

"How so?" asked Tioga, acting intrigued.

Kopi continued, "Chief Tundra would surely reward the warriors who rescued her from the Mononga."

Tioga paused and contemplated the idea. "Very good, Kopi. You are right! The chief would reward the man who saved her—and quite handsomely. He might even promote *me* to be his personal assistant."

The scouts nodded in agreement.

Tioga turned to the prisoners. "If we set you free, and you caught up with the war party, do you think you could free the girl and bring her back to us?"

"Yes!" said Bongo. "We can do that!"

Tioga abruptly spit in the man's face, and growled, "Do you think I'm an idiot?" Kopi was shocked at the move, but guessed it was a necessary part of the act.

Tioga continued, "We will let the Mononga bring the girl home for us. Then they will see that the fort is well guarded and an attack is pointless. At that time a parley might be possible. A trade. Two captured Mononga scouts for the Allegewi girl. Chief Tundra would surely agree to it. Would your commander accept such a deal?"

Pox stood frozen. Bongo opened his mouth, then paused.

"Would he?" screamed Tioga.

"Yes, sir" mumbled Bongo. He was boldly lying, but he had no other choice. Their commander would never trade a valuable hostage for two dishonored scouts. They had been captured by two little Allegewi boys! Their only hope was to live long enough to escape and kill the boys in the process. Then they might be able to rejoin the force without anyone ever knowing of their embarrassment.

"But, sir," stuttered Kopi, "for such a trade to work, we would have to arrive at the village first. To convince the chief of the merits of the deal."

"Quite right, Kopi," said Tioga. In reality, he knew Shingas would never go for such a deal. For him to trade away Hanna, it would take a much sweeter prize than two disgraced scouts. But maybe the men didn't know that.

"Sir," said Pox. "We know the path of the war party. If we take the southern route, through Ambush Gulch, we can beat them to the village."

"Do you forget that I am Allegewi?" screamed Tioga. "I already know the fastest way to the village!"

Bongo looked down at the ground. He tried to think of something more to say to ensure their survival. "Sir, we know many other weaknesses of the Mononga force. For example, the warriors have been fighting strong intestinal demons. They must frequently stop to relieve their bowels in the bushes. We also had such pains, but they have improved since we left the camp. We know much about the plan of attack."

"And we know that they fear your ghosts," added Pox.

"Interesting," said Tioga. "You may be worth more to us alive than dead. But we cannot waste any more time talking here. I will give you a chance to prove you are telling the truth. I will let you lead us to the village by the fastest way possible."

"Yes, sir!" said Bongo.

"But, if you are lying," said Tioga smiling, "if there is even the slightest deviation from the shortest route, you both will suffocate by the choke snare. And I will enjoy watching you squirm like a worm in the dirt."

"Yes sir," said Bongo. "We believe you."

"Very well then!" bellowed Tioga. "We leave immediately!" He replaced the gags in the captives' mouths. They couldn't believe their good fortune. They had lived to see another day.

Kopi leaned over and whispered in Tioga's ear, "Can we ride them home? My lungs still aren't back to normal."

Tioga pulled Kopi away from the men. "Too risky. We run behind, with a firm grasp on their leashes."

"Alright," said Kopi in disappointment. "But wait a moment." Kopi raced over to the remains of last night's fire and grabbed two handfuls of ash. "Time to do our makeup," he said, smiling.

"Not only ours, but theirs too. If we stumble into a Mononga sentry, we'd all better look the part."

A few minutes later all four of them were covered in ash and charcoal. Kopi stepped back to view his artwork. "Two ghost warriors and two ghost prisoners. Soon we will have a ghost army!"

# *Twenty-Five*

Shingas sat beside the spring, watching his men fill their canteens. He rubbed his shoulder in satisfaction. The Allegewi boy-healer had cured him. His stump was nearly back to normal. He could still feel the effects of his morning medicine tea. At times it made him so dizzy that he had to be carried on the trail. That fat boy knew his stuff. His medicine was much more potent than that of the old Mononga healer back in the castle. It would have been nice to have had Kopi as his personal doctor, but death had taken him away. At least he wouldn't be healing the Allegewi any longer.

Chemung strode up beside him. "The men are refreshed and ready, sir!"

"Refreshed? They stink! What's that smell?"

Chemung hesitated. He slid the garlic bulb necklace he was wearing beneath his shirt. "Garlic, sir. It grows naturally in these parts. The men took the opportunity to gather some."

Shingas looked at his warriors through his blurry vision. Nearly every man was wearing a garlic bulb around his neck. Shingas growled, "Superstitious fools! They think garlic will protect them in battle?"

"Well, not in battle sir. It's just a precaution to make sure we get to the Allegewi village safely."

"They are afraid of forest spirits? I've never seen such cowards." Shingas stood up with a grunt. Something didn't look quite right. He nervously called out, "Head count! I want a head count!"

Chemung immediately complied. The war party stood at attention. A minute later Chemung returned. "Sir, forty warriors, one elder, two slaves, one hostage, one commander, and one *assistant commander*!" Chemung was especially proud of the last title. He had been promoted just before they left the fortress.

"Forty warriors?" bellowed Shingas. "We left home with eighty!

"Yes, sir! That is correct."

"Where are the other forty?" asked Shingas, slurring his words. The war party looked at him with concern.

"Why, sir, by now, they are probably near the Forks."

"The Forks? Who told them to go there? I will skin him alive!"

Chemung stood there frozen. He was afraid to answer.

"Who gave the order?" screamed Shingas, turning beet red in anger.

Chemung said softly, "Why, you did, sir."

"What? Why would I do that?" asked Shingas, perplexed.

"To look for the bodies of the Allegewi boys who drowned in the Angry River," said Chemung. "You insisted that they be found. When we reached the fallen bridge, you sent half our men down the valley and told them not to come back until they found their corpses."

Shingas sat down in confusion. His head was spinning. He vaguely remembered the scene at the rope bridge. *Did I order half my army down the river in search of two dead boys?*

"It's that Allegewi warlock, Kopi!" screamed Shingas. "He put a spell of confusion on me!"

One of the men moved forward. "Sir, permission to speak? It is urgent."

"Yes, what is it?" moaned Shingas, holding his head in his hand.

"Sir, I do not think it was a spell, but rather a toxic substance."

"He poisoned me?"

"In a way, yes. I noticed the way Chemung has been making your medicine tea. It includes some very strong mushrooms that only a shaman can safely use."

"Chemung, you have been poisoning me!" screamed Shingas, as he pulled his knife.

Chemung quickly tried to save his neck. "But, sir, you told me to make it exactly as the boy-healer instructed."

Shingas did remember that. Nonetheless, he was steaming. *What other decisions did I make on that evil brew?*

"No more medicine!" growled Shingas as he stood up and regained his composure. "That Allegewi devil will pay for his tricks... Troops, move out! At double time! We will crush the Allegewi today, before nightfall!"

Chemung wondered if it was a wise decision. The men would be in much better shape for battle in the morning. And more importantly, he hoped that his commander's head would be clear by then. It would also give them time to conduct some surveillance on the enemy. With the disappearance of the scouts, they had no information on the Allegewi fort.

But Chemung didn't dare raise these issues. Instead, he watched Shingas stumble down the trail and round the bend. He immediately ran after him, concerned that the boss might fall and hurt himself. The men wearily picked up their packs and followed.

An hour back from the war party, the boys trotted behind their ash-painted prisoners on the well-beaten path. They were making good time, but now they came upon a fork in the road. The main path branched to the left, but it was clear the army had taken the less traveled trail to the right. Bongo signaled as best he could that something was amiss.

"All stop!" order Tioga. "Kopi, lower their gags."

Tioga held their leashes while Kopi handled the task.

"What is it Bongo?" asked Tioga.

"This is the fork in the trail," said Bongo. "The war party went right, but we must go left to take the shortcut."

"Through Ambush Gulch," added Pox, nervously.

"Very good," smiled Tioga. "I was waiting to see if you would tell me. Kopi, given them a drink of water to reward their honesty."

The scouts gulped from the canteen as Kopi raised it to their lips, but their eyes never stopped scanning the landscape.

Tioga noticed their anxiety. Something strange was going on. "We will rest here for a moment," said Tioga in Mononga. He tied Bongo securely to one tree and Pox to another. Then he led Kopi just out of earshot of the captives.

"What's going on?" asked Kopi in Allegewi.

"The scouts seem nervous," whispered Tioga. "I need to check out the path ahead of us. They could be leading us into a trap. You stay here and watch them for a few minutes."

"You can't leave me here alone with them!"

"They are well tied. And you have a bow and a full quiver of arrows. It will only take me a few minutes. Just don't go so close that they can grab you."

"What do I tell them?"

"You don't need to tell them anything. They're your prisoners!"

Tioga turned and moved cautiously down the trail. He kept a keen eye out for prints or any other sign of human activity. As the path fell downward into a valley, rocky cliffs emerged from the earth and bracketed the route. The valley became a canyon. *This is it. Deadly Dell.* A strange feeling came over him. He yearned to explore the historic battlefield, but his mission now was to make sure it hadn't been setup for another ambush. Maybe Chemung had reported seeing them after all. The war party could be hiding on the cliff tops waiting for them to pass below.

Tioga stopped and backed up. To make sure it was safe, he needed to check the high ground. He branched off to one side and paralleled the valley from the top of the bluffs. He could see why the Allegewi called it Deadly Dell. From this position, a single archer could pick off a dozen targets below without even breaking a sweat. Twenty archers would have turned the gulch into a bloodbath. A wave of sadness came over Tioga. After all, those who lost their lives here were just trying to save his mother.

Satisfied that there was no sign of recent human activity, he turned and headed back. Kopi didn't hear Tioga as he walked up behind him. He was too busy conversing with the scouts.

"He won't be too much longer," said Kopi to the men. "You see, Tioga has this thing about relieving himself in public—around other people. He's quite shy that way. So, when he has to go, he wanders off and finds a quiet place."

Bongo couldn't help but chuckle, then he noticed Tioga behind Kopi.

"Silence!" shouted Tioga, trying to regain the appearance of a ruthless warlord.

"See! I told you he'd be back soon," said Kopi with a smile.

"Kopi!" interrupted Tioga. "Enough talk. We need to get moving. Replace their gags and hand me Bongo's leash."

"Yes, Great Leader," said Kopi, remembering his role.

Bongo spoke up before he was re-gagged. "Sir, it is best to move through Ambush Gulch quickly. Blood has soaked the soil. The spirits of the fallen still haunt the canyon."

Kopi got a wide-eyed look, but kept his mouth shut.

Tioga answered, "We will walk—not run. To the Allegewi, Deadly Dell is hallowed ground. The site of a great victory."

Before long, the four travelers were moving into the canyon. Spooky cliffs towered over them on both sides. A small, braided stream trickled through the valley beside the path. As they passed under the dark bluffs, Tioga pictured dozens of Allegewi eyes watching from above. He could almost see his father lying in wait, like a mountain lion stalking its prey.

Their footsteps echoed eerily off the walls like a strange, rhythmic song. Tioga could only imagine the cacophony of bloodcurdling screams that had once filled the death zone. The canyon would have been a nightmare for the ambushed Mononga rescuers. Tioga wondered how Shingas had made it out alive.

In various places, Tioga could see faded symbols etched in the eroding sandstone. He knew these had been made decades ago by the victorious Allegewi warriors—the tale of the battle was literally carved in stone.

The shallow stream cut rudely across their path. At the eroded edge of the creek, something shiny caught Tioga's eye.

"Stop!" he ordered in Mononga. The scouts and Kopi halted and turned to watch him. Tioga reached down and pulled a mysterious object from the soil—an arrowhead made of swirling, red and blue, glossy flint. The hair on Tioga's arms stood up. This wasn't a typical arrow tip. This was made of exotic flint. Whomever had shot it in battle, no doubt believed that it held special power. Bongo swallowed hard at the sight.

Kopi also recognized the artifact and spoke up. "Tioga, don't handle that. There could still be poison on the tip."

Tioga ignored the comment and studied the arrowhead as if in a trance. He wondered whether his father was the one who had launched the deadly projectile. He slipped the point into his pocket and looked sternly at the scouts.

"Move out!" he ordered.

The men quickly complied. Ten minutes later they emerged from the canyon. Tioga ordered the men to resume trotting. The prisoners continued to lead the way.

While Tioga was intrigued by the historic site, his thoughts returned to the problem at hand. While the scouts might be glad to be through the gulch, Tioga's anxiety was increasing with each step. He was dreading the coming conflict and felt powerless to stop it. He struggled to appear calm. He had to maintain an air of command in front of their prisoners. If he showed any weakness, the scouts might try an escape—or, even worse, lead them in the wrong direction. So, Tioga acted like he knew the way.

After another fork in the trail, he stopped the procession and bluffed. Tioga said aloud in Mononga, "Kopi, they think this is the fastest way!" He chuckled and turned to the scouts. "You think you know these trails better than an Allegewi?" Tioga pulled out his knife for dramatic effect. The captives looked back nervously. "Kopi, remove their gags."

Tioga pointed over his shoulder to the darkest part of the forest. "Do you not know the secret passage?"

Bongo responded humbly, "No, sir. This is the fastest way that we know."

"Ha! Stupid Mononga," said Tioga. "Well, you are lucky this time. The secret passage is shorter, but it goes through a difficult rocky pass."

Kopi quickly picked up on Tioga's deception and decided to add his own touch. "Yes! And a cave. A dark tunnel full of spiders, bats, and bears!" Kopi took on the pose of an angry bear.

"I am not afraid of bears!" bellowed Tioga. He stared down Kopi, hoping he would leave the acting to him.

Tioga held up the rope attached to Bongo's choke collar. "The secret passage is wet and dark. One slip, and your neck..." Tioga grabbed his own neck and gagged with his tongue sticking out. The captives immediately understood the gesture. "Since the secret passage is dangerous to you, I will allow you to continue with your route. But it better be almost as fast."

"Yes, sir!" said Bongo.

Tioga was about to put the gag back in the man's mouth when Kopi stepped forward.

"I want to ask him something," said Kopi to Tioga in Allegewi.

"Go ahead," said Tioga. "But make it quick."

Kopi addressed the lead scout in Mononga, "Bongo, do you know the healer called the Gangas Witch?"

"I do not know her personally, but she is famous in the north," said Bongo. "She is elusive, but many try to find her. Those needing a miracle."

"Why do they seek out a witch?"

"She commands powerful magic. She can heal any ailment, if she so desires. She can even command fire."

"Command fire?" questioned Tioga, overhearing the statement. "How so?"

"She can make the fire jump, and dance, and change colors—all at her command," said Bongo. "Or so I've heard."

Pox added, "It's true!"

Tioga was surprised by the answer. He had heard of shamans and healers doing magical things, but controlling fire was beyond supernatural. Whoever could command fire, could rule the world. He suddenly saw an opportunity to enhance Kopi's reputation.

"Kopi the Sorcerer can also control fire!" boasted Tioga. "You saw him bring down the lightning bolt in the fortress, yes?"

Both scouts nodded.

"It was Kopi who enabled our escape," said Tioga, patting his friend on the back.

Both men looked at Kopi with new found respect.

"Bongo, where does the Gangas Witch live?" asked Kopi, ignoring the praise.

"I do not know," said Bongo. "But there was a rumor she was in the headwaters of the Allegewi River not long ago."

"Yes, your commander asked her for a new arm, but instead she poisoned him," said Kopi.

"The witch put a deadly curse on him," said Tioga. "But Kopi saved him and broke the curse."

"Really?" asked Pox. "You broke the curse of the Gangas Witch?"

Before Kopi could answer, Tioga stepped forward, "Yes! Shaman Kopi has many powers. He can even read minds."

"I can?" asked Kopi.

"Yes, you can! You just forget because you are in a trance when you do it," said Tioga, realizing things were getting a bit out of hand. "Enough talk. Back on the trail! And no tricks or you will feel the choke snare and Kopi's lightning bolt!"

Tioga reinserted their gags and motioned for them to proceed. The two scouts looked at each other and led them on.

Tioga turned to Kopi and whispered in Allegewi, "What was that all about?"

"I was curious," responded Kopi.

"About a witch? There has to be more to it than that."

"Well…" Kopi paused. "Someone once accused my mother of being a witch."

"Really? Why?"

"A trader brought in his boy who had fallen into the river. By the time he reached my mother, the child was blue—he looked dead. But Mom used her skills to revive him. The boy woke, but was never the same again. The trader accused my mother of witchcraft. He said she had turned his son into a zombie."

"That's a serious charge. What happened?"

"Chief Tundra defended her and sent the man away. But ever since then, I realized that healing can be dangerous. If someone doesn't get well, the family might think it's the healer's fault. I guess it's a risk every doctor takes."

"So, this Gangas Witch isn't really a witch at all?"

"I don't know. But if she's good as they say, she must know a lot of cool stuff," said Kopi. "Someday, I'd like to meet her. Hey! When this is all over, can we seek her out?"

"You think she might share a few of her secrets?"

"You never know. She just might."

"Or she just might turn you into a zombie."

"A zombie?" said Kopi, with a fearful look.

"Yeah. She might put a cherry pit up your butt."

"That wouldn't be so good," said Kopi, rethinking the plan. "Maybe she really is a witch."


Two hours later, the path entered a clear field of jumbled rocks, left behind by a melting glacier in the last ice age. It felt strange to be out in the sunshine after walking under the forest canopy for days. It was tricky business working their way through the jagged granite rubble. As Tioga stepped on an unstable stone, it gave way and he crashed to the ground. He let out a yelp as he fell. He instinctively let loose the choke snare, so it wouldn't engage on his prisoner's neck. Although he was injured in the fall, he quickly regained hold of the leash before the surprised captive realized what had happened.

"Are you alright?" asked Kopi.

Tioga sat on the ground and held his ankle. "Tie them in the trees," he groaned. "Make sure they don't escape."

After Kopi finished the task, he returned to his patient. "Let me see it," said Kopi.

Tioga pulled his hand away and revealed a rapidly swelling ankle, which was quickly turning blue from the trauma.

"That doesn't look good," said Kopi. He manipulated his friend's foot while Tioga grimaced in pain. "Do you want the good news, or the bad news?"

"The good news," responded Tioga.

"Well, it's not broken."

"And the bad?"

"It's a wicked sprain. There's no way you can walk on that, let alone run."

Tioga moaned, more from the emotional pain than the physical. "This is a disaster."

"Stay here," ordered Kopi, as he walked away. He approached the prisoners and drew his knife. Both Tioga and the men were shocked at the sight. It was a particularly sharp blade taken from Pox back at the Bending Oak.

Kopi approached the lead scout and commanded, "Bongo, raise your arms." The man complied and stood at attention. He knew from the boy's determined expression that his luck had finally run out. He closed his eyes and bravely began to speak his death prayer.

Tioga had no idea what had gotten into Kopi. His friend had turned from a compassionate caregiver into a remorseless butcher in a matter of seconds. "Kopi, no! Don't do it!"

Kopi ignored him and put the blade against the man's stomach. Then he began to cut. The sound of ripping skin echoed off the rocks. But it wasn't human skin that was being sliced. The shocked scout looked down in surprise as Kopi cut a long strip of soft leather from the bottom of Bongo's buckskin shirt. He walked around the man as the blade did its work. After about five rotations, Kopi stopped. Half of Bongo's tunic had been peeled away, leaving him bare from the chest down. It looked like he was wearing a strange new fashion to go with his ghost makeup.

Kopi strolled back to Tioga. "Let's see what we can do."

Tioga watched as Kopi expertly wrapped his sprained ankle with the supple leather strip. "This should stabilize it and limit the swelling," said Kopi. "But keep off of it for a week."

"A week?" said an exasperated Tioga. "We've got to get home tonight!"

"Well then, you'd better saddle up. We're just wasting time sitting here."

Tioga immediately understood what he had to do. With Kopi's help, he hobbled over toward the prisoners.

"Hey, I think this wrap is helping," said Tioga, still in pain but able to move slowly under his own power.

"Good," said Kopi. "If I see any natural painkillers along the way, I'll grab them."

"Kopi, I don't know what I'd do without you and your witchcraft. Thank you."

"Ha! My pleasure."

Tioga approached Bongo, the bigger of the two men. "You will carry me on your back," he ordered in Mononga. "No tricks."

Bongo nodded and kneeled before him. Tioga climbed aboard. Kopi untied the leather leash from the tree and handed the reins to his friend.

"Giddy up!" said Tioga to Bongo.

A moment later, Kopi had the leash of Pox securely in his hands. While he would have loved to ride, he remembered Tioga's comment about the risks involved. He trailed behind Pox and maintained the maximum distance the rope would allow.

The group picked their way through the rest of the boulder field. When they finally cleared it, the path became much smoother. Bongo and Tioga went first, followed by Pox and then Kopi. Now that Tioga was hurt, General Kopi had taken command. He kept a keen eye out for any escape attempts.

As they jogged through the forest, Kopi also looked for medicinal plants. When he spotted a willow tree, he stopped the group and shaved off some bark for Tioga to chew. Back on the trail, he grabbed the leaves of various plants without even breaking stride. Tioga took the medicine as instructed. Before long, the throbbing in his ankle subsided to the point that he began to feel drowsy.

The next thing Tioga knew, Kopi was shaking him by the arm. "Wake up, General!" Tioga opened his eyes and was shocked to see the back of the Bongo's head inches in front of him. He had fallen asleep while riding!

"How long was I out?" asked Tioga with concern. He knew he had dodged an arrow.

"Close to an hour," said Kopi. "I would have let you sleep until dark, but I wanted to tell you the good news."

"The good news?"

"Come down and take a look," said Kopi, pointing toward a small river.

Tioga dismounted and stretched his stiff limbs. With Kopi's help, he was able to walk without too much difficulty. The boys secured their prisoners and shuffled to the bank. The river was shallow enough to walk across, but otherwise unremarkable.

"It's a river," said Tioga, rubbing the sleep out of his eyes. "What's the big deal?"

"Don't you know what this means?"

"No," said Tioga, still feeling groggy.

"We aren't lost anymore!" said Kopi excitedly. "I know this river. It's the Runestone."

"The Runestone River?" Tioga knew the name but didn't recall its waters.

"Yes! My father took me fishing here once," explained Kopi. "I hated it. So, I got out of the canoe and walked home. It merges with the Allegewi River above our village. I know the way home from here! We just follow the Runestone until it reaches the Allegewi. Then we cross the Allegewi River at the north ford and the village is right around the bend."

"How far is it?"

"Not far. A few hours at most."

Tioga's mind kicked into action. He extended his arm toward the sun and used his fingers to measure the distance between the bottom of the sun and the horizon. The gap covered the width of two fingers. He knew from experience that each finger represented about an hour of daylight.

"The sun will set in two fingers—I mean two hours."

"Then we should be home by sundown!" said Kopi with a giant smile on his face.

Tioga dropped his head in despair.

"What's wrong?" asked Kopi.

"That means Shingas could also be at our village by dark. We've got to get going."

As they hobbled back to the scouts, Tioga stopped dead in his tracks.

"Oh no," he mumbled, as he stared at the ground.

"What now?" asked Kopi.

"We walked right by and never noticed," said Tioga, as he dropped to his knees. Even Kopi could see the footprints in the mud.

"Are they Allegewi?" asked Kopi, hopefully.

"No, I'm afraid not," said Tioga. "The war party beat us here. They got ahead of us. It's my fault. If I hadn't twisted my ankle…"

"They took the river trail," said Kopi. "It follows the waterway, which winds back and forth. There is faster way! We can take the ridgeline."

"The ridgeline?"

"Yes, it's usually quicker. And you don't have to get your feet wet crossing streams. Let's go!" Now Kopi barked the orders, suddenly realizing the seriousness of the situation. For the first time in the journey, he fully accepted the responsibility thrust upon his shoulders and stepped forward as the leader.

Tioga climbed aboard Pox to give Bongo a break. Kopi led the way to a rarely used path that ran on the high ridge that paralleled the Runestone River. The elevated path cut out many of the twists and turns of the river trail, but had more than its fair share of fallen trees, vines, and brambles. It was rough terrain, and the sun slowly sank in the sky.

As Tioga rode the rugged trail toward home, images of his mother flashed through his mind. For the first time in his life he truly appreciated her strength, her wisdom, and her love. Her overprotective nature was just a result of all she had been through. Tioga was so lost in reflection that he didn't notice Kopi had stopped dead in the path. Thankfully his mount was watching and jerked to a halt.

"Oh, no," gasped Kopi in Allegewi, as he looked toward the falling sun. Tioga squinted in that direction and saw water shimmering in the distance.

"The Allegewi River!" said Tioga. "We made it!"

"Look in the tall grass above the bank."

Tioga dismounted and limped forward, keeping a firm grasp on Pox's leash. He spotted a human head moving through the waving stalks. Then another and another. Their red and black Mononga war paint was unmistakable.

"They beat us to the north ford!" said Tioga.

"There're going to beat us to the village," said Kopi in horror.

"They haven't crossed yet," said Tioga. *If there was only a way to slow them down.* Tioga looked at the captured bow and quiver of arrows looped over Kopi's shoulder. It was the primary weapon every tribe used in battle. *We need something more powerful than arrows,* he thought.

Kopi seemed to read his mind. "If we pray hard enough, maybe the Great Spirit will wash them away when they cross the river."

Tioga understood why Kopi had made the comment. Such things could happen. Kopi had lost his older brother in a flood. But today the sky was crystal clear. In fact, it appeared that the valley had dodged last night's storm. The mud was cracked and the grass was bone dry.

"You really think they'd attack tonight?" asked Kopi.

"The more time they wait, the greater the chance of detection."

Tioga knew this area like the back of his hand. The village was around the bend on the other side of the river. His brain ached as he tried to come up with a miracle. He was just about to give up when his father's voice echoed in his head. *"Use the logjam!"* He suddenly remembered that his dad had taught him to trap muskrat in a huge logjam just upstream.

"They're about to head in," said Kopi. The war party crouched in the tall grass as they assembled for the crossing.

Bongo had also spotted his tribemates. He wished he could run down the hill and join them, or at least shout out a warning, but the choke snare and gag prohibited both. *Kopi the Sorcerer is a fake!* he thought. *If he could really control fire, he would strike the army with a lightning bolt!* He shook his head in disgust.

"Follow me," said Tioga. "I have an idea." Tioga climbed on Pox's back and ordered him to go back up the path. Then he directed the group down a gully toward the river. They arrived at the riverbank, a few hundred paces upstream and around the bend from the war party.

"There it is," said Tioga. "The logjam." A mountainous tangle of brush and dead trees was piled high along the shore. As they moved toward the mass of logs, Tioga remembered it was the Great Flood that had deposited the mammoth heap. The same flood which had taken Kopi's brother.

"Kopi, give me Bongo's leash," said Tioga, as he dismounted from Pox's back.

Kopi handed it to him. "Now what?"

"Go into the river and try to pry a log loose from the jam. Don't worry, it's shallow there," said Tioga.

Hoping that his friend was being truthful, Kopi set down his bow and arrows, as well as his war club, and splashed into the waist-deep water. He carefully waded to the giant pile of driftwood. With a grunt, he pulled a log from the mass, and set it adrift.

"Good! Now keep at it," said Tioga.

"I get it," said Kopi, pulling a stump loose. "A bunch of junk comes floating out of nowhere, right while they are crossing the river. They'll think the ghosts are still haunting them!"

"Hopefully. It probably won't stop them, but it might slow them down. Then we can swim the river and beat them to the village."

"Swim the river?" said Kopi apprehensively. He could tell that the water was much deeper beyond the logjam. Although the Allegewi River was flowing at its normal level, it was still plenty dangerous to Kopi. He yanked another branch from the pile and tossed it in the water.

Tioga looked downstream. The few floating logs that Kopi had released were so far apart in the wide waterway that they probably wouldn't even be noticed.

"If I could only get some of these big ones out," said Kopi as he tugged at a twisted pine. The trunk barely budged.

"It's not enough," said Tioga in frustration. "I'll swim across and head to the village. You stay here."

"Now wait a minute," said Kopi. "You're not leaving me with two dangerous men and the enemy just around the bend. And what about your ankle?"

Tioga realized his mobility was going to be an issue. "Well, then you'll just have to come with me," said Tioga. "I'll tie them to a tree. We can't afford to waste any more time."

"What if we put the scouts to work?" said Kopi, pointing to the logjam.

Tioga immediately grasped the possibilities. He barked orders in Mononga. "You will pull the logs free and set them adrift! Otherwise you will face the consequences!"

Bongo nodded enthusiastically, and mumbled through his gag. He held up his bound hands. They couldn't do much work with their hands tied.

"Kopi, I'm cutting their hands loose," said Tioga. "But don't worry, I've got a tight grip on their leashes."

Then he said to the men, "Help Kopi break up the jam. But no tricks. I will be holding your lives in my hands!" He snapped their reins to emphasize the point.

The men flexed their muscles and moved toward the log pile. Tioga followed them into the water, but stayed as far back as their leashes would allow. Bongo grabbed a large trunk and rolled it off the top. It splashed into the water and floated away.

"Now that's more like it," said Kopi. He sprang into action beside the men. The results were impressive. With the three of them working together, log after log tumbled into the river. Some bobbed along on the surface, while other waterlogged trunks submerged in the current.

The logjam began to come apart under its own power. Tioga was amazed and wondered if the Great Spirit was helping to untangle the jam. Soon the river looked like a caravan of driftwood, branches, and dead trees.

Bongo reached down and grabbed hold of a thick branch. Then he looked at Pox and grunted.

Tioga recognized the threat too late. Bongo twirled and slammed the log into Kopi's side, while Pox charged Tioga. He was knocked into deeper water and went under with the warrior on top of him. He lost his grip on Bongo's leash during the struggle. Tioga pulled on Pox's leash with all his might, but Pox was too close to engage the snare. The scout grabbed Tioga's neck. He thrashed in panic, breaking Pox's grip. They tumbled in the current as Tioga fought for his life.

Pox was more powerful and pushed the boy deeper, pressing his foot into Tioga's chest until he was pinned to the muddy bottom. The churning silt blocked out all light. The air in Tioga's lungs grew stale. He struggled wildly but the foot was winning. Something brushed by his left hand. He grasped the cord in desperation and pulled in an attempt to reach the surface.

He was about to inhale the murky water when his opponent's leg jerked. The foot slipped off his chest, and Pox fell away. Tioga swam upward, his lungs aching. He broke the surface and gasped for air. He saw the scout clawing at the choke snare, which was digging into his neck. Unknowingly, Tioga had strangled his attacker. Pox stumbled backward and vanished beneath the churning water.

Tioga frantically looked for Kopi. The only person in sight was Bongo, who was swimming away toward the middle of the river. Tioga was about to begin an underwater search when a turtle shell broke the surface, with Kopi's soggy head beneath it. He coughed up some green water and staggered to the bank.

Seeing that Kopi was alive, Tioga turned back to where Pox had slipped beneath the surface. He probed the murky water until he felt a leg, then grabbed hold and pulled the man in. By the time Tioga and

Kopi got him up on the beach, Pox was unconscious and turning blue. Tioga cut the choke snare free and watched to see whether he would breathe. Pox's chest heaved upward, and air entered his starved lungs. The color slowly returned to his face. It was clear the unconscious man wouldn't be a threat to them anytime soon.

"My ribs," said Kopi. "I think they're broken."

"Don't worry," said Tioga. "Your mom will have you patched up in no time. Now let's cross this river."

Tioga looked downstream toward the sunset. He could clearly see Bongo clinging to a floating log. The swift current quickly carried the ash-colored scout and the haunted driftwood around the bend.

# Twenty-Six

The war party quietly moved into the chest-high water at the north ford. The men were exhausted after the long day of running. Many of them were suffering from a mysterious intestinal illness, which made the forced march even more miserable. They looked forward to a much-needed rest when they reached the Allegewi River. When Shingas passed down the order to press the attack, a murmur of discontent traveled through the ranks. To top things off, the river was proving surprisingly difficult to cross. It seemed to be unusually choked with debris.

"Where is all this stuff coming from?" muttered Chemung, as he battled a particularly troublesome limb. At first, the driftwood had gone unnoticed. It wasn't unusual to see a dead tree floating down a river as large as the Allegewi. But now something strange was going on. Thorny branches were ripping their arms, while submerged logs took out their legs.

Shingas fought his way through a thick tangle. This was too much to be a coincidence. He and the other warriors watched the steep hillsides for signs of a possible ambush. Had they been detected? The men were nervous.

Old Ötzi clung to the side of the stretcher on which Hanna was tied. It took four men to carry her across. When one of the men was knocked away by a tree stump, Ötzi took his place. He decided to voice the thought which was running through the minds of many of the fighters.

"It is the work of the Allegewi ghosts!" barked Ötzi. "They have brought forth the spirits of the dead timber!"

"The mission is cursed," agreed one of the warriors. Just as he said it, a crafty branch snatched the bow from his shoulder and vanished with it below the surface.

"We should turn back now before we are all possessed by demons," said another man.

Just then, a mysterious moan carried over the water from upstream. It called out to them from a tangle of driftwood. An arm and then an ashen face appeared within a knot of bewitched limbs. The apparition was floating straight toward them.

"A river ghost!" cried one of the men.

The war party scattered in panic. Most of the fighters turned back and ran for shore. Shingas watched helplessly as his battle-hardened troops screamed like frightened children. He looked up river and strained to identify the mysterious figure.

The ghost's groans suddenly became clear, as the escaped prisoner freed the gag from his mouth. "It's me! Bongo!" yelled the raspy voice.

"The ghost of the murdered scout!" cried Ötzi. "He has come to feast upon our flesh!" He looked up at Hanna and winked as he led her stretcher back to shore. All but Shingas and Chemung ran from the specter. If it was up to him, Chemung would have headed for the hills, but he knew better than to leave his commander's side.

"Help me!" cried out the river phantom. He spotted Chemung and swam toward him. "Chemung! Get this snare off my neck!"

Chemung began back peddling, but the spirit closed the gap. As a last defense, Chemung raised his bow and fired an arrow at the ghost of the dead scout.

Bongo cried out as the arrow skipped over his head. "Chemung, are you crazy? It's me, your brother-in-law!"

A puzzled look came over Chemung's face. The ashen head was too lifelike to be of the spirit world. As they came together, he reached out and felt the man's painted face. "Bongo, you're not a ghost!" said Chemung in astonishment.

"Of course not."

"Did the ghosts torture you?"

"There are no ghosts, you idiot! You have been tricked by two Allegewi boys! The same boys who escaped from the fortress. They are the ones haunting the war party."

"How did you resist their evil powers?"

"They have no evil powers!" said Bongo. "They are just ordinary boys! They are trying to scare you."

The warriors watched with suspicion as Chemung and the ghost scout headed toward shore. When they saw that Bongo was still a living man, they slowly reassembled and listened to his tale. The seasoned warriors were embarrassed that two little boys had outfoxed them for nearly a week.

The debris that had clogged the river had mostly passed. Shingas regrouped his troops into an angry fighting force. Just before he was about to lead them back in, Elder Ötzi stepped forward and addressed the men.

"Do not be ashamed of falling for the deception," said Ötzi. "Those boys are smart and cunning. The one named Tioga has Mononga blood running through his veins. We should all respect his bravery. He carries the power of his ancestors!"

Shingas roared, "What power? Your ancestors were weak and spineless! When I was a child, we were starving just like all the other tribes. I vowed then that I would take what I wanted. Strength through force is the only way!"

"Don't mistake wisdom for weakness," said Ötzi. "It was a difficult time, when Mother Earth was sick. We shared what we had and there was peace in the valley."

"Who needs peace when you can win in war?" boasted Shingas. "Since I have ruled, we have not lost a battle. All of the tribes, except for the Allegewi, bow down before me. And in a matter of minutes, they will be gone. I will rule the rivers and the mountains!"

"The other tribes may bow down to your face, but behind your back they loathe you," said Ötzi. "You have soiled the good name of the Mononga people. And at what price? We have lost many men in your pointless wars, just to take more food than we could ever eat."

The old man's comments struck a chord in many of the men's hearts. All of them had lost fathers, brothers, or friends in the countless battles.

"You do not appreciate the food I put in your mouth?" said Shingas, his eyes bulging.

"I do not eat your stolen food," said Ötzi. "Mother Earth provides more than enough nourishment in the forest. I could never eat food stained with the blood of innocent women and children."

"Who cares if they die?" laughed Shingas. "They are not Mononga."

"They were made by the Creator, just like all of us. The day will come when you will answer for your cruelty."

"I answer to no one!" bellowed Shingas. "Especially not to a cowardly old man." He slapped Ötzi to the ground. "Enough of your weak-hearted ramblings!" he screamed. "No more delays. It is time to destroy the enemy!"

Shingas waited for the cheer that always followed his speeches. This time there was only silence. "Come!" he yelled. "The village is ours to take!" He splashed into the river and led the way. But he didn't hear the sound of his men entering the water. He looked over his shoulder and paused.

The confrontation between Ötzi and Shingas had a pronounced effect on the troops. Ötzi was a respected elder and a powerful mystic. To strike such a sage was prohibited and would surely anger the spirits of the ancestors. The mission was cursed—if not by ghosts, then by bad luck. The men mulled around at the water's edge, uncertain of what to do.

*Why aren't they coming?* thought Shingas. Chemung finally set an example and followed his leader into the river. Soon the rest of the warriors fell in line. The war party moved forward for the attack. But for the first time in his life, Shingas wondered if his men were truly behind him.

# *Twenty-Seven*

Tioga and Kopi heard a clamor of distant voices downstream. It went without saying that their secret was lost. The time for tricks was over. All they could do now was make a mad rush for home. With Tioga's injured ankle, and Kopi's inability to swim, they knew they needed each other. They had begun this trip together, and they would end it together.

Tioga grabbed a rope from the ground and looked to Kopi. "Can you give me a ride?"

"Sure. Where are we going?" asked Kopi, as his friend climbed on his broad shoulders.

"Head up river as fast as you can," said Tioga.

They left Pox, who was still unconscious on the beach, and moved to the north. Tioga knew they needed to get further upstream before they attempted the crossing. Otherwise, they would be swept around the bend right into Shingas's grasp.

After a few minutes, Tioga called out, "Stop at those reeds." When they reached the spot, he added, "We're making you a float."

Kopi and Tioga used their knives to cut free the dry stalks. They soon had a sizable bunch. Moving as quickly as possible, Tioga lashed together the bundle of reeds and handed it to Kopi.

"This should hold you up," said Tioga, as he splashed into the water.

Kopi hesitantly followed and tried out the float. Tioga grabbed the rope at one end and swam with all his might toward the far shore. Kopi did his part by kicking.

"Hey, watch what you're doing," said Kopi. "You might pull it apart."

"Shingas will pull us apart, limb by limb, if we don't hurry up and get across," said Tioga. They moved into deeper water and the strong current took hold of the craft.

Tioga knew the terrain on the other side of the river all too well. It would be a challenge to get to the village first, as the path home followed the river and went right by the north ford. A tall rocky ridge stood in the way of any other route.

Tioga looked back at the shore to judge their progress. They were already even with the log pile and were only halfway across. Suddenly, a shiver ran up his spine. He could see their former prisoner, Pox, sitting on the beach. The man had returned to the world of the living. They had left a powerful bow and a full quiver of arrows right beside him!

"Get ready to duck!" said Tioga. He knew they were well within the range of an accomplished archer.

Kopi turned and saw the threat. "I'm glad I've still got my helmet. It's arrow proof." With that said, Kopi kicked like his life depended on it.

Pox looked out at the river and spotted the two boys splashing up a storm. He slowly rose to his feet, but rather than grabbing the bow, he made a surprising gesture—he saluted Tioga in the Mononga fashion. The boy had defeated him in a fair fight and deserved his respect.

Tioga instinctively saluted back, then went back to swimming. The scout quickly faded into the distance.

"Keep kicking!" shouted Tioga. The trees rolled by at a disturbing rate. The current was picking up speed.

"It's too late," said Kopi. "We're not going to make it. Here comes the crossing spot."

Kopi was right. The shallow stretch of water known as the north ford came into view a hundred yards downstream. It was loaded with Mononga warriors. Hanna was in plain view on top of a stretcher carried by four men, and beside them was Grandfather Ötzi.

"You go on ahead," said Kopi. "You can still make it to shore in time. I'll stay and distract them."

"I'm not leaving you, Kopi."

"Then they'll get us both."

"Not if we go under," said Tioga. "Hold onto the raft and get as low as you can in the water."

Kopi did as instructed. He stopped when his lips touched the waves. "This isn't going to work. They'll still see us."

"Not if we're submerged," said Tioga, as he thrust his hand into the stalks of the float.

"I can't hold my breath that long," said Kopi. "My lungs can't do it."

"You won't have to. When I was cutting, I saw some thistle reeds. Ouch! I think I found one." Tioga pulled out a dry, prickly stalk. He looked Kopi straight in the eye. "Do you trust me, Kopi?"

"Of course, I trust you."

"Then you've got to do what I'm about to tell you. There is a way we can get by without being seen."

"How?" said Kopi, hoping for a miracle.

"It's an old scout's trick to hide underwater." Tioga quickly broke the reed in two, and ended up with a pair of straws, each about two feet in length. He held them up to the light to make sure they were clear. "See? They're hollow." He handed one to Kopi. "Here's your air tube."

"Air tube? I don't like the sound of this."

"You move to one end of the float and I'll move to the other," said Tioga. "Lift your feet up and hook them into the ropes under the raft."

Tioga moved into position. Kopi hesitantly did the same. Tioga took one last look at the war party. He could see Shingas clearly in the lead. They hadn't been spotted—yet. The water was getting rougher, as the current sped up at the shallow ford.

"Here we go," said Tioga. "Put the reed into your mouth. Hold your nose with one hand and the bottom of the raft with the other. Then lower your head underwater and breathe through the tube."

"It's not big enough!"

"Yes, it is," said Tioga. "If you breathe slowly. Just stay under and we'll float right by them and on to the village."

"But…"

"Get under," hissed Tioga.

Kopi reached up to his head and took off his turtle shell helmet. He gingerly placed it atop the raft.

"Forget the helmet," pleaded Tioga.

"Turtles ride logs all the time," said Kopi.

"Alright, just get under," said Tioga.

Kopi saw Shingas up ahead. The sight of the warlord did the trick. He shoved the reed into his mouth, pinched his nose, and dunked his head under. Tioga quickly did the same.

Breathing through the tube while hanging upside down was challenging. Tioga fought off the urge to surface and tried to relax.

Things were quiet under the water. The brilliant sunlight danced on the surface in a thousand different patterns. Tioga tried to focus on peaceful images, like the serenity of the forest and the flight of the eagle.

Kopi was having a more difficult time. He struggled to breathe through the tiny opening. It seemed that every breath was shallower than the last. Time seemed to stand still. His ribs ached. He was running out of air.

Shingas paused in the middle of the river. He scanned the valley for signs of movement. Something wasn't quite right. He could sense it. He watched the approach of a bunch of reeds bobbing in the river. A lone turtle clung to the top, sunning itself in the last warm rays of the day. If it felt threatened, he knew the turtle would slip off the float and vanish beneath the surface. The trouble he sensed must be in the other direction. Shingas turned his attention downstream.

Tioga felt his back slip over a moss-covered rock. He could see the riffles above them. He knew they must be near the center of the shallows. In a few more minutes they would be past the war party.

Elder Ötzi also spotted the reeds with the turtle on top, as well as the rope that bound the float together. *It must be the boys! I must create a diversion.*

Ötzi grabbed the side of Hanna's stretcher and let out a scream as he intentionally fell. As he went under, he pulled on the side of the pallet, causing it to tip over. Hanna shrieked as she hit the water and submerged.

Shingas turned back at the commotion. "Get the girl!" he commanded. He grimaced at the ineptitude of his men as they wrestled with the overturned stretcher.

Several other warriors sprang into action and quickly raised the bound hostage up out of the water. Ötzi surfaced and noticed the reed raft was right behind Shingas.

Kopi was terrified. His heart was pounding. The air wasn't coming fast enough. The feeling of suffocation was more than he could stand. He moved the tube aside and broke the surface with his mouth. He stole three quick breaths and went back under. He put the tube back between his lips and breathed in. It had filled with water! He choked as the fluid rushed into his lungs.

Tioga felt Kopi panic. He had been thinking about surfacing anyway. Breathing through the narrow tube was next to impossible in such trying conditions.

Tioga burst through the surface and stood up in the water. He grabbed Kopi by the arm and helped him stand. Kopi coughed up some water and struggled to his feet. The two boys stood exposed only yards from Shingas.

"Are we there already?" asked Kopi hopefully. He grabbed his turtle-shell helmet off the raft and crammed it back on his head.

"Run!" ordered Tioga. Then he let out an ear-splitting war cry. "Ya-wee, ya-woo!"

Shingas turned to the sound behind him. He was shocked to see two river goblins. Then he recognized it was just ashy war paint.

"It's those ghost boys!" he screamed. "Get them!"

"Kopi! This way!" yelled Tioga. He pushed through the pain and stumbled toward shore. Kopi was about to pass him, but reached back and pulled Tioga along. The boys splashed through the shallows as arrows whisked by their heads.

"Head for the cattails!" said Tioga. They dove into the cover of the reeds just as one of Shingas's lances hit Kopi in the head. It deflected off the side of his helmet and vanished in the grass.

"My shell!" cried Kopi, reaching up to feel the damage. "He cracked it!"

"I need help," huffed Tioga, as he struggled to climb the muddy bank.

"Climb aboard!" ordered Kopi. "Just watch my ribs."

Tioga jumped on Kopi's back and they moved out of the water and into the forest. They clearly heard Shingas bellow, "Warriors, cut them off on the trail! There is only one way to the village. Don't follow them into the trees. It could be an ambush!"

Most of the fighters angled downstream to beat the boys to the path. But two overzealous young men either ignored the call or didn't hear the order. They ran into the forest in hot pursuit. For once Tioga wished the men had followed Shingas's order.

"There is no way we can outrun them on the path," said Tioga. "We've got to take a short cut. Over the ridge!" He pointed Kopi toward a steep hillside in front of them.

Kopi ran full speed ahead but slowed when he looked up at the mountain towering over them. "You call that a ridge? It's more like a cliff."

"Come on! We can do it!"

Kopi started to climb, but quickly stalled.

"It's too steep!" said Kopi. "You've got to get off."

Tioga slipped from his friend's back and grabbed a sapling. The trees actually made it easier for him to climb, as his arms did most of the work. Kopi followed Tioga's example, and they soon reached the top of the ridge.

Tioga turned and scanned the forest. He had a commanding view of the terrain below them. He spotted two warriors approaching. They hadn't seen the boys yet—they were too busy following Kopi's tracks.

"Shouldn't we keep going?" asked Kopi.

"Shh..." said Tioga. "Get down. Here they come."

The two men arrived at the base of the hill and swiftly began the climb. As soon as they reached the steepest part, Tioga pushed over a large rock. It bounced down the steep slope and flew over the lead warrior's head. Kopi followed his example and sent an old tree stump over the cliff. It thundered down the hill toward the men.

"It's an ambush!" yelled the lead warrior, taking cover.

Before the other man could react, the stump crashed into his chest, knocking him in somersaults back down the hill.

"Nice shot," said Tioga.

"Thanks!" said Kopi, laughing. "It was a pretty good shot, wasn't it?"

"Look, they don't want to play anymore," said Tioga. They watched as one warrior dragged his injured comrade back toward the river.

Kopi surprised Tioga by letting out blood-curdling ghost shriek. The haunting scream echoed through the trees.

"Ouch," said Tioga, rubbing his ringing ear. "Was that really necessary?"

"Tioga, you can't just look the part. You gotta act scary too."

"I guess you're right."

"Climb on my back. We've got to beat them to the village."

Tioga jumped aboard and Kopi moved to the far side of the ridge. They stopped abruptly at the top of a cliff. Kopi could see the glistening waters of Slippery Stone Creek far below them.

"You're gonna have to get off," said Kopi. "I can't climb down with you riding me."

"We can't go down here," said Tioga, eyeing the landscape. "It's too steep. Bear Cave is directly below us."

"Too bad we don't have a rope."

"A rope?" said Tioga. Kopi's comment jogged a memory in his head. "Good idea! Head west along the ridge. There's another short cut!"

Kopi followed the instructions and trotted along the knife edge of the ridge. He had only gone about a hundred yards when Tioga shouted. "There it is! The zip-line!"

Kopi looked up and saw what his friend was referring to. Six months ago, Tioga had strung up a long thin rope from a tree at the top of the ridge to the valley below. The distant end vanished in the leaves on the far side of the creek.

"Oh no, not that thing," huffed Kopi. "I wouldn't do it before, and I'm not doing it now."

"Come on," pleaded Tioga. "It will be way faster than climbing down. And easier on my ankle."

Kopi stopped beside the taut rope and shook his head. "I wasn't born to fly. Plus, there is only one harness."

Tioga realized that was true. The harness could only take a single person. And if Tioga rode on Kopi's back, the combined weight of both of them would probably snap the rope.

"You take the zip-line, and I'll go down the old fashioned way," said Kopi. "Whoever gets to the bottom first should warn the village."

"Deal!" said Tioga. The words had hardly left his mouth when Kopi bolted down the hill as if a race had just started. But Tioga knew this wasn't a game. The fate of the tribe was in their hands.

Tioga stepped into the harness and checked the loop that was strung over the top line. The harness was uncomfortably tight. He realized he must have grown a lot in past few months. Tioga ran his eyes along the length of the span. The rope was covered in green moss and was frayed in several spots. It dawned on him that he was taking a serious risk. If the rope broke, he might fall to his death.

He considered aborting the plan, but Kopi was already half way down the hill. With his bad ankle, Tioga doubted he could climb down without help. But if he called Kopi back, they would lose valuable time. He decided the risk of falling was worth the reward of saving the village.

Tioga said a quick prayer, checked his bindings one more time, and pushed off into thin air. The zip-line did its job and he was quickly flying down the hill between the tree tops.

As Kopi flashed by beneath his feet, Tioga yelled, "If the rope breaks forget about me! Keep going!"

If Kopi answered, Tioga never heard it. He was picking up speed at an alarming rate. An involuntary shriek escaped his lips. He decide to embellish it with a full blown war cry. It empowered him in an out of control situation.

The waters of Slippery Stone Creek rushed by beneath him. Tioga looked up as he sped toward the thick canopy of trees. He suddenly wondered if the pile of straw he had placed at the end would still be in place. It was essential to cushion the impact. Before he could think of it further, he burst through the leaves and slammed into the straw. Thankfully the pile was more or less in place, although somewhat deflated from exposure. The collision knocked the wind out of Tioga's lungs.

It took him a minute to recover and step out of the harness. Even then, it was clear he had beaten Kopi to this point. Tioga looked into the thick forest in the direction of the village. His ankle was throbbing, but he prepared to move ahead as they had discussed. Just then, Tioga heard the sound of water splashing and a familiar thud.

Kopi's cursing echoed through the trees, "Darn it! Not again! I hate this creek!"

"I'm over here!" yelled Tioga.

A moment later Kopi's dripping form appeared in the trees. He ran to Tioga to make up for lost time.

"You slipped and fell in the creek again?" asked Tioga.

"I figured I was wet from the river anyway. So why not take a dip? How was the ride down?"

Tioga climbed on his best friend's back. "Awesome. I forgot how much fun it is to fly like an eagle. We should do that more often."

"Yeah, right," said Kopi sarcastically.

Kopi picked up speed and charged through the timbers. He even leapt over a fallen log without missing a beat. He burst from the trees into a field of waving tan grass. The village wall gleamed in the sunlight at the far side of the meadow. Tioga could see the Allegewi flag waving to them in the strong breeze.

"Home sweet home!" cried Tioga.

"Give the warning cry," gasped Kopi.

Tioga screamed, "Whupa! Whupa! Woo!"

The boys listened for the expected response, but heard nothing but the leaves rustling in the wind.

Kopi slowed down and looked concerned. "Maybe they saw the war party coming and ran off."

"To where? This is the Allegewi homeland."

Just then a welcome call floated across the meadow. Kopi cried out and dashed for home. A tear slipped out of Tioga's eye at the sight of the village. He never thought he would be so glad to see its humble walls. Kopi ran to the main gate, which was opened at their approach. Tioga could hear the buzz of news rushing through the village as Kopi stumbled through the portal.

"Close the gate!" said Tioga to the old guard as he slipped from Kopi's back. "We're under attack!" The elder complied, but didn't recognize the ghostly warrior giving the order.

The boys were greeted by expressions of shock and disbelief. Several children screamed and bolted at the sight of the phantoms, but thankfully several adults recognized them. Word of their return spread like wildfire through the tribe.

Tioga scanned the crowd as they rushed to greet the lost boys. His heart sank at the lack of men in the village. The hunters had not yet returned.

"We're under attack!" yelled Tioga. The noise of the excited mob drowned out his warning.

Kopi's father ran up and swept his son off his feet. "Kopi, you look like a skeleton!" said Pocano. "You're just skin, and bones—and muscle! Where did you get all these muscles?"

Kopi's mother, Nairobi, joined the embrace. Kopi yelped in pain at the double bear hug. "Ouch, my ribs!"

"You're voice!" said Nairobi. "It's so raspy! Do you have a sore throat?"

"It's a long story," croaked Kopi.

Just then Candowsa's voice rose above the clamor, "Tioga?" She burst through the throng and wrapped her arms around her only child. "Oh, Tioga, I thought you were dead."

"Mom, I'm fine, but we're about to be—"

"Look at you," interrupted Candowsa. "You look like you were wrestling a bear!" Realizing the poor choice of words, she quickly added, "I mean a mountain lion!"

"I'm fine," said Tioga. It felt good to be back in her arms, but he broke from her embrace. "Mom, I've got to speak with the chief. We're under attack."

"Attack?" said Candowsa. Fear spread through her muscular frame. "By whom?"

Tioga was afraid to tell her. After all these years, her nightmare still wasn't over. "Don't worry, Mother. I will protect you." Before she could respond, he pulled away and limped toward the chief's lodge.

As he struggled through the crowd, Lenni appeared and blocked his path. "Well look who finally found his way home," taunted Lenni. "Claw, you look like death warmed over!"

Tioga punched Lenni in the gut with a strength he didn't know he possessed. The taller boy crumpled to the ground and rolled aside. "I owed you that," said Tioga as he stepped over the bully. Then Tioga spotted the chief emerging from his lodge.

"Chief Tundra!" said Tioga breathlessly. "The Mononga are on our doorstep!"

"Tioga? Is that you?" Before the chief could say more, a Mononga war cry shrieked from the forest and a flaming arrow fell from the sky. It landed in the village plaza just yards from them and stuck in the dry ground.

The villagers gasped at the apocalyptic omen. Fire was the most feared force in the village. Once one house was ablaze, the others usually followed—especially if the wind was as strong as it was today. There was little the tribe could do to defend against an attack by fire. The only hope was to meet the enemy on the field, before the village was bombarded.

The crowd held their breath and waited for the barrage to begin. Instead a lone Mononga voice carried over the palisade walls. "Allegewi? Peace?"

"It is Shingas... the Mononga Devil," said Tioga to the chief. "He's using Hanna to lure you out. But he can't be trusted."

"Hanna?" responded Chief Tundra. "She is here?" He left Tioga, climbed the tower, and looked out over the stockade wall. He was visibly shaken at the sight of his daughter with the infamous warlord. He barely recognized her skinny frame and short-cropped hair. Like the boys, she was painted in ash.

Tioga pressed his face to the wall and looked through a gap between in the logs. Shingas stood at a safe distance holding Hanna beside him. She looked terrified. Shingas still wore Tioga's bone charm around his neck. Tioga felt his mother arrive by his side. She was trembling. He wrapped his arm around her shoulder.

"Chief Tundra," said Shingas, "do you speak Mononga?"

"A bit," said the chief, understating his fluency. "What evil do you bring us this day?"

"It is a pleasure to finally meet you in person," said Shingas with a smile. "I believe we have met on the battlefield before, correct?"

"Perhaps," said the chief. "I have fought more than I care to remember."

"Yes, of course," said Shingas, secretly insulted that the Allegewi leader didn't remember him. "At your age, your memory must be weak."

The chief didn't respond to the insult.

Shingas was annoyed that he had to play games to get Candowsa back. Part of him wanted to unleash the firestorm now to show the old man who was boss. But he didn't want to end up holding Candy's charred torso. He wanted to hold her warm, fragrant flesh, as he had done so many years before.

Shingas resumed his charm offensive. "For many years our tribes have battled. And at what price? Both sides have lost many good men... and women. It is time to finish the conflict between us. The Mononga have made peace with all the other tribes in the valley. Now it is time to do so with the Allegewi."

"You have made slaves of the other tribes," said the chief. "We would rather die in battle than by starvation."

"I see," said Shingas. "I did not come here for your food. I came to propose a trade. Your daughter for the Mononga woman you call Candowsa."

Tioga cringed when he heard his mother's name and Candowsa gasped. He had figured that Shingas might propose such an exchange, but watching it happen was a nightmare. "Don't worry, Mom," whispered Tioga. "You are safe with me."

Shingas continued, "Candowsa's aging father anxiously awaits her return." He pointed to the tree line behind him, and on cue, Ötzi the Iceman stepped into the meadow. Each of his arms was held by a warrior. It was clear to Tioga that his grandfather was being used against his will.

Candowsa strained to recognize the disfigured old man in the distance. "Father?" she mumbled to herself as she peered between the logs.

"It is our tradition to honor an old man's dying wish," said Shingas. "You see, he will be dying very soon. I assure you it is the truth."

"Candowsa is Allegewi," said the chief. "I do not value one tribe member more than any other. The trade cannot be made."

"Surely a young girl is worth more than a middle-aged woman? Especially if the girl is the chief's only child."

"Only the Creator can judge the value of one's life," said Chief Tundra. "The trade cannot be made."

"I don't think you understand the situation," said Shingas with a smile on his lips. "Look to the field behind you. My warriors stand ready to help you with your decision." Then Shingas bellowed a single war cry, "Moon-aaaan-gaaaa!"

The chief studied the large, grassy meadow that overlooked the village. For many years the field had grown bountiful crops. Then the soil had soured. Now only waist-high scrub grass grew there, bending in the breeze.

The villagers gasped as an impressive force of Mononga warriors emerged from the trees and marched into the meadow. Every fourth man held a flaming torch. The others stood at the ready to light their flaming arrows With a single command, the village would be engulfed in a firestorm. Later, the victors would round up any who escaped the flames.

Tioga studied the enemy force with particular interest. The flaming torches glowed against the backdrop of the darkening forest. *Of course!* thought Tioga. *Why didn't I think of it sooner?*

"May I have council with the village elders?" asked Chief Tundra to the warlord.

"You have until the sun drops over the horizon," replied Shingas. He didn't want to delay the attack, but he wanted Candowsa back in his arms before the village burned.

"The time is too short," said the chief. "The sun is ready to fall into the trees."

"Well then, you'd better hurry," said Shingas, "or fire will take the place of the sun in lighting up your pathetic village!"

The chief climbed down with Master Dudley's assistance and quickly huddled with his council.

Candowsa was numb. She fell to her knees in shock. Tioga held her tightly. "I won't let them take you," he said. "I'm going to stop it."

Candowsa responded weakly, as if in a trance, "We must abide by the council's decision." For years she had feared Shingas's return. Somehow, she had known that day would eventually come.

Tioga watched the village elders gather at the base of the wall. In the past he had always trusted their judgement. Now they looked old and frail.

"Mom, I'll be back," said Tioga. He left Candowsa and limped over near the council.

Elder Gron saw him coming. He greeted the boy who had died and returned as a man. He bowed before his protégé and pulled something from his belt. "Tioga, you fought bravely." He formally presented Tioga with his war hatchet. "I have won many battles with this. Now it is yours to keep."

"Thank you, Elder Gron. This is a great honor," said Tioga as he accepted the weapon. "But you might still need it. The battle isn't over."

"I'm afraid it is," said Gron. Tioga could see the sadness in the old man's eyes. "The vote was unanimous."

Tioga looked at the council as the chief addressed the circle of elders. He moved forward to eavesdrop.

"We are in agreement," said the chief. "We have no choice but to turn Candowsa over."

Tioga was stunned by the statement. Before he knew it, he was moving forward. He burst into the sacred circle.

"It is a trick!" shouted Tioga. "The Mononga Devil has not come for peace. He has come to destroy us!"

The council was shocked at the boy's bold intrusion. Dudley grabbed Tioga and pulled him away. But Tioga twisted free from his grasp and hopped back to the elders.

"I know this man," said Tioga. "I have seen into his heart. He is wicked and evil. If we give in to his demands, he will take what he wants and then burn the village. But there is a way to stop him!"

The council erupted in renewed debate. Dudley barked, "The boy is just trying to save his mother! Angering the Mononga warlord will ensure our destruction! With our fighting men gone, we are in no position to negotiate."

"Look at our flag!" said Tioga, pointing to the pole. "The wind blows to the north. We must meet them on the field of battle. Fire against fire!"

Everyone was talking at once. The chief cut through the chaos. "Silence!" The group grudgingly obeyed. "It is decided. There is no way we can fight against fire. We must hope that the Mononga leader is good for his word. Go get Candowsa. I will take her out myself."

Tioga slowly backed away. He watched as the chief headed toward his mother, who sat alone at the foot of the wall. Even from a distance he could see her trembling. Tioga wanted to run to her, but instead he turned and hobbled to the farthest end of the village.

# Twenty-Eight

Chief Tundra opened the main gate just as the crescent sun vanished over the horizon. He moved forward with Candowsa, who bravely tried to control her fear. She looked over her shoulder and frantically eyed the crowd, searching for the son she had lost and then found. She let out a wail, "Tioga!"

When Kopi heard Candowsa's cry, he snapped into action. He left his family and ran through the crowd looking for his best friend. The village was in chaos. He couldn't spot Tioga in the mix of shouting old men, crying women, and shrieking children.

The chief led Candowsa through the front gate. She could see Shingas smiling in the waist-deep grass in the middle of the field. The sight of the grotesque warlord sickened her. Then her eyes fell on young Hanna. So alone and afraid. Candowsa calmed. She knew it was better to sacrifice her own life than to leave the child with such a monster. She stood tall and walked down the path without hesitation.

Kopi climbed the guard tower and scanned the crowd. Tioga was nowhere in sight. But he did notice something strange. An elderly guard was closing the rear gate of the palisade. Kopi jumped down sprinted through the village. He nearly collided with the man at the back gate.

"I guess you're going out too," said the sentry.

Kopi nodded and squeezed out the exit. He immediately spotted Tioga's tracks in the dirt. He followed them around the wall and noticed the footprints changed to scuff marks. *He's crawling*, thought Kopi. He smelled burning oil. Kopi dropped down and followed the trail into the tall grass. He spotted Tioga's rump up ahead and snuck up behind him.

Kopi pinched him in the butt. "Want some help?"

"Kopi!" said a startled Tioga. He nearly burned himself with the flaming lamp in his left hand. "Don't scare me like that."

"What are you doing with the ceremonial flame?" asked Kopi. "Only a shaman is supposed to carry it."

"Here, then you hold it," said Tioga, handing Kopi the mystic's lamp. "Don't set the grass on fire—yet."

"What are we doing?"

"I've got a riddle for you," said Tioga. "What's the only weapon a boy can wield that's powerful enough to stop an army dead in its tracks?"

"Fire?"

"Kopi, you are beginning to think like a warlord!"

"So, what are we burning?"

Tioga licked his finger, and raised it into the air. "If this breeze holds, you'll be burning up a Mononga war party. They're standing right in the middle of a field of dry tinder."

"But that field is my favorite place to find box turtles," lamented Kopi.

"Come on!" groaned Tioga.

"I'm kidding."

Tioga shook his head in disbelief. Kopi was remarkably calm under the circumstances. "Do you think you can handle the army while I deal with Shingas?" asked Tioga.

"Yes, sir!"

"Then crawl into the field and wait for my signal," said Tioga. "Make sure no one sees you. If we can, I want to avoid this. It's a big risk to take. If the winds shift, we'll burn down the village."

"Oh," said Kopi, swallowing deeply. "What's the signal?"

"The eagle's cry. If you hear it, light the grass and get out of there fast. And don't worry about the turtles."

"You're going after Hanna, aren't you?"

"Not just Hanna. I'm going after Mom too."

"I just got a vision," said Kopi. "We're going to have a victory celebration tonight. Complete with turtle soup!"

Tioga flashed Kopi a smile and crawled into the underbrush. When he glanced back, his best friend was gone. Tioga wondered whether it would be the last time he ever saw him. He knew the odds were stacked against them. Tioga pushed the thought out of his mind and moved deeper into the meadow. He crawled through waving grass and worked his way toward the voices. As he moved closer, he recognized the chief's distinctive tone.

"You are unarmed, correct?" asked Chief Tundra.

"Of course," said Shingas. "I would not bring a weapon to a family reunion."

"Candowsa must mean a lot to her father for you to come all this way," said the chief. "Or maybe you are the one who wants her so badly?"

"Quit stalling," said Shingas. "Give her to me now or I might get angry. And you don't want to see me angry. Right, Candy?"

Tioga inched closer. During the last week he had become an expert at stealth. It somehow came very naturally to him—like a cat stalking a mouse. He stopped twenty feet away the chief. Peering through the grass, he could see his mother's moccasins on the dusty path.

"An even exchange," said Chief Tundra. "Candowsa for my daughter."

"That's right," said Shingas.

"And then you and your men will leave here in peace, as you promised?"

"Of course," said Shingas, smiling. "Now send over my bride."

Tioga snaked his way forward until he caught a glimpse of Shingas's grizzly-bear cape. He saw Hanna's bare legs trembling. Tioga's upper lip twitched unconsciously as every muscle in his lean body tensed.

The chief stayed in place and guided Candowsa forward. She walked emotionlessly toward the man of her nightmares.

Shingas stood proudly before her. The last time she had seen him he had been just a boy. Now he was the most powerful man in the land! *She must be impressed!* he thought.

"Send me my daughter," said the chief. Shingas released Hanna. She sprinted past Candowsa and fell into her father's arms. Tioga could hear Hanna's sobs of joy.

Tioga snuck forward so he could see the warlord's face. Shingas's eyes were locked on his mother. The tyrant glowed with the euphoria of another conquest. But there was also a softer side in his stare—the hope of fulfilling an eternal dream. He smiled and pulled her to him. He tried to kiss her on the lips, but she turned away. It was a reaction he clearly didn't expect. For a moment he stood there like a hurt child. His face wrinkled up and his lip trembled. Then his jaw grew tight. He exploded in anger and threw her to the ground.

Tioga held back the urge to charge. He would bide his time. Even if it meant following Shingas all the way back into the mountains.

The tyrant turned from Candowsa and looked back at Hanna and her father. The sight of their emotional reunion disgusted him. He grabbed Candowsa by the hair and dragged her violently behind him. Then he reached into the tall grass and manipulated something with his powerful right hand.

A chill ran down Tioga's spine when he saw a villainous smile curve over Shingas's lips. Tioga's suspicions were confirmed when the warlord stood up with a spear in his hand. Tioga slowly pulled Elder Gron's hatchet from his belt. He stayed low, but rose to one knee.

In a flash, Shingas cocked his arm and aimed his lance directly at Hanna and Chief Tundra. They were unaware of the danger. Tioga envisioned the spear running them both through. Shingas stepped forward to launch the deadly weapon.

Tioga exploded from cover and threw his tomahawk at Shingas's head with all his might. At the same instant, Shingas fired his lance. The hatchet spun through the air with impressive speed as the spear flashed by in the opposite direction. The hatchet struck Shingas's throat with a *thud*, but the butt end of the handle made contact, rather than the blade! It bounced off the stunned victim's neck and vanished into the grass.

Tioga turned and followed the lance's flight. In the blink of an eye it closed the distance, heading straight toward Hanna and her father, who were still in a tight embrace. She screamed as the spear passed through them.

Tioga waited to see who would fall first, remembering the elk killed by the river. Instead Hanna lifted her arm and exposed a thin red groove along its length. Blood began to run from the wound. The chief picked up his daughter and ran for the village gate.

Shingas staggered backward from the force of the blow to his windpipe. His hand grasped his neck, and a weak croak escaped his lips. Then he locked eyes with the ghost boy.

Tioga pulled his knife and charged the man in a fury. Shingas deflected the blade as Tioga collided with the barrel-chested warrior. He bounced back and landed into the dirt and the knife flew from his hand and vanished in the grass. The attack distracted the tyrant just long enough for Candowsa to jump up and kick him in the crotch.

"Run, Mom! Run!" yelled Tioga as he scrambled to his feet. Candowsa had never heard her son's voice boom with such power. She obeyed his command and sprinted for home.

Shingas stumbled for a moment and then took off after her. He quickly closed the gap as they ran into the shadow of the palisade. He was almost to her when a barrage of arrows fell between them. Shingas skidded to a stop, narrowly avoiding the projectiles.

"Come no closer!" yelled Lenni from the tower, with his bow drawn tight, "or you will feel the flint of my arrow!"

Shingas moved back out of range and watched in frustration as Candowsa, Hanna, and her father disappeared behind the thick oak door. *Enough of this foolishness!* he thought. *Let them burn in hell!* He looked up to the field where his stunned warriors stood, still holding their flaming torches. He opened his mouth to give the order to fire, but all that came out was a weak *croak*. He tried again but his damaged vocal cords sounded like a lonely bullfrog. The cheering of the villagers drowned out his command. Shingas waved his arm in an effort to signal the attack, but Chemung and the others waited in confusion. They wouldn't dare to launch the flaming arrows without the agreed-upon order.

Shingas turned in anger towards the demon boy who had ruined his moment. Tioga was searching the grass in vain for a weapon. He looked up and stared into the warlord's bloodshot eyes.

"You will be the first to die," rasped Shingas in a coarse whisper. "But the rest of your tribe will soon follow."

Tioga responded with the piercing cry of the eagle. Its sharp, clear tone cut through the turmoil and echoed through the valley. The eagle's shriek surprised Shingas. By the time he regained his composure, Tioga was running north, straight for the forest. Adrenaline had numbed the pain in his ankle. He wasn't up to his normal speed, but he was moving.

Shingas grabbed his last spear and charged after Tioga with the fury of an angry bear. Chemung and the others were frozen with indecision. They didn't know whether to hold their position or join the chase.

Before they could decide, Tioga ducked into a hemlock grove. Shingas wasn't far behind and soon vanished into the forest.

Tioga darted through the trees like they were his second home. He stopped for a moment to check whether he was being followed. The crack of branches answered the question. A sense of calm came over him. Hanna and his mother were out of the tyrant's grasp, at least for the moment. He wondered if Kopi had heard his signal.

Tioga was surprised to hear an eagle's cry from above. He looked up through a break in the trees and saw the silhouette of the raptor floating high in sky. He laughed out loud at the sight of the unexpected companion. If the eagle had heard him, then hopefully Kopi did too.

He turned his attention back to his course. This was his playground. He knew every bush, tree, and stone. He grabbed a stick to use as a cane and limped through the forest. Without hesitation, he splashed into the waters of Slippery Stone Creek. He carefully crossed the stream without missing a step.

Tioga emerged from the creek and stood among the boulders on the far bank. He paused and looked up at the cliff above him. It was almost a fatal mistake. Out of the corner of his eye, he thought he spotted a bear. A speeding lance missed his chest by inches and impaled a sapling with a *crack*. The bear was Shingas!

Tioga began climbing the rocky slope toward the cave where he and Kopi had played a lifetime ago. Shingas charged into the water after him. Tioga heard a heavy splash and a grunt. Slippery Stone Creek had lived up to its name.

From the cover of a boulder, Tioga secretly watched the one-armed man struggle to regain his footing. *He's out of spears! That was his third shot!* If the warlord climbed toward him, Tioga could drop rocks on his head. Would it be enough to stop a charging bear?

Shingas stumbled across the creek and immediately went to the tree that held his last lance. The tip had passed clean through the trunk and emerged from the other side.

*There is no way he is getting that spear free*, thought Tioga. But Shingas grabbed the sapling and worked his fingers into the crack. With a grunt he split the tree from top to bottom and the lance fell free. It was an impressive feat of strength that shook Tioga's confidence. The man was now re-armed and Tioga had no weapons. But he did have a plan. He turned and resumed his climb, making sure to leave a clear trail.

Just as he reached the narrow plateau in front of Bear Cave, Tioga's ankle gave out. It twisted in grotesque fashion, and he crashed to the ground. He shrieked in agony and grabbed his leg. But it wasn't enough to stop him. He pushed through the pain and crawled forward to the mouth of the cave. The cool breath of the cavern spirit blew in his face. He took one last look at the bountiful green forest behind him and crawled inside.

As the darkness enveloped him, he paused to allow his eyes to adjust. The musky scent of beaver oil lingered on the stale air. He could hear Shingas climbing up the loose gravel outside. Tioga moved forward through a thick spider's web. He smiled as the sticky threads blanketed his face. It was a good sign. A bear hadn't taken the bait—yet.

"There's no escape, little boy," hissed Shingas from outside the crevice. "Come out now and I will spare your life."

Tioga kept crawling.

"Are you afraid of the dark, little boy?" asked Shingas.

Tioga inched through the narrowing passage. Though he could barely see, he knew exactly where he was. He stopped and gingerly touched the suspended log. He breathed a sigh of relief. *It's still in place!* He carefully crawled under the dead fall trap.

"Well, I am not!" bellowed Shingas's voice, recovering all its former fury. Several bats dropped from the ceiling and swirled over Tioga's head. He ignored them.

"Do you think a man with the bear as his totem is afraid of a cave?" asked Shingas to the darkness.

Tioga thought about the question and responded, "No, I think the little boy inside the man is afraid. And that fear is stronger than the bear's spirit."

Shingas growled in anger at the ghostly voice emanating from the cavern. He dropped to his knees and clawed his way into the den. As he moved forward, a bat brushed over his back and disappeared out the entrance. He gasped and swung his spear at the flapping phantom.

Shingas's body blocked out all the remaining light. Total darkness swallowed the opponents. Tioga felt a large spider crawling across his cheek. He was too focused to move. It burrowed into the thick hair behind his ear.

Tioga heard the sound of heavy breathing as the warlord came closer. A strange scraping sound echoed through the cave. A white spark flashed in the darkness as Shingas's flint spear tip contacted the sandstone wall. He was probing the cave with his hand-held lance. The sparks moved forward like fireflies in the night. The spear's tip skidded by Tioga's cheek. He heard it retract and then rush forward again. If the lance triggered the trap, the game would be over.

Tioga coiled and waited for the next thrust. He heard the point glance off the wall and pass by his ribs. With the quickness of a cat,

Tioga's right hand grabbed the shaft. He twisted with all his might in an attempt to snap the lance in half.

"You want to play?" said Shingas. He yanked the spear back. Its jagged flint tip ripped through Tioga's palm.

Tioga yelped and fell forward into the dirt. The heavy log teetered over his head.

Hearing the boy fall, Shingas dropped his weapon and reached for his opponent. As Tioga struggled to crawl back, a viselike grip grabbed his left wrist. Tioga knew he was a hair away from tripping the log and having his spine shattered.

He wedged his foot against the wall and pulled back, gaining a few inches. His wrist seemed to catch fire as Shingas's sharp fingernails dug into his flesh.

Tioga's strength was fading. He knew he could never out muscle the giant before him. The next pull would send him hurtling forward. Though he couldn't see Shingas's face, he knew the sickening smile would be upon it.

Shingas laughed at the sound of the boy's useless thrashing. He had won! No captive ever escaped the Mononga Devil! As soon as he could pin the boy beneath him, he would cut off his head and leave his body to rot in this hell hole.

Shingas leaned forward to strengthen his grip. As he did, Tioga felt his opponent's arm slacken. He pulled back with all his might, and caught the man off guard. The tyrant lost his balance and fell head first into the dust with a grunt. For a moment, the two adversaries were face-to-face in the darkness.

"Boo!" shouted Tioga as he lurched back, bumping the support stick.

A strange sound above him caused Shingas to pause. It was the groan of splintering wood. An instant later a thunderous crash vibrated through the cavern. Tioga heard bone *crack*, followed by a painful cry.

The Devil's grip fell away from Tioga's wrist. A faint beam of light cut through the swirling dust. Tioga could see the heavy log in front of him with a hand sticking out from under it. Just beyond it was Shingas's head. It raised up and cried out, "Help me! My arm! My only arm!"

Tioga sat back and watched the surreal scene. The battle was over. He couldn't believe it. He had won! He had beaten the Mononga

Devil in hand-to-hand combat! He thought of his father and his first war trophy. Now Tioga had earned the right to take his own prize.

As Shingas whimpered, Tioga crossed the log and climbed onto the back of his victim. He reached down and pulled Shingas's huge knife from its sheath.

The warlord burst into tears and pleaded, "Please spare my life. I will be your slave!"

Tioga ignored the comment and calmly put the knife to Shingas's throat—then sliced free the necklace that was rightly his. He took back the bone relic and climbed off his prisoner.

Tioga sat back against the cold stone wall and tied the necklace around his own neck. It felt good to have his father's charm back where it belonged. Then he remembered the old arrowhead in his pocket. He pulled it out and held it up. Was it just a trick of the light, or was it glowing? For a split second, he thought he saw Dad's face smiling at him from the shadows. Then his father's voice entered his head. *"Well done, son! You wrestled the bear and won!"*

Tioga watched the fine dust swirling in the air. It reminded him of the way smoke sometimes danced around his hut in windy weather. He wondered if he still had a hut to go home to.

# Twenty-Nine

Tioga crawled from the mouth of the cave, holding one end of the hemp rope that he had salvaged from the bear trap. He gave it a light tug and Shingas snaked forward with a freshly made choke snare around his neck.

Tioga had smelled the fire from inside the cave. Even so, he wasn't prepared for the sight before him. A thick gray cloud enveloped the entire forest. A blood red sky was visible through the treetops. The drifting smoke burned Tioga's eyes. Tears ran down his dusty cheeks.

"Stand up," said Tioga to his prisoner. Without a working arm, Shingas couldn't even do that. Tioga pulled him to his feet and climbed onto his back. "You know the way," said Tioga.

Shingas gingerly climbed down the rocks with his arm dangling uselessly beside him. He had broken down inside the cave and begged for mercy. His spirit had been shattered as dramatically as the bones in his arm.

As Shingas carefully crossed the creek, Tioga could hear the frantic cries of his tribemates in the distance. In the fading light, ash floated down from above like snowflakes. The shock of the unthinkable ran through Tioga's brain—the village had burned. He had tried his best, but now it was over. The Mononga had won. A life without his tribe was unthinkable, so he rode Shingas forward to join his people and their fate. Finally, the trees thinned and a blackened field appeared before them.

"No... it can't be," coughed Shingas as he viewed the final indignity to his legacy. The tone of his voice surprised Tioga.

*Could it be?* thought Tioga. He peered through the smoke—the village stood untouched in the distance! The palisade walls seemed to shine in the twilight. He closed his eyes and gave thanks to the Creator.

Tioga turned his gaze to the smoldering meadow in front of them. A few minutes before it had been filled with waving tan grass. Now a thousand glowing embers twinkled there. "You did it, Kopi," he said to himself. "I wish I could have seen their faces."

The Mononga warriors had been shocked to see the fire spring up before them. It came out of nowhere, like the lightning bolt that shattered their fortress wall a week before. Carried by the strong winds, the flames jumped across the dry field in a matter of seconds. Although the fighters had lost view of their commander, they still waited for his order to attack. When the heat became unbearable and the command still had not come, they scattered and ran for the lush forest. The mysterious fire was further proof that the mission was indeed cursed. It moved so quickly that most of the men suffered serious burns.

Chemung had waited a moment longer than the rest. He had always relied on his commander, who had never failed in battle. He finally turned and ran for the trees, but the fire beat him to them. By the time he tumbled into the green ferns, his legs and lower torso were aflame. His men doused him with water, but the burns were severe. He moaned and passed out from the unbelievable pain.

The flames finally slowed when they met the moist green leaves of the forest. There they stopped, leaving the steaming black earth as the only sign of their fury.


Kopi emerged from the smoke as the savior of the village. As he stumbled through the rear gate, a crowd of ecstatic villagers surrounded him. Little Naunu beamed with pride at his big brother's rout of the enemy. Kopi took off his helmet and placed it on Naunu, who instantly stood six inches taller.

Kopi coughed out an urgent question to those around him, "Where is Tioga? Is he here?" The tribe was too preoccupied with their unexpected victory to answer. They lifted Kopi on their shoulders and carried him through the village. Try as he might, he couldn't break free from the throng. The wild celebration continued for several minutes.

An urgent cry from the guard at the front gate interrupted their revelry. Everyone turned and watched in silence as the oak door opened. A strange apparition materialized from the haze. A two-headed man? The crowd gasped as they recognized the Mononga

Devil. Atop his back rode a dirty, disheveled figure, with a ghoulish face.

"Tioga!" screamed Hanna as she burst through the crowd. Shingas dropped to his knees and Tioga dismounted, as the huge gate closed behind them. He wanted to run and meet her but the best he could do was hop on one leg. Hanna hugged him with such force that she knocked him backward. The two fell arm-in-arm to the ground.

"Tioga, you're alive!" said Hanna. "I was afraid I'd lost you—again!"

"I'd never leave you, Hanna. I'd travel to the ends of the earth just to be with you."

"You already did!" she cried.

Schnitzel the dog went wild licking his master's face. When Tioga open his eyes, he saw his mother smiling down at him over Hanna's shoulder.

"Hello, Mom."

"You are quite a man, Tioga," said Candowsa. "A true warrior!"

She and Hanna helped him to his feet. He held them both in a big bear hug. Tioga felt a tap on his shoulder.

"Aren't you forgetting someone?" asked Kopi.

"Kopi!" Tioga pulled him into the embrace.

Tioga was shocked at Kopi's appearance. The fire had scorched his pants, blackened his face, and burned away most of his hair, except where his helmet had been. It only added to his mystical appearance.

"Didn't your mother ever tell you not to play with fire?" laughed Tioga.

"Did you see the way it jumped across the field?" said Kopi. "It was like magic!"

"No. I was busy with something else at the time."

"It was like the fire followed my very thoughts," said Kopi excitedly. "Maybe I am a mystic!"

"Oh, I can see it now," joked Tioga. "Kopi the mystic, predicting the winner of the next turtle race."

Kopi laughed at the thought. Just then, a raspy old voice rose up over the palisade wall. "People of the Allegewi, the Mononga wish to speak of peace."

Candowsa stared at Tioga. "That voice…"

Tioga smiled.

"Father?" said Candowsa.

"Grandfather Ötzi!" yelled Tioga.

Kopi helped his friend hobble to the front gate, with Candowsa and Hanna following close behind.

"Open the gate!" ordered Tioga.

The chief arrived beside them and nodded. The guard quickly complied.

Ötzi stood alone on the path in the still smoldering field. Dozens of unarmed Mononga warriors—those that could still walk—waited in the distance behind him. With their commander captured and Chemung out of action, the men had turned to Ötzi the Iceman for leadership.

"The Mononga wish to bury the hatchet with the Allegewi," said Ötzi. "It is time for peace in the valley."

"Ötzi, is that you, old friend?" asked the chief.

"Yes, Tunny, it is."

"Ha! Please come in. We will talk of peace."

Tioga hopped forward and embraced his grandfather.

"Tioga, you are as cunning as a fox, as stealthy as a cougar, and as brave as a badger!" said Ötzi. "And Kopi, you are something special too. You've got to teach me how to command fire!"

Just then Ötzi spotted the silhouette of his daughter against the maroon sky. A teardrop rolled down his cheek. She rushed forward and fell into his arms.

"Oh, Father, you came back to me."

He wiped the tears from her eyes. "I never left you, my child. I've always been with you in spirit."

She reached up and softy touched the scars on his face. "Oh Father, they tortured you! All because of me!"

"No child, that is the work of the north wind. But those old scars are only skin deep. It is not the body, but the spirit that is one's true self."

"Grandfather, what is your animal spirit?" asked Tioga.

Ötzi smiled. "The eagle, of course. No creature can see as far and wide."

Tioga looked up in wonder at the old man. The three generations of family walked arm in arm toward the chief's hut, as the crowd of villagers parted before them. The chief and Hanna led them to the entrance of their home.

Ötzi asked Chief Tundra, "May my grandson join the peace talks? All of my men are talking about the courageous young fighter who commands a tribe of ghost warriors."

"Certainly," said the chief. Then he muttered, "ghost warriors?"

"I am honored at the invitation," said Tioga. "But I'll stay with Mom for now. Besides, I'm no warrior. I'm just a simple trapper."

"A trapper of men!" laughed Ötzi.

Chief Tundra chuckled and the two wise men proceeded into the chief's lodge to begin the peace process.

# *Thirty*

Later that night, the Mononga warriors were welcomed into the village and the peace celebration began. A wonderful feast was prepared, complete with box-turtle soup and fresh roasted grasshoppers that had been collected from the scorched field. Tioga, Kopi, and Hanna—all freshly bathed and in new cloths—were honored with seats on the stage with the tribal leaders. After Kopi had wolfed down more than his share, he left to help on his mother, who was treating the injured. Most of the Mononga warriors had suffered burns in the field. Those that were able, joined the festivities.

Tioga had never seen the village so joyous. As the children danced around the blazing fire, Tioga leaned over toward Chief Tundra.

"Excuse me, sir," said Tioga, humbly. "May I ask you a question?"

"Of course, Tioga," responded the chief, with a smile.

"Back at the gate, when you first greeted my grandfather, you called him 'old friend.' "

"Yes. A very old friend. Isn't that right Z?"

"Indeed. Good memories," chuckled Ötzi.

"How is that possible?" asked Tioga, a bit confused. "Weren't the Allegewi and Mononga enemies?"

"Not when we were young," said the chief. "It wasn't until later, when food was scarce, that the fighting began. Stupid competition that led to conflict. And once lives were lost, it spiraled out of control."

"How did you two wise men meet?" asked Hanna.

"We were not wise men back then," laughed Grandfather Ötzi. "We were just children!"

"We both use to fish the Runestone," said the chief.

"I'd run into him on almost every trip," added Ötzi.

"Before long, we were sharing a canoe," said the chief.

"There is no competition among fisherman," said Ötzi. "The fish choose whom they want to go home with. We were just young boys, about your age, enjoying time on the river. We'd fish, skip stones, and make forts in the woods. What fun!"

Kopi, never one to miss dessert, rejoined the group just as the berries and honey were served.

"Z, tell them about *the adventure!*" laughed Chief Tundra.

"Ah yes, *the adventure!*" said Elder Ötzi. "One day on the river, Tunny convinced me that we should canoe down past the Forks and spy on the Dracul fort above the Emperor's Skull. He said we would be heroes if we found a weakness in their defenses!"

"The Emperor's Skull?" asked Tioga. "The cliff that looks like a face?"

"Why yes," said Ötzi, surprised that Tioga knew of the place. "Have you been there?"

"Yes, briefly," said Tioga. "But the only one who lives there now is a cougar."

"Well, back in the day, it was a big Dracul settlement," said Ötzi. "Those people have since moved south. But trust me, you don't want to mess with the Draculs. They're a rough bunch."

*That's quit a statement, coming from a Mononga warrior*, thought Kopi. He did not want to run into the Draculs there or anywhere else.

"What happened when you spied on their fort?" asked Hanna.

"Well, we made it to the overlook and hid there," said Chief Tundra, looking to Ötzi.

"The overlook? We were there too!" exclaimed Kopi.

"You two sure get around," said Ötzi.

Chief Tundra looked puzzled. Where had Tioga and Kopi been for the last few weeks?

"Back to the story, urged Hanna. "What happened at the overlook?"

"The Dracul sentries spotted us," said Ötzi.

"They chased us for two days!" laughed Chief Tundra. "I've never been so scared. If we hadn't lost them in that swamp, I swear they would have eaten us!"

Ötzi chuckled at the memory. "What a rush!"

Tioga's jaw dropped and he looked at Kopi in astonishment. Hanna burst out laughing at his funny expression. Kopi suddenly got an attack of the giggles.

"Ouch!" groaned Kopi. "Don't make me laugh. It hurts!"

"Broken ribs are very painful," said Grandfather Ötzi, noting the bandage around Kopi's chest.

"It's not my ribs, it's my stomach," said Kopi. "I can't eat another bite. I think we ate all the food in the village."

"Don't worry," said Ötzi. "There is plenty more in our fortress, including food that needs to be returned to the people of the valley." He looked down at Tioga's foot. "Grandson, I hope your ankle heals quickly. Then you and your mother can come visit us."

"Definitely," said Tioga. "I know the way."

"Can I come too?" asked Kopi. "I love it in the mountains!"

"Of course, Kopi," laughed Ötzi. "It wouldn't be the same without you."

Chief Tundra spoke up, "Tioga, I seem to recall you turned thirteen a few weeks ago, correct?"

"Yes sir!"

"Well, then. You've got something important to do soon, don't you? Before the next moon?"

"My spirit quest!" gushed Tioga.

"That's right. The passage to becoming a man and an Allegewi warrior," said the chief. "We can't wait to add you to our force."

"Congratulations on your birthday, Tioga," said Ötzi. "During your spirit quest, your animal guide will show itself. Then you can tap into its powers."

"What do you think it will be?" asked Hanna.

"I'm not sure," said Tioga sheepishly. But deep down he felt sure it would be the eagle, like his grandfather. After all, his left hand did look like a talon. And he did have good vision.

"It better not be a turtle," interjected Kopi. "That one's taken!"

Just then an Allegewi warrior's call floated in from the night. It came from outside the wall and was quickly followed by another and another. The gate opened, and excitement spread through the village. A few moments later the hunting party stumbled through the entrance. The women and children of the village rushed to greet their husbands and fathers.

The lead hunter staggered up to the chief. "Chief Tundra, we were on the way home when we saw smoke in the distance. We dropped everything and ran the final leg of the journey. What is going on?"

The chief looked over at Tioga and said, "Thanks to Tioga and Kopi, we are at peace with the Mononga. Come join the feast. We will tell the story of *The Ghost Warriors* long into the night."

The exhausted hunters joined the celebration. Tioga had never seen the village so alive with hope and happiness. He scanned the crowd, looking for his mother. There was so much more he wanted to know about her life with her father. He was beginning to get worried when he spotted her kissing one of the hunters in the shadows.

"I can't believe it," said Tioga. "Mom has been keeping secrets!" Satisfied that she was in good hands, Tioga's thoughts turned to Shingas. He was glad the fallen warlord was no longer a threat. He certainly deserved his fate. But somehow, he couldn't help but feel sorry for the man. Shingas had lost both of his arms, his tribe, and the woman he loved.

Tioga leaned over to Ötzi and asked, "Grandfather, what will become of Shingas?"

"He is your prisoner. It is up to you to decide his fate."

"I think he should live in peace with the Mononga."

"An interesting proposition... Since he was disgraced in battle, he will never be allowed to rule again. It is possible that the elders may spare his life."

"When his arm heals," said Tioga, "he could start a garden and live as a farmer. Kopi could teach him what plants will grow in the mountains. He could learn to nurture his crop and be patient for the harvest."

"You are wise beyond your years," said Grandfather Ötzi. "I think that is an excellent idea."

Tioga turned to the chief. "Esteemed Leader, may I be excused for a moment?"

"Of course, Tioga."

"Thank you," said Tioga, as he picked up his newly crafted crutches and a roasted turkey leg. He moved to the steps and gingerly climbed down from the stage.

As he worked his way through the crowd, two Mononga warriors approached him. Tioga recognized them as Bongo, the lead scout that escaped on the river, and Pox, his comrade.

"Sir, do you need assistance?" asked Bongo, trying to make up for any hard feelings. "You are welcome to climb on my back. I shall transport you wherever you wish to go."

"Thanks for the offer, Bongo. I'll be okay. How is your neck?" Even in the torchlight, Tioga could see it had been rubbed raw from the choke snare.

"To be honest, I'm glad to be free of that snare. You tie an excellent knot!"

"Thanks," said Tioga, blushing at the complement. "That Mononga rope is amazing. You must have a master ropemaker back at the fortress. I'd love to meet him."

Bongo and Pox looked puzzled.

"But sir, you already know him," said Bongo. "Ötzi the Iceman—your grandfather—he is our master ropemaker."

"What?" blurted out Tioga with a smile. "I can't believe it! I'm starting rope-making lessons in the morning. Right after Kopi's swimming lesson."

"Sir, may I say something?" asked Pox in a raspy voice.

"Of course Pox. Are you feeling better?" asked Tioga. "Kopi is excellent at treating lung ailments if you need him."

"I'm fine, sir," said Pox awkwardly. Then he lunged forward and hugged Tioga, as he burst into tears. "Thank you for saving my life at the river! You could have left me in a watery grave. Only a saint would spare the life of a man who just tried to kill him. I am forever your servant."

"Oh Pox. I'm no saint. When I see suffering, I just try my best to stop it," said Tioga, borrowing Kopi's motto. "Now you two go enjoy yourselves. I'll be back in a moment."

Bongo and Pox bowed and stepped aside.

Tioga limped to the back of the village, where the famous captive was tied. He hoped an offering of food would be the beginning of his rehabilitation.

As Tioga moved into the shadow of the stockade, a strange feeling came over him. Something was not as it should be. He noticed the rear gate was slightly ajar. The old guard must have joined the celebration when the hunters came in.

Tioga examined the ground in the faint firelight. He instantly recognized the large footprints that led to the exit. Tioga limped over to where Shingas had been tied. All that remained was a pair of gnawed leather straps—chewed clean through. Shingas had escaped!

Tioga thought about calling out the alarm. With bright torches and a full moon, the warriors could quickly track down the run-away prisoner. But Tioga stayed quiet. A man should have the right to die in peace. It was plain to see that Shingas was on his way to the spirit world. No one could survive alone in the wilderness without arms. *Or could he?*

Tioga's thoughts were broken by Hanna's approach. "What are you doing, Tioga? I miss you," she said.

"Oh, nothing," he said. "I just wanted to bring some food out for the dogs. That little one over there is just skin and bones." He placed the turkey leg on the ground. The little dog trotted over with her tail wagging.

"You're always thinking of others," said Hanna. She gently clasped Tioga's left hand and led him toward the palisade.

"How is your arm feeling?" asked Tioga.

"It's fine," said Hanna as she raised her left wrist to the light and pulled back the bandage. "Kopi did a great job sewing up the spear wound."

Tioga could see a string of stitches running the length of her inner arm. "That's gonna leave a scar."

"I hope so," smiled Hanna. "Scars tell the tale of an interesting life." She pointed to a ladder that led to the top of the wall. "Will you go up on the catwalk with me?"

"Of course. It's a beautiful night."

They climbed to the wooden walkway that rimmed the stockade and stared at the moonlight reflecting off the river. She laid her head on his shoulder and pulled him close. Now that it was clean, her purple hair glowed in the moonlight.

"Do you still want to follow the moon over the horizon?" she asked.

"What did you say?" asked Tioga, a little embarrassed.

"One night, before this all started, I overheard you talking. You were up here all alone. And you were talking to the moon. I stopped to listen. You said you wanted to run away with the moon over the horizon. I felt sorry for you."

"You were spying on me?"

"No, I was just out for a walk. You see, sometimes I come up here too—to think about my problems."

"Problems? What problems could you have, Hanna?"

"My father, for one," she said. "He is always telling me what to do. Like whom I should marry—when I am old enough."

"Oh, yeah," said Tioga. "That will be a hard choice with so many good warriors to choose from."

"Not really," said Hanna. "I have my eye on someone."

"Oh," said Tioga sadly.

"He is a wonderful man," said Hanna. "Strong, brave, smart, and my father thinks very highly of him. I just hope he'll want me."

"Who wouldn't want you, Hanna? You're the best girl in the world!"

"I hope he does, because there is no one else I could imagine myself with."

Tioga looked up at the thousands of stars glimmering in the night sky. Tears welled up in his eyes. The thought of Hanna with another man was more than he could bear. He pulled away from her.

"Tioga, it's you, silly! You're the one!"

"You want me?" he asked in amazement.

She smiled and nodded.

"Yes! Yes! Yes!" exclaimed Tioga. "Oh, Hanna, you'll see. I can learn to use that spear-thrower weapon that Shingas had. I'll become the toughest warrior in the village. I'll protect you!"

"You're already my warrior, Tioga. My ghost warrior! Don't change a thing. I love you just the way you are."

"But my hand," said Tioga. "And my scars. They don't bother you?"

Hanna reached down and held his twisted fingers. "I love that you're different. This wonderful hand is just the beginning. There is so much more about you that is so special."

She looked into his eyes and kissed him for the first time. Tioga's heart jumped like the festival drums that pounded behind them. But his soul was as tranquil as the boundless forest that surrounded them. He had never felt so whole and complete. He held her close and vowed to never let go. For the first time in his life, there was peace in the valley.

Coming soon:

# The Ghost Warriors: Battle for the Emperor's Skull

## Book II in The Ghost Warriors Series

To learn more about the facts
behind the fiction visit:

### TiogaAndKopi.com

If you enjoyed this book, please post a review
on Amazon.com and Goodreads.com.

Made in United States
North Haven, CT
01 November 2021